BEST
MURDER
of the *Year*

ALSO BY JON P. BLOCH

Finding Your Leading Man

BEST MURDER of the Year

JON P. BLOCH

ST. MARTIN'S MINOTAUR ❧ NEW YORK

www.minotaurbooks.com

Library of Congress Cataloging-in-Publication Data

Bloch, Jon P.
    Best murder of the year / by Jon P. Bloch.—1st ed.
      p. cm.
    ISBN 0-312-28090-4
      1. Academy Awards (Motion pictures)—Fiction.   2. Hollywood (Los Angeles, Calif.)—Fiction.   3. Motion picture industry—Fiction.   4. Gossip columnists— Fiction.   5. Gay men—Fiction.   I. Title.

PS3602.L63 B47 2002
813'.6—dc21

                    2001058855

First Edition: May 2002

10 9 8 7 6 5 4 3 2 1

For Tristan Robin Blakeman

Artist
Director
Actor
Poet
Renaissance Man

You have brought the Renaissance
to my heart and soul.

ACKNOWLEDGMENTS

Thanks to June Clark of the Peter Rubie Literary Agency and to Peter Rubie himself for their invaluable guidance and encouragement. Ditto my editor at St. Martin's, Keith Kahla, whose rather acerbic reference to "Margaret Dumont" proved to be the most important advice I received. And, of course, I would also like to thank the members of the Academy . . .

BEST MURDER
of the Year

*E*ven before all the fuss about murder, I knew that it just wasn't going to be my night.

There I was, Rick Domino, America's number one gossip columnist, hosting a live pre-Oscar telecast outside the Shrine Auditorium. Amid the usual hysteria of screeching fans, honking limos, and scads of TV journalists competing to be heard, I chatted cavalierly with every big name in the business. Flashbulbs popped as Sharon Stone rushed across the red carpet to kiss me on both cheeks. Harrison Ford put a brotherly hand on my shoulder. Tom Cruise said he'd be sure to tell his kids that "Uncle Rick" said hi. Obnoxiously bright and splashy colors made a comeback that year—I privately called it the Bad Acid Trip Look—and each actress tried to outdazzle the last with her gaudy hot pink gown and de rigueur rented diamond necklace. The humid, Palm Springs-ish twilight air was thick with the smell of thousand-bucks-an-ounce designer fragrance. It was the smell of money, and even on a phony-baloney smog-filled night in Hollywood, money smells mighty good.

Millions of people would've given their eyeteeth to be me. Yet all I could think about was how soon the whole thing would be over. I wasn't cynical so much as in love. That's something you learn after ten hard-boiled years of reporting on the Hollywood scene: All the Oscars and million-dollar contracts in the world add up to zip when you're just another schmuck suffering the pangs of unrequited love.

The object of my affection was none other than Best Actor nominee Shane Kirk, nee Eddie Sharnovsky. For the past few years he'd been considered a "hot young hunk" and "rising heartthrob," which was a fancy-schmancy way of saying he couldn't act his way out of a paper bag. Why should he have to? He was the boy toy of every dirty old man producer in town—which is no short list, by the by.

Eddie—excuse me, Shane—got his big break playing an intro-spective jock (i.e., no acting required) on a short-lived *90210* wannabe series on a WB wannabe cable network, attracting the so-called serious attention of several heavy-hitter producers. Yada, yada, yada, and the next thing you knew, he was cast as an intro-spective jock in a major motion picture called *Light My Fire*. It was one of those parts that played itself. The moment of his suicide, when you found out his character was a case of still waters running deep, happened off-screen. But a few important critics—coinciden-tally enough, gay male critics—praised his "subtle underplaying." The studio publicity machine built upon the big box office Shane had generated in a couple of teen market flicks over the past season, and bingo, you have a Best Actor nomination.

Shane faced formidable competition: Billy Bob Thornton was up for his performance as a president of the United States who is also a serial killer in the controversial Oliver Stone–Quentin Taran-tino collaboration *Oval Office Massacre*. Tom Hanks scored as the first astronaut with Down's syndrome in the Spielberg sci-fi weeper *Beyond the Blue Horizon*. Kevin Spacey played to perfection a priest with an obsession for flashing himself at nuns in the Coen Brothers' newest quirky comedy, *Saint Thang*. Last, but not least, Robert De Niro stretched his acting muscle by playing a gangster in his lat-est Scorcese flick, *Neighborhood Thug*. (Sarcasm aside, critics said that he'd surpassed his work in *Taxi Driver* and *Raging Bull*.)

Unfortunately for us all, Hanks, Spacey, and De Niro each already had won two Oscars, so it was unlikely any of them would win again. Thornton won before in the screenplay category, but *Oval Office Massacre*—not to mention Billy Bob himself—was pos-sibly a bit too off the beaten path to signal victory. Incredulous as it seemed to industry insiders, no-talent Shane Kirk actually was considered the front-runner.

When I first met Shane, he was still Eddie. He worked as a parking valet at Planet Hollywood, which was a polite way of saying he was a prostitute. It was one-sided love-at-first-sight. One look at that finely sculpted bod, short jet-black hair, and those penetrating hazel eyes, and you'd have thought I was some sappy adolescent twit. Or, even worse, one of those ninny stars I wrote about who just got married for the zillionth time after meeting the so-called love of their life at their second-to-last stay at Betty Ford.

Within a matter of days we were talking in terms of me turning Eddie into something. I was thinking along the lines of making him some sort of all-purpose "assistant" who got me my coffee and maybe even did a little digging up of dirt behind the scenes.

Eddie, though, had other plans. Eve Harrington had nothing on him. Next thing I knew, he was under contract with some Dream-Works wannabe, getting glorified walk-ons in teen market movies starring Jennifer Love Hewitt wannabes. He'd play the hunky quarterback that the girl *thought* she loved only to realize he's just an airheaded, self-absorbed nothing. It wasn't exactly a major leap out of character for the newly christened Shane. Then came the short-lived cheap-O TV series, and, before you could say "KY," a star was born.

In the ensuing years, Shane ignored me when he didn't think I could advance his career. Then, interestingly enough, he'd come crawling back whenever he needed a good jolt of publicity. The acting he did off-screen far exceeded anything he did on-screen. Every single time I ended up taking him back. Once he got an Oscar nomination, he all but promised to get a sex change so that we could legally marry. But in another amazing coincidence, once the Academy voting period was over, Shane could barely even grunt in my direction.

Not helping matters was the fact that I was a totally out-of-the-closet gossip columnist while he was a totally in-the-closet movie star. Shane was ultraparanoid about even being seen with me in public. The secrecy of our relationship—if you could call it that—very much reinforced the overall shabbiness of it. Since it was unlikely that we'd ever become an "official" couple, Shane could move in and move out without thinking twice.

Well, it's always the no-good bums who break the hearts of nice boys like me. A day or two before the Oscars, I reached a breaking point of sorts.

I blathered away about who in Hollywood had a good relationship and what I thought a good relationship *was*, and *why* a good relationship was important to me (hint-hint). In response, Shane gave me a frigidly silent routine such as the sort you'd reserve for a crazy person talking dirty to you on a public bus. Could one of his famous speeches about "needing more space" be far off? Realizing that anything was better than this relentless purgatory of off-again passing for on-again, I decided to go for broke.

"Good afternoon, ladies and gentleman," I stated sardonically, stirring my Campari daiquiri with a hand-blown Venetian swizzle stick. "This is Rick Domino coming to you from my ridiculously pretentious neo-art-deco Bel Air home. I'm interviewing Shane Kirk, Oscar nominee for *I'm Capable of Thinking About Someone Other Than Myself for a Single Instant of Existence.* Tell us, Shane, how did you prepare for this amazing performance?"

Shane gazed tirelessly at his ultraperfection in my vintage thirties beveled wall mirror. Decisions, decisions. Was he more irresistibly gorgeous with one or two wisps of hair falling onto his forehead?

"I'm sorry, Rick. Were you saying something?"

I stared numbly at my bittersweet drink. "Shane, I can't believe what you've reduced me to. I'm actually going to say that things can't go on like this. That we need to have a serious talk. And what's even worse, it's all *true.*"

"'Serious talk?'" His brow furrowed in awe. He had heard the word "talk" before—it was what his agent told him to do during interviews—and photogs told him they needed a "serious" publicity shot to complement a smiling one. But he marveled that the English language was structured in such a way that the words "serious" and "talk" could be used beside each other, having never before considered the possibility.

"What do you want to talk about, Rick?" Before I could answer, he added, "You know, this *has* to be my favorite mirror in the whole wide world. Boy, I sure do like this mirror."

I took a hefty swallow of my drink. "I'm glad you like it, Shane. If we ever tie the knot, we can put it in the prenups that the mirror is yours even if we divorce. Hell, even if I die of leprosy."

His face lit up. "Are you serious, Rick? I mean, you'd let me have the mirror?"

"Sure. What the hell." I poured myself a tall refill.

"I have a press conference in about an hour," he informed me, as if further contributing to the general theme I introduced. Apparently this was Shane's idea of serious talk. "The last big one before the Oscars. Your network's sending somebody else. I forget who. But I gotta be good." Translation: He had to *look* good. Which of course he already did. Yet I couldn't blame poor Shane for being unable to resist his own face. Would you fault Narcissus for being narcissistic?

I semichanged the subject. "You know, I got that mirror at a charity auction. Chinchilla Rights, I think. They say it was owned by Carole Lombard. Just before her plane crashed."

Shane did a double-take of pure ecstasy. "Wow, no *wonder* I always liked this mirror so much," he generously shared, as if I sat on pins and needles awaiting explanation for his approbation of it. "I swear, Rick. It's like I can *hear* Carole telling me, 'You go for it, fella.' She sends me good luck whenever I look at myself. I just know it. I mean, they say all that psychic stuff is true, don't they?"

His pathetic Lombard impersonation was more than matched by his faulty logic regarding the laws of karma, since poor Miss Lombard could hardly be considered the Patron Saint of Good Fortune. Besides, the steely determination with which Shane gazed at his own magnificence gave you the idea that luck had nothing to do with it. He psyched himself up for press conferences like a brain surgeon about to operate on the president of the United States.

What happened next was so shocking, you could've knocked me over with a feather. As he hurried out the post–op art door to suck up to more reporters, he said, almost as an afterthought: "Sure.

We'll talk. But after the Oscars." He added cryptically, "So much can change between now and then. We just have to wait, okay?"

Of course, he said this while sneaking one last glance at his god-like self in the mirror, like a schizo from a forties horror movie telling his own reflection that they needed to talk.

"*When* after the Oscars? A hundred years?"

Shane sighed with exasperation. How I tried his patience with my endless demands.

"Uh, right afterwards. How's that?"

"You mean, like before the parties and stuff?" Shane not only made me suspicious, but often reduced me to speaking Valley Girl–ese.

"Sure. Why not?" His smile caught me off guard.

"Great. Let's say backstage. Right after Best Actor."

For about two seconds after Shane zoomed off in my silver BMW, I was so elated I felt like Tom Hanks's mentally deficient astronaut. I even staged my own private little celebration with a fairly decent Dom Perignon '56, and an altogether decadent container of Ben & Jerry's Chunky Monkey.

But then I got this throbbing, sinking feeling in the pit of my stomach that stayed with me long after my hangover. For one thing, my nutritionist was going to have fit when I told her about the Chunky Monkey. More to the point was the realization that of course Shane wanted to talk, because he wanted to tell me to get lost—as in, permanently lost. Win or lose, the Oscar nomination did the trick. He was on the "A" list for film roles. Clearly, he had no more intention of getting serious with me than he did in learning how to act. True, I was the one who said things could not go on, but obviously the dim-witted Shane took things a bit too literally.

Like someone on trial for murder awaiting the jury verdict, I both dreaded and couldn't wait to find out what Shane had to say. Come Oscar night, it was all I could do to smilingly interview the glittering parade of celebs that passed before me. The sidewalks were a virtual land mine of cables and wires, and I was so distracted that I almost tripped straight into Brad Pitt—which, as not-so-Freudian slips go, would not have been half-bad.

As I lamely apologized on camera to Brad, a shot was heard above all the clamor. I figured it was just a car backfiring, or some dopey adolescent fan setting off a firecracker.

Then, as if through some psychic bond between lovers, I intuitively turned to see Shane Kirk some thirty feet away as he slumped to the sidewalk. The door to his limo was still open; he'd only just arrived.

The crowd shrieked. Then, like a swarm of vultures, Shane's teenybopper devotees rushed forward, ravenous for one last souvenir of their favorite heartthrob. Only a protective circle of police officers prevented poor Shane's body from being all but cannibalized.

Ever the trouper, I fought in vain to make my way through the mob. I managed to swallow back a flood of emotions to ad-lib that there seemed to be commotion coming from Shane Kirk's limo. As a TV reporter, you *never* say more than what you know for absolute certain. I was careful to keep my facial expression one of proper concern, without registering unnecessary alarm.

"Let's try to see what's happened to Shane Kirk," I bravely told the TV millions, wondering how many more seconds I could last without going hysterical with grief and rage.

2

*M*iraculously, Shane stood up.

Houdini himself would have been envious.

Shane was aw-shucks jokey with reporters as he brushed himself off and winked and waved to his shocked but relieved fans. Never missing a beat, he even threw in a plug for his forthcoming action flick, *Mercenary Clone*, stating that his little mock death scene was a but sneak preview of the thrills and chills his fans could expect from said epic.

But as I mentally replayed the rapid serious events, I realized that at the moment the tire blew—or whatever—Shane simply tripped while stepping out of his limo. His rapid-fire showbiz instincts were working overtime as he turned slapstick pratfall into top drama. What could have been a Dick Clark blooper of a Gerald Ford magnitude became the splashiest star entrance of the night. Some no doubt would question Shane's taste and judgment (amen), but the old saying about the only bad publicity being no publicity was only too true. And since Shane was a guy, he could get away with so blustering a publicity stunt. After all, it was just his young, irrepressible testosterone at play.

Hollywood being Hollywood, things instantly returned to normal—if you could call Oscar night normal. I smiled into the TV camera to reassure the world that its favorite new movie star, Shane Kirk, was alive and kicking (among other things). And, as if that weren't thrilling enough news, we broke for a word from our sponsor: Fountain of Youth, Skin Exfoliate to the Stars.

My pre-Oscar show cohost, the "lovely" Mitzi McGuire, was no slouch in the smile department herself. Mitzi was always doing these supposedly "hard-hitting" TV specials called things like "The Truth About the Casting Couch," or "Does Money *Really* Talk in Hollywood?" She wanted to come across as doing something on a higher level than mere smut magnets like me. But to call her a snake would be like calling Godzilla a teddy bear. Plus, she was hopelessly lost without cue cards, so when you did a show with her, you always had to be ready to ad-lib. I'll bet that even when she was home in bed with her third (supposedly straight) husband there was a teleprompter in the room.

Mitzi once showed me a photo of herself as a kid, and even at age ten she somehow looked like she'd had a facelift. She favored strapless low-cut gowns (tonight being no exception), yet she always seemed to be showing off not so much her figure as the price tag of her latest boob job. She was the Minnie Pearl of plastic surgery. You half-expected to see stamped onto each enormous plastic appendage: *My husband makes a killing in cosmetic dentistry.* Her wig de jour was in her trademark shade, which I thought of as Hair Spray Blonde.

"So, Rick," Mitzi read flawlessly, "this is your seventh year covering the Oscars for the Hollywood Network. Doesn't it get a little *old* after awhile?"

The way she said it, you knew the bitch wanted to do the show by herself and hog all the glory. I frowned with a guy-type sincerity; when you're a male TV personality, one of the first things you learn is to smile less often than your female counterpart. It gives you a kind of edge or chemistry with her. I also turned slightly to keep Mitzi from crowding me out of camera range, which was another one of her famous little tricks. "Not at all, Mitzi," I read from a cue card. "Each year is *more* exciting than the one before it, because each year the film industry manages to outdo itself. The stars, the movies—it all just gets bigger and better."

Mitzi laid her hand on my forearm, as if overcome by the profundity of what I just said. "Oh, Rick, how very right you are." She thrust her chest forward to signal that the movies were not the only things getting bigger and better.

The short lag in star arrivals was over, thank God. "Oh, look," Mitzi cried, her shrill nasal voice competing with the screaming fans. Once silently reverential in the presence of the gods and goddesses of the silver screen, in more recent years the gawking masses seemed to think they were at a boy band concert. "It's superstar Best Actress nominee, Tara Perez," Mitzi breathlessly informed the universe, as if everyone didn't know that of course it was Tara Perez. Would you need to explain to people that Cher was Cher?

"*Tara,*" Mitzi enthused, as if greeting her dearest friend, "only someone with your inimitable flair could pull off such a sequinny look. You *have* to tell me who you're wearing. But first let me say, you were *so* believable as a drug-addicted sexaholic in *Do That to Me One More Time.* You just continue to *stretch* as an actress. And I see your escort this evening is none other than the equally gorgeous and talented Best Actor nominee—*and* practical jokester extraordinaire—Shane Kirk."

"Hi, Mitzi, Hi, Rick!" chorused the gleefully nominated twosome. Just out of camera view, a female fan carried a sign that read: *Tara, get lost! Shane belongs to me!*

"Thank you, Mitzi, for the lovely compliment," added Tara.

"I'm wearing a new designer tonight named Sookie Sims. You don't think it's *too much*, do you?"

Mitzi gave a dismissive bend to her wrist, indicating that no statement on Tara's part possibly could've been more ludicrous. "Tara, this particular combination of purple and orange and pink and chartreuse *is* you. Wow, just imagine. From the fashion runway to the red carpet of the Academy Awards. Of all the super-models who've attempted acting careers, you're the only one to have succeeded—and how! Now tell me, with this being your . . . uh . . ."

There was a brief lag in the cue cards. "It's her third nomination!" I put in brightly. Speaking of numbers, what I counted to be the fourth police siren since we went on the air blared through the thick hum of gossip. A fairly slow night in L.A. I guessed at least a few people figured they'd hold off on bumping someone off until after the show.

Mitzi slapped my face in mock indignation, deftly rubbing her fingers afterwards to signal I was wearing a bit of on-camera foundation. "Really, Rick. I know this is her third nomination." She turned from me like an iceberg that just struck the *Titanic.* "As I was *saying,* Tara. Are you nervous about winning?"

Shane leaned into the mike to gallantly answer for Tara. After all, he hadn't been the center of attention for at least thirty seconds. "We both feel it's an honor just to be nominated," he bellowed in his low-key, guy-type way, slightly creasing his forehead as he dared the faintest wisp of a grin out of one side of his mouth. He looked to us all for approval, as if he'd just said something very clever and now deserved a blue ribbon.

Mitzi laughed with her head titled back. "*Honestly,* Shane. You're incorrigible. Such a dry, subtle wit. Tell me, is it true what they say about the two of you? Do I hear wedding bells chiming in the distance?" She made a point of stepping on my foot.

In this totally convincing, hetero butch way, Shane shrugged nonchalantly and said, "I'm waiting for her to ask me." No doubt the world was thinking, *He can't possibly be gay because he's so unclever.*

As Mitzi shrieked with laughter, Tara gave Shane a good-natured dig with her elbow. Ah, yes, love was in the air. What an adorable couple they made.

Seizing the moment, Shane crouched in close to the mike and wore his most sincere expression. "Actually, Mitzi, if I can get serious: When I first came to Hollywood, I didn't have a cent. A friend called and said, 'I have something for you.' I thought to myself, 'Is it a job?' You know, a walk-on in a commercial—anything at all, and I'd have been so grateful. Well, this friend presented me with a *mirror*, of all things. This may sound strange, but I just don't like mirrors. I've never been comfortable looking at myself."

Mitzi managed to brilliantly ad-lib, "Oh, you." She cutely pinched his cheek.

"It's true," confirmed Tara, nodding her lacquered head with conviction. "Shane is the *least* vain man I've ever met."

Shane effectively pretended to ignore their compliments. He was too much of a modest, everyday guy to acknowledge them. "Anyway, ladies, as I was saying—"

I cleared my throat.

"Oh, right. And you too, Rick. Anyway, my friend told me that this mirror had once belonged to that great lady of the screen, Miss Carole Lombard, who, as we all know, died so tragically while helping our nation's war effort. My friend said that the mirror would bring me good luck. I thought to myself, 'Yeah, right.' I mean, I'm not the kind of guy who goes in for all that mumbo-jumbo. But I have to say that everything changed after that. Every day I'd give the mirror a quick little wink, and I'd get this *confidence* I never had before. So in case I don't win tonight—and being in the company of four such great actors, I think that's a pretty safe bet—I wanted to take this moment to say a special 'thank you ' to the great Miss Lombard, whose spirit lives on. Believe me, I *know*."

A sniffle was emitted from Mitzi's surgically corrected septum. "Why, Shane. You're *such* a sensitive man."

"Truer words were never spoken," Tara proclaimed.

"You'll get no argument out of me," I concurred. "Everyone in town says that Shane Kirk is one very, *very* sensitive fellow. Tell us, Shane. Who was this friend who gave you the mirror?"

"Well, Rick. I'm afraid I'd better not say. She's a very private sort of gal."

"Oh, Rick," laughed Tara, reaching over to pat my hand. "You *never* stop working, do you?"

"Okay, I'm busted," I genially agreed. "You know, Tara, speaking of doing my job, please help me set the record straight. Tell me you weren't turned down for the lead in *Don't Leave Me This Way*, because the producer, Truman Shea, said no one would believe you as an ingenue. *Please* say it isn't so. You look as young and fresh as you did . . . goodness, has it really been *twenty years* since you first graced the screen? And I'm sure you could be convincing in any part you played. Heck, looking at you right now, I'm thinking you could even play a sumo wrestler and get away with it."

The glare in Tara's eyes spoke volumes. I knew she was outraged that I'd gotten the scoop on a supposedly secret meeting. But that's what made Rick Domino the most widely read and watched gossip columnist in all the land. Say what you like about how I made my living, but I was good at it. I knew how to get things out of people.

"Why, Rick," Tara smiled. "Since when do you pay attention to such silly rumors? But thank you for the compliment, just the same."

As the glamorous twosome moved on, Shane slipped me a note. Without missing a beat, I glanced quickly at it: *The men's room, far left side, as soon as you're done. I'm ready to talk now.* I could feel my heart racing.

"Oh, look!" enthused Mitzi. "It's Jewel, who's going to be performing one of the nominated Best Songs tonight with Placido Domingo and Meat Loaf—'I Can't Find Me Anywhere,' from the full-length animated feature *Where's Waldo?*"

Somehow, I got through the rest of the pre-Oscar show, and hurried to the men's room on the far left as if I'd been seated at the dais at a U.N. banquet for the past six hours. Normally, I would've been eager to linger in the lobby to listen for scoops in the veritable stock exchange of innuendo circulating amongst the hundreds of wannabes and has-beens milling about, but first things first. Every year, there's some sort of "theme" to the ceremonies that nobody pays attention to, and this year it was: *Oscarland . . . Where Dreams Come True.* Or so claimed a series of tacky banners in the otherwise-nondescript lobby, which, architecturally speaking, was what you might call High Airport Waiting Room. I couldn't decide if the slogan mocked or reassured me.

The men's room Shane elected for our meeting was way, way down one wing of the polyester-carpeted corridor—and presumably less populated. I wondered how Shane would know about this meeting place until I remembered the obvious. Indeed, in a moment reminiscent of his original profession, Shane was waiting next to the urinals. He had a huge smile on his face. Shane was one of those guys so totally gorgeous that you could never decide if he was handsomer when he was smiling or serious.

"You were brilliant," I noted, looking dourly away from him.

"'Brilliant?'" Shane was perplexed as he rolled the unfamiliar word along his tongue. Besides, it *was* pretty hard to remember something that happened all of ten minutes ago.

"The limo," I snapped impatiently. "When you fell. Plus that little added touch about the mirror."

His face lit with recognition. "Gee, thanks." He grinned with pride, like a boy scout receiving a key to the city for getting plasma to the hospital on time.

"You look great, Rick."

"Not bad for pushing forty," I marginally concurred, frowning as I gazed at my reflection.

Looking quickly about the men's room to make sure no one was watching, Shane cupped my chin in his hand and kissed my mouth. In theory, he had nothing to worry about. Two men (leading action film director and Oscar-nominated character actor) emerged from a stall as Shane and I kissed, indicating that this was some sort of cruise hangout. But Shane was paranoid to the point of pathos. I wondered if this men's room was always this cruisey, or if it was just some secret little Oscar night tradition. Not that having sex in men's rooms is what you'd call my cup of tea. But, professionally speaking, it annoyed me that all this might have been going on for years right under my nose. Maybe I wasn't as good at my job as I thought.

But mostly I tried to ignore the thrill shooting down my back.

"Well, Shane. They say you're going to win." I ran my fingers through my hair to encourage the proper tousled effect—and to conceal my mortification for having made such an inane remark.

Shane grinned, as if all the cameras in the world were upon him. "It's an honor just be nominated."

"I assume your publicity manager told you to say that?"

Again making sure the coast was clear, he quickly nuzzled my neck. "There's just no fooling you, is there?" Hearing a stall door swing open, he let go of me so quickly you'd have thought he suffered from multiple personality disorder, and just did some abrupt switcheroo.

"Oh, I wouldn't say that. I certainly have been played for a fool in my time."

"What—you mean like false leads on a big scoop?" There was a chuckle in his voice, like he was really enjoying our conversation.

I turned away from the mirror. "Yes, Shane. Exactly. You really are as dense as you seem, aren't you? Sometimes I've wished that it's all just an act. That you're capable of noticing that people have feelings. But I guess it's a lost cause. You really do belong in Hollywood."

"Rick, please keep it down," Shane whispered, indicating with a quirked eyebrow that the other guys in the men's room might be listening. Just then, three more men walked by. One of them gave Shane the wolf whistle. Another demurely grabbed his tuxedo'd ass.

"Well, what did you want to tell me?" I braced myself, figuring I might as well get it over with.

Someone tapped me on the shoulder. "Why, Rick, good evening! And Shane—we all have our fingers crossed, you know."

It was none other than the rotund Chauncey Riggs, rival columnist with a rival network, and who, I was reasonably certain, was in cahoots with Mitzi to get me ousted. Then Mitzi would have my job all to herself, and Chauncey could proceed to make mincemeat out of her. If Mitzi was a cobra, Chauncey was the unlikely mongoose that could defeat her in battle.

"Rick," Chauncey continued, "I had no idea you even *knew* Shane." In other words, he heard everything we just said.

"We go way back." Shane winked at Chauncey, who flustered to a bright balloon pink. Though Chauncey was decidedly on the fem side—I came across like John Wayne in comparison, and "Butch" was not exactly my middle name—he was one of those heavyset fellows that makes you think of a bull, because his emotions flowed through him so powerfully he all but blew smoke from his nose.

Chauncey splashed cold water on his heavily perspired face, then patted it dry with a paper towel. "Shane, I've heard you've been having some not-so-secret meetings with the folks over at Big Dipper. An action series about a space cowboy to the tune of eight figures, I'm told."

As the song goes, I turned a whiter shade of pale. Not only had Chauncey scooped me, but it was about *Shane*, who obliviously lacked the decency to let me hear the news first—which boded ill on so many levels it made my head swim. And, of course, I knew that Chauncey knew exactly what I was thinking.

Shane did his all-American humble bit. "It would be an honor to work at Big Dipper even as an errand boy, Chauncey. I've had so much unbelievable good fortune come my way, I don't want to tempt fate too much. I guess we'll just have to see." He held up two sets of manicured crossed fingers.

Shane's charms had worked their magic; Chauncey turned red as a chili pepper. "Well, you fellows will want to take your seats. The show's about to start."

Shane and I eyed each other meaningfully. "I guess we should," Shane said softly. "Um, I'll talk to you more later, Rick."

"After Best Actor," I concurred.

Shane wore a surprisingly impassioned expression as he said, "I look forward to it."

Could it be that he had good news for me after all? Were we about to elope? Be a real couple? Or was the SOB just mind-fucking me?

I heard Chauncey mutter the word "prick" on his way out the door. He could've meant me, but he also could've meant Shane. I had no proof, but I certainly wouldn't have been shocked to learn that Shane was so desperate for fame that he even put out to Chauncey Riggs. Who knows? Maybe Shane even promised to marry him, too. And maybe Chauncey, like me, had been dumb enough to believe him.

As I saw the trail of frowns and grimaces Shane left behind him as he made his way through the lobby, I wondered if there was anyone in town he hadn't screwed in either or both senses of the term. I felt ironically at peace. Even in Hollywood, you shouldn't make *too* many enemies, and in his desperate climb to the top, Shane just might have won the battle but lost the war.

3

*S*hane sat down in the front row beside Tara, and I took my aisle seat toward the back. Like a child punished by the teacher for talking too much in class, it was the best the Academy would allow me. Still, at least I wasn't banished to the humiliation of the balcony, where the lucky few noncelebs in attendance were seated—as were reporters of lesser stature. I felt a little jab of pleasure as I noted that Chauncey was seated in the section next to me, one row behind and in the middle, making him even less visible than myself. (Poor Mitzi had been very self-righteous all week about how she would scoop the "real story" of Oscar night, for what was Oscar without fans?, etc. In other words, she was stuck upstairs.)

Otherwise, things seemed par for the course as we took our seats. The men in their ten-thousand-dollar tuxes were appropriately relaxed—cheerful, charming, but let's-not-get-carried-away dude-ish about the whole thing. The women at their sides were predictably more animated, smiling delightedly as if about to get married or take their final vows as nuns. Though needless to say, the former was the more likely scenario of the two.

A special stage curtain had been designed, presumably out of scraps from the hundred ugliest gowns of the night. In an exercise reminiscent of an ophthalmologist testing you for color-blindness, I made out the insipid slogan about dreams coming true in Oscarland in the gaudy folds of fabric. "Oh, *now* I see it," you heard this or that person mutter, as someone next to them air-traced the letters with their finger. The biggest phonies even clapped their hands together in mock glee, making it seem like this was some sort of amusing parlor game on the Academy's part, and not just an instance of a set designer doing too much Ecstasy.

Only hours beforehand, Billy Crystal had to bow out as master of ceremonies—his plane was snowed-in in Estonia for a location shoot—so they found a last-minute replacement in Alec Baldwin. I think everyone in the audience felt sorry for poor Alec when he had to take center stage and pronounce, "Welcome to Oscarland, where dreams come true!" Then his extended ringmaster-like arm ushered in, via a sort of giant Lazy Susan, an assortment of otherwise unemployed dancers who bored everyone to the point of catatonia with their antics.

First, an allegedly biological female was done up like Dorothy from Oz. Off to the side, we saw the TV camera zoom in on her ruby slippers, which compelled the audience to obediently burst into applause. One of those innocuous, hopelessly outdated songs that you hear once and never again piped in about "the land where dreams come true." Next thing you knew, there were a whole bunch of dancing Scarecrows and Tin Men and Cowardly Lions, their choreography apparently lifted *en total* from the Anaheim Gay Square Dancing Club. Some dry ice on red lights ushered in the appearance of the Wicked Witch. Her camouflaging green makeup did little to diminish the shocking realization of just how hard-up for cash Marilyn Quayle had become. Then white lights and more dry ice gave us the Good Witch, who was less Billie Burke than a cross between Tammy Faye and the Bride of Frankenstein.

Dorothy clicked her heals repeatedly, as if afflicted by an autistic tic, as she rose on a pedestal that, we quickly saw, was this giant-sized Oscar. One wondered if the eager lass would straddle herself on top of it, but instead the cloying clicking of heels gave way to a frenetic tap dance, as the other performers made a tribal swoon of devotion around the massive phallus. Presumably, somebody's dream came true. Then, thanks to the Wonders of Technology, Dorothy did this computerized dance with Fred Astaire in *Top Hat*, and then partnered with John Travolta in *Saturday Night Fever*, and Patrick Swayze in *Dirty Dancing*.

Grateful for one day's work a year, the sweating, out-of-breath dancers clasped hands to rapturously take their bow. Just when we thought it was (thank God) all over, a cutesy Toto dog barked across the barren stage. Everyone felt compelled to laugh, as if it were a delightful little denouement.

Then came the awards, which, like women in childbirth given drugs to forget their pain, we all manage to forget until the following year is mighty tedious business, what with all those schlep technicians droning their long-winded speeches and more godawful production numbers. A so-called highlight of the evening was when Angie Dickinson presented the Lifetime Achievement Award to so-called living legend, Miss Francine Quick, who, back in her heyday, apparently lived up to her name and then some.

If truth be told, Francine's credentials were middle-drawer at best. She took parts that fifties suds queens like Hayward, Wyman, or Kerr couldn't be bothered with—indeed, her roles no doubt also had been rejected by the likes of Mala Powers. But like other people who managed to kick around the industry for decades, ol' Francine now was touted as a "real star" from the "golden era," which was a bit like saying that a bottle of Welch's grape juice that's been in your cupboard for a while is a rare vintage wine. Plus, a few years back, some people thought she'd win for Best Supporting Actress when she played the older version of prim, idealistic missionary Jennifer Lopez in *I Will Survive*. There was a minor scandal when Francine failed even to be nominated.

So here she was accepting her award to a standing O, while audience members pantomimed back and forth as to who owed whom money in lost or won bets as to whether she'd be sober enough to make it across the stage. Originally from Brooklyn, Francine had taken on a vaguely Asian appearance for having had nearly as many facelifts as husbands, and it was part of the deal that the TV cameras couldn't pan in too close. In fact, the cameras were pulled so far back that had you just tuned in, you'd have thought you were watching a Discovery Channel special on the mating rituals of killer red ants. As red gowns go, however, Ms. Dickinson was a study in understated elegance beside Francine's frock, which seemed to have been inspired by prop balloons in a burlesque show. Good taste did not rest easily on her shoulders. Francine claimed to be sixty-five—she was sixty-five like I'm Princess Margaret—but her speech got right to the point: "I love you all!" she proclaimed, as indeed she had. Rather tackily, she blew us kisses with both gloved hands, and thankfully was led offstage before any sort of mishap occurred.

Suspense-wise, Francine's trek across the stage marked the high point of the evening. It had hardly been a banner year at the movies, and, predictably enough, the intense but overrated family drama *Butterfly Kisses* swept category after category, making for few if any surprises.

What made it all fairly revolting were the constant references made by this or that winner as to the "courage" of hardball producer Truman Shea, kingpin of mighty Big Dipper Films. Tru responded with a steady stream of smugly pensive stares, hands clasped before his lips, as if treating the TV masses to a few fleeting moments of his Genius at Work. You'd have thought it was a huge gamble to make a movie out of a number one best-selling novel, cast it with more big-name stars than there are toys in Toys R Us, and then give it the biggest publicity campaign since Happy Meals. Plus, of course, pay off a few well-placed critics to praise the film's "tasteful and sensitive" handling of incest between identical twins, whatever that's supposed to have meant.

Truman himself was one of those fortunate souls so totally insecure about himself that he could do nothing but blow his own horn. Apparently, this was true in the literal sense, given his natural talent for contortionism (he first entered showbiz as a child novelty act via his pushy stage mama), not to mention his self-righteously open bisexuality. It would seem Tru genuinely was bi (as opposed to semicloseted gay), and he conducted his personal life with the same chaotic greed of his professional enterprises. He was like a fire-breathing dragon on speed bemoaning that nobody understood him. Why did a rival producer just publicly call him an SOB? Was it really necessary to get so *personal* about it, when all poor Truman did was steal a major project when the other producer was out of town because his son died of a brain tumor? And that starlet who broke off their engagement just because Truman wanted her to do him with a dildo while he blew some guy—what was all *that* about? Wasn't there *anyone* who could accept him for the simple, loving man he was?

Ironically, I found myself hoping that *Butterfly Kisses* indeed would win Best Picture, as there would be no end to Truman's ranting and raving if it somehow lost—how it was all a plot, how Hollywood had lost its integrity, how he courageously proclaimed to the world he liked both men and women (albeit neglecting to mention a few choice tidbits thereof) and that *this* was how "they" rewarded him in return, and on and on and on.

At long last, it was time to present the major categories. Last year's Best Actor, Bob Raflowitz (who unlike the Shane Kirks of this world, had the contemporary style and class not to change his name), stepped forward to present the award for Best Actress. Bob was that rare bird in Hollywood: a good, solid actor on whom no one could find any dirt. He showed up to work on time, and never pulled any monkey business. At night he went home to his common-law wife, Cleo Simone, a minor actress who spent most of her time raising their five kids and being a kind of yoga-astrology guru to the stars. But Bob was no Pat Boone. He was an outspoken superliberal—a stable fellow with an edge. The kind of genuinely straight man that you wished were gay.

The same could not be said, alas, of his highly closeted frequent costar in buddy-buddy action flicks, Jeep Andrews. His hyper-macho image notwithstanding, Jeep was such a friend of Dorothy's that he made Toto seem like the Wicked Witch of the West. A popular underground joke: *How do you know when you're dreaming? When you hear Jeep Andrews say, "I want to be the top."*

Still, box office is box office, and Bob couldn't resist making one of those ambiguously gay-ish, meant-to-be-funny references to his frequent male costar before presenting the award. "Jeep, I feel naked up here without you," Bob quipped. The TV cameras zoomed to a reaction shot of Jeep in the audience, who blew back a supposedly jokey kiss. But those of us in the know always assumed that poor Jeep was hopelessly in love with Bob.

Bob and Jeep enjoyed a symbiotic relationship, professionally speaking. Long the fave of critics, Bob broke into big-league box office a few years back when paired off with Jeep in an opus of blood-and-guts brain candy entitled *Detonation*. Playing the more complex character, Bob proved he could carry a big-budget action flick while keeping his reputation as a serious artist in tact. Jeep's status was likewise enhanced when he demonstrated he could "hold his own" (with a little help from a script that gave him all the good lines) acting against a powerhouse like Bob. Jeep was an only-his-hairdresser-knows-for-sure blond with a killer smile, while Bob emoted away with his brooding dark features. Audiences responded to their platonic "chemistry" to the tune of billions of dollars. They went on to costar in a string of smash-kaboom box-office triumphs, most recently the highly imaginative *Detonation VII*. No doubt they'd eventually make a movie called *101 Detonations*.

Jeep was a genuinely butch guy who could "pass" for straight in real life. Yet they say the movie camera picks up *everything*, and if you watched Bob/Jeep epics closely, you could unmistakably observe Jeep giving Bob the eye—for lack of opportunity to give him something else. But Bob was such a subtle actor he knew just how to dissipate Jeep's leapin' libido. So they weren't just good box office together; pairing Jeep with Bob meant fewer retakes than with other male costars, and time of course meant money on a movie set. With other action stars, Jeep could come across as so frisky a gay blade that he made Jeff Stryker look like the Singing Nun. Endless retakes—plus all sorts of tricks in the editing room—were needed to convince audiences of Jeep's hetero-ness.

Finally, the big moment came: "And the Oscar goes to . . . Tara Perez!"

To appease the TV audience, Shane reached over to give Tara a kiss. The whole world saw his smooched-up lips in close-up as Tara ignored him, standing up in a frenzied euphoria. She was like Sissy Spacek in *Carrie*, only instead of getting drenched in red Karo syrup she seemed drenched in liquid gold.

For me, it was one of those times in which you hope against hope that the odds-on favorite would lose. It had to do with her supposedly dating Shane, even though I knew she was just his fag-hag beard—the poor dear was slightly older than I was, and Shane was only twenty-seven. But I also honesty didn't care for her work in *Do That To Me One More Time*. It seemed like a consolation prize for not honoring her performance in *Kiss from a Rose* three years earlier, and I never liked it when the Academy did this. Still, I joined in giving her a standing ovation. The former fashion model truly had paid her dues. Besides, it would have looked bad if I'd remained seated.

Tara had become increasingly Queen Shit regal over the years, and I practically expected her to give her Oscar the white glove test before deigning to accept it. But she was surprisingly human about the whole thing, sniffling and giving us her famously charming million-watt smile while she thanked God and the usual litany of mortals who made it all happen for her.

"I have worked for this moment all of my life," she shared, consistent with the trend in recent years to regard the Oscar podium as a kind of encounter group hot seat. "Now that it's happened, I feel so overcome with *love!*" Well, that was one word for it. She spread her arms as if she were the Great Earth Mother, and somehow made it backstage to meet the press.

Then, in keeping with the trend to spread out the major awards a bit, Dwight Yoakum and Roma Downey performed the last nominated song—"The Beast is Yet to Come" from the animated version of *Dr. Jekyll and Mr. Hyde*. After the trillionth commercial break, none other than Shane Kirk came on stage to announce the award for Best Song. (In an obtuse reference to Marilyn Monroe and Shane's earlier publicity stunt, Alec introduced him as the "*Nearly late Shane Kirk*.") Shane presented the Oscar to the dweeby composer of "Revolution in My Heart" from the animated version of

Doctor Zhivago, which we'd had the treat of hearing performed by Lorna Luft, Jon Bon Jovi, and Lisa Hartman Black. The little twirp song writer unsuccessfully tried to cop a feel from Shane, but presumably he would learn to make do with his gold statuette.

During yet another commercial break, I spotted a pair of rising young stars I wanted to interview—I'd heard their marriage was on the skids—and walked toward them. Spotting me, they smiled and waved, and mouthed that they'd talk to me after the show. The commercial was over, so I stayed put where I was, standing along the wall in the far-righthand aisle. It was an interesting angle—you could see a lot of apprehensiveness, eye signals, boredom, and intoxication in people's profiles. I felt like I could write an entire column just on this alone.

Last year's Best Actress and I-don't-discuss-my-personal-life lesbian, Cinda Sharpe, stepped forward to present the award for Best Actor. She was more highly respected actress than star per se. The films she made were chock full of important sociopolitical messages and integrity, so needless to say people did not stand in line to see them—except maybe in Greenwich Village, parts of San Francisco, and an allegedly secret lesbian enclave in Teaneck, New Jersey. But she was a damned good actress, and thankfully, the Academy knew it.

There were no little cutesy jokes; Cinda (who was far more vivacious in person than on film) got straight to the point. When they showed a clip of Shane from *Light My Fire*, the audience inexplicably went gaga with applause. Curiously, the TV cameras couldn't locate Shane; there was a blank above his name on the TV projection when we should have seen him smiling sportingly in anticipation. He was not in his seat, nor was he still backstage for having recently presented Best Song. Well, obviously he was *someplace*, and the show had to go on.

"And the Oscar goes to . . . Shane Kirk!"

The full-piece orchestra broke into a rockin' rendition of "Light My Fire" as the crowd cheered. But still no Shane. The music stopped, then started again. Still no Shane. Now, Shane was hardly a genius, but even he knew enough to accept an Academy Award—

especially since he was already there. In spite of myself, I was worried. Cinda shrugged charmingly and stated, "Well, Shane. We saw you just a minute ago and we all love you, but I guess I'll just have to accept this for you and say thank you to everyone, as I know you would've done." There was an unplanned cut to another commercial, which gave everyone in attendance time to wonder aloud what was happening.

Amidst the general buzz of conversation, I quietly sneaked backstage to see what in the blazes was going on with Shane. After all, that was the last place he'd been seen. Behind a large heap of music stands and unmarked boxes, I spied an exit door. According to some intimidating big red letters, the door was supposed to be kept shut except in emergencies, yet it was opened. On my way to the door, I bumped into a glitzy blonde—or rather, she bumped into me. She looked like a badly-used *Playboy* centerfold—the kind of girl who still looked great when they airbrushed her unhappy life out of her photos. She seemed slightly familiar, like a starlet Hollywood briefly enjoyed a few years back, but now could not remember her name. But it wasn't the time to be asking her who she was.

I made my way through the verboten door. I stood in a kind of alleyway that was perpendicular to the back parking lot.

It had gotten dark.

4

There was no sign of Shane out back, unless—instead of accepting his Oscar—he felt a sudden urge to play hide-and-seek in a Dumpster full of very ripe garbage. The poetic justice of said action notwithstanding, it seemed an unlikely possibility at best. Flies buzzed greedily amidst the overpowering stench. It struck me as an apt metaphor for the glitzy showbiz fluff coming from inside, which—let's face it—had all the heartfelt sincerity of canned laughter. There was a loud humming from some sort of overhead generator, which made a steady drip onto the cracked black pavement. I looked down to notice that the sooty drops of water were splattering beside a pistol. A thin trail of smoke rose and curled from its barrel, like a cigarette smoldering in an ashtray. As it lay there gleaming menacingly in the moonlight, for some reason I was reminded of the small, compact gun that Nancy Reagan used to carry in her purse.

I called for Shane, but nobody answered. I wondered if I was being set up for one of those Dick Clark practical joke things.

Then I saw the body.

It's a funny thing about stumbling onto a corpse. You find yourself thinking all sorts of bizarre things. Chalk it up to shock, but the first idea that flashed into my head was how the reality of seeing someone you knew lying there having been brutally murdered went way beyond anything the movies could achieve. The eeriest thing was how the lower torso was covered by the shadow of the alley, while the yellow glow of the parking lot lights cut across the upper body, one arm extended as if rushing toward the light. Awash in a pool of its own blood, the corpse's mouth and chest wounds were an especially bright red. By contrast, the stomach wound was a glistening black. I could faintly hear the dark blood gurgling down the alley. I looked up at the moon; a cloud passed over the ring of smog surrounding it. I let out a sound that was neither a laugh nor a cry but some freakish third alternative that I'd never made before.

I heard another police siren, followed by an ambulance, and I figured help was on the way. But the sounds quickly sped into the distance. A cat in heat called out, and another cat answered its cries, padding about the Dumpster. From inside, I heard the muffled voice of Jeep Andrews proclaim, "*Butterfly Kisses!*" and the sound of wild applause.

Then I heard a gunshot.

From the other end of the alley, a lurking figure took aim at me. It seemed to be nothing but shadow, a gaping emptiness with no purpose other than to kill me.

I lunged for the pistol like there was no tomorrow—and maybe there wouldn't be if I was an instant too slow. I was no expert marksman, Lord knew. In fact, I'd never before fired a gun, and had always been afraid of them. But my adrenaline urged me to aim the pistol straight ahead. Gulping down hard, I butchly pulled the trigger. The shot made an echo that rang in my ears, and when a cat screamed I wondered if I'd shot it by mistake. I nearly lost my balance from the kickback of the fired gun. I felt like I was back in PE class, my spaz body somehow unable to do things that other people's bodies took for granted. Only this time my klutziness was literally a matter of life and death.

The generator began humming louder. I regained my bearings, only to note that whoever took a shot at me had disappeared. Was this homicidal maniac coming after me? I didn't feel like sticking around to find out, thanks just the same. As if helplessly spiraling through a bad dream, I hurried back to the auditorium, one hand firmly gripping the smoking gun. Each second seemed to last a hundred years as I neared the door.

Someone grabbed my shoulder. I practically leapt out of my skin. "*Shane!* Jesus, what happened? Don't tell me that you . . . ?"

He jumped back, defensively putting up his hands. "Rick, be careful with that thing. You could hurt someone real bad." He started to cry. I knew Shane wasn't enough of an actor to be faking it. "I *swear* I didn't do it, Rick. Please believe me. I have no idea why—"

A police siren sounded, getting closer by the instant. Shane looked at me with panic, then started running. His years as a high school track star came in handy. In nothing flat, he bounded over a fence and was nowhere to be seen. He might as well have evaporated into the faint night mist that was forming. Besides, too much was happening too fast for me to have even thought to go after him.

The exit door slammed open; I saw a million gaping faces.

I was still holding the smoking pistol. A big bear of a police officer came forward. His blue-black jacket gleamed in the dark, and it seemed to me just then that cops were a species of vampire—or maybe rodent—that came fully to life only after the sun had set. He looked around gingerly, greedy to pounce on his prey, and all but salivated as he stated, "Drop your weapon."

I carefully set down the gun and raised my hands. The cop

frisked me, then turned me around and frisked me again. I felt my heart sink down to my stomach as I saw him take out a shiny pair of handcuffs. For some reason my throat grew parched as he locked the cuffs to my wrists. Extreme fear, I was rapidly learning, produced all sorts of weird body reactions.

"Don't be a crybaby," admonished the cop, sounding like a disappointed high school gym teacher. As if the worst thing happening was that my sudden tears were spoiling his fun. I'd always thought of myself as a moderate, law-abiding guy, but this jerk was so unfeeling that for the first time I understood why people hate cops. My tears hardened into stone cold rage and tenacity.

The mean, burly cop rudely dragged me over to the parking lot. By this time, virtually every TV camera in the universe was poised on the two of us. The yellow parking lot lights made me all the more visible. I felt like I was having one of those dreams in which you're naked in public.

Newspaper reporters scribbled away as Mitzi bravely found the strength to express her "utter shock" to the millions tuned in to watch. "I can scarcely believe what seems to be happening to my good friend and colleague, Rick Domino," she shared. Mitzi and about a million other news people rushed toward me for comment, but the stone-faced cop kept me moving along. Needless to say, I was not about to make a statement.

Hundreds of bejeweled celebrities had come outside to gawk, but I don't recall anyone looking sad. Instead, they all seemed to be smirking. Rick Domino was getting a taste of his own medicine. So what if someone just got murdered?

The cop cleared his throat. "You are under arrest for the murder of Tara Perez . . ."

But after that I didn't hear what he was saying. While most eyes were upon me, I couldn't help noticing that off to the side were several famous sets of peepers most decidedly upon each other. Namely, Francine Quick, Cinda Sharpe, Bob Raflowitz, Jeep Andrews, and Truman Shea, who exchanged sidelong whispers and meaningful glances like schoolchildren being disobedient during a fire drill.

I instinctively tried to run toward them, to eavesdrop on what they were saying. When the cop quickly restrained me, the frustration of being a prisoner took on a whole new meaning.

The brute shoved me into a waiting police car, its hood light spinning. Then he crawled in next to me and said, "Maybe I should start over. You are under arrest for the murder of Tara Perez. You have the right to remain silent—"

"Look, I know the drill," I snapped. "What—you think I've never seen a *movie*, for Crissake?"

Undeterred, the cop droned on: "Anything you say can and will be used against you in a court of law . . ."

5

*N*ever again will I have a prison fantasy. Not that it was ever my steady diet. But in theory, anyway, I always understood the turn-on of being at someone else's mercy. I'm no shrink, but I figure that's why Hollywood boasts the highest rate of kinkiness per capita in the world. You pretty much *have to* eroticize being in bondage to survive in this town. Because in one form or another, anyone connected with showbiz is a glorified slave, totally beholden to powers much greater—be they producers, stars, the press, or even just that fickle entity known as Johnny Q. Public.

But take it from one who knows: the *reality* of being handcuffed and thrown into a cage ain't no fun at all. Especially when you can't just say after a few minutes, "Cell phone's ringing—gotta run."

From the moment I got Mirandized, I felt like one of those tough guys James Cagney used to play. I wasn't going to give the coppers a moment's satisfaction. They could fry me, but I was damned if they'd have any fun doing it. (Okay, so it was really James Cagney in *Angels with Dirty Faces* crossed with Susan Hayward in *I Want to Live!*, but you get the idea.) Even riding over to the slammer, I made it clear that nobody messes with Rick Domino.

"Turn that crap off," I heard myself kvetch at the driver, who, between the squawking sound of APBs, hummed along to a merry country-and-western tune about the freedom of the wide-open prairies. Having been arrested for murder, the last thing I needed was for someone to rub it in. The driver's response was to turn up the volume. I pretended to have no reaction.

About a million TV network vans were following us along the monotonous infinity of the L.A. freeway. Whenever a van came window to window, its bright lights upon me, I defiantly stared straight ahead. The world was waiting to see me hide my face so that I'd be at the mercy of my own game. I was damned if I'd give everyone the satisfaction.

Besides, it really *wasn't* my game. I was tops in my field because the stars trusted me. And one of the ways I earned their trust was to never crowd them. Had someone else just been arrested, I'd have sent a sympathetic card asking for an interview when he or she felt "ready" to see me.

Ordinary people in their cars honked as they sped by, savoring the thrill of seeing for a fleeting second the latest celebrity murderer. From the corner of my eye I saw a lot people give me the finger, but I also saw someone give me the thumbs-up.

"What kind of music do you like?" asked the big guy cop who arrested me, and who sat beside me on the back seat. I looked away from him, saying nothing.

"What—you need to have your attorney present in order to answer?" he tried to cajole.

"Charlie, turn off the radio," he finally told the driver—who reluctantly reached for the knob.

But the radio newscaster was saying something I wanted to hear.

"No, wait. *Please*," I quickly added. The newscaster droned on: *So far, the whereabouts of Best Actor Shane Kirk are not known. The Oscar won by Ms. Perez was not found at the crime scene. Mr. Domino has not yet made a statement . . .*

"The Oscar is missing," I found myself thinking out loud.

"Is that a problem?" asked the Neanderthal cop sitting next to me. "Did you stash it someplace?" Like I was going to just up and tell him if I *had*.

"I want your name and badge number," I said to the big guy, not about to fall for some stupid "good cop/bad cop" routine. "I'm filing charges of police brutality. I'm suing the LAPD for every dime it's worth."

You could tell the big Bozo was trying to conceal a smirk. "I'm Officer Terry Zane. You can see my badge number for yourself." He tapped on his shiny badge.

"I'm glad you think this is so funny. No wonder you're a cop. You get off on making people suffer."

"Hey, watch what you're saying," admonished the driver. "At least cops don't go around murdering innocent people."

"Not according to the newspapers."

In the rearview mirror, I could see the driver tremble with rage. "That's it. You've crossed the line, buddy. I'm pulling over." The right-turn signal blinked ominously, setting in motion a near-collision of two TV vans. Can't say I felt too relieved when they managed to avoid hitting each other.

"*Charlie,*" stated Officer Zane, with a sharpness that suggested a long-standing problem between the two men. "You keep right on driving."

The turn signal stopped blinking. "Yeah, well. Okay. But no more wise cracks against police officers. Got that, smart aleck?" Our eyes met in the rearview mirror. Even in the dark I could tell he really wanted to club me or something.

"Mr. Domino," said the big guy, "everything's been strictly by the book, I can assure you. When someone is a murder suspect, it's my job to contain them as matter of public safety. Frankly, I'm a little surprised you don't seem to know this. Surely in all the movies you see they explain these things."

I shrugged—or tried to, anyway, but the way my hands were cuffed behind me, moving my shoulders shot a pain up my neck. "That's the technical stuff," I answered, resisting the urge to wince. "I never pay attention in movies when they're talking too technically." That wasn't true, but it sounded bratty and uncooperative.

"Huh. Interesting. See, that's the only part I ever like. I'm not really into movies. Don't know the first thing about them, actually. My wife drags me out to a show about once a year. Usually on our anniversary."

"How romantic. Do you make her pay for your ticket?"

Officer Zane laughed, womping me so hard on the shoulder that I wondered if it wasn't his passive-aggressive way of blowing off steam. After all, as a cop he must've hated murderous gay scumbags like me.

It occurred to me to be frightened for my life. Charlie the driver was a small guy who talked big to puff himself up. But this Officer Zane was a good six-four, and weighed at least two-fifty. It was your typical blue-collar blend of flab and muscle. You could tell he was naturally strong, but had never stepped inside a gym. Broad as his shoulders were, and beefy as his arms were, his head still seemed slightly too large for his body. I could imagine him resting it in his wife's lap at the end of a hard day like some sort of giant dinosaur egg. He had big thick bushy eyebrows over his big brown-black eyes. Big thick lips. Probably a size 14 shoe. When he took off his cap to scratch his head, there was maybe a week's worth of dark brown stubble on top. But it wasn't in a stylish way. It looked more like a Marine Corps drill sergeant to whom it never would occur to do anything with his hair other than keep it as short as possible. If you were a casting director, you'd take one look at him and think, "Incredible Hulk."

It was as if the only Good Fairy to show up at his christening was the one in charge of size, because the only thing you noticed about this Zane guy was just how very *large* he was—and no, I don't mean "down there." I couldn't have been less interested in sneaking a look, as those big bear bruiser types did nothing for me, thanks just the same. Give me a genteel, "A" list (preferably gay) man who summered at Cannes and sported a trim, solid physique. And while we're at it, a man who showed some nominal amount of brain activity, and a knowledge of wine that extended beyond which type of cardboard box sealed in the most bouquet. Someone like Shane Kirk was a man of the world when compared with this Officer Zane clown. He was like so many uncouth dolts I left behind in Iowa, thumbing my nose all the way.

"You're a funny guy," commented Officer Zane. "I can see why people like your column so much."

"I'm also on TV," I belligerently shot back. Back in Iowa, I'd learned to squelch the schoolyard bullies through sarcasm and an uppity attitude, and I figured it was worth another try. It was the only defense I had, since, even had I not been cuffed, I wouldn't exactly have been able to fend off Officer Zane with my prowess in the martial arts.

We were momentarily blinded by the floodlights from a TV van. Charlie damn near drove us off the road. "Jesus!" he remarked, honking at the van angrily. "Fuckin' reporters." Officer Zane gave me one of those downward smiles, the ironic corners of his ample mouth intending to indicate that we were in on some sort of joke together about the hapless Charlie. I coolly looked out the window to ignore him.

"Say, since you're the big Hollywood reporter," suggested Charlie, "maybe you can settle the score. Isn't Clint Eastwood married to Barbra Streisand?"

I thought I must've heard wrong. "Isn't what *what?*"

"You know. Dirty Harry. Isn't he married to Barbra Streisand? I could've sworn I heard that someplace, but ol' Terry over here says she's not."

Officer Zane wrinkled his bushy eyebrows with sincerity. "She's married to Marcus Welby, M.D.—isn't that right?"

It should have been simple enough to correct him, but somehow it felt difficult, like explaining something to a very young child or a very old adult. "Well, she married Jim Brolin, who used to *be* on *Marcus Welby, M.D.*, but he played Dr. Kiley."

"See?" triumphed Officer Zane. "I told you, Charlie."

"You told me *what?*" countered Charlie. "He just *said* you were wrong."

"Well, I was closer than you were." Officer Zane winked at me. I hoped it didn't show that I was flattered—though *why* I was I couldn't imagine. What is it about these dumb-fuck straight guys that can get under your skin, in spite of all your better judgment?

"Yeah, yeah, yeah," articulated Charlie. "Say, Mr. Reporter—"

"His name is Mr. Domino," corrected Officer Zane. Obviously, the only reason he was being so superpolite was that he was hoping I wouldn't sue him.

"Yeah, whatever. I have a question for you. They say that Barbra Streisand is a fag lover. What's the story? I mean, she's a normal woman, right? So why would a lady who likes men hang out with some faggot?"

"Charlie, that's *enough*, dammit." Officer Zane turned to me—though I noticed he couldn't quite look me in the eye. Gay-wise, he obviously still had a lot of hang-ups himself. "Mr. Domino, I apologize for my fellow officer's remarks. He just likes to give people a hard time. Please don't take it seriously. It doesn't reflect the policy of the Los Angeles Police Department."

"So, you're some sort of big-shot detective, I suppose?" I asked Officer Zane, eager to change the subject. A frenetic honking of horns indicated that yet another TV van was unsuccessful in cutting over to our left side.

"Maniac drivers," commented Officer Zane, shaking his head as if unable to comprehend the insanity of it all. If aggressive driving threw him for such a loop, I wondered how he'd do, say, after five minutes at a private Hollywood digs.

He turned to me with his good-cop cheery face. "No, sir. I told you, I'm an officer. If I were a *detective*, that would be my title. I'd like to make detective, though. Homicide," he pleasantly added, leaving little doubt that he was President of the Tact Society of America.

"You don't say," I said in my most sarcastic tone of voice.

"I think I'd be good," he continued, as if I had nothing better to do than listen to him wax on about his career goals. "I *know* I'd be. But there's a huge waiting list. I'm just another cop without a face. For twelve years I've been working overtime every chance I get, volunteering for every cruddy job no one else wants, and where has it gotten me? Nowhere, that's where. But hey, what can you do?"

His clear dark eyes crinkled as he grinned. As much as I hated to admit it, the devil earned his due: Officer Zane had a great-looking smile. I could see how someone more naive than I was could be manipulated by him.

"Well, Sherlock, I'd say you're a long way from your goal. For starters, you arrested the wrong man."

"That's for the court to decide," Officer Zane replied evenly, all serious again. "Just out of curiosity, Mr. Domino, who *should* we have arrested instead?"

"Shane Kirk." It felt good to say this out loud, even if only to some big bruiser cop. My feelings for Shane had made me do all kinds of things against my better judgment. But apparently I wasn't a total loser. I drew the line at protecting him after he bumped off Tara—or at least knew who did—and then vanished to let me take the fall. When a guy does this to you, you find yourself not caring about him as much as you thought you did. Life's funny that way.

"Shane Kirk," pondered Officer Zane. "Should I know who he is?"

"*Duh.* He just won the Academy Award for Best Actor. I mean, *hello?* It's Oscar night, for crying out loud. It's only the most important occasion in Hollywood. The crowning achievement of the entire film industry."

"Wow. That's impressive, I guess. This Shane Kirk fellow must be a great actor."

"Ha! Shows how much you know. He couldn't act his way out of a used condom."

I looked to see if I grossed out Officer Zane's uptight heterosexist sensibilities, but I have to hand it to him. He didn't miss a beat.

"I'm confused. If it's the most important award in Hollywood, why would they give it to someone who can't act?"

"How the fuck should I know? It's not like I get to vote, or anything."

"But it *is* your job to find out that kind of stuff, isn't it?"

I could feel my eyes practically rolling out of my head. "Trust me, Shane is a long story. But the point is, he knows what really happened. He was outside in the parking lot about one second before you got there. In other words, when Tara was getting shot, and when

Shane should've been inside accepting the Oscar he just won. Who knows? Maybe the prick got so greedy, he bumped Tara off just to get *her* Oscar, too."

I was about to tell him about someone taking a shot at me and the rest of it, but I got this terrible jittery feeling as I saw that we were pulling into police headquarters. I could barely even swallow. Ironically, I was almost glad to be in handcuffs for the steadiness they provided.

"Looks like we're here," Officer Zane remarked brightly. You'd have thought we were old pals who just arrived at our weekend fishing lodge. "Stay with me, okay?, and I'll get you inside without all these no-good reporters eating you alive. No offense," he quickly added.

"Did you hear what I just *said?* Shane Kirk knows who killed Tara. He even might've done it himself. *He's* the dangerous one."

Officer Zane smiled. "I'm sure you'll have plenty of opportunities to tell your story, Mr. Domino. Chill out a little, okay?"

"Chill *out!?* Gee, what a good idea. I'm going to fry for a crime I didn't commit, but, hey, let's just relax. Let's have a good ol' time as they lock me up on Death Row."

Officer Zane rubbed his temples. "You know I didn't mean it like that. I'm only trying to do my job."

I was beyond endurance in dealing with this nitwit. "Let's just get it over with."

Plowing through the mass of reporters was like a scene out of a million different movies: "Mr. Domino, did you kill Tara?" "Rick, tell us what really happened." "Do you think you'll get the same cell as O.J.?" "Is it true that you were in love with Tara, and that you shot her in a jealous rage to keep her from marrying Shane?" (Now *there* was a reporter who'd done her homework.) The lights were blinding, but I kept walking straight forward, refusing to even blink.

Officer's Zane's size came in handy, I must say. He forced us on through like a Sherman tank.

Once we got inside, Officer Zane removed the handcuffs. For a second or so, he shuffled about uncomfortably, like he wanted to say it was a pleasure meeting me or good luck, but knew there was no way to do so. Or maybe he was waiting for me to thank him for protecting me against Charlie. I saw no reason to kiss Officer Zane's feet just because he hadn't been blatantly antigay. That should be a given all the time. Certainly I had better things to worry about than the feelings of some Nowheresville cop.

"Mr. Domino," Officer Zane began. I looked up at him defiantly. "Never mind."

6

$\mathcal{I}$ barely had a moment to relish the freedom of having my hands back when I heard the unmistakable, booze-and-cigarettes voice of Francine Quick. Still decked out in her *vogue à la Minsky's* regalia, she called out to me like Diane Keaton lunging through the Communist masses for Warren Beatty's embrace in *Reds*. "My darling Rick, this cannot be," she cried, one gloved arm outstretched.

It was hard to separate fact from fiction when it came to such an entrenched showbiz vet as Francine. Was she really overcome with emotion, was it an act, or was there even a difference anymore? Only the gin bottle knew for sure.

I didn't mind that a thick, chaotic hive of police officers prevented me from reaching out to her. It always felt a little icky to embrace Francine, like being forced to kiss some awful relative when you're a kid.

Still, I was interested in what she had to say.

"Rick, you must call me," she bellowed desperately. From the way a pair of cops led her to the doorway, you'd have thought she was Norma Desmond. She gestured subtly to indicate cognizance of the many reporters. "Just call me," she repeated with self-importance. "*Do it!*"

Our eyes met as the cops shoved her outside. Through the glass, I could see her regaining her star poise: shoulders back, chest out and out and out, and throat cleared as TV cameras whirred and she made some innocuous statement.

I was pretty sure that whatever she had to say to me was connected to the loving little huddle of whispers I saw her engage in back at the crime scene with Bob, Jeep, Cinda, and Tru. But I wasn't given much time to think about it all as I found myself in the enlivening company of three police officers. I strongly suspected their training video was the scene from *Blue Velvet* in which Dennis Hopper gets all chummy with Isabella Rosellini.

Two of the three cops could've been Officer Zane's triplet brothers. I confess that I found the third so-called peace officer attractive. (Think Ethan Hawke crossed with Matt Damon.) True, he wore a wedding band, but under the circumstances I was getting my jollies wherever I could find them. As if my luck were changing a little, it was Ethan who took pictures of my hands and put this goo stuff on them that he kept saying was soap.

I also found solace in seeing other suspects being brought in. Call me egotistical, but it was balm to my soul to see that I was not alone in my plight. Plus there was the lively hum of the police station, like something out of countless black-and-white movies: the incessant talking and paper shuffling, the old-fashioned typewriters clamoring to the rhythm of two-finger typists, the gurgle of the water cooler, and the smell of stale coffee and day-old donuts. It all suggested some sort of continuance of life beyond the misfortune at hand.

Okay, so life is not an Esther Williams musical, I told myself, *but that doesn't mean it's an Ingmar Bergman filmed nightmare either.* There was reason not to lose hope.

When we entered into the holding area, I did not expect to see sets designed by Cedric Gibbons. But I was unprepared for just how grim it was. Once you stepped into the jail corridor, it was as if every bad smell in the world had been locked inside. No amount of off-white paint could disguise the essential creepiness of the cinderblock walls. I felt as if I were being led through the catacombs to Hannibal Lector, like some unassuming mouse about to be devoured by a boa constrictor.

Getting strip-searched was not exactly a laugh riot, either. In fact, it was about as unfunny as you could get. Unless, of course, your notion of humor is a near-petrifying fear that this roomful of cops is going to brutally gang-rape you, and since you're a gay man, no one will believe you. Me, I prefer knock-knock jokes.

"Easy there, fella," I encouraged Ethan, doing my best to smile through my grimace as I stood stark naked on dirty, mildewed linoleum, bent over for inspection. "I can assure you, there is no secret passageway behind a bookshelf up there." After what felt like decades, it was over. Hardly a turn-on, it was more like a bunch of bullies torturing the neighborhood sissy.

Ethan—whose appeal was diminishing by the second—looked me over for a moment before tossing me bright orange coveralls and a dime store pair of rubber thongs. "I guess you're a *medium*," he commented with a smirk, as if I were really a "small" in some telling, male sort of way, but he'd humor me. The coveralls smelled of strong detergent, flecks of which clung to the course synthetic material.

"Hurry up and get dressed," Ethan scolded. "It's just a prison uniform. It won't bite."

"Only the other inmates do *that*," added one of the big cops. "Better watch out for your pecker." The other big cop laughed. Then he whispered something to his lookalike, who roared and gave his pal a playful punch on the arm.

Needless to say, the little witticism did not exactly inspire confidence. Would I be put in some sort of communal cell? As an out gay man, I hardly relished the possibility. I wondered if I should say something, but decided it was safer not to.

"Just out of curiosity, Mr. Big Shot Reporter," Ethan began, scratching his cheek with his index finger like it was some sort of in-house joke. "I was wondering if you could give us the latest hot scoop. Just what did you have against Tara Perez, anyway? She was my little girl's favorite movie star. She looked up to her as a role model. You have no idea how much you've made my daughter cry. Thanks a lot."

I zipped up the stiff coveralls. "I didn't do it."

Ethan nodded his head sadly, as if I were just too pathetic for words, and actually replied: "That's what they all say." The cinematic qualities of the moment were not lost on me, but Ethan and Co. looked dead serious.

"No, really. I mean it, guys," I slightly stumbled as I slid my feet into the thongs. Out of force of habit, I caught the trace of my reflection in the barred window. Rick Domino, Jailbird. I wasn't exactly inspired to burst into a rousing chorus of *If They Could See Me Now*.

Apropos of this sentiment, Ethan set me up for my mug shots. "Smile for all your fans, you prick," he meanly encouraged. He didn't exactly bring back fond memories of the Sears photographer holding up puppets and lollipops.

One the big cops stated: "They said her Oscar's missing. Did you steal it? Were you planning on hocking it for drug money?"

"Probably some kind of faggot sex toy," contributed his sidekick.

So the press was making a big to-do about the missing Oscar.

"Turn to the left," commanded Ethan.

"And what about Shane Kirk?" continued the big cop. "Did you kill him, too? Just because he was a normal guy?"

"Probably you knew about the engagement ring," contributed the other big guy.

I hoped it didn't show that my ears were practically on fire. *What* engagement ring? For Tara? For *me*? Or was it just a made-up story to throw me over the edge and confess all?

"Now turn to the right," Ethan dictated.

I literally bit the inside of my lower lip to keep from speaking.

"Yeah, Shane Kirk proposed to her," elaborated the third cop. "We've already found a diamond ring backstage. With a receipt made out to Shane Kirk."

Ethan gave him a dirty look, though for all I knew it was an act.

"Hey, it's already in the news," the big mouth cop protested. "That reporter guy found it and turned it over. Whatshisname— Chauncey something."

So there really was a ring. I wanted to believe that Chauncey didn't hate me enough to have planted it, that he wasn't in on the whole thing. But recent events were making it hard to trust anybody, let alone an arch rival.

"You fags always have to spoil things for normal people," observed Ethan.

Needless to say, my mug shots looked like hell—and were instantly broadcast all around the world. From the expression on my face, you'd have thought I was still being strip-searched.

"Would you like to make a statement? Let's talk about it." Ethan's good-cop smile was far less convincing than Officer Zane's had been. I got the impression that Ethan never smiled in his life until the police academy taught him to do so for interrogation purposes.

"You know I won't. You know I'm going to wait for my lawyer."

Ethan turned ugly again, his true colors shining through. "Yeah, I know how you rich folks operate. You think you're better than everyone else. That you're above the law. We've already heard about the hard time you gave poor Charlie. Like you're some big important person, like Mr. Howell on *Gilligan's Island*, and we're just your flunkies who do as we're told. Well, after you do a little hard time, you just might come down from your Beverly Hills ivory tower, Mr. Thurston Howell. Yeah, that's what we should call you—Mr. Howell."

"*Mrs.* Howell is more like it," cleverly opined one of the big guys.

"Mrs. Howell?" pondered the third cop. "Oh wait—I get it. Hey, that's pretty good." He chortled for his delight. "Mrs. Howell. That's a good one."

On that cheery note, I found myself led down still another corridor, more dank and stinky with every footstep, and staring at a stark, decrepit cinderblock cell. The first thing I noticed was that there wasn't a seat or lid on the metal toilet. From the barred window high above, the headlights of a car beamed striped shadows across the iron bunks. Lurking in the slant of zebralike darkness were a pair of inmates. With a politically correct TV-movie perfection, one guy was white and one was black.

"Ladies, I'd like you to meet Mrs. Howell," Ethan declared with relish.

"You know—from *Gilligan's Island*," elaborated the cop who first made the joke.

The inmates made wolf whistles as Ethan turned the key.

"Welcome to your new mansion, you murdering shit." He gave me a shove.

As the chortles of the cops echoed in the distance, I stared straight ahead as the two big convicts approached me. Their shadows loomed large across the tiny cell. I tried to speak, to maybe promise that I'd give them all my worldly possessions if they left me alone, but my fear seemed to paralyze my throat. The two men stood over me, grinning in anticipation. I hoped it wasn't too obvious that I was trembling. If I saw my fear, they'd go even rougher on me.

"You're that Hollywood reporter guy, right?" said the black cellmate.

"Uh . . . yeah."

He smiled ear to ear. "I'm Calvin. This is Ed." They each offered their hands. "Can we get your autograph?" inquired Ed. "Next time we can use a pen, that is."

"And tell us if it's true about Cinda Sharpe. Is she a les?"

"Are Jeep Andrews and Bob Raflowitz pals in real life?"

"Do you think Spielberg's new movie is going to fly?"

"I've heard Tom Hanks is headed for divorce. Is he seeing Meg Ryan?"

"What about Whitney Houston and Bobby Brown?"

"Whoa," I said, sitting down on the edge of a bunk. "One question at a time, guys."

Calvin and Ed were such an attentive audience that I was almost disappointed when my attorney finally arrived. Corny as it sounds, I kept thinking how it said something about the indomitable human spirit, the way simple human companionship could lessen the horror of being behind bars. I didn't know why they were in jail, but I had to say they were two of the nicest guys I ever met.

"Say, you're Benji Malone," noted Ed, highly impressed. "You aren't by chance taking on any *pro bono* cases?"

It wasn't surprising that they knew who Benji was. He was a high-profile mouthpiece to the stars, and a minor celebrity in his own right. Stars being stars, they were always getting divorced and committing felonies and whatnot. So Benji's face cropped up regularly on TV to make innocuous statements about how his client was working things out "amicably" with his/her ex-, or "amicably" working out a deal with the DA over some drug bust or drunken assault charge. A legal jack-of-all-trades, he'd successfully defended a minor screenwriter and an even more minor TV actor on a murder rap a few years earlier. I knew I was in good hands.

Speaking of divorce, Benji was short, thin, and balding in a cuddly sort of way, and insecure starlets found him irresistible. To date, he'd been to the altar five times. What made his breakups especially pronounced was that each and every time thus far his ex-wife would make some abrupt life change upon divorcing him. You would've thought they married him to get ahead in their careers, and maybe they had, but by the time they divorced him they decided to chuck it all to live on a lesbian kibbutz, or something. They'd always say how "sweet" Benji was, and how even though the marriage didn't last, he taught them what was really important in life. I always wondered how this could've been the case, since the Benji I knew talked the same polluted showbiz crap as everyone else in town. But I guessed when you knew someone in an intimate context, you saw other things.

"Sorry, guys," Benji cheerfully told my cellmates. "I'm afraid your pal, Mr. Domino, is going to be taking up all of my time. But, tell me, what are you in for?"

"I beat my grandmother with a hammer," Ed informed us, as if politely responding to a routine question. "Only I didn't do it," he quickly added.

"I tried to poison a kindergarten class," added Calvin. "But it's all a misunderstanding."

"Well, best of luck to both of you." Benji offered his hand. "Now, Mr. Domino and I are going to talk in private." He snapped his fingers for the guard to open the cell.

"It was an honor meeting you, Mr. Domino." Ed offered his hand.

"It sure was," agreed Calvin.

"Uh, gee. Thanks."

I saw no choice but to shake their hands.

7

A guard inanely whistled "Strangers in the Night" as he led Benji and me into a small, windowless room with a rickety card table and two metal folding chairs.

Just seeing Benji lifted my spirits; corrupt as he was, he always had this effect on me. I wasn't sure why, though I'd heard other clients say the same thing. Maybe it was that he seemed so singular of purpose—represent anyone for anything, as long as they paid big bucks—that he lacked any sort of complicating moral conscience. You never had to worry that Benji would end up at Betty Ford, because he obviously had no inner self to conflict with the superficiality and greed that was at the essence of Hollywood.

Benji put on his creepy-looking reading glasses and took out a file folder with my name on it—actually, it said, "Rick Domino, No. 47," given all the various lawsuits he'd helped me wiggle out of over the years. "Well, Rick, you've certainly outdone yourself this time. Now what on God's green earth really happened?"

Since Benji already knew about Shane's presence in my life, there wasn't much to tell. But even so, Benji interrupted me about fifty thousand times. Usually, when people cut you off a lot it makes for mistrust; but when Benji did it, you felt reassured. Once I was finished, he grew quiet just as he always did. Like Elvis unable to fall asleep without the TV on, Benji did his best thinking while someone else was talking.

"Well, it doesn't sound very promising," he finally remarked. "You're *sure* you didn't see who was shooting at you?"

"I guess life would be a lot simpler right now if I had. But, honestly, I couldn't see a motherfucking thing." I found myself unable to resist staring at a file folder in the briefcase with a different client's name on it.

Benji turned the folder name-down. "*Really*, Rick. You're not on assignment."

"Sorry. Force of habit."

"Well, stop it," he scolded, like a father trying to get his son to stop biting his nails. "Back to this person in the alleyway trying to send you to that great big Oscar show in the sky—height, male or female, clothing, type of gun, *anything?*"

"I keep telling you—it was dark in the alleyway, I was panicked, the whole thing took like two seconds. Maybe they'll find a bullet from the other gun. That'd *help*, wouldn't it?"

"Maybe, maybe not. The DA could say it's unrelated—that there's a shooting every ten seconds in this dump of a town. Or that to alibi yourself you fired from another gun, and tossed it someplace. Or that someone took a shot at you in self-defense. Or just about anything they fucking feel like—*if* a shell turns up, that is. They're wasting no time, incidentally. They already know that the bullets came from the gun you were holding. Lots of nice gun residue on those manicured hands of yours, too. Not very bright of you, Rick, I gotta say."

"Shit."

He rearranged the papers in my file. "Couldn't have said it better myself. Of course, the press doesn't know that Shane was in the alley, too. All they're saying is that he's missing—though they're saying it like he's this lily-white who's not at all to blame. Who were you sitting next to? Could they verify that you were in your seat until Best Actor? It all happened so fast, it probably wouldn't matter. But, hey, it might be worth a shot."

"I sat next to some nobody—I don't even remember who it was. It wouldn't make any difference, though. I brilliantly got out of my seat *before* Best Actor. I saw a scoop. I was leaning against a wall in the back, way out of camera range." Thinking one step ahead, I added with considerable regret: "Then, of course, I didn't even walk up the main aisle to go backstage. I slinked down this empty hall-way, and through a side door. I remember thinking how clever I was that nobody saw me."

"So there's *no* filmed record of where you were when Tara got shot. Gee, what a lucky break."

I nervously tapped the table top like a drum. "Actually, there was one person who could help. Maybe. At the exit door, just before I went outside, there was this second-string blonde. You know the type: Takes the Greyhound to Hollywood a week after high-school graduation. Over the hill six months later. Keeps hoping that this latest producer will make good on his offer to give her a bikini walk-through. Probably did a few favors under the table in the literal sense to get invited tonight. Could've been twenty-five, could've been forty-five. Looked a little familiar, though I couldn't place her. She seemed in a hurry. Bumped right into me, though she could've just been wasted. Or in a hurry to touch up her roots."

"Gee, a faded bottle-blonde at the Oscars. That should narrow the list down to about half a million. Besides, if she saw you at the door for like one second, who's to say you were coming or going, or what?"

Benji began pacing back and forth, a sure sign that his brain was on a roll.

"Its all very simple," he explained. "Shane bumps Tara off, and leaves the gun on the ground for someone else to pick up—hope-fully you. After all, Lady Luck's been on his side so far. He figures—and correctly, I might add—that first and foremost you'd be the one to go looking for him. I mean, he knows you pretty well, am I right?"

I lamely nodded affirmatively.

"But even if someone else beats you to the punch, he's got an extra gun, and he takes pot shots from the alley, knowing that who-ever he was shooting at would pick up the other gun and fire back. He even was kind enough to put the gun near the body, where it couldn't be missed. And the open exit door . . . why, it's pure *genius*."

I was tempted to say something sarcastic about how if it was an act of "genius," then Shane couldn't possibly have done it. But Benji's nose for where the stink was coming from was not a talent to be taken for granted. Besides, Shane *was* extremely clever in some ways, wasn't he? I mean, how dumb could he have been to have gone from common street whore to Best Actor? Dumb as the proverbial fox.

"Sure," Benji continued, "Shane can say he heroically missed accepting his Oscar because he was trying to stop you from shooting Tara. He could even say you had a motive. You were jealous of Tara because of her torrid romance with Shane. And if you told the truth, who would everyone believe? The slime-bucket gay gossip columnist, or the ha-ha hetero, fine young all-American success story?"

I wanted to say something, but no words came out of my mouth.

"And now there's even this talk about an engagement ring," Benji relentlessly persisted. "And I already know what you're thinking. *No*, Rick, I don't believe Chauncey would go so far as to set you up. Anymore than I'd believe for a minute that the ring was really for you. I'm sorry, Rick. But I have to practice some tough love here. You need to face up to things. Or at least face up to the strong possibility of them."

"But if Tara just got engaged to Shane, why wouldn't she be wearing his ring? Why would they find it backstage, with the *sales* receipt?"

Benji frowned, and took out his Palm Pilot, keying in an entry. "In point of fact, it was found on a folding chair."

"That doesn't answer the question."

"Think about it, Rick. Shane proposes, Tara accepts—only they're going to wait for the exact right moment to make the big announcement. Why shove it into Oscar night, when it could be a major scoop on some other day? So she wouldn't be wearing the ring. Who knows? Maybe it was such a calculated business move that he brought along the sales receipt to get reimbursed."

"But he left the ring backstage, on a *chair*. Why wouldn't he take it with him?"

The Palm Pilot beeped; Benji returned it to his suit coat pocket. "To play the grieving fiancé, of course. And to point out how innocent he is. After all, if he wanted to kill her, why would he have just proposed?"

"Well, what if she turned him down, so he flipped out and killed her?"

Benji wore an expression that communicated a profound lack of confidence in my mental prowess.

"I mean, the *police* might think that, since they don't know Shane's gay."

"Maybe. But people believe what they want to about movie stars. You, if anyone, should know that. And believe it or not, cops are people, too. As far as the world is concerned, Barbie met Ken. Last year's Barbie with this year's Ken, to be sure. But I'm sure you get the general idea."

For a moment, I literally thought I was going to faint. I know that sounds wimpy of me, but the reality of hearing someone say out loud just how dastardly Shane might be was more than I could stand.

"So you really do think it was Shane, then?" I finally muttered.

"I'm saying let's start with Mr. Kirk and see if one plus one reasonably resembles two. Sure, keep digging. But right off the bat, we just might have a winner, folks. What do *you* think, Rick? You gotta admit it sounds reasonable. As much as murder can be reasonable, that is."

"Kind of," I allowed. "I mean, he definitely knows *something*, and Lord knows he's not the nicest guy you'd ever want to bring home to meet Mom and Dad. Only why would he do such a thing? He was about to win the Oscar. Tara was covering his gay ass. He had his whole future in front of him. Why would he want to kill her? For that matter, why would anybody?"

Benji made a dismissive snort. "The bitch claws her way from poverty to superstardom, and you don't think anyone wishes her dead?"

"Of course people wished her dead. Hell, I wished her dead myself when I'd see her with Shane. She really got off on rubbing my face in it. But in this town everyone wishes everyone dead all the time. But that's as far as it goes. We just savor the fantasy."

"Usually, but not always. Tonight being a good case in point."

"But at the *Oscars*? I mean, if you're going to kill someone, you do it when no one's around. You don't do it in front of an audience of a billion people."

He peered at me with his glasses down to his nose, looking very homely in a pleasant way. "Apparently, that's just what someone did, Rick. And so far so good. They're getting away with it. As for Shane's motive, think about it. It begins with a 'P' and ends with a 'Y.'"

"Publicity," I numbly stated.

"You got it. He not only wins Best Actor, but is the brave hero mourning the loss of Tara, his one great love. You might as well mandate that every tabloid in the world has his picture on the cover for the next decade. Plus he gets rid of two albatrosses around his neck at the same time. Pseudo-fiancée Tara, of course, and as much as I hate to say, it, Rick—*you*."

"But he could've just broken up with me. I'm a big boy. I can take it."

Benji tapped a pencil. "And risk that in a moment of pique you'd out him to the world? Or ruin him via some other nasty rumor? Face it, Rick. Shane is very, *very* protective of his career. In all my years in this town, I've never seen anyone so singularly determined to make it, and Lord knows I've witnessed my share of hardball. Who knows? Maybe Tara threatened to out him herself unless he married her. Maybe he got a little too pissed off, and *whammo*."

I traced the fake wood-grain pattern of the card table with my finger. My thoughts were racing a mile a minute. I kept trying to think of something about Shane—some little moment of genuine vulnerability or gesture of kindness—that contradicted all that Benji was supposing about him. But I came up blank. I could've been one of those heroines in a Lifetime Movie whose husband is obviously some sort of crazed rapist/killer, only she's the last to know.

Benji let me be alone with my thoughts. Finally, I said, "The blonde at the door is a start, right? I mean, what would I have to lose by finding her? And I *will* find her, Benji. That's exactly what I'm good at. Like I said, she even looked vaguely familiar."

He made a face at a contract of some kind in a different folder. "Who doesn't look familiar in this town? Good luck tracking her down just the same." He scribbled onto a yellow Post-It, then carefully placed the Post-It on the right-hand corner the contract. "You might want to locate that missing Oscar while you're at it. Naturally, you already thought of that. And a million other things, if I know Rick Domino."

I leaned back in my chair, attempting to feign a state of calm, but instead almost losing my balance. "As a matter of fact, Francine stopped by to chat. They wouldn't let her see me."

"That must've broken your heart."

"Be kind, Benji. I think it was very sweet of her. When I was arrested, I saw her talking with Bob and Cinda and Tru and Jeep kind of off to the side, like they were all in on something. And I think she was going to tell me what it was."

"Well, whatever it was, I doubt that it was what to buy you for your birthday. They were all hanging around at the time of the killing, weren't they? Presenting awards, receiving awards, fucking awards. And of course they all had the pleasure of knowing Tara quite well. Go for it, Rick. Let me handle the courtroom crap, but you're still the gossip kingpin. They won't want to alienate you, just in case you get off. So they'll talk. Not a *lot*, of course. But enough for you to rub two sticks together. Shane is sitting on the goodies big time. But don't let him cramp your style. Do what you can without him."

He peered at me through his reading glasses significantly, as if to say I'd be wise to do without Shane in other ways, as well.

"So, Benji—what's your strategy in the meantime?"

"Strategy? At this point, Rick, my strategy is to get on my knees and beg." He clicked his briefcase shut. "You have to realize that a beautiful movie star just died young. And was *murdered*. There's already like a million flower bouquets piling up in the parking lot where she died. Tara T-shirts. Tara baseball caps. Tara French ticklers, for all I goddamn know. How the hell people crank this junk out so fast—well, it's ingenuity, you have to admit it. Makes ya proud to be an American.

"But don't worry. Half the town's offered to help you post bail. Assuming the judge lets you, of course. We've got a woman on the bench, Ruetha Hopkins, and she's got bigger balls than any of the men. So don't hold your breath."

Assuming I posted bail? I couldn't even think that way. I *had* to get out of this place.

Still, I had my pride if nothing else. "I won't accept a dime of charity."

Benji gave me a mocking spatter of applause. "How noble. Look, I put in a call to your accountant. You're cash-poor, my friend. Seems you've been making too many charitable donations to the needy on Rodeo Drive. Unless you want to mortgage your house, I'm afraid you have no choice."

"When you say 'half the town' offered to help, who exactly do you mean?"

Benji stood up and straightened the knot on his tie. "Why, your old pal Chauncey Riggs, of course. Did I say half the town? Sorry, I exaggerated." He absently brushed his Italian-cut lapels. "Pure Hollywood politics. Chauncey not only wants to come out of this smelling like a rose, he wants to be Pope. If you're not guilty, he looks good. If you're guilty, he can sing his story to the tune of millions about his shock in having trusted you, and cry all the way to the bank. Incidentally, the old guy's a pretty good singer. Bass baritone, believe it or not. Heard him once after he'd had about a million Rob Roys at a party. The drink, that is."

I did some quick mental arithmetic. "Tell him thanks but no thanks. Chauncey will have it all over the papers, and if I'm perceived as broke on top of everything else, then I really will be marked as a loser. All I'll need is a drug problem and a *People* magazine cover story, and they might as well start digging my grave."

Benji snapped his fingers to get the guard's attention. "The arraignment is at nine A.M. I'll drop by a suit for you in the morning. In the meantime, I'll do my lawyer intimidation thing to get you a private cell."

"That's *it*? You really can't get me out of here tonight?"

Benji took a deep sigh. "Think 'Movie of the Week.' That ought to help you keep your sanity. Count royalty checks instead of sheep." He cleared his throat. "But I'm afraid that's not *quite* it."

From the phony showbiz smile he wore, I knew that he had some pretty crappy news.

"Okay, lay it on me."

"It won't look good if you don't cooperate *at all*. So I agreed to let you talk to a shrink."

"You mean to help me get in touch with my feelings? I have my own shrink for that."

"I mean a *cop* shrink, you idiot. No, I can't be in the room. It's not official questioning. He just wants to see if you're nuts enough to kill."

"How wondrous. How ideal."

"Look, Rick. I BS'd you out of having to meet with this detective who was foaming at the mouth to a beat a confession out of you. Count your blessings."

And so I was whisked off to yet another cell, where I met with a somber, robotic police shrink who had all the personality of Dan Rather under anesthesia. I was determined to give him nothing to work with. He showed me inkblots; I insisted that none of them looked like anything. Actually, that wasn't such a leap from the truth. They looked like *inkblots,* for God's sake. He asked me about my childhood. I said I didn't remember it. He asked me if I killed Tara. I said no. He asked me I were a violent person. I said no. He asked me what I did when I got angry, and I replied, "I beat off." He was quiet for about two full minutes as he shuffled through papers; I literally could hear him breathing. Then he said the interview was over. And to think that hardworking taxpayers gave this ninnie a paycheck.

It was well after four in the morning before I finally nodded off to a few fitful hours of sleep. I was grateful for a private cell, yet I didn't know it was possible to feel so alone. Psychotic as it sounds, I found myself feeling a little homesick for Calvin and Ed, even jealous of their companionship.

So much anxiety was swimming through my brain that I honestly don't know if I was dreaming, or if I really was hearing a man shouting from down the hall. He sounded like he was kicking smack cold turkey. But it blended in with a dream in which *I* was the one who was shouting, and the Ethan Hawke cop was strapping me into an electric chair to make me confess. Officer Zane from the car ride was saying to him, "But if he's *dead*, he can't talk." To which Ethan replied, "Oh, he'll talk all right. Death won't shut *this* one up."

Which, I guessed, signaled a healthy survival instinct on my part.

8

*J*ust my luck, the arraignment was broadcast on live, international TV. The courtroom was jam-packed with press, while hundreds more clamored to get in. I looked like crap, naturally. The prison mattress was about as comfy as a bed of nails. My back was killing me, and I didn't even have any fun to show for it. I passed on the prison cuisine, thanks just the same. (Fortunately, Benji brought me a cardamom latte, half-decaf, with a mocha-kiwi croissant.)

I ignored these relatively minor annoyances. Like a rabid Monopoly player, my only thought was to get the hell out of jail. The torture of confinement wasn't even the point anymore. Benji was a genius at pulling rabbits out of hats, but I didn't want merely to be found not guilty through a bunch of legal red tape. I wanted every man, woman, and child in America to know that I was one hundred percent innocent. And like the Little Red Hen, I was going to have to do it all myself. I didn't become the gossip kingpin for nothing. I could find dirt like a hog sniffing out a truffle. I would not only find who the killer was—I'd find him or her before I even had to *go* to trial.

Just as Benji warned me, the DA opposed bail. "Your honor," she remarked, clicking about the marble courtroom floor in her professional black pumps, "The People are firmly convinced that

Mr. Domino poses a serious threat to society. The very public nature of this crime signals a highly unstable character." She wore a navy blue blazer with a gold butterfly pin on the lapel, and a blue and gold scarf tied about her gray blouse. As a gay man, I have long been mystified as to why a woman would actually *choose* to dress this way.

I studied her for a moment. "Hey, wait a second," I whispered to Benji. "I *know* her. Caroline Caruthers, am I right? She met Jeep Andrews at some sort of benefit for free-range goldfish or whatever, and offered to be his eternal sex slave. Needless to say, Caruthers wasn't his druthers. But apparently she's got quite a thing for doing it blindfolded while shackled in a broom closet. And there was something about crushing raw eggs between her knees."

Benji grinned, and scribbled something into his notepad. Imperiously standing to speak on my behalf, he slipped the note to Ms. Caruthers. The poor dear turned white as a spoonful of Kaopectate as she read the contents, and then made eye contact with me. Her short, unbecoming, mousy brown curls—no doubt intended to indicate yes-I'm-all-business-but-not-really-I'm-also-soft-and-feminine—wiggled at me menacingly, like Medusa's snakes.

"Your Honor, my client is innocent of all charges," asserted Benji. "Hence, he poses no threat to society at all. He has no previous criminal record. The only evidence against him is purely circumstantial."

"Circumstantial? I think not," posed the DA co-counsel, a nerdy young guy named (I could not help gloating) Marion Goober, who looked like a Marion Goober, and who came across as hopelessly wet behind the ears. How he ended up in L.A. rather than, say, Beaver Dam, Ohio, shall remain one of Fate's cruel jokes.

Young Mr. Goober was so nondescript he literally seemed neuter, lacking in any sexual urges whatsoever. Yet I guessed that eventually he'd marry some unfortunate woman and have the proper 2.2 kids, like someone at Baskin-Robbins unable to make up his mind before settling on one scoop of vanilla.

"I hardly think being found at the crime scene holding the smoking murder weapon is merely circumstantial. We have a iron-clad case against the defend*ant*"—he made a point of pronouncing the last syllable with a short "A" sound—"and strongly protest the way counsel is attempting to discredit—"

"Your honor, may we approach?" interrupted Ms. Caruthers.

There was a stir of mumbles that Judge Hopkins, from atop her lofty pedestal, saw fit to stop with a bang of her gavel. Her Honor was quite stunning—Felicia Rashad could've played her in a TV movie. Not that she was all sweetness and light. From the no-nonsense way she shuffled through papers, as if daring a single "T" not to be crossed, I got the impression you'd rather get on Hulk Hogan's bad side. But I trusted in her fairness immediately.

Benji and Carolyn briefly conferred with the judge; when Benji walked back over to me, he winked.

"Bail is set at one million dollars," declared Judge Hopkins.

Before I had a chance to react, Carolyn Caruthers announced, "The People would like to begin jury selection two weeks from yesterday."

Two weeks? That hardly gave me loads of time. Obviously, Carolyn was making a mere token gesture; in reality, it no doubt would be *months* before a trial of this magnitude began.

Sure enough, Benji voiced his objection.

"Your Honor, as a public figure my client will find it difficult to do his job during this waiting period. Therefore, we request that the date be changed. Let us begin *one* week from yesterday."

Carolyn looked dumbstruck. Marion dropped a folder, sending papers scattering across the floor.

"Benji," I hissed through clenched teeth, "what the hell are you doing?"

He whispered back, "Relax. We're totally freaking them out."

"Do the People object?" asked Judge Weinberg.

"Your Honor, one week does not give the People a great deal of time to—"

"Given the State's 'ironclad' case against my client," Benji smoothly interrupted, "this should not pose a problem."

"Well, Ms. Caruthers?" asked the judge.

"Uh . . . fine, Your Honor," replied Carolyn, as Marion tugged on her blazer and pantomimed the word *No*.

The judge briefly conferred with the bailiff.

"Very well, then. One week from yesterday." She banged her gavel and took her leave. On the way out of the courtroom, I made a point of holding up my wrists in a shackled position, licking my upper lip at Carolyn. She pretended not to notice.

Marion, though, looked ready to spit ink. I could tell he didn't just consider prosecution a job that had to be done, but that he truly hated *all* defend*ants*. Carolyn at least had a human side (or so claimed Jeep Andrews).

Benji and I ducked into a private conference room, away from the swarm of press.

"Benji, what the hell was that about? Are you nuts?"

He smiled to himself, like he just remembered a funny joke. "It's simple, Rick. Supposedly they're absolutely certain of your guilt. You were holding the murder weapon. Gunshot residue on your hands. And let's not forget motive. After all, the entire world saw you be a first-class bitch toward Tara at the pre-Oscar show. Slam dunk. Or so they think."

"Well, isn't it?"

"As soon as I learned Judge Ruetha's docket was empty starting next week, my instincts told me to go for it. How many experts do you think the State can scrounge up in one measly week? How can they build such an air-tight case that the jury can't believe there's reasonable doubt? They can't. They know they can't. And what's more, they can't admit it.

"In the meantime, we act like it's taken for granted that they have no case. That the trial is a waste of taxpayer's money. We just want to get it over with as quickly as possible because the whole thing is ridiculous. Remember, Rick—the longer we put it off, the more time there is to canonize Tara. Even one more week could make a huge difference."

Benji saw our strategy as follows: He'd keep the complications of my personal life out of things. Outing Shane, Benji reasoned, could turn the industry against me, and I needed all the friends I could get. Plus of course it could turn *Shane* against me, and who knew what his next move might be? So instead we'd simply shoot holes in the circumstantial evidence: I was famously bitchy with everyone, not just Tara; I was gay but single (technically true); I shot the gun because I saw someone shoot at me, and so on.

Once he explained his reasoning, I realized Benji was right. And I had to admit I looked forward to getting the whole thing over with. Nonetheless, I wondered if six days would be enough for me solve the case. To date, I'd never missed a deadline, but I feared that when it mattered most there just might be a first time that I did.

"Just remember, Rick. I've already spent the bonus you're giving me for a job well done." He whistled as he followed me out into hall, and the drooling press that awaited.

While posting bail, I put my house up for collateral. I didn't need any favors from Chauncey. Satan would've had fewer strings attached, had he come to my aid. I no-commented my way down the corridor, feigning a need to enter the off-limits holding cells, and then stealthily made my way out a side entrance. I quickly revved up the unfamiliar, degradingly tacky Ford Escort that Benji rented for me. I understood his logic: no one would've guessed in a million years that Rick Domino would drive a Ford Escort. Still, it had all the horsepower of a yo-yo, and was painted this awful color—a kind of puce crossed with ecru. I thought longingly of my silver BMW, or even my knockabout black Cherokee.

I drove around aimlessly for a while to make certain I wasn't being tailed. Once I felt safe, I pulled the flimsy car over to a newsstand.

I couldn't wait to see the morning edition of *Variety*.

Of course, I was the superstar headline story: "RICK NAILED, JAILED, BAILED." The subhead stated: "Shane Missing, Benji Dissing, DA Hissing." A second headline story cleverly conveyed: "Oscar Lost, Engagement Ring Found." There was a photo of Tara accepting her Oscar, and one of Shane waving to fans upon arrival, but the fact that they won Oscars was subsumed by the murder. Pictures of me—the mug shots, alas—were twice as big. Discussion of the Oscar winners per se was relegated to lowly page 3.

There was also a special insert entitled: "Tara Perez: Good-by to Screen's Most Beloved Star." The photos showed her doing things like signing autographs at a children's hospital and playing softball for AIDS research. The difficult superstar who once had an underling fired because her hair color was too similar to Tara's, and who had it stipulated in her contract that she must be served fresh white-chocolate black-bottom cupcakes every day at four from a particular bakery in West L.A.—and if she was on a location shoot they had to fly them in each day because the cupcakes had to be *fresh*—suddenly never existed.

I was sorry Tara got murdered to the extent that it just isn't nice when someone's life gets cut short. But, frankly, I was having a hard time mustering up any tears.

Throughout the paper were a million different articles that all began the same way: "It started like any other Oscar night: the usual production numbers, strained jokes, and too-long acceptance speeches. But then something happened that topped the drama of any movie," etc.

Chauncey was quoted as saying that I'd been "under tremendous strain" as of late, but that he was sure the whole thing was some terrible misunderstanding. He added that we all needed to pray for the safe return of Shane. With transparent false modesty, he dismissed his turning the ring over to the police by stating it was "his duty as a good citizen."

Mitzi claimed to be too shocked to comment, though she couldn't resist throwing in a plug for her upcoming special: "Hollywood Burnout: The Perils of Fame." In a last-minute storyboard change, I was to be featured alongside Margot Kidder, Farrah Fawcett, and the cast of *Dif'rent Strokes*. (The special also touted probing personal interviews with Lauren Tewes, Joyce DeWitt, and Vicki Lawrence Schultz.)

Natch, the featured Oscar players from the night before were asked to comment. I hardly expected heartfelt sincerity out of hard-bitten showbiz veterans. What was strange, though, was how unnecessarily dishonest the things they said were.

Francine managed to blurt between hiccups that it was all just too dreadful as Tara was "the jewel in the Hollywood crown," and that she hoped I was innocent and that Shane was safe. All of which was predictable. But then she went on to say that she personally coached Tara in her star-making role twenty years earlier: *That Girl—The Movie*. She claimed that her greatest joy had been seeing her "protegee" make good on the enormous potential she saw in her.

Francine was entitled to her hallucinations. But it wasn't just idle gossip that she fumed when her featured role as Lou Marie's September love interest was reduced to a glorified walk-on after Tara raised a fit—among other things—to then-junior producer Truman Shea. Francine actually attempted to sue both Tara and Tru, but her case was thrown out of court. (Insiders claimed she gave an inspired comedic performance that would've won her a Supporting Actress nod.) Something about untimely death makes people think that they can rewrite history, but this was way over the top.

The other stars followed Francine's lead in stating that they *hoped* my nose was clean. Jeep Andrews was quoted as saying, "Tara, we'll always love you. Shane, come home. Rick, please tell me you're innocent, buddy." Then he added: "Tara and I were the greatest of pals. We loved to pull practical jokes on each other. And she was *so* generous. When we starred together in *You're So Vain*, the big joke was how vain she wasn't. She kept giving me close-up after close-up. She'd say, 'But you're the pretty one, Jeep.' Imagine saying that about a guy like me! But that was just how she was."

Nice try, Jeep. But that was just how she *wasn't*. Indeed, if Mr. Andrews thought about it, perhaps he'd recall the nasty litigation that ensued when he and Ms. Perez had a veritable cat fight over who was getting the most—and best—close-ups. Each accused the other of personal familiarity with the cinematographer to this end. Ultimately they actually had clauses inserted into their contracts over "equal number of close-ups." Given that Hollywood favored male stars, Jeep had more consistent box office power, and so had been slated for more close-ups—until Tara, bless her, sweetly threatened to out him to the world.

Cinda Sharpe said how Tara Perez was a true artist, and Shane was a gifted young actor. She said she'd known Rick Domino for years, and had always believed him to be a man of integrity. Whatever the relative merits of these assertions, little store could be placed by what she went on to say: "Tara was the sort of friend in whom you could confide *anything*. We'd get together for slumber parties like a couple of giddy teenagers, and gossip and giggle. I'll miss her the most when I put on my favorite fuzzy flannel nightie."

But in truth Tara was the sort of "friend" in whom you could confide nothing. Unless your idea of trustworthy was confiding your intense lesbian love for Tara—as did poor Cinda—only to have Tara reply that she wasn't interested unless it meant a three-way with Truman Shea so that he'd give Tara the lead in *Don't Leave Me This Way*. Broken-hearted Cinda furthermore had to endure Tara's insistence that Cinda herself back off from the coveted part when Tru offered it to her. Allegedly she said that Cinda would do this if she truly loved Tara. But whenever Tara was present the word "blackmail" was as likely to be involved as the word "syphilis" was likely to be employed in a story about the Old South.

Contemplating just where to stick his Best Picture Oscar for *Butterfly Kisses*, Truman Shea told reporters it was especially tragic about Tara because he was planning on starring her in his next film, *Don't Leave Me This Way*. Accurately, however, he was planning—if I may tone down his actual words a notch—to run her ass out of town when she threatened to sue for "professional damages," given his assertion that she was too old for the part. To top things off, Tara and Tru—though it was difficult to even remember, given their cut-throat animosity—had once upon a time been hubby and wife.

I was pissed that on top of everything else Tru couldn't resist making a liar out of me from the night before. What reason would he have to fabricate all this I could only imagine. (Ever the humanitarian, Tru also expressed worry over Shane's safety. Surely the fact that Shane was tied up in a mutlimillion-dollar deal with Tru couldn't have been farther from his thoughts.)

Only Mr. Squeaky Clean, Bob Raflowitz, seemed to be striving for honesty. Not that his Hollywood hieroglyphics were easy to decipher. "Tara led a complicated life," he carefully began. "If her Oscar could talk, we'd know the truth, which I'm sure had nothing directly to do with Rick Domino. When Shane surfaces, as I'm sure he will, we'll know the whole story."

Bob was prone to truth-seeking, tempered with goodwill and a dash of schmaltz. But the way he said the murder *directly* had nothing to do with me that made me wonder if he didn't know more than he was letting on. As if *indirectly* I was connected to it—meaning my relationship with Shane? Or something else? And what about the Oscar "knowing" what happened—was it in the alley with Tara, only to be taken by the killer? Why did Bob seem so sure that Shane would not only surface but would know what really happened?

I didn't know what these five people were hiding, but clearly they all were hiding something. And I determined to talk to each of them until I found out what it was. I was certain Benji was right: they'd all be willing to talk—maybe even go out of their way to wine and dine and flatter me.

My cell phone had a dozen different messages from the assortment of personages that normally populated my life: my agent, my trainer, my fashion consultant, my limo service, my shrink, my astrologer, my this, that, the other. They'd all have to wait. Even my beloved Hollywood Network, whose corporate VP thereof conveyed in her professional monotone that I was to consider myself "on immediate leave of absence until further notice." (This sentiment was echoed by the newspaper syndicate that ran my columns.) It was a neat legal tactic to avoid lawsuits should I be found not guilty, but as much as it pissed me off I couldn't be bothered for the time being.

I didn't even bother going home. I knew where I needed to be.

I was headed to Shane Kirk's place.

I was about a block from his pad when my cell phone rang. I figured it was Francine, number two on my list of Things To Do Today.

"Hey, Rick, my amigo." I recognized the Actor's Studio mumble of Bob Raflowitz.

"Hi, Bob," I replied with my best showbiz cheeriness. "Hear any good gossip lately?"

Bob laughed. "I gotta hand it to you, Rick. You never miss a beat. Say, how'd you like to drop over before the memorial?"

The memorial? For Tara, I assumed. Hollywood worked fast, I'd say that much. Now there was an event I would've *loved* to attend—and for so many reasons—but obviously there was something a bit too evil-fairy-godmother-at-the-christening about it. If Tara had any family to speak of, they probably weren't exactly looking forward to having me kiss them on both cheeks. So I knew I'd have to make do with watching it on TV.

"Uh, sure. Is now good?" I was guessing the memorial would be held in the mid-afternoon, to make the evening news back east.

"Now would be perfection," he replied, in what mildly could be termed an exaggeration. It wasn't like Bob to be quite so gushy-wushy.

But whatever the reason for his eagerness, I intended to use it to my advantage. I couldn't wait to get to Shane's, but I guessed that I was going to have to.

"Great, I'll be right over." I skillfully made an illegal U-turn. Then I chastised myself, realizing that it was one of many habits I'd have to break, now that I was out on bail.

9

The Escort could barely climb the steep, arid hills up to Bob's digs. Bob and his partner, Cleo Simone, lived in sagebrush country high above Laurel Canyon. Their humble twenty-room abode was a Jetson-like menagerie of solar-paneled spires and domes that was ecologically welcoming to the endogenous coyotes and rattlesnakes, who, to Bob's activist way of thinking, were People Too. When TV journalists like Mitzi tried to fake maternal instincts by asking Bob if he worried about his five kids in such an environ, Bob guilelessly replied that by being At One with Nature, his children had nothing to worry about.

So far, so good. The kids, who all had hyphenated first names like Ezekiel-Sky or Naomi-Flower, were said to be obnoxiously well-adjusted mini–Ralph Naders who spent their summer vacations protesting the Wall Street monopoly on sperm whales, or whatever.

Cleo operated her own "how to" enlightenment center from a giant glass teepee on the property. Her kinky, colorless hair piled indifferently atop her head, she contorted her body into pretzel-like positions that would've made Linda Blair in *The Exorcist* turn green with envy, and Om'd all the way to the bank. Known for her "inner beauty," Cleo played occasional second leads in indie films. A year or two earlier she registered with critics for supporting Cinda Sharpe in a modest epic entitled *Both Sides Now*, which rivetingly chronicled the compelling world of a feminist recycling center. The politically correct extravaganza made a whopping fifty cents at the box office.

I knew that Bob and Cleo meant well, but after about a half-hour with them I usually wanted to shoot up with absinthe.

When Bob greeted me at his sliding front door, the first thing he said was: "An energy-efficient car. I'm proud of you, Rick." As if he'd ever be caught dead driving anything so tacky as a Ford Escort. In his custom-made Birkies and hemp T-shirt, he seemed light-years removed from any such earthly foible as an unsolved murder.

On screen, Bob had one of those malleable faces that could seem dashingly handsome or creepily psycho, and a wide range of ethnicities. In person, he just sort of looked like a guy, neither handsome nor ugly. He had a reserve about him that came as surprise, given the intensity of his acting and his very public political stance. Like many people larger than life, one-on-one with another person did not come as naturally as performing before the masses.

But let us not forget his body.

Bob had one of the most Adonis-like physiques in Hollywood—and that's saying something. Firm, muscular, toned, he was a walking and breathing essence of Greek statue. Everything was perfectly and beautifully proportioned. He rebelliously refused to shave his body hair, and just the right amount of virile black chest hairs poked through the collar of his T-shirt, which clung to his rock-hard torso with a faint electricity of manly sweat. His solid nipples moved with the muscular flow of his abs as he walked.

As a serious method actor, Bob got very irritable when inter-viewers asked him to comment on his superb physique, how did he like being such a hunk?, and so forth. And since he was a man, reporters tended to respect his feelings, and seldom broached the subject. Still, it's not like he stopped working out. He must've enjoyed having such a great body much more than he admitted.

"I'm *so* glad you came Rick." He gave me a tentative, straight-guy half-hug with his hairy, rippling arms. I could smell his male aroma, and was annoyed by my sudden hard-on. "And I'm glad you could meet us before the memorial."

Cleo eagerly ran to greet me, like I was Lassie and had finally come home. She was all giggles and good vibes, whereby she sought to remind me of the One Cosmic Joy beyond the happenstance of the moment. *Because I am spiritual,* she seemed to be saying, *I do not judge you.* Her peasant skirt and blouse gave her a plain girl's sensuousness.

Nonetheless, I was relieved to lose my hard-on.

"Please sit down, Rick," Cleo enthused, leading me to the rustic living room. "I'll be right back with some goodies." "Goodies," I knew, meant yummy seaweed-soy cookies, or some such. My sensi-tive taste buds braced themselves.

"Yes, my friend," Bob agreed, grinning as though he's just won another Oscar. "We haven't had a chance to talk in such a long while."

The first thing I always noticed was this amazing fresh-air qual-ity to the Raflowitz–Simone domicile, as if there were a bottled fra-grance sold only to them called Breezy Sunlight. Yet in a way, everything smelled *too* good. Like you wanted to see them step in some dog shit once in awhile like everyone else.

Inside the house, form diligently followed function. Mother Earth was too precious for them to waste space. Each of the twenty rooms had a specific purpose—e.g., Bob's method acting room ver-sus Cleo's method acting room—and the numerous living room sofas compassionately folded out to what Bob and Cleo called with straight faces "sleeping modules." You'd have thought that the multimillion-dollar domicile doubled as a homeless shelter—though, needless to say, such was hardly the case. Moreover, these were not your run-of-the-mill futons from strip malls. Each module was custom-designed and made from top-drawer purest linen and teak. The wind chimes that wafted gentle notes in the faint desert breeze were flawless abstract figurines of delicate, hand-blown Florentine crystal.

Bob and Cleo boasted that they bought only from small, independent craftspersons and so-called fair traders who strove for economic democracy. Or at least they did in theory, since the cost of a single item in the home would have busted the life savings of your average middle-class family. Everything in the house Made a Statement, though the statement made was not necessarily the one that Bob and Cleo strove to make. If you weren't in the home of ostentatious people, you still knew rich when you saw it.

Mr. Hunk sat across from me, a hand-crafted zebrawood chest between us that was resourcefully used as a coffee table. On the chest was a tag explaining that it had been crafted from a tree felled by natural causes. Presumably its solid gold hinges simply fell from the sky. Bob quickly grabbed a handful of brochures from atop the chest. He opened the lid (inlaid with mother-of-pearl from Madagascar, according to the tag) to slip them inside of it, as if to signal that as his guest I of course had his full attention.

"Vacation garbage," he explained. No doubt they were astral projecting to wherever it was so as not to pollute.

I hoped he didn't notice that I was staring at the outline of his nipples through the T shirt.

"So, Rick. What shall we talk about?" He slipped his muscular feet out of their five-hundred-dollar sandals and put them up on the zebra chest.

It seemed so ludicrous a question I couldn't contain myself.

"Well, Bob, I'm trying to figure out who killed Tara so that I don't die on death row. But actually, I came over to borrow a cup of sugar."

Bob laughed, scratching his foot. "Really, Rick. You need to do something about your attitude. It's so . . . *anti-life* past a certain point." He nodded his head with exasperation. "Though I have to confess I enjoy it in small doses. 'All things in moderation,' as they say."

Cleo serenely appeared with a tray of snacks and a steaming pot of tea. She sat on the arm of Bob's chair and put her arm around him as I helped myself to tea and biscuit, politely taking a nibble of the flavorless, kibble-like morsel. I brightened when I noticed a small obelisk of Galiano in the corner of the tray. Like many alleged health food nuts, Bob and Cleo's worries over drugs and chemicals in foods did not extend to alcoholic beverages, especially when they were foreign and expensive.

Still, I resisted the urge for a drink. I needed every last one of my wits.

"Rick, I want you to know something," Cleo instructed. "Tara's spirit is *whole*. She is very, *very* happy where she is. I can hear her laughing. You know—that marvelous laugh she's always had. And that smile. Her smile is *so* radiant right now. Tara is saying that she always knew she wasn't long for this world, and at her soul's urging, she strove to achieve all she could with what little time she had. So she's content now. So very content."

Cleo held out her hand to me. It was my cue to stand up and reach over to take it. "I'll be saying all this at her memorial," Cleo related. "Tara was one of my best students, as I'm sure you know. Such a spiritual person. Perhaps *the* most spiritual person I have ever met. But since you *obviously* won't be able to attend, Rick, I wanted to say this to you personally. As a gift." She looked at me meaningly.

"Thanks, Cleo." Our hands grasped tightly.

These types of scenes embarrassed me, but I figured I'd best play along.

Cleo let go of my hand, and I nearly lost my balance. "Not to in *any way* rush you, Rick," she assured, "but we *do* have to start getting ready for the memorial."

When Cleo talked about "getting ready," I knew she didn't just mean mascara. She needed time to Merge with the Cosmos so that she could be impressively blissed-out when addressing her flock.

"I'm speaking at it, too," Bob added, glancing at his casually styled Cartier watch. "Tara was one of my *dearest* friends. But then, for whom was she not? Jeep's speaking, as well. And Cinda. And Tru and Francine." He said this as if each name was joy added to joy, and I should be overcome by how rapturously thrilling it all was.

But what I was really thinking, of course, was that they were my suspects.

Cleo kissed his cheek. "I'll leave you two to your fondest memories of our beloved Tara." She winked at me on her way out.

Bob clasped his hand behind his head. "You know, Rick, when I think of Tara, I find myself remembering first and foremost her extraordinary generosity. One time, when she first came to Hollywood, there was an extra on the set who was about to get fired. The assistant director told her to walk across the street. Well, this zealous extra walked across the street *again,* even though she hadn't been directed to. Completely spoiled the shot, obviously. It wasn't believable that she'd be walking across again two seconds later. But you know the type—can't wait to get discovered and become a star. The poor kid started crying. But Tara was just great. She took the girl aside, and told her she'd be a big star one day. Tara said she just *knew* it. Imagine how inspired that girl must have felt. But that's just how Tara was."

"Just out of curiosity, Bob. Who was this girl Tara talked to?" I wondered if this was one of those "heart-warming" stories in which the extra girl later became a major star.

"I don't know. Nobody." Meaning she wasn't a celebrity. He looked about the room distractedly, as though he'd run out of patience for having to deal with me, but was too polite to say so. "I wasn't there when it happened. I just heard about it later."

I lightly pushed aside my refreshments. "I'll get right to the point, Bob. When I got arrested, I saw you talking to Francine, Cinda, Jeep, and Tru. What was everyone saying?"

Bob considered, then shrugged his sculpted shoulders. "That we were sad to lose Tara. And also sad for you, Rick, to be so obviously falsely accused."

"Look, Bob, if you're going to be evasive, I don't see why you asked me up here. I have a lot of work to do in a very short time, and I—"

"Rick, relax. You're right. I did ask you up here, because I do want to help you. I consider you a *friend*. But really, you need to stop being so suspicious. We felt bad for you. And for Tara. That's the whole story."

"How do you *know* I didn't do it?"

Bob gave a low chuckle, as if my mundane little question tried his cosmic patience, but he graciously would condescend to my level. "C'mon, Rick. You, a murderer? Gimme a break."

Ironically, I felt insulted. What did he think—as a gay man I wasn't "macho" enough to kill someone? I was tempted to point out with pride the impressive number of gay men who were convicted murderers. *We are everywhere*, and all that.

Instead, I changed the subject. "Did you see anything from the time you gave Tara her Oscar to—well, when everything happened?"

Bob flexed his mighty leg joints, which crackled with pleasure.

"Sure did. That's what I wanted to tell you. After I gave her the Oscar, she went off to meet the press. I went into the green room. Francine was there, so I congratulated her, and visited for a few minutes. Then I left, and bumped into Tru—he was lurking around backstage, I guess wheeling and dealing as usual. We talked for a minute or so. And then I saw Tara, off in a corner. She and some other woman were having it out. They were whispering, so I couldn't hear what they were saying, but it was very intense. At one point she even tried to grab Tara's Oscar away from her."

"Who was this woman, Bob?"

"That's what was weird. I didn't know who she was. Kind of familiar, though. Blonde. I'd say a kind of rough-around-the-edges forty-something."

"What was she wearing?"

Bob looked at me with bemusement.

"It's *important*," I insisted. "I'm not doing a fashion report."

Bob considered. "I don't know. Black, I think."

Well, it was a step in the right direction.

"Did you see Shane backstage?"

"Nope. Though I imagine he went back there after Best Song. By then I'd gone off my merry way. It's not the world's greatest feeling, watching two people arguing. My parents—" Bob gave a nervous laugh. "Well, let's not go there. But it's tragic, isn't it?, the way we let petty squabbles get in the way of the things that really matter. Tara was *radiant* when I gave her the Oscar, and now, only a few minutes later, she was distraught. What is it, Rick, that prevents us from staying focused on the *real* purpose of life?"

I didn't bother to answer, choosing instead to leave Bob to his "real" gold hinges.

"So when you told the press that if Tara's Oscar could talk—"

Bob frowned, snapping his fingers and pointing. "Not now."

For a second I thought he meant me.

"Hi, Daddykins. Hi, Mr. Domino. Murder any movie stars lately?"

It was the oldest Raflowitz son, Ezekiel-Sky. Looks-wise, Bob and Cleo made for a genetic crap shoot, but Zeke rolled sevens all the way, getting the very best from both parents. He had his father's build and the sharp, aquiline features of his mother's face, which were more becoming on a male. At eighteen, he was physically a fully grown man, and a classically handsome one at that. (Some of his siblings were not so lucky.)

More than good looks, Zeke had something else—there was a strangeness about him, an enchantment, if you will. There was something in his eyes that made you think of a baby looking at a mobile high above its crib, or maybe a young prince looking at the stars. You got the impression that wherever Fate would direct him, it would not be down a well-traveled road.

However, like many a gifted youth, he first would have to survive being a teenager.

Zeke's sardonic greeting was like a slap across the face, but I figured he was just being a smart-aleck teen. Besides, I couldn't afford to alienate any of the Raflowitz clan. "Hi, Zeke," I gamely answered back. I gave him my friendliest midwest smile.

Bob scowled at me. "Not now, Rick. Zeke knows better."

"But Dad, can't we at least *talk* about it?"

"You're being a brat. Now *go*." He pointed at his son as if bestowing the death sentence upon one of his henchmen in *Mob Don Juan*, one of Bob's more celebrated films.

Zeke flustered with anger. You could see that emotional intensity ran in the family, though as far as I knew Zeke had no interest in showbiz. "But that's just it, Dad. I don't *want* to go. Why can't I just stay here? I won't make a big deal about it ever again. I *promise*."

"Young man, we've already talked about it."

"But we haven't. You've talked about it and Mom's talked about it. What about *me*? Stop treating me like I'm just some embarrassment to your career. I'm *eighteen*. I'm old enough to make my own decisions."

Mr. Pacifist Bob trembled with fury. "*I said that's enough.*"

Zeke burst into tears. "I hate you!" he shrieked. "I hate you!"

So much for Blissville. Bob's family was promoted as being a kind of post-hippie Ozzie and Harriet, but up close and personal they clearly had graver concerns than who ate the cookies.

As if things weren't groovy enough, Bob threw one of his custom-made Birkies at his son as though shooing away a stray cat. It missed, but Zeke took the hint and fled the room; I heard Cleo go after him. "You *know* how your father feels about this," she lectured. "Don't you *know* how hard this is for him?" Zeke cried back, "Oh Mommy, Mommy."

Bob and I were quiet for a moment.

"As you can see, Rick, Zeke's been having problems. He's a highly strung young man. Brilliant people often are, of course. And he *is* brilliant, you know—a genius, if he ever finds himself. By the age of five Zeke was reading and talking like someone three times his age. He skipped two grades in school. Cleo says he's a very wise old soul. That, of course, is his entire problem. He's so very *aware* on all levels, he has problems fitting in with people. He flunked back the two grades he originally skipped—flunked out, period. We can't even get him to take his GED. He's a teenaged mess. A great big glorified pile of shit. Undirected, unmotivated, un-everything. Except of course for sex and drugs."

". . . and rock 'n' roll?" I helpfully interjected.

Bob chose to ignore my little witticism.

"Cleo and I have decided that he needs a change of scene. There's a marvelous alternative college in northern California. A communal setting that teaches global consciousness. But Zeke is not amused. He wants to sail the Yucatán and I-don't-know-what-all. It makes things a bit dicey at times. But he is hardly mature enough to make his own decisions."

Ay, yes, the classic young man's conflict between a spendy, do-nothing college and sailing his yacht.

"What did he mean by not making a 'big deal' about it any-more?' A big deal about *what?*"

Bob sighed, clasping his hands to his chin in thought. "It's his personal life. An inappropriate partner." Our eyes met. "He's not *gay*, Rick. And Cleo and I would hardly mind if he were. It's a female. She took advantage of his naïveté—not to mention his precarious emotional state. It's hard enough to tell your son he has to go away to school, without some selfish little you-know-what telling him that all he needs is her undying love."

"It must be hard to be parents," I commented judiciously.

"A much-oppressed minority." As Bob laughed, his gorgeous abs undulated.

I tried to be subtle as I crossed my legs—and placed my hands over my crotch.

Under the circumstances, Bob obviously wouldn't have minded a shift in the conversation back to Tara, delightful topic that she was. So I seized the moment.

"As you were saying, Bob—about how if Tara's Oscar could talk . . . ?"

He stretched into a manly yawn. "Just that the Oscar must've been there when it happened. Let's face it. We both knew Tara. Do you think she'd have gone anywhere without it? That blonde might've lunged for it, but Tara was not about to hand it over without a fight."

"Do you think maybe this blonde . . . ?"

Bob smiled to himself. "Imagine someone committing murder just to steal an Oscar. I guess anything's possible in this crazy world. But there was *something* going on with Tara and this blonde, and you deserved to know about it."

"What about saying that Shane would turn up and that he knew the truth?"

"What about it? That's pretty much a no-brainer, isn't it? Don't *you* suspect that Shane knows what happened? Do you really think he'll stay invisible for long?"

I had to admit it seemed a reasonable argument.

"You didn't by any chance hear anything more about the engagement ring?"

"I already told you, Rick. I didn't hear or see anything else. But I'll bet anything that Shane's diamond ring was for *you*, silly." He grinned at me sportingly. "Cleo is *sure* that it was, and I trust her intuition about these things. Think about it. That ring sure as hell wasn't for Tara. If Shane wanted a cover marriage, he'd have picked someone wholesomely more his own age. Not some older . . . well, let's not even go there."

I wasn't sure how to respond. The notion that Shane almost asked me to marry him was devestating, rapturous, and infuriating all at once.

"It's no secret that Tara once made a pass at you." I couldn't think of what else to say.

Bob stared at me evenly. "You're right, Rick. It isn't."

Well, that didn't seem to lead me anywhere.

"The main point, Rick, is that you know how this town works. It's like that childhood game of 'Telephone,' where the rumors get more and more outrageous with each retelling. That's something I've always admired about you—the way you stick to the facts. Sometimes the facts aren't ones we like to read about ourselves, but they *are* the facts. For more than twenty years people have tried to pin some kind of dirt on me, and they're ready to pounce on the fact that my life was slightly intertwined with Tara's. Then you have your Francine Quicks of this world—so desperate for any form of attention that they'll say anything to anybody. So be careful, Rick. Be mindful of the truth. Check with me before jumping to *any* conclusions about *anything* to do with me or my family. And please take anything Francine might tell you with a grain—no, make it a ton of salt. Do you promise?"

"Sure, Bob," I replied without hesitation, wondering if he really thought it was that simple, that I'd trust my entire fate to a casual acquaintance such as himself.

"I really need to get ready." Bob looked at his watch as if quarreling with it. "But if I think of anything else, you know you can count on me. Like I said, I can't sit back and let an innocent man suffer."

Indeed, it was worth a good five minutes of his time to try to prevent it from happening.

We shook hands. Then Bob gave me a meditative hug with closed eyes, as though we'd just shared something so meaningful, so beautiful, that the moment would live on long after my fatal injection from the State.

10

I was halfway down the hill when I turned the car around to drive back up.

There were a number of questions I had from my talk with Bob. But I didn't want to confront Bob with them—who, in any case, had sped past me down the hill with Cleo, honking genially as he all but drove me off the edge of the mountain road. Heaven forbid he should be two minutes late for a televised broadcast.

I wanted to talk to Zeke. Alone.

It wasn't difficult to arrange. Like most teenagers, Zeke was more forthcoming when not in the company of his parents. That his psychiatric medication had kicked in didn't hurt matters, either. As Zeke candidly explained, he took a giant hit of Zoloft once a day for depression, and baby hits of alprazolam six times a day for anxiety. I got the impression that waiting for his next alprazolam was a bit like Linus waiting for his blanket to come out of the dryer. Indeed, the heartwarming Father-and-Son episode I witnessed transpired in those risky minutes of purgatory between pills.

We met outdoors, in the private garden. For all their fancy talk about being endogenous, Bob and Cleo paid a small fortune to have a minitropical paradise grafted onto their backyard. Sagebrush and clay were tortured into leafy palms, climbing ivy, and grape arbors. Hand-crafted blue and gold leaf tiles from Naples and a rather predictable Ming Dynasty Buddha completed the effect. I think they liked having a mulchy outdoor area that kept away the rattlesnakes, though of course they'd never admit as much.

Zeke kept waving his finger under a delicate sheet of water from a Zen-inspired fountain. For a fleeting instant, I saw something flicker within him—maybe he kept a poetry journal, and had just thought of a line.

"I feel like this tree." He stared at a red maple bonsai. "So *meticulous*, the way they keep cutting it back."

"I felt that same way, Zeke, at your age. I couldn't wait to move out of my home."

Like a lot of adults who didn't have kids, I didn't bond with teens often, but when I did I spoke frankly and listened nonjudgmentally.

Also, of course, I wanted Zeke on my side.

"Do you think I'm crazy, Mr. Domino?"

"No, Zeke. I don't."

"Oh." He seemed disappointed.

"I think you're a very intelligent young man who—"

"Who's not living up to his potential." He lowered his voice in sarcasm. "'Now, Zeke, we know it's hard for you. We were your age once, too. But you can't let your grades slip.'"

There was anger and pain in his glazed-over eyes as he mimicked a dozen different authority figures.

"That wasn't what I was going to say, Zeke. You're an intelligent young man who just needs to realize that eighteen doesn't last forever."

"Oh, right. That's another good one. 'When you get older, you'll understand better.'" He stared at me challengingly. "Tell me something, Mr. Domino. Just what do you understand about life right now?"

"That's not a fair question, Zeke. And I think you know it isn't. Yesterday, I could've given you an answer. But today—"

"What great answers do you have to share?" He stood over me in his *Save the Spotted Owl* T-shirt, Levi cut-offs, and hiking boots. "What are you going to tell me—'Everyone needs a goal in life?' Or better yet: 'You only *think* you're unhappy.'"

"Or how about this one?" I offered. "'You can't spend your whole life moping around the house.' I used to get that *all* the time."

Zeke laughed, surprised by my comeback. "Or what about: 'Don't you know how much your parents care about you?'"

"My favorite used to be: 'You have so much to thankful for, young man.'"

He affectionately flicked water at me with his fingers. "You're okay, Mr. Domino. Let's go inside."

Zeke led me into the living room.

"Live it up, Mr. D." He opened the zebra wood chest, and tossed me the brochures Bob had hidden. The pamphlets were not about vacations, or even about alternative schools.

They were all about a private mental hospital.

At last, some dirt about Bob Raflowitz. Now all I needed was a job.

"Is it crazy to like older women?" Zeke peered through an expensive, handmade kaleidoscope. "I do, you know. They say it indicates an unhealthy psychological adjustment. Adjustment to *what*? It seems to me life just sort of happens."

"You might be on to something there." I set the brochures aside. "Do you have a girlfriend?"

"Two," he answered with a sly grin, setting down the kaleidoscope. "I mean, one."

"What is she, a Gemini?" I joked.

Zeke grew sullen. "It's really not funny, Mr. Domino. It's just so hard to get used to—it's like it isn't even *real*. Maybe that's why I can't cry. Because I don't believe it happened. I thought it was my medication, but my shrink says that shouldn't matter."

"Zeke, I'm not sure I understand."

"*Tara*. I still can't believe she's dead."

My mind was humming like a CIA computer. "You were dating Tara Perez?"

"My dad says you didn't kill her. That's the truth, isn't it?"

"Of course it is, Zeke."

"I'm sorry. I just needed to hear you say it." He gave a sad, scared laugh.

"I understand."

He played with the frayed edge of his cut-offs. "I *loved* her, you know. Or at least I thought I did. So many people keep saying I didn't, that I was just confused. That Tara was using me in ways I couldn't begin to understand—that's how my dad put it. I don't know. Maybe it's just easier if I tell myself I didn't ever love her. Then it doesn't have to hurt."

Tara sure did get around, I'd give her that much. It would seem that Shane played beard for her in return, so she could rendezvous with the studly, barely legal Zeke. As for how she might be "using" him, it wasn't hard to figure out. "Over forty" were not exactly two little words that made producers offer actresses their life savings to appear in their movies. And for Tara, the writing was on the wall. Some years back, Bob had played her older brother. Then a few years later they starred as lovers—playing the same age. A couple of years ago, she turned down a script in which she'd play Bob's older sister. Rumor had it a project was in development in which she'd play Bob's *mother*. At forty-something, Bob had a good twenty years left as a leading man—if not more—but as a female the same age, Tara had a much shorter shelf life. Call it sexist and unfair, but them's the facts.

By dating Zeke, another actress might've simply been trying to keep herself youthful in the eyes of the public. But Tara, I felt certain, was killing at least a least one more flamingo with the same stone: exacting her crazed revenge on an industry that would cast her as Bob's mother. That it was not Bob's fault per se—let alone poor, disturbed Zeke's—had begging little to do with it from Tara's point of view; did it matter to the Wicked Witch of the West that Dorothy's house fell on her sister by accident?

"Did your father know you were seeing Tara?"

"Boy, did he ever! Tara broke the news to him on Oscar night."

"*Did* she?" My ears tingled. "And when was that?"

"After he gave her the award. Backstage. I know, because I was there. My dad brought me along this year—he said it would cheer me up. What he didn't know was that Tara and I decided to tell him about us. By the time I got there, she was already into it. She told my dad how there was nothing wrong with me—nothing that some TLC couldn't fix, and that she was determined to give it to me. She said how the two of us wanted to sail off together to the Yucatán, and how that would be better for me than . . . that other place my dad wanted to send me to. It was pretty cool the way she stood up to my dad—she looked him right in the eye."

"And what did your dad say?"

Zeke rubbed his temples, like he had a headache. "He said if she messed with me ever again, he'd—you know, like, *kill* her."

I figured I'd go for broke: "Do you think he did, Zeke?"

He smiled with a naughty relish. "Boy, that would be something, wouldn't it? But no, Mr. Domino. My father would never do that. It was just—you know—a figure of speech."

"I see." But of course I didn't see it that way at all. Bob was a prime suspect. Tara could've made him so angry he snapped. And the only thing that kept Cleo off my suspect list was that I knew she never left her seat during the Oscars. Even at the last moment, before I made my way up the hall, I could see her frizzy hair in front of me.

"But in a way," Zeke continued, "it's like he's been killing her ever since. When you saw us fighting—it's because he's told me that under no circumstances am I to even so much as say Tara's name. That the whole thing was just a bad dream, and we'll forget it ever happened. That I had this neurotic obsession for older women, but he'd see to it that I got help. I don't think that's fair. Tara was *important* to me. It wasn't just that she awakened me sexually. When she held you, you felt so . . . enveloped. Like she really could change everything bad into good. She was Aphrodite. She didn't just love. She had the *power* of love."

I was tempted to explain to Zeke that most people idealize their first sex partner, but thought the better of it.

"What about your other girlfriend, Zeke?"

"She's off-limits, too. Another older woman. I told my parents about her last night when we were fighting. I said to my dad, 'You think you can stop me from seeing older women? Well, I have another girlfriend besides Tara. And she's just as *old*.' It was awful, to see how my dad overreacted."

I regarded him skeptically. "Are you sure you didn't enjoy getting a rise out of your dad just a smidgen?"

He laughed sportingly. "You understand me pretty well, Mr. Domino. Anyway, we've only just started seeing each other. It hasn't been real serious. At first I felt guilty—you know, like I was cheating on Tara. But I guess these things just sort of happen, don't they?"

"Yes, these things do just sort of happen," I concurred. "Who is she, Zeke?"

"Connie Kellogg," he replied. Seeing my blank face, he added: "The *actress*."

Master extraordinaire of showbiz trivia that I was, even I had to thoroughly scan the corridors of memory to recount the obscure Connie Kellogg. Twenty years ago, she got a few two-line parts as a sexy receptionist or a poolside masseuse in TV movies. Too tacky for the likes of *Playboy* or *Penthouse*, she did nudie spreads in lesser girlie mags with titles like *Big 'Uns*. In more recent years, she popped up in nonsex cameos in porn movies. I could only guess how she'd been supporting herself all these years. Or rather, I didn't have to guess at all.

It alarmed me to think that Zeke was attracted to such a person; I could just imagine how it must've been for his parents. He was like a beautiful young stallion, while Connie was like a Tijuana donkey show. But then again, as her photo spread in *Big 'Uns* no doubt indicated, perhaps there was reasonable explanation for his attraction for her. Zeke was complicated as hell, but he was still an eighteen-year-old male—and truly a straight one, it would seem.

Once upon a time, anyway, Connie Kellogg had been a blonde. As I thought back to the blonde I saw by the exit door . . .

"Zeke, did Connie go to the Oscars?"

"Absolutely. You should've seen her with Tara backstage. See, I saw them fighting, and it kind of freaked me out, so I wandered around for a while. It was when I came backstage the *second* time that Tara was talking to my dad." He smiled with a quiet relish. "He got very, *very* upset with me last night."

"What exactly did Connie and Tara say to each other?"

"Oh, it was all about how Tara knew Connie was just trying to get back at her through me, but how she knew she had nothing to worry about because Connie could never compete with her. And then Connie telling Tara how she could see how scared she was, and that it was making her look older by the second. Catty stuff like that."

So Bob Raflowitz was a liar. He may not have known who the mysterious blonde was at the time—I couldn't quite place Connie, either—but surely he made the connection once Zeke told him about her. And it would seem that Bob hung around backstage just a teensy bit longer than he recalled. I guessed he figured I'd be poking my nose around anyway, so he might as well tell me just enough of the truth to lead me away from his own stink. Plus, he may well have thought he was doing some sort of twisted good deed by trying to "help" me. So what if he was only telling me about ten percent of what he knew? At least he was keeping things simple for himself. Not to mention his ass out of jail, if in fact he killed Tara.

Unless of course Connie did it. To be part of the Bob Raflowitz universe meant an immeasurable boost to her reputation. Not that it had anyplace to go but up. And with Tara out of the way . . . Unless it was Zeke, who, likable tyke though he was, was not exactly Mr. Stability. Still, what motive would he have had?

Zeke chuckled. "They say it's from my mom. I mean, they don't say it, but they *do*."

"What do they say, Zeke?"

"My being like—brain weird."

I absently glanced at one of the brochures. The mental hospital boasted all sorts of goodies like shock treatments. ("The most restful and soothing state-of-the-art technology in EKG therapy," bragged the pamphlet.)

"How do you mean, Zeke?"

"My mom goes wacko every so often," he explained. "That's why she never acts much. I think my dad lets her have her little psychic school to humor her. They've never come right out and told me I take after her. It's that way parents have of never saying anything but saying everything." He improvised a little game with his shoelaces. "I don't think my parents have sex anymore. Because of me."

"You don't know that, Zeke. Sometimes, when couples have been together awhile—"

"Do you believe in suppressed memories, Mr. Domino? Do you think it's possible to be convinced that something never happened, yet also be convinced that it did?" He walked over to the handmade grand piano.

"I think my mom had sex with me." He began playing the slow and melancholy "Moonlight Sonata." "Or started to, anyway. I was about three years old. She pulled down my pants and *touched* me and then . . . then they grabbed her and took her away." He stopped playing, and looked at me searchingly. "The memory feels so real. But then it feels so made-up somehow, like when my dad tells me I'm being a nuisance and I feel like I don't know anything."

"Have you discussed this with your parents? Or with a doctor?"

"I told one of my shrinks. Then he called to tell them about it. I wasn't supposed to know he did, but I could tell. My mom went totally hysterical and my dad . . . well, he looked like he was *broken*. I heard all this muffled talk about how the doctor said they weren't supposed to say anything to me."

"And so they've never talked to you about it?"

He snorted with cynicism. "My parents—*talk?!* Lecture, sure— constantly. Pontificate platitudes? Day and night." He looked proud of his way with words. "But talk about something important? I don't think so. The next day my shrink increased my medication."

"Interesting," I politely commented.

"Last night, I heard my dad yelling at my mom about how I had this older woman fixation, and my mom yelling back what was he going to do, blame it on her? He said that blame wasn't the point but how they had to take drastic measures—that was what he said, dras- tic measures—to save me from myself. Like I'm two separate people, or something. I think it's silly to think my mom had anything to do with it. The women I'm attracted to are *nothing* like my mom."

"You have a point," I admitted. And yet, given that he thought Cleo molested him—not to mention maybe she really had—what if he somehow confused her with Tara last night . . . ?

"It's time," Zeke announced, aiming a remote. From behind a hand-carved teakwood relief of Merlin there appeared a wide-screen digital TV. With another flick, we were watching Mitzi McGuire somberly hosting special coverage of Tara's memorial. She wore a low-cut black sheath with a sheer black veil "tastefully" draped across her shoulders and collar. It was as if she were signaling to the world that her tits were in mourning.

The memorial was held—with an irony not lost on Mitzi, or rather the person who wrote her cue cards—at the very same Shrine Auditorium that had seen Tara's triumph only the day before. In back of the stage were flashing images of Tara, one after the other. Glamour shots were used sparingly. Most of the photos showed her either in a movie role doing something humanitarian (i.e., playing a nun or a selfless, courageous mother), or else shaking hands with ghetto youth or hugging a senior in a wheelchair in so-called real life.

We were just in time to catch the tail end of Bob Raflowitz's speech. He proclaimed that Tara was ". . . furthermore, a remarkable intuitive actress." This meant that though unlike himself she lacked years of formal method training, he allowed that she had a modicum of skill. He then went on to say: "As she matured as a person, we saw her youthful exuberance tempered by wisdom, making for an irresistibly charming screen persona. Few could not fall prey to it."

"You see what he's doing?" Zeke pointed at the screen. "He's trying to cover every possible base. So that if people find out about Tara and me, he can say, 'Well, as I said she was charmingly mature and young and irresistible,' or whatever he just said."

Zeke's imitation of his father was remarkable. This kid had acting talent all right, though who could say he'd ever be focused enough to use it? However, I doubted that shock treatments would prove just the ticket for helping him come into his own.

As the program broke for a commercial, there was a photo of a jubilant Tara holding her Oscar with outstretched arms, and her final words to the crowd—"I feel so overcome with love!"—ironically emblazoned across it. (This was the standard logo for each commercial break.)

Back on the air, Mitzi nodded gravely for the still-unbelievable shock of it all. "Next on the program," she softly announced—softly for her, anyway—"we are supposed to be hearing from Truman Shea. Yes, here comes Cleo Simone again, so beautiful and gallant in the face of this unspeakable tragedy, as she introduces her dear friend—and Tara's dear friend—Mr. Shea."

Cleo and Tru hugged for a mawkishly long time at the podium.

Finally, with Cleo holding his hand the entire time, Tru found the strength to speak:

"Once upon a time, a boy with many dreams and a girl with many dreams happened to find each other along the path. They had no magical powers. There were no fairy godmothers to grant their every wish . . ."

"Oh please," I complained. "Who wrote his speech, Kathy Lee Gifford?"

Zeke thought what I said was hilarious. His laughter gave way to a cough as he leaned back in a heap, zonked out by his medication.

"What they did have," Tru continued, "was a lot of good old-fashioned American determination. Most of all, they had each other. He was a struggling photographer, and she was a fairy princess who had never been crowned . . ."

"What's with all this fairy shit?" Zeke commented.

"I *know*," I agreed.

". . . And so they build a life together. He snapped her picture, and they both made good. A few years later, he stopped taking pictures and began producing them. And she became a celebrated actress. Although they walked down different paths, the love never died."

Tru paused. He swallowed dramatically and let out a little sob.

"Nor will it," I predicted he'd say next.

"Nor will it," Tru continued, as Cleo squeezed his hand. "In my life, love has been like a rainbow of beautiful magic colors. And you, my Tara, are like a marvelous spirit that weaves through all of them, giving them brilliance and luster, for now and all time."

"What, no more fairies?" Zeke commented. "You notice he forgot to say how Tara threatened to sue him if he didn't give her that part she wanted."

I was intrigued. "You mean in *Don't Leave Me This Way*?"

"Nah. The other stupid movie." He reached into his pocket and popped a pill; he obviously wasn't due for another one. "The piece of shit she got the Oscar for."

"Do That To Me One More Time?"

"Yeah, that was it. Last year, Uncle Tru came to meet with my mom for spiritual counseling. Seems he was having a bitch of a time with his enlightenment when Tara was sticking it to him every other minute. Or at least that was how he said it. Somehow, when Tara explained herself, you could always see why she did what she did. And it wouldn't seem nasty at all. Tara told me it was the easiest part she ever played. How all she had to do was act coked up and horny, so she could've just sent in some home movies. She was so much fun."

I wondered what else Zeke would tell me.

Cleo next introduced Cinda Sharpe. For the benefit of the TV audience, Mitzi commented favorably on the black, high-necked pantsuit Cinda wore. "Always so understated," Mitzi noted. " 'Like captured moonlight,' wrote one critic. That's our Cinda."

"What a fucking dyke," Zeke elaborated. "No offense, Mr. Domino."

"None taken, Zeke."

"Hey, lesbians are great. Seriously."

Cleo kissed Cinda on the cheek. In returning the gesture, Cinda's mouth brushed provocatively close to Cleo's.

Cinda was a fine, subtle actress, and when she smiled at the audience, she communicated the right tone of underlying sadness. "So, Sis," she began courageously, "we've shared out last bowl of M&M's. We've had our last slumber party doing each other's hair and watching Frankenstein movies. We've split our last container of Cherry Garcia. We've had our last pillow fight . . ."

"We *get* it, okay?" Zeke muttered. "Christ, get to the point."

And, indeed, there seemed a virtually endless list of things that Cinda and Tara used to do together at their "slumber parties," albeit with one activity in conspicuous absence. Yet I had to hand it to Cinda for being such a pro. She must have been dying inside, recounting the pain of her unrealized love for Tara, especially when Tara was willing to use her as a sex partner just to mend fences with Tru.

"Tara, you are irreplaceable," Cinda decreed. "As an actress, and as a human being. But most of all, as the sister I never had. As the sister that every girl wishes she had."

I supposed that could be true, if all the girls in the world were shot up with some strange new drug that permanently rendered them total masochists on all levels.

"Tell me, Zeke. Did Tara ever mention anything about using Cinda to get the lead in *Don't Leave Me This Way?* You know— blackmail, three-ways. The usual."

"Tara didn't like Cinda," he replied, as though answering my question. "She said Cinda made her nervous. 'She never relaxes around me,' Tara used to say. 'I don't trust her.' I wonder how Cinda felt about the letter."

"You mean the letter Tara wrote to Cinda to . . . ?" I had no idea about any such letter, but I didn't want Zeke to think I was interrogating him. No teenager likes to feel interrogated.

"The one where she said she didn't want to know Cinda anymore. That Cinda was giving her the creeps. Not because she was hot for her. Women were always coming on to Tara. But Cinda took it too far. You winced when you saw them together. Cinda would be all smiley-smiley, but you could see her heart breaking right there in front of you. It was just too intense. It was icky. Tara said, 'I have to be cruel to be kind.' So she told her to bug off."

"And Tara sent her this letter . . . ?"

"She gave it to her personally. At the Oscars. Once Tara wanted to do something, it was like she couldn't wait an extra second to do it."

Further contributing to the naked honesty that was Hollywood was our own Jeep Andrews, whom Mitzi described as "the heartthrob of every red-blooded female in the country. But today, Jeep is just another friend of Tara's mourning the loss of her irreplaceable friendship."

Jeep didn't hug Cleo very long. *Will and Grace* stereotypes to the contrary, Jeep appeared to be gay out of a kind of hypermasculine sensibility, and he got along better with straight men than he did with women—or for that matter, overly frou-frou gay men. He was the sort of gay man who really *didn't* like women, and got a mild case of the creeps having to touch them at all. Supposedly there are tribal cultures where the warriors have to purify their huts if a female has entered into them, and in a way, that was Jeep. It was as if loving men meant a total rejection of the female world.

Jeep was such big box office in action films that no one seemed to notice that he couldn't carry a romance. For Jeep to have a non-action hit, he had to play the supporting, romantic interest of a female protagonist. The audience got to see Jeep through her worshipful eyes, and he could be Prince Charming in small doses. He still got star billing, and was frequently cited for his "generosity" toward actresses, every year or two handing one a big hit on a silver platter. (Women's magazines frequently mentioned this when placing Jeep on their 10 Sexiest Men lists.) But Jeep got suspiciously few close-ups during make-out scenes, and it was written into his contract that both he and the female lead had to wear transparent body stockings during bedroom interludes so that he didn't have to actually touch her.

"Tara, you made it hard for a guy like me to be a gentleman," he so credibly began. "And yet you made it easy."

"Huh?" pondered Zeke.

"I think I see where he's going," I assured him.

And I was right: "You were just so beautiful, and just such a *lady*, Tara, that all I could do was be in awe of you . . ."

"In awe of her boyfriends is more like it," Zeke corrected. "Poor Uncle Jeep. I just don't see how living a lie can be good for you, you know?"

". . . One of my most memorable—no, I take that back—*the* most memorable experience I ever had was costarring with you in

Passionate Kisses. You taught me so much—not just about my craft, but about professionalism itself, and how to be a better human being . . ."

"Yeah, yeah, yeah." Zeke dismissed Jeep's speech with his middle finger. I felt he was expressing ire not toward Jeep so much as the world of adult deception that, like many a teen, he was firmly convinced he would never have any part of.

Jeep paused. Then he started sobbing. It looked like it was for real, though maybe it wasn't. "Last night," he managed to say, "after you won your Oscar, I wanted so much to tell you . . . that is, I wanted . . ."

The mike went dead. Since Bob and Cleo were pretty much running the show, I wasn't exactly convinced it was a coincidence.

Within about one and a half seconds, Cinda and Cleo were putting their arms around Jeep to "comfort" him—though I couldn't help thinking it was to shut him up. Obviously, they were destined to be only moderately effective. But then Bob, the great love of his life, came forward, and gave him this huge, long bear hug of support. Bob was whispering something to Jeep, who appeared to weep copiously onto Bob's shoulder.

Mitzi pretended to be utterly moved as she explained: "As you have just seen, Jeep Andrews was overcome with emotion, and unable to continue with his speech. There also might have been some technical difficulty with the sound. His dear friends Cinda Sharpe and Cleo Simone rushed to his side. Then his very best friend of all, frequent costar Bob Raflowitz, exchanged a deeply felt moment of brotherly support with Jeep. I must say, as a woman, it is so *very* touching when men are able to reach out to each other in friendship in this way. Tragic as today is for us all, there is a silver lining to the cloud, and that silver lining is pure and simple love."

As if the pile of fertilizer was not yet piled high enough, there was a commercial break, announcing the "Tara Perez Story," which would be broadcast later that night. In a preview, we saw Tara telling Chauncey Riggs: "You might think I'm crazy, but in all honesty my life hasn't gone the way I planned. What I wanted for myself was something very simple, and very honest and sincere. And no matter what sort of adventures I've had in this world, I've never found what I've been looking for."

Zeke flicked off the TV. "Sorry, but I can't take any more."

I felt the same way, though I'd expect for different reasons. "Zeke, do you have any idea what Jeep was trying to say about last night?"

He thought for a moment. "Not really. I guess he was backstage before presenting Best Picture, but so what?"

"What about Tru?"

"Uncle Tru—hell, he's everywhere at once, if you know what I mean."

Zeke became gloomy, maybe because of some reaction from his medication. "You know, Mr. Domino, it sure is a drag when you're smarter than your parents, only you're so much smarter than they are that they don't even know it, so they end up thinking you know nothing at all."

I smiled in remembrance of being eighteen. "Yes, Zeke, you're right. It *is* a drag."

We were both quiet. I listened to the soft wind chimes, and thought of Bob and Cleo's desperate quest for perfection as contrasted with the reality of their lives. Zeke, for his part, seemed lost in a world of his own.

Finally I said, "Are you going to be committed, Zeke?"

He looked away from me, and stared at the wall. "When I was a kid, I used to have this bad dream where these faces came out of the wall next to my bed. Like the wall was sort of a movie screen. I always slept facing the other way so that they couldn't get me. The Wall People." He delicately traced the wall with his fingertips, like a blind person reading Braille. "Now I'm not afraid of them."

Zeke walked over to me, staring intently. "If you'd like, you could have me, Mr. Domino. You name the price. I've never had a guy before, but you could do me however you wanted. If I had some money, I could run away with Connie, and—"

"Zeke, stop it." Handsome teenaged boys who were virgins gay-wise were a bit too exotic a fantasy for my tastes. And being called "Mr. Domino" did not exactly compel me to throw all caution to the wind.

"Yeah, Mr. Domino. I guess you're right."

As I was leaving, I asked, as casually as possible, "You wouldn't by any chance have an address for Connie Kellogg, would you?"

Zeke laughed incredulously, as if I'd just said the most pathetic thing imaginable.

Then he glared at me. He looked like his father did when he played violent characters.

"You leave Connie alone. She had *nothing* to do with this."

"Sure, Zeke. Take it easy. I won't even contact her."

But of course I knew I was going to be doing just that.

11

$\mathcal{S}$hane Kirk still thought like a hustler.

Most people who make it in Hollywood can't wait to buy a big fancy house. But no amount of admonishments from his business manager could compel Shane to muster up the focus and foresight to put down roots. The best Shane could do was rent another star's home, sending thousands of dollars a month straight down the drain. Having his private world in order did nothing to advance his very public career, so he couldn't be bothered with trivial details such as investing for his future. Besides, on some level he needed to feel that it was all beyond him, and that if he really made a mess of things some rich man would come to his rescue.

That was what made Shane truly dangerous. It's one thing to fantasize being rescued, and it's another to fantasize making it in Hollywood. But when you put the two together, they spell trouble. The last thing anyone in Hollywood would ever do is rescue somebody else. And when you try to force the issue, you destroy not only yourself, but who knows how many others.

He liked to tell friends he rented the mansion under a phony name, but paradoxically the lease was in his real name of Eddie Sharnovsky. It stood at the base of Beverly Hills, as if, like a kid doing the bare minimum on a homework assignment, Shane took the first fancy address he saw. Outside, it had a mock Spanish façade framed by palm trees. But inside, it could've been the pad of an eighteen-year-old on his own for the first time.

As a pledge of his supposed devotion, Shane gave me a key to the domicile—and because he was a careless person, the key still worked. Quietly, I let myself in to the stale air and chaos that was my semi-boyfriend's life.

Used to living in studio apartments and the impermanence they stood for—and also more comfortable in small spaces—Shane used but one of the twelve rooms; the other eleven were bare. Entering the foyer that was also the living room-bedroom-study, I could barely breathe in the sweltering air. I turned on the thermostat, and was relieved as the cool air kicked in. The Martha Stewart Kmart shades were pulled down, but they weren't quite the right size for the large bay windows, and you could see out along the sides and bottom.

Dirty clothes were scattered everywhere—though the tux Shane wore the night before was nowhere to be seen. The Kmart futon on the black-and-white linoleum had a couple of paper bags twisted up into its tangle of polyester sheets. Near the window was a dead, shriveled ivy plant in a plastic clay-colored pot. A hot-pink price sticker indicated a lowered purchase price from the white one underneath.

There was a Salvation Army dresser that Shane bought years ago because it had three large mirrors, so he could see himself full-face and at both a right and left angle all at once. Shane painted about half the dresser with trendy bright stripes and stenciled stars (as per an instructional cable TV show) before losing interest, leaving the other half drably oak-stained. A lighted makeup mirror and several hand mirrors of various magnifications sat atop the dresser, as well as an assortment of expensive hair gels, erase sticks, and colognes.

A second-hand love seat blocked off the winding staircase. He had a habit of tossing his neckties and belts onto the ornately carved oak newel.

All four walls had male nude calendars lovingly thumbtacked into place. Any Place I Hang My Porn Is Home.

I was looking for *something*, though I didn't know what. A phone number on a slip of paper, maybe. A torn-up love letter. Or something about Tara. But there wasn't anything to go on—unless your idea of a meaningful clue is a discarded box that once held a plastic approximation of certain body part of a certain popular porn star.

I sorted through the stacks of mail piled amidst CDs with cracked jewel cases, old issues of *Variety*, and—I noted with vague embarrassment—several "Betty and Veronica" comic digests. The CDs revealed Shane's highly predictable, teenybopper tastes. Still in its protective cellophane wrapper was the soundtrack to *Light My Fire*. In a corner of the floor was a stack of real estate brochures, some of them upwards of several years old. Now and then a page was dog-eared, or a property circled with a felt-tip pen.

An old poster of Tara in a bikini from her preserious artist phase was thumbtacked to the wall. Shane had scribbled a Groucho face over Tara's with a Magic Marker. He cryptically wrote "Miss Thang" off to one side, followed by several somewhat girlishly curlicued exclamation points. Did he mean it as a put-down—and if so, how *much* of a put-down?

I looked under the futon, but the only thing there was a condom in a packet.

The doorknob turned.

I ducked into the walk-in closet, a chaos of rumpled jeans and T-shirts; Shane owned few expensive clothes, and often appeared at premieres and the like in loan-outs from designers. *So Shane, you've come back after all,* I thought to myself, as I listened to the jangle of a keychain, and then the squeaky opening of a door. My heart beat rapidly: I realized that I was being a total ninny again. This was the main closet. It was entirely likely that Shane would open it—in which case he'd see me, and in which case, if he *was* a cold-blooded, homicidal maniac . . .

My cheery trend of thought was abruptly halted as my elbow knocked against a hard object. Even in the dark my hands could make out the shape of an Academy Award. Since it seemed unlikely that Shane would've somehow scooped up his own Oscar and then decide to hide it, I could only assume it was Tara's Oscar. The winner's name's were engraved onto the statuettes after the ceremonies, so there was no way to know offhand.

The footsteps grew closer. *Think, Rick, think.* Better just to stay in the closest and keep my fingers crossed. No point in purposefully antagonizing a possibly dangerous man. I'd want to talk to Shane all right, but only with Benji present—if not a few strong-armed cops. I'd wait for Shane to leave, then follow him out to wherever he was going. No—first I'd check real quick see to see if he left any clues behind.

Of course, all this was predicated on him not opening the door to the closet. If he *did* open it, I needed to defend myself. I contemplatively held the Oscar. It was compact and heavy, rather like using the candlestick to kill Colonel Mustard in the Billiard Room. But it also was potential evidence, and I didn't want to tamper with it. Besides, call me crazy and stupid, I just couldn't bring myself to defile an Academy Award. It seemed sacrilegious.

I quickly thought about wiping my fingerprints off the Oscar, but just as quickly vetoed the idea. If Shane's fingerprints were also on the Oscar, it might connect him to Tara's whereabouts at the moment of her death.

If I could find a scarf—you can choke someone with a scarf. But as I rummaged around, taking great pains not to make any noise, the best I could come up with was a wire hanger. If it was good enough for Joan Crawford, it was good enough for me. And as I thought of it, with enough force you could do all sorts of dastardly things to someone with a hanger. Hanger in hand, I listened attentively, and waited.

I was sweating like a pig. I loosened my tie and carefully slipped off my suit jacket.

It was happening. The footsteps were coming straight toward me. The doorknob was turning. Bracing myself, I drew a deep breath. Closing my eyes in terror, and with wire hanger in hand, I thought of Faye Dunaway, and attacked with everything I had.

The hanger was yanked from my hands in about less than one second. Figuring I might as well get it over with, I opened my eyes, expecting to get bludgeoned to death.

It took a moment to adjust to the light.

"Office Zane?" I couldn't believe it.

He was laughing, and nodding his head in exasperation. "Like I say, Mr. Domino, you're a hell of a funny guy."

12

"So what are you going to do, arrest me for assaulting an officer?"

Presumably off-duty, Officer Terry Zane was dressed in a black T-shirt, construction boots, a rugged-looking bomber-type jacket with about a million zippered pockets, and non-Levi, discount jeans. Since the jacket—unlike the cheapo jeans—indicated some sense of style, I assumed it was given to him by his wife. If anything, he looked more commanding out of uniform. He gave me a mock, playful punch to the arm—though his idea of "playful" hurt a little.

"Aw, Mr. Domino—can I call you Rick?—let's get real. I'd be the laughingstock of the LAPD if I reported anything as lame as your goofy little attack." He snorted for the preposterous thought as he set down the hanger.

For the second time in one day, I was angered by the patronizing machismo of a straight man. I knew what he was *really* getting at.

"Plus let's not forget that I'm a fag," I noted sardonically, quickly returning the hanger to the closet. "So why would you ever have to think I was dangerous in a million years?"

My shirt was drenched in sweat. I lowered the temperature on the thermostat. "Don't you remember, Officer? You arrested me for murder. I'm a cold-blooded killer. A gun, a hanger, it doesn't matter. I swat 'em down like flies."

"Really, Rick—"

"I never said you could call me that."

He sighed, and extended his thick-wristed, thick-fingered hand. "Call me Terry, okay?"

I figured I'd best cooperate with the palooka. "Well, okay then. *Terry.*" I tried to make it sound like it was the most absurd thing I could call him, though needless to say the subtleties of my sarcasm were lost on him. I reluctantly offered my hand. Terry's face crinkled into a smile.

"Looking for something, Rick? Anything I should know about?"

"Oh, you mean this isn't my home? Gee, I'm confused. I must've had too much to drink last night."

Terry laughed. "You come up with some real zingers, I'll give you that much."

For an extremely long, awkward moment, we both just stood there. Strangely, I couldn't bring myself to make eye contact with him.

"Jesus, it's hot in here," Terry noted. He took off his jacket. His hairy forearms looked about as thick as my waistline.

Terry leaned his massive frame against the dresser, filling all three mirrors with his darkly attired backside. "As I started to say, Rick, you've got one heck of a chip on your shoulder. You're the one who keeps making a big deal about being gay. Hell, I deal with gay guys all the time. I have *friends* who are gay." He spied one of the male nude wall calendars. "See?" he elaborated, removing the calendar from its pushpin. He unsexily licked his thumb to flip through the pages. "See? I can understand how these are real good-looking guys and that they turn you on. That's cool. I have no problem with it." He paused to take a brief look at Mr. April—who, as it happened, was wearing a cop's hat and carrying a club. "Huh. I wonder if he's a real cop. We have gay cops on the force, you know."

He flustered only slightly as he tried to act nonchalant about the whole thing. By contrast, I could tell that I'd turned redder than Francine Quick's monstrosity of a gown. When straight people decide they Don't Have a Problem with your being gay, your lifetime of being told you were a freak is supposed to instantly evaporate for their convenience.

"Like I say, it's no big deal," Terry continued, returning the calendar to the wall; he even took a sec to make sure it was hung straight. "My wife—" He paused, I assumed because there was the sound of footsteps outside. The footsteps subsided; presumably a neighbor was coming or going.

"Your wife . . . ?" I helpfully encouraged. In a morbid way, I was curious to hear what ignorant, condescending, homophobic remark he was going to make.

He scratched at his sweaty stubble of hair. "Never mind. Anyway, the point is, I know you didn't do it. The murder, I mean."

I regarded Terry suspiciously, and stepped away from him—and nearly tripped over the futon in the process. "What is this, some sort of reverse psychology tactic to get me to confess?" My awkwardness, alas, spoiled the melodrama of the moment. From a nearby house came the mood-breaking strains of Barry Manilow's disco extravaganza "Copacabana."

Terry tried unsuccessfully to swallow back a chortle, though I couldn't tell if he was making fun of me or Barry Manilow.

"Look, Rick, call it a sixth sense, but I *know* you're not a murderer. Not in a million years. You like to say nasty things you don't really mean. But I can see it's just your way of fighting back, and everyone has to fight back one way or another. You're not a *bad* guy. You're not the type of man who could live with yourself if you ever truly hurt somebody."

Now I was really pissed off. What an arrogant son of a bitch he was, thinking he could rattle off some bottom-drawer psychobabble, as if the magnificently complex personality I worked so hard to cultivate could be so easily deconstructed. Excuse me, but I got my head shrunk only by two-hundred-buck-an hour top Beverly Hills professionals—just like I only got my hair cut on Rodeo Drive or on Manhattan's East Side.

"Thank you, Dr. Joyce Brothers." I waited to see the shocked expression on Terry's face, that such a butch guy as himself would be likened to someone of the female persuasion.

"Joyce Brothers? I don't get it."

I was truly exasperated. "Never mind. Just spare me your trivial insights into my poignantly disturbed character. What about all that peachy circumstantial evidence that compelled you to arrest me?"

"I know that's all it was—circumstantial. And after your lawyer told the press someone shot at you in the alleyway, it was all I needed to hear. I decided to follow you."

I had no idea I was being followed. I was impressed. But I wasn't about to admit it.

"Didn't you have anything better to do? Surely there's some little old lady whose hamster is stuck in a tree, and she's just waiting for you to make her day."

Nothing could deter his demented enthusiasm. "Rick, I know *exactly* what you're doing. We're totally on the same page." He grinned ear to ear, holding up his index and middle fingers close together, presumably to suggest some sort of revolting bond he felt the two of us shared.

"You're exaggerating, to put it mildly," I stated evenly, hoping my faint shudder didn't show. "By the way, what in the world are you talking about?"

He stood up from the dresser, having never once sneaked a peak at his reflection. And to think that some people would say that he was the same sex as someone like Shane.

"Rick, I thought you were a smart guy," he chided, walking about the room. "It's staring you right in the face. This is my big chance—*our* big chance. Let's work together. Find out who really killed Tara Perez. You cover the showbiz angles, and I do the police grunt work. I have an inside connection for finding things out. And I'm *great* on the computer—I've read all these survivalist-conspiracy theory books on how to hack into just about everything. I've already started doing my homework. I know that Shane rents this place under a phony name—Eddie something."

To say his suggestion had "doom" written all over it would be like saying that rumor had it that not all the men in West Hollywood had taken lifelong vows of celibacy. It was like a nightmare within a nightmare—on top of everything else, I now had this lunatic cop getting in my way. Unless of course the whole thing was a hoax— part of his good-cop routine to earn my trust and then fuck me over.

Still, he *was* a cop, and I needed to be tactful. "Terry, I really don't think—"

"Think about it," Terry interrupted. "Everyone wins. You clear your good name. And I'll finally get noticed for promotion. Wow, after all these years of rerouting traffic, I finally stumble on a *murder*." From his elation, you'd have thought he just said, *I finally found a cure for cancer.*

If Terry thought I'd be happy upon hearing his idea, he was sorely mistaken. He may well have wanted a promotion, but I wanted to be spared a lethal injection. This wasn't just some fun little lark from my end of things.

"But won't you get into trouble for not following procedure or sticking to your beat or whatever they call it?"

"With all the publicity, they wouldn't dare do anything but reward me. You know—cop shows true American initiative, and all that jazz."

If I didn't know better, I almost would have thought that Terry had a trace of showbiz savvy about him. Probably he was just trying to win my trust.

"Well, what about having the time to do it? You have to work, right? And go home each night to wifey."

"I'm one step ahead of you there," Terry replied pleasantly, ever the engaging salesman. "I'm taking a two-week vacation starting today. I told them I had an emergency situation. I've got enough seniority to get away with it."

"What about your wife?"

"What *about* her?"

"Well, in the strict sense I've never been married, but I'd assume that your life-partner would appreciate it if you spent your vacation time with her. Call me nuts, but it was just a passing thought."

Terry shifted his weight about with a vague embarrassment. For all of his bulk—or maybe because of it—there was something touchingly vulnerable about him at times. "What can I say? Darla Sue and I—well, we *understand* each other. I put my career first. And she's busy with her own life quite a lot."

"A cop's wife," I suggested helpfully, resisting with all my willpower the urge to comment on the name "Darla Sue."

"Yeah, I guess so. A cop's wife."

So Terry, in his hetero way, was clearly no better than Shane. His career was all that mattered. *Men!* What a hopeless lot they were.

And yet, as much as I hated to admit it, there was an integrity about Terry told me that it wasn't quite that simple, that something very real must have happened in his marriage. I wanted to ask if he had any kids, but figured he hadn't, or else he would've mentioned them already. As a gossip columnist, my spider sense was tingling. My guess was that he and his wife had lost a child. Maybe the poor kid got murdered, and that was why Terry was so into being a cop. But I thought the better of prying—at least for right now.

Besides, what was I doing, starting to wonder about this *cop* who might as well have lived in some parallel universe? The main task before me was to shake him off my tail. I had no desire to turn my life into some misbegotten remake of *In the Heat of the Night*. Especially when: a) I didn't trust him, b) I didn't need him, and c) I didn't trust him.

Terry invasively clutched me by the shoulders. "Rick, face it. We live in different worlds. But that's what's so great about it. We're doubling our chances for success. I'm investigating this case whether you like it or not. Wouldn't it make sense to work with each other, instead of against each other? And if I fail—if *we* do—then what has either of us lost?"

A phone rang. "That's me." Terry took out his cell phone. I was pleased to have an extra moment to chose my words.

A glance out the bay window made me glad of something else.

Lurking across the street and a few doors down was none other than Officer Charlie, the delightfully homophobic pig of a cop from last night—and, of course, partner to none other than Terry Zane.

I knew better than to trust Terry, but seeing Charlie made me realize just how sound my instincts had been. Terry *was* out to set me up. I scolded myself for having taken any interest in anything he had to say at all.

Well, two could play this little game.

If Terry thought he was leading me along, I could play right into it—though of course I'd be one step ahead of him. Better not to have this jerk for an enemy. And who knows? Maybe his police smarts *could* be put to good use. Maybe he'd even start to see the truth, and it would never hurt to have a cop on my side . . .

"Yeah, Darla Sue. That's fine." Terry rolled his eyes, indicating we were in on some joke together. "I'll see you in a couple of weeks, okay? Fine, make it three. Yeah, give my love to your folks." He folded the cell phone back into his jacket pocket. "Boy, *women,* huh?"

I couldn't tell if he was forgetting a slight detail about me, or if he truly felt that all males were brothers under the skin for having to deal with those "impossible" females in some way, shape, or form. I was oddly tempted to commiserate, starting with my woes with Mitzi, but quickly thought the better of it. As a contemporary gay man, I lived beyond the realm of simplistic gender stereotypes. In any case, I was not about to fall for any of Terry's attempts to flatter me into thinking we were pals or partners or whatnot.

"You're right, Terry. We should work together."

The look on his face was so innocently happy that if I didn't know better I would've felt sorry for him. What a lying, conniving prick.

"Rick, that's great. Now tell me. You've obviously cased the joint top to bottom. Come across anything you should share with your partner here?"

I shrugged. "Wish I could say that I had."

"You're *sure?* I don't want us to keep any secrets from each other. If we're going to crack this case together, we can't be—"

A key was rattling in the door.

"Holy shit!" I topically remarked, my voice inconveniently cracking so that I sounded like Robin the Boy Wonder. "*Shane!*" The neighbor presumably was treating us to Barry Manilow's greatest hits, because now we were hearing, like it or not, "I Write the Songs." I quickly looked out the window; Charlie was down at the end of the street, looking in the other direction. Thanks, Charlie, for being so useful.

"Be *quiet!*" Terry forcefully whispered. "Are you a total idiot?" For a flash of an instant I saw concern register on his face. I guessed he was wondering what Charlie was up to.

Terry quickly reached into his jacket. "Here," he whispered urgently, handing me a gun. "It's a Luger, so the safety—" My baffled look must have given me away. Terry sighed, and clicked something on the gun. "Just *hold* it, okay? Try to make it look good. And try not shoot anything. How you managed not to do any damage last night is a miracle." He blessed himself with a gun in his own hands, in what I took to be a serious gesture.

I hated guns as much as ever, but I felt insulted yet again. I mean, I *did* manage to fire the thing last night. But here he was, taking even that away from me, so that I felt more incompetent gunwise than when left to my own ingenuity. As an adult, I often felt that the male world of bullshit no longer posed a threat to me. I could transcend it or fake a connection to it when need be—sometimes even feel that it was a *part* of me. But Terry was taking me right back to square one. I felt as hopelessly unbutch as when I was twelve years old in Iowa.

Still, I had better things to worry about. Barry Manilow was crooning that he'd been alive forever, but I wanted to survive until lunchtime, if not longer. Maybe it wasn't all bad, having a competent police office on my side with Shane about to enter the room and do who-knows-what to me. Of course, maybe Shane wasn't dangerous, but better safe than sorry.

The door opened. Shane entered.

"Police," Terry informed him. "Hands up." With his free hand, he flashed his badge.

Shane quietly set down his overnight bag, and raised his hands as told. Yet he didn't seem especially surprised. It was more like he was shocked to be in the house at all, and we were just one aspect of this larger bafflement. In fact, he looked completely disoriented, as though he just awoke from a fifty-year coma, or landed on Mars.

"Officer, I know what you must be thinking," Shane began, striving to sound calm and reasonable, though I sensed his nervousness. He reached down toward his bag.

"Easy now," Terry warned, waving his gun. "There's nothing you need to grab."

13

$\mathscr{S}$hane sighed, and returned to his hands-up position. "Please, Officer. You don't understand."

In the last twelve hours, Shane managed to change out of his tux. He sported the squeaky-cleanest of casual clothes, looking as refreshed as if he'd just returned from a weekend at a health spa. While I'd been rotting in jail, he'd apparently taken the time to get a haircut. It was a much less trendy version of his usual cut, as if in an act of penance he went to a regulation barbershop instead of his zillion-dollar stylist. You'd never guess that he fled the sight of a murder only the night before. Some tidbit of the art of acting was rubbing off on him; he knew how to emphasize his innocence in every possible way.

"Officer, please let me explain—"

I was losing patience fast—not that I had much to begin with. "Can it with the fake politeness, Shane. Save it for next year's Oscars. 'Oh, but *Officer*,' '*Please*, Officer.' If you're Mr. Law and Order, why didn't it behoove you to stick around last night? Now you tell us what's what, and you do it *now*." I extended my gun for emphasis.

Terry looked at me with annoyance. "Mr. *Kirk*," he stated, in manner of one seeking to eradicate what was previously spoken by another, "I apologize for Mr. Domino's behavior."

He rose, and methodically frisked Shane.

"Officer, is it standard procedure to have accused murderers assist you in your work?" Shane's remark seemed so cruel that I almost got sick on the spot. Benji must've been right. There were no limits to the crazed evil that Shane was willing to commit.

Terry stopped pawing him. "It's okay, Rick. Set your gun down."

I set the gun aside as told. Terry, though, kept pointing his gun at Shane. "Never you mind about police business."

"But Officer, I—"

"Do you mind if I search your bag?"

"Not at all," replied Shane in a cheerful, even voice.

I had to admit that Terry had his smooth moments. He zipped open the satchel and emptied its contents onto the floor. There were a couple of changes of clothes, all neatly folded, a wallet and—of all things—a Bible and rosary. Shane may not have been much of an actor, but in the props department he'd done his job. Imagine Shane with a Bible!

"Excuse me," Shane politely interjected, "but you both are quite understandably mistaken. You see, I'm not Shane, though I have of course come to find him."

Now I'd heard everything.

"Please, Shane," I admonished with a snort. "Spare us. You're not a good enough actor to be pulling this off this schizo routine. As usual, you're overplaying."

It was true. Shane's Acting 101 approach to drumming up an alternate personality was to go from one extreme to the other, as though suddenly playing Gallant instead of his usual Goofus. He was like Cathy Lane on Quaaludes. What was truly insulting was that he actually thought he could fool us with such an amateurish performance.

I walked up to Shane, looking him straight in the eye. "I have to say, though, that's it's refreshing to see you at least fake some semblance of decent manners. I didn't know you had it in you at all. What's with the Bible and rosary? Some sort of kinky new sex fantasy? Do you play the priest or the altar boy? Whose cock do you—"

"Rick, cool it." Terry tossed me the wallet. Inside it was a driver's license from Ohio, noting its owner as one Brother Dennis Sharnovsky. Even in the cruddy DMV photo, I recognized Shane's movie-star looks.

"Wow, you even got a phony ID," I stated caustically, tossing the wallet aside.

"But it's not," protested Shane. "That's what I've been trying to tell you. I *am* Brother Dennis Sharnovsky. I'm a Jesuit out of Columbus. Eddie's twin. I mean to say, Shane Kirk's twin. Last night, when he turned up missing after the—the *incident*, I flew right out. Now I think I'm entitled to some explanation. I'm not surprised to see a police officer doing his job to find my brother, but I recognize Mr. Domino, and I must ask what he's doing here."

Now I'd *really* heard everything. My entire life was degenerating from a bad movie script to an even worse one. An identical twin brother—and a Jesuit *brother* at that?! One twin a man of the cloth, the other a man of the bedsheets; one a man of the collar, the other a man of the dog collar and leather harness . . . well, you get the idea. Not that I was a hundred percent sold that Brother Dennis wasn't Shane. But if he was really Brother Dennis then he was utterly without guile, oblivious to the ways in which his mere existence made life imitate pulp.

But then, that's how things so often played out in Hollywood. One way or another, everyone's life turns into trash, and now it was happening even to the likes of Brother Dennis.

"This license is real," Terry affirmed. "Rick, I think you owe Brother Dennis an apology for—you know, those things you were saying."

Brother Dennis laughed. "Please, Mr. Domino. No apologies are needed. I work as a guidance counselor in our high school. Young people today have so many questions about sex."

He spotted the porn calendar, then averted his eyes from it. If he *was* Shane, it was the greatest piece of acting he'd ever done. Asking Shane not to ogle porn was like asking the Pope not to wear gold lamé.

"Now, then. An explanation, please."

"Mr. Domino has agreed to help find Mr. Kirk," Terry answered carefully, "who, after all, is both missing and a likely key witness."

"And you have him pointing guns at innocent people?"

Terry laughed. "Wasn't loaded." He reached for the Luger and opened the barrel, demonstrating that it was indeed empty. "Just wanted to be intimidating to whomever was coming in."

"You prick! You no good motherfucking—"

"Easy, Rick," Terry advised with a smile. "I had you covered. And watch your language." He tilted his head toward our man of the cloth.

Brother Dennis walked to thermostat, raising the temperature without asking us if we wanted him to. "That's perfectly all right, Officer . . . ?"

"Zane. Terry Zane." He extended his hand. "And this, as you know, is Rick Domino." He obviously took pride in introducing someone to a celebrity. So what if it was under the sleaziest, most duplicitous of circumstance?

"Mr. Domino." As Brother Dennis offered his hand, he regarded me with a detached pleasantness, reserving judgment of my soul to God but not exactly asking for my autograph, either. For my part, I wanted to see if his hand gave off some sort of familiar Shane vibration. It didn't seem to, but I could swear that in the split-instant Brother Dennis made eye contact with me, he knew exactly what I was thinking.

"How'd you get a key?" asked Terry.

Brother Dennis smiled sadly as he looked about the messy room, as though the squalor of his movie star twin was disappointingly familiar. "My mother used to leave an extra key taped to the backside of the mailbox. I assumed that Shane would do the same thing."

"What if he hadn't?" I wanted to know.

"I suppose I would've had to break in." He said this as a matter of fact, that it would have been just and right to have done so if needed.

He gazed at the graffiti'd poster of Tara, and smiled with a sad gentleness. "She must have been just a delight. What a marvelous sense of humor, to have a poster of herself with a funny face drawn on."

"Yeah, she was a card alright," I tactfully replied. I didn't bother pointing out that it was Shane who drew on the face—which action, incidentally, I hardly thought indicative of "marvelous" wit.

Brother Dennis studied me. "You're not guilty, are you, Mr. Domino?" he asked forthrightly.

"No, I'm not," I replied with some force, as if venting my anger toward Shane.

"I believe him," Terry boldly shared. The conviction with which he lied gave me shivers—and as a Hollywood columnist I didn't shiver easily.

"I could tell," Brother Dennis naïvely stated. "Now, Mr. Domino, tell me everything. Please don't worry about offending me. I already know quite a lot about my brother. We are twins, after all." He briefly looked at his three images in the dresser mirror, then turned away, seemingly ashamed of his momentary lapse into vanity. "Not to be boastful before the eyes of the Lord, but I think Shane found something cleansing in sharing with me, given my vocation. I have done my best never to judge him. Anything you say will go no farther, I can assure you. Unless of course Officer Zane has any objections?" He sat himself on the edge of the futon, indicating that I should join him.

For some reason, I looked at Terry, like I needed the jerk's approval.

"Go ahead, Rick," Terry answered quietly.

And so I gave Brother Dennis the lowdown of events since the night before. I was vague about my relationship with Shane—I actually described him as my "special friend"—and avoided all mention of the way the shit had used me. I hinted that perhaps once or twice a producer was *interested* in Shane, without getting into just how reciprocal the frisky young lad could be. I said there was a rumor that Shane had been a prostitute, but hey, rumors—who believes them? Yet I was straightforward about what counted: the gun, the body, Shane's disappearing act, and the alleyway shooter.

Annoyingly, Terry kept whistling "I Write the Songs" the whole time I spoke. At one point, he absently sang a snatch of the lyric, though he erroneously thought it went: *I write the songs that make the whole world king.* It made no sense, but I didn't bother correcting him. He had a mildly pleasant cop-type tenor voice.

I acted nonchalant when Terry walked over to the window—I assumed to give some sort of signal to Charlie.

When I finished talking, Brother Dennis stretched into a yawn. "Pardon me," he murmured. "Those red-eye flights." He stood up and repaired to the Spartan kitchen for a drink of water. "Now then," he called from the other room, "let's see if I understand. Shane was a prostitute who slept his way to the top, and used you badly." He came back to the main room. "I must say I was proud of Shane last night. Up to a point."

104

Before Terry or I could speak, Brother Dennis added, "Now, Mr. Domino, am I to assume that you and Officer Zane are secretly working together to solve the case?"

"Brother Dennis," Terry offered, "this is special police business. It's—"

"It's two people trying to get at the truth, when the system has failed." Brother Dennis smiled. "Don't worry, gentlemen. Your secrets are safe with me. I admire you for doing what needs to be done." He looked at the Kmart digital clock. "But I must leave you now. I have to find my brother. I assume you can let yourselves out?"

"Not so fast."

"Of course. Forgive me, Mr. Domino." Brother Dennis smiled. "You're wondering why Shane never mentioned me, aren't you?"

"Not really," I answered bitterly. In point of fact, Shane told me three completely different stories about his childhood, and when I finally called him on it he never brought it up again. There was an official bio given to reporters, but I assumed it was a bunch of BS. Though for the record, it mentioned nothing about having a twin.

Terry started whistling again.

"Will you *stop* that?" I beseeched him. I must have asked more forcefully than I realized, because Terry and Brother Dennis looked at me with this *and-did-we-forget-to-take-our-Prozac-this-morning?* condescending alarm.

"Sorry," I heard myself amend.

Terry gave me a dose of his fake concern. "I'm getting the impression that Shane is a man of many secrets."

"Too many," remarked Brother Dennis firmly. "He has caused

damage to others as well as to himself. And now I fear his life is in danger. Not just because of what he might know about the murder. Or even if he committed it."

"*Did* he?" Terry inquired, as if Brother Dennis worked for the Dionne Warwick psychic hotline.

Brother Dennis looked through Shane's pathetic CD collection, like a parent snooping through his teenager's bedroom. "I would certainly like to believe he did not."

"That's not much of an answer," Terry remarked.

So even the twin brother thinks Shane did it. If I wasn't being charged with first-degree murder, I might have been upset.

There was a screech of brakes coming from outside. Brother Dennis opened the window shade a crack to peer outside.

"Anything out there?" I asked as innocently as possible.

"I'm sure it's nothing," Terry stated.

"I didn't see anything," Brother Dennis concurred. He turned to look at us, then looked back out the window. "There's a great deal neither of you know about," he quietly remarked. "When we were twelve years old . . ."

He faltered, then went on. "Sadly enough, it's an all-too-familiar story. There was a stranger with a ski mask. He had a gun. He walked us into the woods. He looked us over. God in Heaven only knows why, since we looked exactly the same, but he told me to run for my life. Eddie—I mean Shane—had to stay."

"Poor kid." Terry bowed his head.

"Shane never talked about it. Except to me, of course. Our father had died. And our poor mother could not deal with very much. Drinking problem. Countless boyfriends. She only lived a few more years. Shane made me promise never to tell her. No one else ever knew."

He turned to face us. "Not until now—isn't that funny? I never even mentioned it to my fellow Jesuits. You two, whom I've just met, are the only ones I've ever told. But there's no more time for secrets."

Something sounded fishy. "So this weirdo with a gun just decided to let Shane go?"

"Maybe."

Terry and I looked at each other. "You think Shane might've—"

"Yes, Mr. Domino. I think he very much did. I think he was violated, and then somehow got hold of the gun, and shot the perpetrator in self-defense."

The room was getting warm. I turned the air conditioning back on high, feeling like I was rebelling against my parents. "You *think*? I thought you said you were close to your brother."

"I was. I am. Only this . . . I simply never asked Shane about it. Not just out of respect for his privacy. You see, I really didn't *want* to know. The next day, the papers reported a man in a ski mask who'd been found dead of a gunshot wound. The police assumed it was over some sort of botched robbery. I find it heroic that a twelve-year-old boy could fight for his survival so gallantly.

"Later, of course, I was disturbed by Shane's prostitution, though I understood what he was reacting against. And considering the fate that could have awaited him after such an ordeal, I'd say he's done quite well for himself. Imagine—an Academy Award. When I watched him playing that troubled young man in *Light My Fire*, I marveled and how he was able to draw upon all those depths of pain and anguish inside him. I'm sure that's what made it such a riveting performance. Quite on the par with the young Brando or James Dean, wouldn't you say, Mr. Domino? The Lord does indeed work in mysterious ways. From the worst of sorrows can come the greatest gifts of beauty and truth."

"Uh . . . yeah. I guess." It was the best I could muster. Clearly, the Mother Church's gain was not the film critics' loss. If Brother Dennis thought Shane was comparable to Brando and Dean, one could only wonder what else he might opine. Perhaps that Anna Nicole Smith would be the next Garbo?

I was anxious to change the subject. "Well, they say once you kill, the second time—" Terry's scowl stopped me from finishing the sentence.

"I'm very sorry to hear about Shane." Terry shook his head in sympathy. "Sorry for you both. But how does that put him in danger now? Is someone blackmailing him?"

"Quite likely. If not worse. You see, when Shane was turning tricks . . . well, a hungry young man wants to get a little sympathy."

Terry took out a notepad and wrote something down. "I don't follow you."

Brother Dennis sighed. "When Shane first started hustling, he told me not to worry, that he had everything under control. Something about how he told the person or people he was working for 'everything' about his past. How this information had won them over, and how Shane now had them wrapped around his finger."

"And what did Shane mean by 'everything'?" Terry asked.

"I regret to say I didn't ask. But I assumed . . . well, let's just say it was dangerously naïve of Shane to think he could trust some john or pimp or whoever it was. You see, I never even asked for a name. Or *names*. I simply didn't want to know anymore than he told me."

"But what does all this have to do with Shane now?" I asked.

"Shane called me last night. It would've been about an hour after the Oscars. He was using his cell phone, and there was a great deal of static. He had to repeat himself a few times for me to hear what he was saying. But it was something about how it was all over. That everything from the past was about to unravel. That when he started to make it as an actor, someone who knew 'everything' told him that he'd bide his time until he could use the information against Shane to his best advantage. And that because of Tara's murder, this other person was ready to cash in. They were going to go public with it all, unless he cooperated."

Terry registered puzzlement. "'Cooperated?' I assume he meant money?"

Brother Dennis nodded sadly as he perused one of Shane's real estate brochures. "I'm afraid that's all I know. Shane said that no matter what happened, he wanted me to know that he loved me. Then he hung up. Or at least, I *hope* he hung up, that he wasn't . . ." He looked meaningfully at us both. "I have no idea where he is right now. But I have to find him."

Terry looked at me, and then at Brother Dennis. "It's very touching, the way you've dropped everything to help your brother," he began. "But Rick and I are already looking for him. I'm a police officer. Rick knows Hollywood. Please, leave it to us. Go back to Ohio. We'll call you if we learn anything. If we find Shane, we'll make sure he's safe. Isn't that right, Rick?"

I had to hand it to Terry. I didn't want this sanctimonious Brother Dennis hanging around. He was just another body to get in the way. Now, if I could only get someone to make a similar speech to Terry himself, I'd be free to work on the investigation unencumbered by nuisance hangers-on.

"Sure, Terry. Brother Dennis, Terry is right. Wherever Shane is, it's no place you should be. You can trust us."

Brother Dennis closed his eyes, his hands clasped near his face. He might've been praying, but I believe he was simply deep in thought.

"You *will* keep me informed?" He looked at us beseechingly.

"Absolutely," Terry assured.

"Then you're right, of course," Brother Dennis decided. "Thank you for being the answer to my prayers." He extended his arms, indicating that he wanted that most deplorable of contemporary phenomenon, the group hug.

Oh well, I figured as a Jesuit brother he didn't exactly Get Any, and this silly hug would probably mean a lot to him. With the reluctance of one about to undergo a dentist's drill, I grimaced as I stepped into the inane little huddle.

"I think we ought to take a moment to pray," Brother Dennis offered. "To pray and give thanks." I guessed he was so used to being around Jesuits he didn't realize that "Prayer" was not exactly everyone's middle name.

"That sounds like an excellent idea," Terry agreed.

And so I wincingly prepared myself for the mawkish little moment of Sunday School.

"Heavenly Father—"

My cell phone was ringing. Ironically, I found myself thinking: *Thank you, God.*

"Hold your horses, Brother D."

Terry scowled at me as I answered the phone. It was Benji.

"Well?" Terry asked, when I got off the phone.

"My attorney wants to meet with me."

Actually, Benji said that Francine had been calling him ad nauseum for her urgent need to speak with me, and that if I didn't get the old bag off his back he was dropping my case. It was typical of old drunks like Francine to involve extra people in whatever was happening, and so turn it into a crisis all about *her*. There was no reason why she couldn't have called me herself.

But Francine was on my list, anyway. If she could help me, I was all ears.

Besides, it gave me the ideal excuse to ditch Terry the two-faced cop and the vapid Brother Dennis. Once I had them off my tail, I could come back and scoop up the Oscar.

14

*T*erry agreed to take Brother Dennis out for lunch before driving him to the airport. I felt an amazingly intense sense of freedom to be away from them both.

I had zero desire to go home before meeting with Francine. You might think it would be fun to lounge around your Egyptian mosaic pool that's catty-corner to your Zen meditation pool that overlooks your Swiss postmodern sauna. But somehow, when the tabloids have helicopters circling your property with telephoto lenses, even swimming pools lose their charm.

Yet I knew I had stalled long enough.

I needed to change my clothes before meeting with Francine. But, more importantly, I needed to stop putting off the inevitable, because the pesky reporters weren't going to go away. *Not* facing up to the press was starting to feel worse than avoiding it.

Unlike movies, with their sudden interludes of background music to signal change, real life is a place where courage often happens gradually.

It won't be so bad, I told myself, bravely driving to Bel Air.

But the instant the reporters swarmed me—and they spotted me a good five minutes away from my faux Spanish deco house—I knew I'd made one of my more disastrous mistakes. It took thirty nerve-wracking minutes to drive the few hundred yards to my driveway. Other drivers caught in the riot of press kept honking at me, as though it were all my fault. So many reporters were talking at once, I couldn't have made out any of their questions even if I wanted to. There were even a few protesters amongst them, screaming about how I'd fry for killing Tara. Just as bad were the simple gawkers, who shouted that they wanted my autograph.

All I could think of was the respite of my private garage, from where I could slip inside my home and find some semblance of privacy. They'd all be trying to peak inside, but with the French-pleated linen shades drawn, I could pretend no one was there.

Then I realized that since this was a rented car, I didn't have the gizmo to let myself into the garage. I'd have to park in the cobblestone driveway.

Stepping out of the car was like stepping into the locust storm in *The Good Earth*. A million mikes and TV cameras zoomed in on me, making it impossible to move. Maniacs tore my shirt. Someone yanked hard on my hair while someone else seemed determined to keep my desocketed arm as a souvenir. Another schmuck with far more straightforward goals pulled an expensive diamond ring from my middle finger.

Images of Ingrid Bergman as Joan of Arc came rushing to mind as I prepared myself for my tragic, ironic, and untimely demise.

"Okay, folks, break it up."

The macho voice of Terry Zane boomed over a bullhorn. Like Cecile B. DeMille's Red Sea, there was a parting in the tidal wave of people as Terry stepped forward in his uniform, bullhorn and club in hand. The gawkers had to step pretty far aside to make room for him. Between his bulk and his authoritative policeman's air, he took up a lot of space.

"Let Mr. Domino through," he commanded, clutching his arm around my shoulder as if I were a football and he was taking off to the goal post for a touchdown. I figured it must have really grossed him out to have to touch a fag, but that there were no limits to how much double-crossing he'd do to nab me.

Still, given the circumstances, I was glad he magically appeared.

"My hero," I declared, as we approached my front door. I batted my eyelashes.

"Very funny," he hissed between clenched teeth. "Now stop it. The press might see."

"And we wouldn't want anyone thinking you knew a fag *personally*, now would we?"

"That's not what I meant. I might've just blown my cover. I have to think of something to tell the force if they ask me what I was doing here."

Yeah, I'll bet you will, you no-good louse of a liar.

I could see, though, that I'd embarrassed him. His face was as red as a giant killer tomato.

"Don't worry, Terry. I could tell the TV cameras were all zooming in for a close-up of me. Your secret is safe, unless any of your fellow officers are on intimate terms with your right hand."

"Ha-ha," he replied eruditely.

I fumbled for my keys; I found them, dropped them on the terra cotta steps, then picked them up. Terry tried to stifle a mean grin, like he couldn't believe what a clumsy dweeb I was.

"By the way, what are you doing here?" I opened the front door and hesitated. Apparently, I was inviting Terry inside. Or in any case he was inviting himself in.

"You could say I had time to kill. Brother Dennis hopped out of my car at Santa Monica and Wilshire. He shouted at me that he was sorry, but he just had to keep looking for Shane."

"Where did he go?" I stepped into my foyer, Terry right behind me.

"I have no idea. Hopefully, he'll turn up at Shane's place."

I set my keys down on the decorative zinc table. "Well, maybe a whiff of reality, Hollywood style, will send him flying back to Ohio on his broom."

"That wasn't very nice."

I didn't even dignify that with a reply—imagine Terry telling me what was *nice*. "So what happened—you just decided to follow me here?"

"I didn't *follow* you. I just assumed you'd come here before meeting with your lawyer, to change clothes and stuff. I figured you could use some help getting into your house in one piece."

How unselfish of the two-faced motherfucker. What would it take to get rid of him?

It was unbelievable to me that it had been less than twenty-four hours since I'd been home. Everything looked so unconnected to who I was, as if it belonged to some long-dead ancestor whom I'd never known. What a simple life I'd had only yesterday.

"Wow, this is some place," Terry remarked. He gave a wolf whistle to signal his approbation. "It's like a palace. I could never afford to live here in a million years."

Dasher, my black cat from the pound, expressed the profoundest indifference at the sight of me. He leapt creatively across the steel foyer table and chairs to leave the room—after all, *anyone* could simply walk across the inlaid floors—and thereby bypassed the annoyance of my invasive presence.

"Oh, a cat," Terry wittily remarked. "I like cats. Dogs, too," he revealingly added. Ever the gentleman, he took off his cap. He'd given his head a fresh shave, and his large, well-shaped head glistened. He wasn't at all my type, but I had to admit he looked kind of okay, in a big trucker sort of way.

"Hey, fancy mirror." He grinned into the beveled Carole Lombard looking glass. "Looks kind of old, though. Funny, I didn't take you for the antique type." He studied his reflection with a shade more scrutiny than I expected from him.

"By the way, Terry: Yes, you may come in."

He ignored what I said. I was getting the impression that the realm of the sardonic was beyond his mental capacities.

"Here, kitty, kitty." He knelt down, softly whistling as he rubbed his fingers together.

"My cat hates everyone," I informed him, sorting through the day's junk mail. "Its part of his charm."

Terry smiled kind of crookedly. "I guess they say the same about you."

"Thank you so much."

"Aw shucks, Rick. That's not how I meant it. Guys you meet in bars and stuff probably think you're funny. I mean, ha-ha funny. I mean—I wasn't trying to make it sound like you're just some runaround kind of guy, or anything."

"Tell ya what? Let's say we change the subject big time."

"Are you still in love with Shane, Rick? You can talk to me about it, I don't mind."

I took a deep breath to signal *The End*, and sat myself down in my beige, geometric settee. "Now then, why don't you go try to find poor Brother Dennis?"

Terry sat across from me in the matching window seat. "I do worry about him. I doubt that he has much in the way of street smart. Not like us cops. We know how to pull it over on those lowlife slime buckets."

"Sounds like you make friends and influence people everywhere you go." I examined my torn shirt sleeve, wondering if it was worth repairing.

"All in a day's work," Terry replied evenly, not missing a beat. He was superdefensive about being a cop. "Anyway, he may be naïve, but he's not stupid. I'm sure he'll call if he needs us."

If I had a nickel for every awkward silence between Terry and myself, I'd be rich enough to be made King of the Universe.

"So, don't you need to get ready for your lawyer?" Terry finally asked.

"I changed my mind."

"C'mon, Rick. You can do better than that. I thought we were *buddies*."

I stood up just to avoid having to look at him. "I'd like to shower and, well, just be *home* for awhile."

"And then what? I suppose you're just going to lean back in your La-Z-Boy and channel-surf for the next week?"

"I'm also going to order a pizza and pet my cat." I shuffled through the mail again.

"Stop avoiding me. You already looked at the mail." He walked toward me in all his hulking six-four-ness.

"You don't scare me."

Terry looked so baffled he seemed hurt. "Good. I don't want to. I'm trying to help you."

In a devilish mood, I had half a mind to totally freak him out and kiss him. Probably he'd arrest me for assaulting an officer, though. Even Terry's fake good-cop act only extended so far.

I resisted the impulse—hardly a challenge—and sat down again.

"You might as well know. I met with Bob Raflowitz this morning. And his son, Zeke."

I figured I'd play things fifty-fifty with Terry. I'd keep the Oscar in the closet a secret, but I'd tell him all about Bob Raflowitz. That way, I could have the best of both worlds: stuff that I only knew that he couldn't botch up, but also info that I shared and maybe would convince him that I really was innocent, or at least that there were other people he should scope out. And in so doing, leave me the hell alone.

As for telling him I'd be meeting with Francine, I'd have to play that one by ear.

"Bob's an *actor*," I added impatiently, figuring that Terry never heard of him.

"I know who he is. I'm not some ignoramus, you know. I even saw one of his movies. With Darla Sue."

I couldn't resist. "Oh, really? And what was it called?"

"I can't remember. I never remember the names of movies."

"What exactly *do* you remember? The numbers on the parking tickets you write? How many 7–10 splits you've gotten in bowling?"

It was difficult for me to comprehend that there were people who didn't *live* for the movies, especially since I so seldom had contact with such entities.

Terry smiled. "Say, you like to bowl, Rick?"

"You think I'd be caught *dead* in a bowling alley?"

"Easy, Rick. No need to shout."

"I wasn't shouting. Anyway, like I said, Bob Raflowitz invited me over."

"Is it interesting to talk to movie stars in their mansions?"

"No, Terry. It's boring as all shit."

"I guess I said that wrong. It's just that you seem—I don't know—so impatient all the time. Like you've never been happy with your life."

I wondered what it would take for Terry to take the hint that I didn't think of him as my chum. It was obviously all part of his pathetic ploy anyway—win the sucker's trust so he spills the beans—so I certainly didn't feel guilty telling him to fuck off. Which I did.

"Jeez, Rick. I'm just trying to get to know you."

"Well, what about you? Are you happy with *your* life?"

I don't know why I bothered to ask him this. It just kind of came out.

I was surprised to see Terry get all little-boyish, shyly looking down and away as he scrunched up his massive frame. "Gee, I really can't say. I'm so used to worrying about other people's happiness that I guess I don't take much time to think about my own. I *guess* I'm happy. I like my work. And my wife and I, we sort of . . . I mean, you know how it is. Marriage isn't what you think it's going to be. It doesn't make all your problems go away."

Cops worried about other people's happiness? Since when?

I was ashamed of myself for having asked the question.

"Anyway, I learned a few interesting tidbits." And I filled Terry in on everything Bob, Cleo, and Zeke said.

I also told him about the conspiracy of sorts between Bob, Jeep, Tru, Francine, and Cinda. I tried not to show how annoyed I was that he'd barely heard of these people.

"Sounds promising," he lied. "Too bad about that kid Zeke, though it's probably best he avoids that blonde lady, Connie Whatever-You-Said-Her-Name-Was. She sounds like trouble. So what's next? What are you *really* going to do now?"

Boy, talk about suspicious. No wonder he was a cop. I figured I was better off telling him what I was up to. Otherwise, he'd probably just tail me and muck everything up.

"Look, you can come with me," I heard myself blurt. "But if you say anything that embarrasses me, or messes things up—"

"Where are we going, Rick?" He looked like a little boy hoping I'd answer, *The circus*. Which in a way was true.

"To Francine Quick's," I replied. "She's—"

"You just told me. She's a famous actress. And I already knew that, anyway."

"How did you know?"

Terry looked very proud of himself. "My mother used to like her. Her favorite movie was called *A Star Is Born*, starring Francine Quick and some English guy."

Needless to say, I felt as if my very essence had just been kicked in the teeth. I was shocked to the point of numbness, and I couldn't have begun to fashion a response.

In any case, I knew it was asking too much of the universe for Terry to know who the bitch was.

15

*C*ynicism, aside, I'm a sucker for old-time Hollywood—even, as in Francine's case, fifth-rate old Hollywood. Besides showering, I changed into a semicasual tie and jacket in trendy dark colors, and slicked back my hair. I believed in showing the old broad some respect.

Terry's clothes would never do, of course, if I were to pass him off as some sort of "assistant." I began to hope wildly. Surely this meant that he couldn't join me after all. Needless to say, there was nothing in my wardrobe that he could've fit his pinkie into.

But Terry, bless his cop soul, thought of everything, and had a change of clothes in his pick-up truck: a blah but respectable ensemble of shirt, slacks, and shoes. He needed a dress jacket, however, so we headed to this awful sort of Crazy Bob's Going-Out-of-Business place on the outer fringes of the Strip. Terry said he shopped there all the time with Darla Sue.

Giving Terry his due, he did prove handy at ditching the press.

After waxing enthusiastically at getting a chance to drive my BMW, he instructed me to crouch out of view as we backed out of the garage. Since I couldn't see out the window, I had to rely on my churning stomach to get a sense of the hairpin turns, sudden reversals, and screeches of breaks Terry successfully maneuvered.

"Watch it," I warned. "I paid big bucks for this car."

But Terry ignored me and whistled as he made a U-turn that made me feel like I was on an amusement park ride.

"It's okay now," he calmly announced. "We've lost 'em."

As Terry shopped, I waited in the car, my lapels pulled up across my cheeks so as not to be recognized. Not that I cared about being spotted as Rick Domino, murder suspect, but that I'd be misidentified as someone who shopped in this store. Even just waiting outside I felt vaguely violated, like when Terry had set down a donut shop Styrofoam coffee cup on my Venetian marble pantry table.

"Uh, Rick, could you come in for a sec?" Terry tapped at the window.

I buzzed it down, furtively hoping I wasn't recognized. "Why?"

For all I knew it was a setup, and I was about to get busted all over again.

"I need your help. Please." He looked very earnest.

I sighed, took a deep breath, and prepared myself for the worst.

I was all but blinded by all the fluorescent green signs indicating sales-sales-sales across the splintery countertops. The salesman looked like the love child of Igor from the Frankenstein movies. His cologne must've been called Halitosis in Spring.

"Which do you like better, Rick?" Terry promisingly held up two sports coats, each of a vibrating checkered pattern, and which I privately christened Polly and Esther. "I know that we're meeting a fancy lady."

"Tell ya what, Terry? Let's go to one of *my* stores."

"But I can't—"

"Look, I'm doing it for me. If we're going to hang out together, you need to blend in with my kind of crowd."

"I couldn't accept that."

"I'll write it off on my taxes."

Terry considered. I guess the idea of outsmarting the IRS big shots appealed to him. "Well, okay then. But consider it an IOU, alright?" He gave me that big, toothy smile of his.

I drove us to a fairly modest, up-and-coming downtown boutique that I knew would be grateful for my "celebrity" business, and not ask any questions. I picked out two simple off-white linen dinner jackets for Terry, asking which he preferred. If I can't be a reporter anymore, I told myself, I could have my own style show. *Entertaining Behind Bars*, or maybe *Death Row Shabby Chic*.

"How about this one?" Terry held up a creamy, palest gray sport coat that frankly was much handsomer than either one I selected. It somehow tied together his shirt and pants, and brought out a virile coloring in his face. Terry was full of surprises, I'd give him that. Ignoring the slight detail that he was out to frame me, I had to admit he didn't look half-bad.

"Say, I look all right." Terry checked himself out from various angles in the store mirror. "Thanks a million, Rick."

"Hey, anything for a bud, right?"

Speaking of being framed, back in the car I looked into the rearview mirror to see Charlie driving a modest Chrysler Imperial. As I pulled into Francine's circular driveway, Charlie "cleverly" drove past us. I noted that Terry quickly looked at the car, then looked away, once he saw I was looking at *him*.

We walked along the brick pathway to the house, the ostentatious topiary towering over us on both sides.

"You know, Rick, when all this is over, I'll have to have you over for some good home cooking. Fried chicken, corn on the cob, watermelon. We have a small backyard with a picnic table. Out in Hemet."

In spite of myself, I was morbidly fascinated. "I'll bet Darla Sue makes that banana pudding out of vanilla wafers. Did you build the picnic table yourself?"

"How'd you guess?" He gave my arm a light punch.

"Oh, us reporters have kind of a sixth sense about these things." I smiled away as I not-so-subtly rubbed my arm.

"I sure do like to build stuff. Darla Sue says it keeps me out of her hair."

"I can relate."

"Really, Rick? You build stuff, too?"

I was hardly surprised that my remark went over his head.

"No, Terry. I'm not much of a builder. I'm too busy fishing and . . ." I faltered, trying to imagine what else Terry liked to do. "And bowling and . . . and fishing."

Terry stopped. He stared searchingly into my eyes.

"What is it, Rick? Why do you keep making fun of me? If I did something I don't know about, just tell me."

"Please let's not have a lover's quarrel."

"See? There you go again. I think it's all just a defense mechanism."

" 'Defense mechanism?' What are you, the Redneck Shrink of Burbank?"

He crossed his hefty arms, staring at me with defiance. "No, but I'm a nice guy, dammit. Why is it so hard for you to treat someone decently?"

What he said was so chockfull of lies and contradictions that I wouldn't have known where to begin. Imagine some double-crossing cop lecturing someone else on being "decent."

"I had a *terrible* childhood," I wailed sardonically. "Plus I have thirty-nine multiple personalities, all of them gay guys. Except for when I think I'm Deanna Durbin."

"It's the jacket, isn't it?"

"What on earth are you talking about?"

"You did a nice thing by buying me this jacket. You can belittle it and say it's just a tax write-off, but you know you were doing something nice for another person. So now it's like you have to cancel it out by acting like a total jerk. I know a lot of guys like you. Joe Average straight guys who never let themselves feel anything. You're not as special as you think, Rick."

I'm embarrassed to say that I couldn't think of a come-back line.

"And incidentally, you don't act all that gay—or effeminate, or whatever you want to call it. You know what I mean, even if my words are less than perfect. You come across like a guy. A nice, normal guy. What is this chip on your shoulder about being normal?"

"I'm nice and normal? And here I thought I was—how did you say it? 'A total fuckhead,' I believe was the phrase."

"I said jerk, not fuckhead. There's a big difference."

"As I'm sure you, if anyone, would know. What's next? Are you going to tell me I'm not really gay? That you know just the right woman who can make me straight? Does Darla Sue have a kid sister? What's her name—Katydid?"

For a second I thought Terry was going to slug me.

"How many times do I have to tell you? It doesn't bother me that you're gay. Gay can be normal, too."

"How generous of you."

"Dammit, you did it again. Twisting around what I say. No wonder you're a *reporter*."

He said "reporter" as if saying "serial child molester."

"And *what*? You mean to tell me that cops never twist around what people say?"

He knitted his thick eyebrows in thought. "I'll admit that unfortunately, yes, there is an occasional misuse of authority. The job is a terrible strain. It makes good people do bad things."

I had to hand it to him—he was superb at playing good cop. Just when you thought you had him, he'd come up with some "intelligent" zinger to throw you off.

"Look, let's just forget it, okay? I don't even know how all this started."

Terry considered. He smiled and offered his hand. "Friends?"

"Sure." It felt a little creepy to shake his hand, but not all that creepy. It was part of my job to shake hands with every slimy SOB in town.

"Holy Moses." Terry stopped in his tracks at the full sight of Francine's home.

I heard myself laugh. "Quite a spread, huh?"

"I guess. But it's kind of—well, kind of an awful *lot*, isn't it?"

He took the words out of my mouth, to say the least. Francine was the sort of aging woman who wore diamonds like they were rhinestones, and the concept extended to her palatial abode. Back in the 1920s, a successful German director built the home to resemble a Spanish mission. But Francine had no sense of these things, and had the stucco exterior painted a kind of lavender-pink (the gay reference would not have occurred to her) and the terra-cotta roof was tortured into sky blue. She had all kinds of little tchotchkes stuck on to the exterior, in the manner of the fringe-and-jingle-bell dresses preferred by Barbara Stanwyck in *Stella Dallas*. Little full-colored cupids and ceramic flowers and butterflies and things. The overall effect was not unlike a suburban home with too many outdoor Christmas decorations.

"Remember, you're supposed to be *very* into showbiz, so don't say anything to give yourself away." I rang the bell, which played the opening notes of "Doggie in the Window."

"Maybe you'd like me to not say anything at all," Terry complained.

"Not a bad idea."

Everyone knew that Francine rented a butler for those rare occasions a guest came over, but all concerned behaved as if the latest temp had been with her for decades.

"Good evening, Mr. Domino," pronounced the proud, rented stranger in full livery. His British accent suggested better times in the past—whether he was genuinely British, or simply an aging, unemployed actor. "Good evening, sir," he bellowed at Terry. "Madam is waiting for you presently."

"Madam" indeed. The foyer featured a fish tank built into the wall, but rather than seem a fun, creative touch, it gave the impression of entering a cocktail lounge. That the tank was stocked with goldfish instead of something more exotic did not help matters.

Muzak wafted in from hidden speakers. The rarified, too-warm air was thick with a pungent, flowery perfume.

The formal greeting by the butler seemed all the more pathetic when one considered that Francine was seated all of ten feet away. Her highball was probably in a crystal goblet, yet it looked like it belonged atop a paper napkin featuring a picture of Andy Capp with the hiccups. Behind her was a genuine Renoir, but the overemphatic way she had it framed and lit gave it the air of a reproduction in a dentist's office. It might as well have been that painting of dogs playing Poker. The furnishings were of a determined French Provincial mode, suggesting neither comfort nor imagination as much as a fear of committing a decorating error.

Reclining on the movie set–like sofa, Francine sported one of her customary champagne blonde wings. A sultry brunette in her youth, she went a few shades lighter with every decade. Bits of face powder had fallen in dandruff-like flakes onto her satin hostess gown. Her purple eye shadow matched her dress, as well as the purple bow in the hair of the bratty Pekinese on her lap whom she called "Angel," though I don't know if that was its name or nickname. Francine's classic red lipstick emphasized the artificial nature of her porcelain teeth. Fresh from another face-lift—for the Oscars, I presumed—her taut skin was virtually without wrinkle.

On the glass coffee table in front of her was a half-empty half-gallon bottle of Beefeater's, an ice bucket, her Salem 100s, a Bic lighter, a cut-glass ashtray shaped like a swan, and her Oscar.

A matching end table featured a photo of Francine with Tara on the set of *That Girl—The Movie*. They had their arms around each other and were smiling away, happy as clams. The photo obviously had been thrown into a frame that very morning, by virtue of the fact that the Wal-Mart price sticker had not been removed, creating the erroneous impression that Francine's left breast was valued at $2.99.

"Mr. Rick Domino," announced the butler, "and Mr . . . Terry Zane, I believe you said?" He stated this with a purposeful rudeness, as though Terry had some nerve being someone the butler hadn't been prepared to meet.

"Welcome, boys," Francine bellowed. Her diamond bracelets jangled like brass charms as she extended both hands. From the way she said "boys," she clearly assumed that Terry was of The Brotherhood. Amused by the possibilities, I did nothing to correct her impression.

I kissed one of her hands; Terry slightly grimaced as he followed suit with the other.

"Rick, I never knew you were so fond of *cavemen*." She winked, then gave Terry a mock-flirty once-over.

Before Terry could say anything, I explained, "He's my new personal assistant."

Francine laughed. "I *see*. But you should say 'bodyguard,' if anyone asks."

She was right, of course. Given Terry's bulk and my current precarious situation, it was exactly what I should say—had Terry actually *been* my boy toy, that is. In her way, Francine was one smart cookie.

Not quite getting the implications of it all, Terry smiled in agreement. "Yeah, that's it. I'm his bodyguard." He nervously added, "I mean, yes, ma'am, I'm his bodyguard."

"He's a sweetheart, Rick." She took a long swallow of booze. "Now Terry, don't you worry about being so formal with your Auntie Francine." She patted the mock satin upholstery. "You boys sit down next to me, and we'll have ourselves a good ol' chitchat."

Terry awkwardly lowered himself to one side of Francine, myself on the other.

"You can touch it, if you'd like, Terry." Francine spiritedly clasped his hand.

"Touch it?" Terry turned pale. He must have thought she meant some sort of sex thing. Or maybe the creepy little dog, who kept snorting and licking its chops.

"The Oscar, silly." She set down her latest Salem to cradle the gold statuette in her arms. " 'The Lifetime Achievement Award to Francine Quick,' " she read, seemingly in a trance. She proffered the award to Terry. "Here, you can hold it," she instructed, as if it were a baby.

I wondered if Terry had an inkling of how many millions of people would've wished they were him in that moment—to actually be able to touch an Oscar.

"It's very nice, Miss Quick." He didn't know what to do with it, and so set it back on the table.

"*Francine* to you, honey."

"Uh, okay. Francine." Terry flustered, though I wasn't sure why.

Francine saw his gaucheries as good, modest manners. "This one's a honey, no doubt about it. Don't let him get away, Ricky-Boy. Believe you me, if there's one thing I know about, it's those bastards called the male of the species." She took a thoughtful, bitter drag on her smoke. "But that's a story for a rainy day."

She poured herself a tall refill. Plopping a couple of ice cubes into the glass, she winked again, took a hefty swallow, and sassily whispered, "Cha-cha-cha." (Only after we left did it occur to me that she never asked us if we wanted something to drink.)

"Now then, boys. Especially *you*, Rick, since you're the one in so much trouble. Though I suppose if it's Rick's problem, it's your problem too, Terry." She looked at me and then at Terry with her most maternal gaze. Then she leaned back, smoking shrewdly. "What have you found out so far?"

"I spoke with Bob Raflowitz—"

Francine put her hand over my mouth. "Say no more. I can just imagine." She made a face of disdain. "This newer generation of stars, you know, takes so much for granted. Back when I was starting out, they never would've tolerated the Commie Zen bit. Though he is a terrific actor. And *nice*, I suppose, if you like that sort of person. The wife I've never cared for. You should've seen him, though, in the green room with Tara. At the Oscars, that is."

"What was he doing, Francine?"

"Oh, it was most unlike the Bob we all know and love," Francine remarked tartly. "But, then, Tara brought out all kinds of things in people. In a way, I suppose I'll miss her. I've always believed life has more oomph when it's a smidgen unpredictable. Don't you agree, Rick?"

"Only up to a point. I can live without first-degree murder raps."

She affectionately patted my knee. "Oh, aren't you just a dear." But she looked at Terry when she said this, as if to show her warm support of our tumultuous love for each other.

"Anyway, you would not believe the things Bob said to Tara. 'Keep your sick, nympho ass away from my son.' His *exact* words, as God is my witness. I must say it was most inappropriate to the occasion. I'd just received my award, and hearing such language—I cannot tell you, boys, what it was like. True, he didn't know I was standing behind a curtain listening in, but if you don't want the public to hear what you're saying, then you shouldn't say it in private either. That's what my very first publicity agent told me, and it was the best advice I ever got. Anyway, Bob went on how his poor son Zachary—"

"You mean Zeke?" I offered helpfully.

"Yes, whatever. How *Zeke* was terribly disturbed, and needed to be hospitalized. How Tara was making things worse, and how he knew it was her twisted way of trying to make things right by him, but that he wasn't going to stand for it. Lord only knows what that was about. Tara, bless her, kept smiling defiantly and saying over and over again, 'Let me make Zeke happy.' At one point Bob made a fist. His hand trembled, like it was taking all of his willpower not to clobber her. He kept saying, 'No, you can't make it right. Not this way.' Bob would *kill* me if I found out I told you all this. He does so want to protect the poor boy's privacy.

"Well, Tara started to cry, if you can believe it. 'I loved *you* once upon a time, Bob, in case you've forgotten.' Dear old Bob was having none of that. I mean, *really*, boys. Imagine Tara actually loving someone besides the face she saw in the mirror. He knew that she tried to seduce him just to get ahead. She wanted that part with him in—oh, what was it called, Rick?"

"*Ticket to Ride.*"

The dog barked, like it was trying to contribute to the conversation. Francine got all kissy-smoochy with it, calling it "Angel" as she muzzled its mouth with her hand.

"Yes, that was it," she agreed. "*Ticket to Ride.* That silly movie about the wife killer posing as a Greyhound bus driver. Tara would've been the sweet little blind girl Bob's character fell in love with. Can you *imagine?* Of course, giving Miss Devil her due, back then she was—well, she was *never* sweet, heaven help us all. Probably the first thing that filthy little tramp did when was born was spread her legs. But this was the start of her career, so presumably there were at least a few men in town she hadn't gotten familiar with. I heard all her stories about growing up without a family, as if that somehow gives you the right to stick every pecker in town up your you-know-what. In *my* day, one was lady."

In her day, one was not all that different from Tara, but I let it pass.

"Anyway," Francine continued, "Tara either gave the performance of her life, or else maybe had some blood in her veins, after all. She got down on her knees and said, 'Bob, I have to have some kind of meaning in my life. Won't you give it to me?' *Meaning!* That's one way of putting it. If I wasn't right there hearing it all, I wouldn't believe it myself. But I swear that's exactly what she said.

"Well, Bob wouldn't even look at her. 'Please, get up,' he said. 'Stop begging, it doesn't suit you.' Tara got all soft and feminine and said, 'I've been a beggar all my life.' Well, you know Bob. It was just the sort of sappy psycho-garbage to melt his heart. Next thing you know, Mr. Family Man is locked in a kiss with Tara. Not a movie grand-finale type of thing, but more than just a peck you'd give to your baby sister. Well, wouldn't you know that at just that moment, none other than Zeke walks in."

Francine clasped her hand together in glee, sending one of her Lee's press-on fingernails flying across the room. Terry and I pretended not to notice.

"Well, Tara grabbed her Oscar to go running after crazy little Zeke. Bob went off to stare at his navel, or who-knows-what. A few minutes later, Tara was dead. Now—you tell *me*, buddy boy."

It would seem that poor short-term memory ran in the Raflowitz family. Just as Bob forgot to mention a few choice tidbits that occurred backstage, so had his son, Zeke.

My mind was racing with rapid-fire Hollywood arithmetic. "You think that Zeke shot Tara, and now Bob and Cleo are trying to protect him?"

"Honey, your Aunt Francine ain't one of them uptown intellectual types. Back in Brooklyn, we didn't *think*. We knew."

"You didn't *see* it, though, right? It's your instinct or street smarts or whatever."

Francine waved her hand dismissively. "Rick, there in the Shrine parking lot Bob had a little chitchat with a few of us who had what you young people would call 'issues' with Tara. In my day, we would've called it something else, but no matter. What he said gave me chills. 'Rick is innocent, of course,' he told us. 'But no matter what happens—protect my boy.'"

Terry wasn't convinced. "Maybe he just meant to protect the kid against publicity about his mental illness."

Obviously, he could not waver in his quest to prove me guilty.

"Terry, you seem to always think the best about people." Francine slapped his wrist. "Shame on you, sweetie."

"Did you see a blonde backstage named Connie Kellogg?" I asked.

Francine snorted. "What about it?" She said this as if though Connie were a form of foot fungus.

"Don't you mean 'her'?" offered Terry.

"Rick, he is *such* a baby." Francine tweaked Terry's cheek affectionately. He smiled like a good sport, but I could tell he was befuddled.

"Little Miss Connie Kellogg," Francine began imperiously, "is a *minor* player in all this, I can assure you. I heard the little ninny telling Tara about how she was the one Zeke really wanted. As if what *Zeke* wanted had anything to do with anything. Connie would not *begin* to know how to fight the likes of Tara Perez, or even Bob Raflowitz. It is *impossible* to conceive of Connie ever getting her clutches on poor young Zeke. Even with Tara gone, there'll be some new Tara to outsmart her." She leaned forward conspiratorially, narrowing her eyes. "You see, boys, she *drinks.*"

"How unfortunate," I commiserated.

"Yes, that's really sad," Terry added, catching on.

The gin bottle gurgled for the vigorous pour Francine gave it. Angel sneezed as its mistress polished off her upteenth drink of the day. "Such a *waste,*" Francine reflected. "The poor dear had a modicum of talent, you know. When I was starting out, her kind would've never gotten even as far as she did. We had something called standards back then. Of course, people like Little Miss Tara Perez are not exactly role models, either. It's just that Tara could still function when she was loaded or getting laid or whatever it was she did."

"But you don't think Connie did it?" Terry inquired. "Kill Tara, that is."

Francine knocked her Oscar over with her elbow. Fortunately, it did not break the glass table top. "Honey, she couldn't have walked in a straight line, let alone aim a gun. Now, Zeke's another story. Crazy people always hit their mark. It's all about demons. The sick of this world are demonically possessed, you know. And so the Forces of Evil help them to succeed at these things.

"Anyway, when Bob made that little speech, my blood ran cold. I *had* to tell you the truth. Sure, he loves his kid. But to withhold information that could save an innocent man's life? That's illegal, isn't it? Not only that, it's just plain sonovabitchin' wrong."

Francine was on the verge of passing out. I snuffed out her latest cigarette while Terry took the dog from her lap. The rent-a-butler told us he'd take over from there. I guessed that he'd been forewarned.

On the way out, we heard Francine being helped up the stairs to her French poodle-like bedroom. As the temp servant led her along, she shouted: "That Perez bitch! My best acting—my *best* acting—cut down to nothing so that Little Miss Whore Bitch could become a star. Well, I should've taken care of her years ago."

"Yes, Madam," agreed the butler.

"Kapow! Bang-bang!" Francine cried. "Did you know I almost played Annie Oakley? They wanted me on Broadway in *Annie Get Your Goddamn Motherfucking Gun*. I could've been the greatest Broadway star you ever saw, buster. Sing, dance—I could do it all blindfolded. But that pervert Truman Shea wouldn't let me out of my contract. So instead I work my twat off, and Miss Tara Perez becomes a star. Hell, I could've played That Girl myself. I *should've*. They even offered me the part." She laughed hysterically.

Terry and I looked at each other.

"Sure are a lot of crazy people in this town," Terry commented.

"Who can say what's crazy anymore?"

We slid into my BMW. I turned the ignition on; then I turned it off.

"Listen, Terry. Maybe Zeke did do it. Maybe Connie or Bob did it. But if *any* of them did it, Bob would have his reasons for trying to obfuscate things—muddle them up," I quickly added, so Terry would understand.

"I know what 'obfuscate' means," Terry protested. "For all your talk about hating stereotypes, you sure do have a lot of stereotypes about cops."

I was in no mood for another Community Outreach lecture.

"Anyway, if Connie did it, Zeke might be chivalrously covering for her by claiming—to his father, anyway—that he did it. Whatever his problems, Zeke is pretty shrewd. Daddykins will keep him out of jail. Of course, maybe Francine did it, and she's just blowing smoke. The thing I really need to do is . . ."

I stopped myself from saying, *I need to get the Oscar out of Shane's closet.* I found myself sometimes forgetting that Terry was not to be trusted.

An idea was forming as to why the Oscar might have parted company with Tara. Or more to the point, why Shane (or someone else?) would want to hide it. Like Bob intimated, maybe it *did* tell the story of what happened to Tara. Or at least part of the story.

I needed to shake loose from Terry, and get back to Shane's.

But I also needed to make sure that Brother Dennis wasn't there. I wouldn't talk about the Oscar with anyone. Except maybe Benji.

"C'mon, Rick. Tell me your ol' partner here what you need to do."

I revved up the car. "Just that I need to figure out who did it." I smiled at Terry. "That we *both* do."

"You said it, bro,' " Terry agreed.

16

*B*y the way, I'm not as dumb as you think."

Between unanswered phone calls to Shane's house, cell phone, and answering service, I was attempting to locate Ms. Connie Kellogg via the Internet. I figured it would take a couple of minutes; then I'd scoop up the Oscar and pay a visit to Connie.

However, Terry was doing his utmost to sabotage my efforts by distracting me with more of his inane comments.

We were in my spacious home office, replete with a fully restored oak icebox cabinet from Charlie Chaplin's old home that I used to store tapes and files. I enjoyed sitting at my zinc-and-steel executive desk and looking out the leaded window at the lemon trees and herb garden. Terry, though, was more bowled over by the fact that I had my own fax and copy machines. To him, this spoke of unimagined decadence. He was to an equal measure disappointed that I did not keep his favorite brand of supermarket coffee in my desk-side coffee maker. The appeal of my various antique film posters—I had originals from *It Happened One Night* and *Grand Hotel* in mint condition—was utterly lost on him.

It was already evening. I was hoping to get in many more hours of work. But as if part of the bad dream my life had become, I was incredibly tired, and had to fight to keep my eyes open. I felt I could sleep for the next fifty years.

"I said, I'm not as dumb as you think, Rick."

"I beg your pardon?" I made no effort to stifle my yawn.

No matter what server I used, there was nada on the Web about Connie. I could track her down through SAG, of course, or could even call the Raflowitz household for her phone number—fat chance—but I wanted to find her whereabouts on my own.

I wanted to surprise her.

"Like when Francine was going on about . . . all that stuff she was saying. I knew what she meant. That you and me were sort of like—um—a couple."

I turned to look at him meanly. "And that you were sort of like—um—gay? How will you ever live it down?"

Terry shrugged unconvincingly. "Whatever it takes to crack the case. Up to and including your dumb little mind games."

He was a fine one to be talking about mind games. All of ten minutes earlier I'd caught him talking on his cell phone with Charlie. He hung up as fast as if I were Darla Sue, and had caught him talking to some slutty policewoman mistress he no doubt had tucked away someplace. "Charlie, my partner," Terry lamely had offered. "Just checking up on how I was doing."

So now he was accusing me of being less than straightforward. Well, who started it?

Dasher picked just the right moment to be sociable, and elected to help me by jumping on the keyboard. The computer froze, and I needed to reboot. I petted my beloved feline under the chin for a job well done. He knew he deserved every moment of lavish praise. Then, having performed his requisite ten seconds a year of being affectionate, he jumped away, knocking over a pencil holder in the bargain.

"Dammit, you stupid thing." I swiveled away from my computer, frustrated over how long it was taking to reboot. "Not you, Terry. It's that Connie Kellogg bitch. Doesn't she even have one dopey fan club out there? There's a *Karen Valentine* Fan Club, for fucking crying out loud."

"Was she the one in that *Airport* movie? Man, that was a good movie."

It took every ounce of patience I had to reply: "No, that was Karen Black." I elected to withhold comment on the merits of *Airport '75*.

Terry's cell phone rang. From the concerned look on his face as he uh-huh'd through a brief conversation, I could see it was something pretty serious. Maybe Charlie had eloped with Darla Sue.

"Brother Dennis," he explained, getting off the phone.

"What about him?"

"He's in jail."

"Come again?"

"In *jail*. You know—metal bars, bread and water. Ringing any bells?"

Was it my imagination, or did Terry have something approaching a sense of humor?

"Very funny. What happened?"

"A mix-up, from what I could tell. He approached a street hustler, who turned out to be an undercover cop."

I took off my wire-rimmed reading glasses to rub my eyes. "What do you mean, he 'approached' him?

"You know—Brother Dennis said something like, 'Can I talk to you?' and I guess the arresting officer misunderstood."

"Misunderstood?! What was there to misunderstand? Last time I checked, 'to talk' doesn't mean 'to fuck.'"

"What are you getting at?" Terry reached for his dress jacket and keys.

"That either Brother Dennis, like all good religious hypocrites, wanted a bit more than talk, or that the undercover cop just couldn't wait to bust some innocent schlep. Neither of which scenarios, I might add, does much to reinforce my faith in human nature."

He straightened his lapel in the mirror. "You know, Rick, the sun does not rise and set on your mood of the moment. Brother Dennis needs our help."

I stared at him challengingly. "Terry, where are you going?"

He looked surprised by my question. "To the police station, of course."

"But won't your fellow officers wonder why you're bailing him out? After all, supposedly no one knows you're doing any of this."

Terry tried to conceal the alarm from his face. "What do you mean, 'supposedly'?"

"Nothing in particular," I answered sadistically, savoring the twinge of panic that flickered in his large dark eyes. "The point is, neither of us should fetch Brother Dennis. Let me call my lawyer."

"You're right." He took his jacket off.

I opened my cell phone to call Benji. "Don't worry, Terry. I'm sure you'll have other chances to show off how gorgeous you are."

"What did *that* mean?"

"You know perfectly well," I teased. "You can't stop looking at yourself in that jacket. Even at Francine's I caught you sneaking peeks. In the tabletop. The windows."

Actually, I didn't recall this at all, but the blush in Terry's face signaled the presence of a guilty party.

"You're as bad as—" I started to say "Shane," but stopped myself. I didn't want to talk about him. Or at least not in a jokey way. "Never mind," I concluded.

I was relieved when Benji answered on the first ring.

"Benji," I began chipperly, "I hope you're sitting down. The plot has thickened."

When I finished explaining about Brother Dennis, Benji hardly expressed delight. "I'm glad your plot keeps thickening," he snapped, "because every time I talk to you my hair thins out a little more."

"That was cute, Benji." I gave a polite little laugh.

He took a deep breath. "Fine. I'll go get the poor lost lamb."

"Gee, Benji. You're swell."

As we waited for Benji to retrieve Brother Dennis, Terry idly attempted a computer search on one "Conn*ee* Kellogg." He hit the search button before I could point out the typo. Well, wouldn't you just know it? There we were at Connie's Home Page—or rather, Conn*ee*'s page. As she explained to her fan(s) at the Web site, she'd recently changed the spelling of her name because a numerologist told her it would bring her more luck. Terry said he had no idea that was how she spelled her name; he was just plain one-in-a-million lucky. As much as I hated it in movies and TV shows when a dumb character lucked out, I hated it even more in real life. There was something so *Gomer Pyle, USMC* about it all.

Ours was only the one hundred third visit to the sad little Web page. And I had a sneaking suspicion that the other one hundred two hits were made by young Zeke Raflowitz. At the top of Conn*ee*'s Home Page was the slogan: *The Kellogg Girl wishes the best to you each morning . . . and night!!!* Featured prominently was an imprint of her lipsticked kiss and a photo of herself smiling wholesomely while a tape measure around her naked breasts ("tastefully" hiding the nipples) confirmed that she was indeed 40 inches around. You could click onto little animated snippets of the Artist at Work, such as her TV commercial some years back for a local gym chain that later folded. She wasn't shown working out on the treadmill, though. Instead, Connee wore a sequinned gown and about fifty platinum blond hair pieces as she sang in her weak voice a campy song about liking men with muscles. She didn't seem to be in on the joke.

There was a listing of her film and TV credits, as well as a pathetic listing of her *cut* film and TV credits. It seemed she had a bimbo-ish walk-on role in the big screen version of *Three's Company II: The Ropers* that—thanks to a special guest appearance by Tara Perez, playing Herself—ended up on the cutting room floor. With shapely Tara on board, Connee's scenes were now superfluous and "slowed down" the movie. (And a mighty fast-paced frolic it was, in case you somehow missed it.) Connee told her fan(s) that it was, after all, her cursed fate to be "such a similar type to Tara Perez."

I could only presume that now that Tara had gone on to that Casting Couch in the Sky, Connee would update her Web page to reflect her strong sisterly ties to Tara. Maybe even how Tara had spoken to her beyond the grave, and for a small charge to your credit card . . . Just like I could only imagine the cheery little conversations that must've transpired between Tara and Connee on the movie set, or what both of them did behind the scenes, as it were, to influence Fate in regard to screen time. Not to mention their sisterly exchange backstage at the Oscars.

The Web page also listed an address of a supposed "business manager." You didn't need to be psychic to determine that it was her personal address, noted for the benefit of what one might call her potential clients.

"Bingo." Terry nudged my arm.

"I guess," I marginally concurred. After all, it wasn't the same thing as having solved the crime.

I yawned again. Dammit, I was tired.

"Listen, Terry. Be a good boy scout and wait for Brother Dennis, while I mosey over to Connee's penthouse suite at Hotel Cockroach. Help yourself to Beluga and Pepsi in the fridge."

But since when had Lady Luck disappointed me? Just at the moment, the doorbell rang, and sure enough it was Brother Dennis and Benji.

Brother Dennis looked a bit worse for the wear. His eyes were bleary for all they'd seen, which I doubted included personal visitations from the Holy Virgin. "Any word from Shane?" he asked. It saddened me—and possibly even Terry, if he had some semblance of a heart—to have to nod no.

As for Benji, I could tell he was pissed. I knew it wasn't just that I interrupted him from whatever he was doing. It was because I was a client keeping things from him.

"He sure does look like Shane, doesn't he, Benji?" I tried to joke. "Bet you thought you were seeing double."

I introduced Benji to Terry, but Benji could scarcely be bothered to shake his hand.

"In private, Rick." Benji was probably the only person who could order me about in my own home.

As Terry gave Brother Dennis a cup of coffee and a sympathetic pat on the back, I retired to the billiard room with Benji. I could shoot a pretty mean game of eight ball, but the real reason I devoted an entire room to the sport was the table itself, which had once belonged to Rudolph Valentino. It was made of the palest blond mahogany, inlaid with gold, and had a peach-colored cloth. The balls were numbered in a deco typeface, and each had "RV" inscribed in tiny letters. A retro, industrial-looking ceiling fan brought the room together.

Benji absently rolled the cue ball across the table, sinking the eight ball. "So, Rick—you certainly have been busy since this morning. What did you think, that with God on your side, the cops could be trusted?"

"It wasn't like that at all, Benji." I got the eight ball from the hole, and tapped it across the felt expanse. "The cop is out to nail me, so I figured I'd keep one step ahead by pretending to work with him. He claims he's working on his own time to solve the case to get a promotion, that he knows I'm innocent and we're just the *best* of buddies. The fucking shit. As for Brother Dennis, you know about as much about him as I do."

"Just out of curiosity, were you planning on telling your attorney any of this?"

"Of course. It's just that—jeez, Benji, I figured you'd try to talk me out of it."

"Tell me everything, Rick. And tell me now."

And so I did.

Benji chalked up a cue stick and set up a game for himself as he listened, occasionally murmuring "yeah, uh-huh" as he made one impossible shot after another. (Benji often said that if he hadn't become a lawyer he could've been a pool shark and made *real* money.)

When I finished, Benji just stood there. I couldn't tell if he was pondering what I said, or how to put a spin on the six ball so that it angled itself diagonally near the three ball and then into the left corner pocket.

"Well, at least you're wise to Charlie. This shows minimal brain activity. But for God's sake, be careful. And get that Oscar out of Shane's before you do anything else." He made his shot. It looked like a miss; then the ball edged over to the hole . . . and sunk in.

"I guess I should turn the Oscar over to the cops?"

"Wrong again. I should, as your attorney. That way, it's less likely to 'disappear.'" He set down his cue stick. "What the hell. I'll get the Oscar for you. I don't trust this Terry Zane character. He'll have you shadowed."

"Would you, Benji?"

He laughed. "Jesus, Rick. You sound like a little kid I just promised to take to the zoo."

"Make it an 'N Sync concert. I have a thing for Joey."

I gave Benji a key to Shane's. Then I told him exactly where the Oscar was hidden.

"I'll leave now," Benji decided. "I'll make a big production to your esteemed guests about how tired I am. Which by the way would not take any great acting on my part."

Spending all day with fake-nice Terry, I'd forgotten how it felt to be with someone genuinely sleazy I could trust. "Thanks, Benji."

He was never much for sentiment, but I could tell he appreciated my feelings. "Anytime, Rick."

As we repaired back to my office, Benji turned to me and whispered, "According to Brother Dennis, it was all a big misunderstanding. According to the arresting officer, Brother Dennis asked him to . . . well, my mother raised me to not say certain words, but you can use your imagination."

"Which one is lying?"

Benji shrugged. "Lie, schmie—I straightened it out. Bad publicity for the LAPD to accuse a man of the cloth."

"What about the missing Shane bit?"

"Brother Dennis told the cops zip. He told me it would cramp your style. Or should I say your and Terry's style?"

"Don't rub it in, Benji."

"Anyway, since his last name's 'Sharnovsky,' Shane never came up. No, wait—I take that back. One of the cops said that Dennis looked a lot like Shane Kirk. Dennis said he hears that all the time."

"You're a pal."

"No, I'm just totally corrupt."

After he left, Terry and I got to hear Brother Dennis's description of the scintillating events.

"Never did I imagine that a police officer could be so unjust," he shared. "I'm sorry if I'm insulting you, Officer Zane, but I must speak the truth."

"That's okay," Terry assured him. "Just tell us what happened after you hot-footed out of my car."

Brother Dennis put his hands to his face, then clasped them to his chin, deep in thought. "I apologize for surprising you like that, Officer Zane. But the more I thought about it, I just couldn't go back to Ohio. For my own sanity, I had to keep looking for Shane. I took a cab out to the Boulevard. I figured I'd talk to some of the street boys. Find out about some of the big customers or pimps. See if any of them had run into a guy who looked like Shane Kirk.

"There were dozens of boys hanging around on different corners. They seemed to know each other, yet I noticed they always worked alone. A few were somewhat older—in their twenties, I'd say. They all had that drug glaze in their eyes. One of them stooped over to vomit, then went right back to working the streets."

Brother Dennis gave a shiver of repugnance, then blessed himself.

"A boy who couldn't have been more than fourteen told me that he saw a guy who looked almost exactly like Shane Kirk late last night. He said that this Shane lookalike was having an argument with an older man. Tall, with curly hair, according to the kid. Drove a white car, though he couldn't remember what type. It looked as if the Shane person was actually forced to get into the car. As you can imagine, my head was spinning.

"I kept asking around. I wanted to see if there was a second young man who could verify the story. Or maybe even tell me something more. One of them did—maybe. He said he saw a fellow who looked like Shane getting out of a white car with an older man. He offered no description of the older man, but he did say he saw them this very morning. It gave me so much hope that Shane was . . . you know, still all right."

Terry took a thoughtful swallow of donut shop coffee—which was, I supposed, to cops what green tea was to Zen masters. "It just doesn't add up," he pondered. "If all this guy wants from Shane is hush money—assuming that it *is* Shane—why wouldn't Shane just slip him a few bucks, and let it go at that?"

There was an obvious angle that my so-called partner wasn't seeing. How to bring it up tactfully?

"Go to the dictionary, Terry, and look up the word, 'fuck.' "

"*Rick,*" he scolded. "May I remind you that you're in the presence of a man of God?"

Brother Dennis laughed. "Don't worry, Officer Zane, though I thank you. I'd like to hear what Mr. Domino has to say. It might help."

"Thank you." I gave a sarcastic little bow. "First of all, in case you hadn't noticed, there was no money tree at Shane's house. He has zero comprehension of how to invest, and like many a red-blooded American Movie Star, a chunky percentage of his earnings get swallowed and snorted. So it just might be that this guy or guys wants more dough than Shane can cough up. And even if money is no object, if we're dealing with some sort of pimp or john we just might be talking about S-E-X. Besides—or maybe instead of—good ol' green stuff, Shane might be taking a little stroll down Memory Lane, professionally speaking. I mean, think of it—a big-time movie star as your sex slave. Though presumably there'd be some sort of statute of limitations. After all, to *stay* a movie star, Shane can't spend the next fifty years putting out to this perv. Or should I say pervs?"

"Congratulations," Terry proclaimed. "You managed to explain all that with the least possible amount of sensitivity."

"Oh, I beg your pardon. Remind me to bring along my copy of *Miss Manners* when they strap me to The Chair."

"Never mind, Officer Zane. Mr. Domino did me a favor. It's just as well that I heard it that way. Without trying to disguise any of the ugliness."

"Plus let's not forget the obvious," I added. "I mean, *hello?* Shane might've killed Tara. So maybe, just maybe, he's not in any great hurry to surface. Even if he didn't do it, he knows who did, and better I should pay with my life than for him to suffer some bad publicity."

Brother Dennis trembled, turning bright red. "I would like to believe, Mr. Domino, that whatever my brother's shortcomings, when faced with the choice of a life of utter degradation and speaking the truth, however disquieting that truth might be, that he would choose wisely."

I laughed ruefully. "You're tellin' me, honey."

"That isn't what I *meant*, and you know it." Brother Dennis, I was discovering, had a smarmy, kindergarten-teacher quality about him when he got upset.

"Now, guys," Terry patronizingly offered. "We're all friends here, right? And we still haven't heard the rest of your story, Brother Dennis."

"You're right, Officer Zane." He offered his hand. "I do apologize, Mr. Domino."

I offered my hand in return. "Apology accepted." I resisted the knee-jerk impulse to say I was sorry, too. I didn't see that I had anything to be sorry about.

"Anyway, it was maybe twenty minutes after I talked to this second boy that a car pulled over," explained Brother Dennis. "The driver called out to me. 'Hey, Shane,' he said. 'Long time no see.' He obviously wasn't the guy who the kid described. And his car was a gray Volvo. But I was intrigued. I had to talk to this man."

"The arresting officer?" Terry nodded his head sadly.

"I told him that it was urgent," Brother Dennis replied, as if answering Terry's question affirmatively. "He told me to get in the car."

"My God, don't you realize how dangerous that was?"

Brother Dennis sighed. "I have to find my brother, Officer Zane."

"Had you gotten killed, you wouldn't have been able to find much of anything," Terry admonished.

"I know, I know," Brother Dennis answered wearily. "I kept telling him I wasn't Shane, but that I wanted to find Shane. He kept saying things like, 'Oh, I get it. That's your fantasy today.' He . . . kept putting his hand on my knee. At a red light he leaned over to kiss me. I put up my hand to stop him. He slapped me across the face, and said I was making him really—you know, horny.

"Then we got to this motel room. I kept saying I just wanted to *talk*, but he just kept laughing at me. He locked the door and said, 'First you want to pretend you're Shane Kirk, then you want to pretend that you're not. But I want you no matter who you are.' He lunged toward me. I put up my hands to shield myself."

"So he busted you when you refused to put out, like he thought you normally did." Terry sounded genuinely angry. Apparently he didn't like it when corrupt cops gave corrupt cops like himself a bad name.

"That's about the sum of it," Brother Dennis confirmed, walking about my office. He paused to admire the icebox cabinet, caressing its smooth wood surface. "He didn't go into any of the details in his report, fortunately—I assumed so that he wouldn't trip himself up lying. I said *nothing* to any of them until I called you, Officer Zane."

"At least you're safe now," Terry reflected. "And the charges have been dropped."

"I didn't think you cops ever were happy about *that*," I couldn't resist noting.

Terry gave me a dirty look. Brother Dennis either didn't notice, or else chose to rise above it all.

"Rest assured it wasn't that bad," Brother Dennis stated. "I was not at all mistreated, once I got away from that arresting officer. And spending a little time in a jail gave me a chance to think." He smiled nervously. "Gentlemen, I have a proposition."

"Go on," Terry encouraged.

"This man in the white car who took Shane—he needs a little shaking up. A sense that he might be outsmarted. And you, Mr. Domino—you need to establish your innocence."

"I think I already know where you're going," Terry announced.

"Well, I sure don't. Anyone care to enlighten me?"

Brother Dennis walked toward me beseechingly. "Mr. Domino, I want to be Shane Kirk. Just for a day or so. Teach me how Shane would dress and so forth. I'll hold a press conference. I'll say that I stumbled upon Tara's body, and then went into shock. I'll say that I know you didn't do it, because I know for a fact you were inside the Shrine at the time. And then I'll talk about the child molester."

I was puzzled. "Well, it seems to me there's one slight problem. You're not Shane. What if Shane is subpoenaed to testify, and the real Shane never turns up?"

"I apologize if I wasn't clear. I said for about a *day*. I'd give this one press conference, and that would be that. Either Shane turns up afterwards, or he doesn't. If he doesn't, I keep looking for him, and praying. But there still would be a public statement as to your innocence."

Picking up on Brother Dennis's idea, Terry added, "And no one would blame you for Shane's second supposed disappearance. If anything, it would point the finger away from you—to the real killer who's out there someplace, trying to stop Shane from testifying."

"I believe it will help Shane to very much turn up," Brother Dennis asserted. "Whoever this man in the white car is, when he sees that 'Shane' has come forward with the story of the molester, he'll have no more hold over the real Shane. And it's not as though this man will publicly declare that I'm a fraud because he personally kidnapped or blackmailed Shane. The crook will have his money, he'll have had his . . . *way* with Shane, if that was part of the bargain. And he'll let Shane go."

"Or else bump him off," I speculated. "Why not? No one would miss the real Shane at that point, and a *living* real Shane could have this guy arrested. Especially if the molester story becomes public knowledge. Shane would have nothing to lose."

"I thought of that, naturally. And it *is* taking a chance. But if we don't try it, my brother could get killed anyway. The man in the white car could still become paranoid. Or, if what you said is true, Mr. Domino, maybe some sort of bizarre sex thing *will* get out of control. At least this way, the perpetrator realizes that people are sniffing around. Which just might scare him enough to cut his losses, and let Shane go free.

"Besides, Shane would still not want to go public with it all, Mr. Domino. Think about it—in having this man arrested, Shane would have to go into grisly details about his life as a prostitute, and whatever sort of things this man made him do."

"Rick, I think it's worth a try," Terry decided.

"But it's not the *truth*," I protested.

"Mr. Domino, you *are* innocent, am I right? You *were* inside the Auditorium during the shooting?"

"That's not the point. This isn't how I want things to happen."

"It wouldn't be forever, Rick," Terry tried to assure me. Like I would trust anything coming from him.

It was ironic, to say the least. There I was, the sleazeball gossip columnist, trying to convince a police officer and a servant of God that honesty was the best policy.

"C'mon, Rick. What have we got to lose?"

"Yes, Mr. Domino. You yourself said not a moment ago that my brother thinks only of himself. If by any chance he *is* simply biding his time, how do you think he'll react when he sees me, his own twin brother, stealing his thunder?"

Now *that* perked my ears up. Honesty and integrity were one thing, but the chance to make Shane Kirk squirm was something else altogether. There was the slight detail, of course, of what to say to Benji at what point in the hoax, but I was a firm believer in crossing each bridge as my Rolls Royce got there.

"Well, it might be kind of fun at that."

And so there we were, going through my walk-in closets, where I kept a few nice changes of clothes for Shane. Unlike the mess at Shane's, here the clothes were neatly pressed and organized by my au pair, and Brother Dennis's eyes grew large just at the perfect creases and folds. I was surprised—yet not so surprised—by the relish with which he tried on all the linen and cashmere and Vicuna.

"Such attention to detail," Brother Dennis marveled, trying on a subtly-embroidered Saville Row vest. But I wondered if he meant the vest or the bevelled Carole Lombard mirror.

I had visions of needing to play Henry Higgins to Brother Dennis's Eliza as I taught him—if not about the rain in Spain—how to talk and walk like a star. But he adapted to the role with an alarming ease. I felt like Jimmy Stewart looking at Kim Novak when she goes back to being a blonde in *Vertigo*. As sure as I lived and breathed, Shane Kirk stood before me. Even Brother Dennis's speaking voice changed. It took on that sexy, testosterone-ish quality that Shane's had.

Terry, for his part, kept saying he couldn't see the difference between the "old" and "new" Brother Dennis. Typical of his kind. (For some reason, I was reminded of a jock back in college, who claimed he couldn't tell the difference between video and film, and when I tried to explain that video looked more "live," he'd give me these blank stares.) But Terry was eager to get the show on the road, and obviously was pleased to have done some heavy-duty cop work, i.e, broken the law to suit his ends.

"Pretty neat, huh, buddy?" Terry enthused. "Now all we do is wait."

"Indeed," I agreed, for lack of knowing how else to respond.

Brother Dennis/Shane emerged from his shower luxuriantly, drying off not with the austere hurry of a man of the cloth, but with the slow, glistening wet look of a star. The radio was playing "Express Yourself" by Madonna, and Brother Dennis moved his hips to the music.

"This shirt with *this* tie, or *this* shirt with this tie?" His gelled, shiny dark hair fell teasingly onto his forehead, a thick white towel wrapped about his torso, as he held up the items in question. "Shane wears such *beautiful* clothes," he commented, stroking an Italian silk tie. Talk about your Freudian implications.

My cell phone rang.

"Rick, what happened?" Terry asked. From the look on his face I could tell the look on mine caused him concern. Like maybe I just found out what a double-crosser he was.

I wanted to think I dropped the phone only because I was having trouble staying awake.

"It's Benji. He's been in an accident."

17

$\mathcal{J}$ was relieved to find Benji sitting up in his hospital bed at Cedars-Sinai, doing a *TV Guide* crossword puzzle.

"'She was Edna Garret,'" Benji read aloud, upon seeing me. "They put that in every week. Boy, what a toughie."

"I'm so glad you're alive." I reached down to hug him. I was a little surprised when Benji firmly hugged back. It was more like him to nastily refuse to do so, but I guessed that almost losing your life makes you a bit more sentimental—at least for a couple of hours.

"Two cracked ribs, a minor concussion," Benji explained. "I'm very lucky. The car was totaled."

"What happened?"

Benji weakly lifted his head to look about the room. "Are we alone?"

"Terry and Brother Dennis are waiting in the car." I felt guilty not telling Benji more than that. But I rationalized that it wasn't the time to be worrying him.

"Are there a lot of reporters outside?"

"Only about fifty thousand."

He flashed his homely but winning smile. "That's down from a hundred. You're losing your touch, Rick. You're strictly yesterday's news."

"I wish. Now, you were saying . . . ?"

"It was the damnedest thing, Rick. I swung by Shane's. No one was there. I found the Oscar in the closet, just where you said it would be. I scooped the damn thing up, careful not to get my fingerprints on it, and headed back to the freeway.

"All of a sudden, this car was tailgating me. The headlights kept getting bigger and bigger. I tried to see the make and model, but it happened too fast. I couldn't see the driver, either. I tried to pull over, but the car rammed into me. Next thing I knew, I was zooming out of control, straight into a street lamp."

Benji closed his eyes, reliving the awful moment.

"It was no accident. It wasn't just some drunk driver."

This was not exactly music to my ears.

"You're saying that someone saw you take the Oscar, and then tried to kill you?"

"No, I'm saying that someone saw the herringbone jacket I was wearing, and thought I deserved to die because it didn't go with my belt. *Of course* that's what I'm saying."

In agitation, Benji shifted around in bed. He winced with pain and clutched his chest.

"Easy, Benji," I consoled. "My stupidity isn't worth dying over."

"I'm okay. Just find out what happened to the Oscar. I had it in the trunk of the car."

"And now the car is . . . ?"

"Impounded by the cops, of course. All I told them was that I got rear-ended. I didn't mention the Oscar. Too risky. It could louse up our whole case if people thought we were blowing smoke. Not to mention that whoever's doing this isn't exactly Mr. Nice Guy. Or Ms. Nice Guy. If words gets out, this psycho might really start to panic, if you get my drift. If anything happened to you, I'd never . . . well, whatever."

It was obvious that Benji needed to rest.

I made my way down the hospital corridor, feeling somewhat accustomed to the stampede of flashbulbs and microphones. As I approached my black Cherokee in the parking lot, I considered the occupants inside it, albeit crouching out of view from the press. (No easy feat for poor Terry.) Thinking quickly, I decided I had to hedge my bets and trust Terry with something—or at least trust him enough to tell him about it.

Once I make up my mind to say something to somebody, I'm a good old-fashioned blurter. Having kept Terry in the dark about the Oscar, I now could scarcely contain myself from blabbing on about it. But I didn't want Brother Dennis to know about it. He had a bad habit of interfering after promising not to. So I had to wait a few agonizing minutes.

I pulled the Cherokee over in front of the Hollywood Network station. The new and improved Shane regally slid the Cherokee door open. He looked like a million bucks.

"Break a leg, Shane."

He winked at me and smiled, and damn if I didn't feel tingly all over. Not a good sign.

Then I drove off with Terry. I vaguely felt like we were "parents" dropping off our child for his first day of school.

"Maybe sometime I could drive the BMW again," Terry wondered wistfully.

It wasn't hard to drum up an instant press conference. Even as we drove off I could see reporters milling about "Shane."

"I can't explain everything, Terry, but you have to trust me. There was an Oscar in Benji's trunk. Tara's Oscar. He got it at Shane's house." I pulled the Cherokee to the side of the road. "I told him to get it."

"And that's why Benji was . . . ?"

"You got it. Only Benji didn't want to report it. He was afraid that it would—well, he was just afraid."

I figured Terry was going to give me a bad time about having kept this from him, how if I'd told him in the first place Benji wouldn't have nearly gotten whacked. But I had to hand it to him. He had the class to roll with it all. Terry might've been out to get me, but as a cop he didn't want to see me or anyone else get bumped off. After all, it would be illegal.

"Let me drive. We're going to police headquarters Or at least I am. It's your turn to crouch under the seat."

Neither of us said anything as we drove to the police station. Despite everything else going on, I couldn't help thinking about how only a day ago he'd driven me here to get booked.

As I waited for Terry, I began to feel really crappy. No wonder I felt so tired. I was coming down with something. Now I was *truly* blessed.

With shivers and chattering teeth, I turned on the radio to cheer myself up. Big mistake.

I listened attentively to Brother Dennis's press conference. The radio announcer kept blabbing on about how Shane never looked more handsome, more confident, more everything.

Brother Dennis/Shane addressed the crowd of reporters: "I have little to say here today, other than that I grieve the loss of Tara Perez."

"Mr. Kirk," asked one reporter, "did you see who murdered Tara?"

"Was it Rick Domino?" chimed in a second reporter.

"Why didn't you accept your Oscar?" inquired a third.

"I have been advised to say more nothing more at this time."

"Fuck," I thought out loud. Was he the victim of stage fright? Or was he just another motherfucker out to screw me over?

A reporter called out, "Did you even know that you won an Oscar yourself?"

"I read it in the papers. I'm deeply honored, of course, and wish to thank the Academy, but . . . well, there's really so much else to think about right now."

A cacophony of reporters began shouting at him all at once. Dennis told them: "Please. Leave me to my mourning. I am available if the police have any questions."

Available to the police?! I could scarcely believe what I was hearing.

The radio announcer stated that "Shane" had left the podium. I turned off the radio, too disgusted for words.

It seemed like Terry was in the cop station for an eternity. That was a good sign, I supposed. It must've meant he was getting information on the accident.

But I was impatient to get going. I still wanted to surprise Connee Kellogg with a visit.

Apropos of this, my cell phone rang. It was Zeke Raflowitz, who screamed that if I got in touch with Connee I would live to regret it.

I hung up the phone without saying anything. I felt too lousy to think of some devious answer to give him.

My cell phone rang again. I almost didn't bother answering it.

"Is this Rick?" inquired the hoarse, unfamiliar female voice.

"Yes, this is Mr. Domino."

"Rick, sweetheart, it's your Connee-kins."

I was so out of it I had to think for a second.

"You remember—we met at the adult film festival. I was a special celebrity presenter."

Obviously, she had me confused with someone else.

"Well, hello anyway," she went on cheerfully. "I've always been your *biggest* fan. Shame on you for not remembering me."

"I remember. I was just giving you a hard time."

"Oh, you dirty boys and your hard times!" she giggled. "Now then, I would *love* to sit down and talk to you. I have all the time in the world. Well, not *all* the time, I do have a very busy career. But I want to tell everyone about my dearest friend in the world, Tara Perez, and I want you, Rick, to have the exclusive."

"Zeke Raflowitz doesn't want me to talk to you." I was not in a million years going to let that stop me, of course, but I wanted to see what Connee would say.

"Oh, Zekie is a riot. He's so young. He still takes himself seriously. Though I'd like to think I'm making him more mature by the hour, if you know what I mean, Ricky-kins." Her melodic voice melted into a kind of mewing titter.

"Would about an hour from now be too late?"

"Not at *all*, Sugar Lips. For you, my little schnookums, *anything.*"

"Great, then. One hour. Your place."

Or so I hoped. Terry was sure taking his time getting out of the station, and I frankly wanted to ditch him before I talked to Connee.

I was getting colder by the second. Terry had left his cop jacket in the car. I put it on for warmth. I felt something in one of the pockets. It wasn't hard to succumb to the temptation to see what it was.

Imagine my surprise. It was a note to Charlie, listing remarks I'd said about the case, though making no mention at all of Brother Dennis or any other possible suspect. Even though I already knew Terry was in cahoots with Charlie, this note was utterly repugnant. Sort of like when you know your spouse is cheating on you, but when you find an actual love letter, the whole thing takes on a new dimension of cruddiness.

The next thing I remembered was someone touching my shoulder.

"Rick, wake up."

The sight of Terry made me jump.

"I've got bad news, sport," he conveyed. "There was no Oscar in the trunk of the car." He smiled at me as he turned the ignition. "But cheer up."

I wanted to cry, but felt too shitty.

Terry was going on about something else, but I couldn't even hear.

"Terry, I don't feel so hot."

And then I remember nothing.

18

I awoke to the familiarity of my bed. Or at least I was reasonably certain it was my bed. I'd recently had my master suite redone in the no-frills, undyed-white-muslin style currently so fashionable, and for a moment I thought I was a patient a Red Cross ward in an old World War II movie. I spent a ridiculous amount of money to have new appointments look like old ones: New wallpaper professionally crackled and faded to have a kind of grandparents' attic affect, new white porcelain fixtures in the master bath designed to look like ones out of the Depression, plain mirrors synthetically treated to be slightly opalizing, wrought-iron bedposts professionally dented with a delicate ball peen hammer, white-painted trim carefully antiqued, and plain cedar chests and dressers stripped of all stain and varnish.

I looked at it all and wondered what I could've been thinking.

I noted it was light outside. A bright sunny day. My plain-looking, made-to-seem-old nightstand clock was being repaired—in an amazing coincidence, Dasher was nearby when it broke—so offhand I had no idea as to the time.

The next thing I saw was Terry. As if intuitively responding to the color scheme, he wore a white T-shirt instead of a black one. Though I realized, of course, it was a coincidence. Besides, he still made a poor substitute for a nurse like Irene Dunne.

"What time is it?" I managed to croak. My throat wasn't sore, it just felt like I hadn't spoken in a while.

Terry considered. Aw, what the heck, he'd look at his watch and tell me. "About one."

Those two little words hit me like a jolt of espresso. I sat up in bed like a jack-in-the-box.

"*One?* Jesus H. Christ, what are you doing, letting me sleep in? It's Wednesday morning. It's Wednesday *afternoon.*"

Terry laughed good-naturedly. "Try Friday afternoon."

I hoped he was kidding. "Friday?"

"By the time we drove back here, you had a whopper of a flu. I found the name of your doctor. He came by and gave you a shot of something. Boy, you must really have what it takes, to have a doctor who still makes house calls. Plus there's this nurse who's been stopping by. The doc said it was caused by stress. Weakened your immune system. Happens to cops all the time. You gotta take care of yourself, my friend."

"Gee, I wonder what I could've been worried about."

"I wasn't putting you down, Rick. It's understandable. Running yourself ragged while facing such serious charges."

"Plus knowing I'm innocent," I couldn't resist adding.

"Oh yeah. Of course that, too." He said this with about as

much conviction as if the mechanic at Jiffy Lube just asked him if in addition to an oil change he wanted to fill-up on windshield fluid.

As I stood up and got my bearings, I noticed I was wearing unfamiliar pajamas. They belonged to me all right, but I normally slept naked.

As if semireading my thoughts, Terry explained, "The nurse got you undressed."

"I would've expected as much."

"What I meant was, I didn't want you to think that another guy—"

The glare in my eyes stopped him from going any further.

"Oh yeah. I keep forgetting."

As I made full cognizance of the fact that it was Friday, I was on the verge of tears for my frustration. "Friday!" I wailed, flailing about the bedroom for a change of clothes. "Two days—no, two and a half days down the drain." I picked the first shirt I saw. "I was supposed to meet with Connee Kellogg the other night. I only hope that Zeke hasn't locked her in an ivory tower, chaste maiden that she is."

"No need to worry about that," Terry conveyed helpfully. "She's dead."

I fetched up a fresh pair of socks and pretended I misheard him.

"I have to call her again," I stated emphatically, though I also tried to sound cheerful. "She's expecting me."

Terry walked closer to me. "Rick, I'm telling you, she's dead. She was found in her hotel room Wednesday morning. They said it was an accidental overdose of pills and booze."

I slammed my underwear drawer shut. "Is that all anyone in this shithole town ever dies of? What swamp gas is to UFO sightings, pills and booze are to Hollywood deaths. Why don't they just get rid of the coroner's office and start saying that *everyone* dies of pills and booze? If you think about it, indirectly everyone does."

"Rick, I'm worried about you. I was hoping the rest would do you good. But you're coming apart."

"Well, then, when they give me my lethal injection, they'll have to do it more than once, because I'll be in so many little pieces."

He had the nerve to put his hand on my shoulder. "Rick, please, sit down for a minute. Let me call the nurse and see if—"

"You stay away from me!" I wriggled free of his touch, electing to pass on his double-crossing tea and sympathy.

Terry's face registered puzzlement and hurt. It occurred to me that cops were highly underrated as actors, even if some of them knew so little about movie stars.

"Rick, what do you mean?"

"Have you been staying here? Sleeping in my house?"

"Well, *yeah.* On the couch in the office. Only I haven't been sleeping much. I've mostly been doing grunt work. Lots of things that we need to go over. Plus I wanted to make sure you were safe. Francine was right. I guess I am sort of like your bodyguard."

"What about that creep, Dennis?" I couldn't bring myself to call him by his proper title.

Terry looked worried. "He left you a note. I'll show it to you. But first you need to *calm down.*"

"And first you need to get the hell out of here. You need to leave me alone. Go away. Never come back. Never speak to me again."

The degree of emotion in my voice alarmed me. I must've hated his guts even more than I realized.

"But *why?* What makes you say this?"

I was afraid to explain. I was afraid of what he might do if I told him just how much I knew about him.

Instead, I started to cry. I mean *really* cry. We're talking a double feature of *Dark Victory* and *Stella Dallas.* Not my butchest moment, but there you have it.

"I was going to talk to Connee," I heard myself sputter between sobs. "She had *information* for me. She was *there* when it happened. I'm sure of it."

"I know, Rick." Terry sat down next to me on the bed. He was careful not to touch me, but he did look at me with concern. I was so desperate for someone to unload on that I didn't even care anymore that it was him. Probably, that's how cops get the job done. They isolate you, and then finally you can't stand it anymore and you tell them everything because you have to tell someone.

"I don't want to go to jail. I didn't *do* it, dammit."

"I know."

I buried my face in the pillow, wailing and moaning. Terry murmured, "That's okay, you just let it out. You'll feel better now." Like he was a shrink in some TV Movie of the Week, and was pleased that the patient had this major breakthrough.

I could feel him watching over me. And as much as I hated to admit it, it felt somewhat comforting. I could see how people who were exceptionally weak or vulnerable could find it soothing to be around someone like him.

My tears subsided. I sat up in bed, took a deep breath, and silently counted to ten.

"I know about Charlie."

Terry looked utterly innocent as he replied, "You mean Charlie my partner? Did something happen to him?"

"Terry, please. I just want to make the best of the time I have left. I know what your game is, and if you're going to keep hanging around, we might as well at least have all our cards on the table. I'm too *tired* to keep pretending."

"Rick, I have no idea what you're talking about."

I was feeling frustrated all over again. So much for my thirty seconds of tranquility.

"Terry, I've known all along that Charlie is following us. That it's all just a setup. You're waiting for me trip over myself. Or trust you enough to confess. Or however you thought it would work."

For all I knew I was totally screwing myself, but for the moment I was relieved to get it out in the open. Since I was running out of time, I couldn't keep worrying about secrets. Plus in a strange way, I felt like Terry *had* connected with me, and maybe he'd cut me a little slack.

"In other words, you've seen Charlie when he's trailing us." He was calm and professional about it all—too much so, which gave me chills.

Terry's cell phone rang.

"Cool," he decided, looking over at me as he talked on the phone.

I could barely swallow.

I guessed they were coming over to take me back to jail, for whatever I'd done to violate being out on bail.

"Here." I defiantly offered both my wrists.

"Here *what?*"

"Go ahead. Cuff me. Let's just do it and get it over with."

Terry turned pale. "Rick, what do you take me for? I'm not . . . you know, into that kind of stuff. Though of course, if that's your thing, I don't want to—"

"Who was that on the phone? What did they say about me?"

"I have some great news. Well, not *great.* I mean, it's not happy or anything, But it sure does shed light on things."

"But what about *Charlie?*"

"Charlie followed us around a few times. He was wise to what I was trying to do. He was worried for me. He said . . ." Terry stopped himself.

"Well, what did Charlie say?"

"He's convinced you killed Tara. That you're the most danger-ous kind of murderer—the type who *seems* nice. The rest is simple arithmetic. Two cops are better than one when fighting off a psycho killer. He meant well, he really did. He just wanted to protect me."

In a stupid way, I was complimented. No one ever thought of me as dangerous before.

"What about the gay bit? Didn't he think I was too whimpy to be a threat to a big ol' guy like you?"

Terry laughed ruefully. "Rick, my good man, a bullet is a bullet. A knife is a knife. Don't make no difference who's aiming it. All that matters is if you get hit."

"Were you ever wounded on the job, Terry?" I heard myself inanely ask.

"Not so far. Ain't too much action there at the parking meters, remember?"

He was a good sport, I'd give him that much.

"So you really, *really* don't think I did it?"

Terry laughed. "I really, really know you didn't. And I really am trying to help you—and myself, don't forget. Though at this point, even if I get canned for all the rules I've broken, I'd still rest easy knowing that I found the real killer. That justice was served."

"Is Charlie going to keep poking around?"

"No way. I started making him a list of all the reasons why I knew you didn't do it. Then I figured, screw it. I'll just tell him to bug off. You remember when you saw me calling him? I didn't give him any of the juicy details, but I told him there was a whole can of wormy suspects, and you really were an all right guy. And to leave us in peace."

"He went along with it?"

Terry gave me one of his playful punches. "Charlie thinks it's an honor to fetch me donuts. I have him very well trained."

I politely, semiphonily laughed. "What about your wife?"

He rubbed his neck like he had a kink in it. "Women have this way of making it seem like you're deciding things, when really they are. It's hard to explain." He smiled at me. "Hey, nothing in this world's perfect, right?"

Terry stretched his massive frame like an eager lion. "Now, before I go over everything with you, tell me. Is there anything else you need to ask me about? Anything at all?"

In the split instant I had to decide, I heard myself answer, "No."

"Good. Let's get back to work." He walked over to my dresser and tossed me a letter. "From You-Know-Who."

The unsealed envelope was addressed simply to "Rick." Inside was a card with a medieval Orthodox icon of the Virgin and Child. Inside the blank card was written:

Dear Rick,
  It is best for all concerned that I work on my own from now on. I have been saying a rosary every night for us all.

                        XXOO
                        "Shane"

The note was neatly printed; Brother Dennis no doubt used to get A's in penmanship. Then, when he oddly signed off with hugs and kisses, the X's and O's were scribbled and jagged, as if he were suddenly on a bumpy train. Contrastingly, the alias "Shane" was signed boldly, in huge letters and with a flourish of curls at the end that would've made John Hancock jealous.

"Pretty weird, huh?" Terry commented.

I set down the note. "That's certainly surprising coming from you, President of the Brother Dennis Fan Club."

"Well, even *I* don't always know everything." He looked pleased with himself, like he was rising to the occasion. "The thing is, I talked with the officer who arrested him, and he's a very clean, upfront, by-the-book cop. I'm not being naïve, trust me. I know perfectly well there's some crooked cops out there. But LeShawn January isn't one of them. He grew up in the projects. Became a cop to clean the dealers off the streets. Family man, active in his church and community. Wife and four kids. He wouldn't lie in a police report."

Of course, the cop still could've been some sort of weirdo closet case, but for the moment anyway I decided not to get into all that.

"What does he say happened?"

Terry nervously scratched the stubble on his head. "It's kind of hard to talk about, but here goes. LeShawn was checking out a drug lead. Dennis came up to him, and said something about—well, you know how they say that black guys are pretty well endowed. Then he said something like, 'Do you think I look like a movie star? Guess which one I am?' According to LeShawn, our friend Dennis seemed like he was high on something—who knows?

"Anyway, LeShawn politely declined, and kept walking. But Dennis wouldn't give it a rest. He kept following him down the street, calling out to him, pulling on his arm. Even begging. He said something like, 'Look, I'll do it for free. Just love me. Please, just love me.' Except when Dennis said it, he was like—you know—screaming. LeShawn had to bring him in. Disturbing the peace and lewd public conduct. But it was also for Dennis's own good, because he was way over the top."

"Well, what do you think?"

"I don't think Brother Dennis had anything to do with Tara's murder. But I think he's having some sort of nervous breakdown,

156

and we better keep an eye on him. He's still popping up as Shane, and could muck things up real bad. I could be out of a job, and you won't be lookin' so hot in the eyes of the jury."

I looked at the note again, as if it would give me the secret to Brother Dennis's duplicity. "So where's the dear boy now?"

"Wish I knew. No answer at Shane's house, and when I've driven by a few times, no one's been there. We just have to keep our fingers crossed that the real Shane turns up. Which, in case you haven't guessed, hasn't happened so far."

Before I could think too much about Brother Dennis, Terry nudged me and asked, "Ready for some fun?"

"I'm all ears."

"Good. Connee Kellogg's death—how does that grab you so far?"

"Sounds like a blast. Whatcha got?"

Terry absently drummed the dresser top with his thick index fingers. "The death itself? I have zip. If someone just happened to put some extra pills in her booze that night, it's impossible to tell. She'd had her stomach pumped on at least seven occasions. It was one of those ODs that could've happened hundreds of times before."

"Still, it's an interesting coincidence that it would happen on *the* night I was due to talk with her."

"Indubitably." Terry looked pleased with himself for saying such a fancy word. "But in the meantime, we can look at everyone's behavior since then."

He turned on the wide screen TV opposite my bed. Then he turned on the DVD player.

"I recorded this myself," he announced proudly.

There before mine eyes was none other than Mitzi McGuire. She wore a different black dress than she did for Tara's memorial— a *very* low-cut V-neck—that got across the same general idea.

"Have I died and gone to heaven?" I wondered aloud.

Terry looked at me quizzically. "Never mind," I answered. "Long story."

"Friends," Mitzi began, trying gallantly to frown when her face lacked the elasticity to do so, "I'm here on this sunny Thursday morning to briefly share with you another tragedy that has befallen a member of our Hollywood family of stars. Delightful comedienne Connee Kellogg, who ironically changed the spelling of her name last year because she thought it would bring her luck, died of an accidental overdose of barbiturates mixed with alcohol late Tuesday night—only one night after her good friend and confidante, megastar Tara Parez, was so brutally murdered. As you know, Hollywood network anchor Rick Domino has been charged with Tara's murder. His trial is expected to begin Monday. We at Hollywood Network hope for a speedy and just resolve to this terrible situation."

"It's weird," Terry commented. "The stuff she's saying sure is articulate and I'll bet she's a nice lady and all, but it just doesn't sound like she's really saying it."

"Terry, you are very astute." Though I begged to differ with the "nice lady" bit.

Mitzi continued: "We have with us now just two of the many, *many* people whose lives were touched by knowing Connee. Jeep Andrews and Cinda Sharpe, who of course also happen to be two of our brightest stars."

"Good morning, Mitzi," spoke Cinda in a solemn yet crisp voice. She wore the same black pantsuit as the other day.

Jeep was all laid-back gentleman, his hands clasped behind him "Hello, Mitzi. How sad that we should have to meet this way again."

Mitzi went seamlessly into her next cue card: "Cinda, Jeep, what can you share with us about Connee Kellogg? I know she had many fans, but some people out there may have wanted to know more about her."

"She was lovely," replied Cinda. "Very *real*. Very down-to-earth. She survived a great many disappointments, yet she kept her chin up and hoped for a better tomorrow. I still can't believe she's gone. This whole thing must've been some dreadful mistake."

"I agree, this whole thing is dreadful," added Jeep. "Like Cinda said, Connee was a funny and honest girl who never harmed anyone in her life. I know this was all just a horrible accident. I was helping set up an appointment for her with Truman Shea at Milky Way for a role in an upcoming film project of mine. She had everything to look forward to."

"C'mon Mitzi," I urged, like a football fan watching a game on TV, "Fuck the cue cards. Ask about the movie deal."

Mitzi moved the mike back to her surgically-enhanced chin. "Well, I'm sure that Connee's memory will live on for millions of her fans."

"Shit." I wanted to throw something at the TV.

"Since I have you here, Cinda and Jeep," Mitzi continued, "are there any new projects lined up that we should know about?"

With a gentle sort of cheerfulness—upbeat about the future, but sad in the present—Cinda related, "Actually, Mitzi, Jeep and I are due to costar for the first time in a new romance called *Afternoon Delight.*"

"Well, I'm sure the chemistry between the two of you will just *radiate* off the screen," Mitzi predicted.

"Thank you, Mitzi," Cinda and Jeep gently replied. She linked her arm with Jeep's, and led him away.

The coverage of Connee's memorial was of course much shorter than Tara's—a five-minute entertainment news spot as opposed to full coverage of Tara's two-hour extravaganza. So there were no more interviews. From the few crowd shots, it did not appear that the Raflowitz–Simone tribe were in attendance, nor did I spot Truman Shea.

I did, however, see "Shane Kirk" in dark glasses, bowing his head in alleged grief. If I didn't know better, I would've sworn he was actually crying.

"He really has lost it," I reflected.

Following Connee's brief memorial clip was a commercial promoting the film, *On the Road Again*, a breezy throwback to the Hope–Crosby–Lamour "road" movies, and which starred none other than Bob, Jeep, and Tara. It was Tru's brainstorm to try to milk the best of both worlds, so to speak, out of the action and romance angles promised by the three stars. Plus the retro "road" bit made for lots of TV fodder (i.e., "Bob, you've had a very serious career. Have you a secret desire to be the next Bob *Hope?*" "Well, Chauncey, it would be an honor to even be compared with Mr. Hope," etc.).

As it happened, this was Tara's last completed film, though the promo made no mention of this, since the movie was touted as a ha-ha, piss-in-your-pants-laughing comedy. The ad showed the merry threesome romping along Tahitian beaches, the Australian Outback, and the Alaskan tundra in classic screwball form. Since this was a contemporary film, however, special-effects action sequences were thrown into the mix, in particular a couple of Tara karate-chopping the bad guys as continents and things exploded in the background. The politically correct filmmakers wanted to make it clear that she was not there just to wear a sarong. But at the same time, of course, there was an alluring (albeit diffused) shot of Tara indeed sporting a kind of bikini sarong. She walked straight toward the camera as she cooed, "Come to mama, you bad little boy!" Then Jeep (sensitive-man update on Bing) was shown throwing a sheet over his face in exasperation, followed by a quick cut to Bob in close-up, laughing with bemusement.

In a cheese puff sort of way, it looked like a fun picture. I don't know if it was because of the good long cry I just had, or that there was something haunting about seeing Tara carousing through a comedy, but I felt truly sorry for her for the first time since the whole thing happened.

Terry seemed to understand. He flicked off the TV and let me be alone with my thoughts. After about a minute I asked, "Well, what did you think?"

"I think that whatever it all is, it's one hell of a mess. Everyone is trying to protect everyone else against Lord-knows-what. Obviously, Jeep Andrews is ready to crack. Maybe we can meet him— boy, I'd sure like that. Imagine shaking hands with such a great guy. Man, I saw him in . . . what was that flick where he played the fighter pilot who wins us the Gulf War?"

"*Born in the USA.*"

"Man, I must've seen that movie five or six times. You remember that scene where Jeep shoves the grenade down the bad guy's throat and all the intestines and eyeballs go splattering on the other bad guy's windshield, so he crashes and you see his arms and head ripping loose as they explode into flames? Man, that's what I call a *movie.*"

Okay, here goes nothing. He's going to have to know sooner or later.

"Terry, Jeep is gay."

Well, Terry thought that was the biggest knee-slapper to come out of my mouth yet. "C'mon, Rick. I thought you weren't going to pull anymore crap."

I guess the look on my face said it all.

I felt like I just told a kid that there was no Santa Claus. It was my turn to be the Strong One, and give him a moment to regroup.

"Well, okay. So he's gay. Thanks for telling me."

"You know, when people are acting in movies . . . well, that's why they call it acting. In real life, Jeep is—"

"Look, I *get* it, okay? It's his business if he likes guys. And it would still be an honor to meet him."

I could see that Terry was trying hard.

Dasher padded into the room, and Terry forced the protesting feline up to his lap. The cat scowled as he tolerated the indignity of being petted. It struck me as Terry's way of latching onto something "normal."

"You know, Dasher is also gay."

"Very funny." Terry tickled the cat and made little baby sounds. "By the way, Rick. Is Cinda Sharpe a lez?"

I nodded affirmatively, logging on to my laptop.

Terry grinned knowingly. "I thought so." Somehow, this made things right again in his world, though I couldn't have begun to fathom how or why.

"Well, straight or gay, Jeep is the one we need to get to next," Terry concluded.

"Shouldn't be too difficult to do." I turned the computer so Terry could see it. Needing to move in closer, he let go of Dasher, who vocalized for the torture he'd been forced to endure. Terry read the e-mail out loud:

"Rick, please come to my beach house on Friday at 4-ish. We simply must talk. I'm having friends for cocktails, but let's meet in private in my area. Use the special entrance in back. I KNOW you're innocent, but you know how these things are. Tru."

"And if Tru is having friends for cocktails," I explained, "you can count on Jeep being among the olives."

"You mean to tell me that Truman Shea is, uh, gay, too?"

"Tru swings both ways. He's open about it."

"So we'll get to kill two birds with one stone."

"Actually, I imagine it'll be closer to three. Something tells me that Cinda will not be too far from earshot."

Terry gave the thumbs-up with both hands. "Great. I tell you, Rick, things are really looking up. And with the blackmail on Bob, and the autopsy on Tara, we're really cooking."

I stop fiddling with the keyboard. "Come again?"

"Wow, you *must've* been out of it the other night. You don't remember, do you?"

Terry sounded disappointed, like a kid whose dad forgot to buy him a candy bar.

"Terry, I had a fever."

"I wasn't criticizing you, Rick. The thing is, at the police station, I stumbled upon a couple of bombshells." He walked about the room, unable to contain his excitement. "In fact, you better sit down."

I looked around to make sure I wasn't missing something. "I *am* sitting down, Terry."

He chortled or so. "Oh, yeah, so you are. Silly me."

I must confess that I find it sort of cute when big ol' guys like Terry say things like "silly me." But the charm of the moment took a decided back seat to more pressing concerns.

"Terry, dammit, what is it? We're talking about my *life*, for fuck's sake."

"Relax. It's good news. Turns out the day before the Oscars, Bob filed a police report. Someone was trying to blackmail him. He wouldn't say *who*, he just had all these questions about how he should handle things. The detective said Bob was very frustrating to deal with because he refused to get specific, even to the point of getting belligerent and kind of know-it-all. It was before Bob knew about Tara and Zeke, but who knows? Tara was always making all kinds of threats at everyone. Anyway, that tells us something, doesn't it? At least maybe?"

"I'd say definitely maybe. What else?"

Terry poured himself more coffee. "Tara didn't die from gunshot wounds."

"Say what?"

"She died from a blow to the head with a blunt object. All those bullet holes were just to make it look good. I assume the DA's told your lawyer by now. By the way, Benji says he wants to talk to you in the morning, as soon as he's discharged from the hospital."

"Terry, the blunt object that killed Tara was the Oscar. I'm sure of it. Why else would someone make sure it was missing from the crime scene?"

"I already figured as much. Now all we need to do is find the little gold booger, and you're off the hook." He took a long sip of coffee. "More or less."

"Try less instead of more," I noted grimly. "Wherever the Oscar is, it's chock-full of my fingerprints."

Terry either didn't get or else ignored my joke. "There must've been blood on the Oscar." He stirred sugar into his coffee; then he poured in more sugar. "Do you remember seeing any blood? Even just a fleck that someone neglected to wipe off in their haste?"

"It was pitch-black in the closet. I couldn't tell."

"Well, we need to find the damn thing in any case. It's a piece of the truth."

I held up the black leather pants I planned to wear to Tru's. "You're right."

Terry scrutinized me. "Those are pretty fancy duds. Is this thing at Truman Shea's going to be some sort of wild party, Rick?"

I smiled innocently. "Of course not."

19

To show what a real person he was, Truman Shea did not always lurk about his forty-room Bel Air monstrosity of a home, which dwelling loomed in my imagination like a massive gargoyle from a bad dream. Sometimes, he preferred the simple pleasures of his twenty-room Malibu beach house. It, too, jutted out like some gaping, staring stone figurine, albeit on a somewhat smaller scale. Heavy weather clung to all of Tru's homes—everything he possessed, for that matter—given his relentless determination to show the world how much power he had over us all. Had I been a child, Tru's houses would've scared me in ways I couldn't have expressed, and even as a sane, rational adult I always dreaded a trek to his turf.

Of course, I never could've said this to Tru. Though highly calculating, he was paradoxically oblivious to the effect he had on people. He strove to be intimidating, yet he would've been devastated to know that he succeeded. He didn't want you to relax for a minute in his company, but it would've crushed him to find out you hadn't enjoyed yourself.

The beach house was a molded stucco affair built in the 1930s by a famous movie mogul for his high-class prostitute mistress—who thanked him by hanging herself from its rafters the first night she moved in. The story was kept out of the papers—the producer had connections, and the mistress was a glorified nobody—but over the years rumors about the house snowballed. (I once heard someone ludicrously claim it was where the St. Valentine's Day Massacre took place.) Knowing the house's history, and the way Tru bragged that he was able to buy it for "almost nothing" (i.e., a mere two million), could only add to my discomfort at being there.

Unlike Francine, Tru could pull off high style—if anything, he pulled it off too well. You felt like you were in some drafty museum for all the priceless, foreboding vases and chandeliers, Rococo decorative tables, heavy carved staircases imported from Spanish castles, authentic medieval stained-glass windows, and the chillingly cold marble floors. All of it was far too formal for the beach.

Entering from the back didn't help matters any. The producer who built the home was paranoid about the double life he was living, and so he had a suite of rooms installed that seemingly could not be entered from the rest of the house. But he had a leading set designer put in a trick wall panel, like something right out of the movies, whereby you could indeed go from the one part of the house to the other. The secret suite consisted of a full master bedroom, bath, and dressing room; an office, a full gym, and a "small" indoor pool, appointed in dark aquamarine tiles. Tru had a sauna and steam room added in. It was a strange, dreamlike feeling to swim in the indoor pool while looking out at the pounding Pacific Ocean that was the backyard—especially at night.

As it happened, the twilight just began. Obviously, when Tru said to drop by at "fourish," he meant about five-thirty. So it was quarter-to-six when Terry and I arrived.

Along the way, I'd had us shop for extra clothes for Terry. He needed more than just a dinner jacket to start blending in with Hollywood. I bought him a couple of pairs of linen slacks to go with his jacket, another jacket, a couple of pullovers, a decent dress shirt and tie, and a cotton sweater. (I also got him a couple of pairs of genuine Levi 501s. Mine is an intense prejudice against "imitation" Levis.) The fashion consultant told us what I already guessed. Terry's color mode was winter: Blacks, grays, whites, silvers and bark-colored browns, with an occasional dash of bold red. It took a little extra digging around to locate interesting size 14 shoes, but I was able to find him some jazzy Italian slippers, rugged sports sandals, and stylish dress shoes. Terry kept rolling his eyes through it all, but he was a good sport, and in the end he marveled at having "so many" new clothes.

"Don't worry, you look fine," I assured him, as I rang Tru's buzzer.

Apparently unconvinced, Terry kept fussing with his lapels. "I just want to make the right impression on such a distinguished producer."

A few seagulls circled over and us squaked in the fresh salt air. There was vivid orange and purple sunset on the ocean, which wore a silken sheen.

"Kinda neat, huh?" bespoke the poet that welled from the depths of Terry's soul. "I don't know, though. Living at the ocean like this—I'd have a hard time knowing how to relate to the real world."

"So who asked you to live here?"

There was a buzz at the door signaling us to enter. Terry made a face at me as we stepped inside.

Like souls having entered into the netherworld, we followed the light in the otherwise dark chamber. It went up the ornate wrought-iron stairs, to the office and bedroom suite.

"I'm over *here!*"

The voice was coming from down below.

We went back down the stairs, and stood before the indoor pool. As our eyes adjusted to the dark, we could make out Truman Shea floating atop an inflated raft.

"The light is to the left of the door," he noted, which of course meant we should serve him by turning it on. Knowing Tru, it wasn't a casual request, but a means of establishing control of the situation.

Terry flicked the switch, and a series of spotlights came on. Collectively, the lights only dimly lit the blue-green tiled room, but it hurt to look up into the glare just the same. Tru, one could not help noticing, was stark naked. Yet from the way he boldly stared at us, it was as though it was our problem that we were so wimpy as to wear clothes.

"My evening meditation," Tru explained. "That's all right—I don't mind being interrupted." Of course, he was the one who invited me over, but no matter. With Tru, it always had to be that he was doing *you* a favor.

Terry started to say something, but I frowned for him not to.

"You should try it, sometime, Rick. It's peaceful, just you and the pool in the dark. No music, no affirmation tapes, no aroma therapy. Just darkness and silence and water, all safe and snug in a secret place. It's *ecstasy.*"

"Maybe they'll give me a prison cell with its own indoor pool."

Tru climbed out of the water, dripping wet as he picked up the first from a pile of black towels. He dried himself off as carefully as a car collector polishing his prized Bentley. The black towels in the dimly lit room made for a magician-like effect as parts of his body seemed to temporarily disappear. His skin was fashionably tanned and—thanks to weekly torturous waxing—virtually hairless. Nature did not give him the most becoming frame—he was naturally thick in the torso, with skinny arms—but to the extent that gym trainers, tummy tuckers, and silicon implanters could succeed,

Tru had an okay build. It was hard to comment on Tru's sharp-featured face, as his personality diminished whatever assets it had. His hairdresser was letting his black hair turn silver only along the temples, giving him a slightly gothic look.

"I wouldn't joke if I were you, Rick. I believe it spreads bad karma." As each towel became even slightly damp, he discarded it for a fresh one. "Who's your friend? Frankly, I thought we'd be talking alone."

"You can trust him. He's my bodyguard, Terry Zane."

"Truman Shea." He smiled as he offered his hand.

Terry tried to just sort of wave howdy, but Tru's eager face and my arched eyebrows told him he was going to have to bite the proverbial bullet, and Shake Hands with a Naked Man.

As their hands joined, Tru stated, "I dropped my towel. Pick it up for me."

I could just imagine what Terry was thinking as he bent down to get it.

"It's wet. I don't want it, after all." Tru dropped it to the floor. "Hand me a fresh one."

Terry's shoulders slightly shook as he complied. Mr. Redneck Cop was pissed.

"Now go stand over there with Rick. I don't like to feel crowded."

For a second I thought Terry was going to pop him one. Or at least shove him into the pool. But he held back, and obediently walked over to me.

"Is he a good bodyguard, Rick? Perhaps you can refer me to his agency."

"Sure, Tru."

I suddenly heard dance music. "The party, of course," True explained. "I'll be joining in shortly. It's always a good sign when the music gets too loud." He gyrated stiffly to the percussive beat; he was an odd, idiosyncratic dancer who made choppy, deliberate movements. "Almost like the old days at the baths. Did you used to be a bathhouse bouncer, Terry?"

"Uh . . . no, Mr. Shea."

"Funny. You look the sort. I'm not often wrong about people. I say this not out of conceit, but as a simple statement of fact. In my business, you can't afford to be wrong about anybody. Not once. Not ever." He reached for what seemed to be an extra-large towel; I then saw it was a black bathrobe, which he tied tightly around his waist. "Poor Tara. Although in a way, I say not-so-poor Tara. She got along quite well, considering she was never right about anybody or anything. She was fearless, but she was always wrong."

"You knew Tara longer than anybody, didn't you, Tru?"

He lay down on a black canvas lounge, and reached for a grape from a bowl of fruit on a black-tiled table. "Do you do massages, Terry?"

"No, I don't, Mr. Shea."

"Then I can't use you." He popped another grape into his mouth. "I require my bodyguards to give me full-body massages on demand. To me, it's all part of guarding my body. Doesn't that make sense, Rick?"

As I took in more of the room, I noticed a few other lounge chairs folded in the corner. It would've been nice to sit down, but I didn't dare ask Tru if we could help ourselves to seats.

"I think it makes *perfect* sense, Tru. You were saying about Tara . . . ?"

He clasped his hands behind his head. "Tara! I met the little shit when we were kids. She was what—fifteen? Sixteen? Seventeen? And I was twenty-four. I'd been this awful child acrobatic dancer. I *hated* having to perform. They told me I was nuts, but I wanted to become a fashion photographer. The best. I'd done a couple of minor shoots for *Vogue* and *Cosmo*, but I needed to really make my name. I've always dreamed *small*, you see. People think of me as a big dreamer, but I realize my goals in stages. One step at a time. So the big thing at the moment was to be *the* fashion photographer. And to do that, I knew I needed *the* face.

"I was living in New York, down in the East Village. My apartment wasn't much, but I invited someone important over for dinner. Funny, but now I don't even remember who it was, only that I had to impress them. So I called this maid service to clean my place.

They sent over this kid. I could tell she was underage. I asked her, 'How old are you,' and with her big, gorgeous, sassy eyes she looked up at me, and said, 'Older than you or anyone.' That was the first time I saw Tara, and I just had this *feeling* about her. She was raw. She needed sculpting. But it was all there. The face, the look, the attitude. Handed to me on a silver platter. I firmly believe this happens to everyone. Most people just aren't smart enough to notice.

"I took my first photos of her that very day. Full of angst and sassiness on St. Marks Place. Dreamy-eyed on the Staten Island Ferry, her hair blowing in the sun. Trendy stuff for its time. All the while, Tara kept telling me about herself. How she was orphaned at three when her parents were killed in a car accident. How they'd fled Cuba, and there were no relatives in the U.S., so Tara was quietly— and probably illegally—let into the foster care system. How Tara ran away to escape being placed in any more homes, because she hated always having to say good-bye. 'From now on,' she said, 'I want nothing but hellos.' She had so much humor when she said it, like she was in on the joke of life. She actually started going up to strangers on the ferry and saying hello to them, waving and laughing and jumping all around like a puppy wagging its tail. She was . . . just so wonderfully alive."

Tru frowned as he scratched his arm, as if someone with his money shouldn't ever itch. "But she was dishonest, too. Even that first day I saw how she didn't know the difference between truth and fantasy."

"What was an example?" Terry asked. He looked at me quickly, as if to say he was feeling out if Tru might treat him as an "equal." Tru didn't seem to notice one way or the other.

"Her parents, for one." He took another grape, then spit it out; apparently it wasn't sweet enough. He placed the slimy, half-eaten grape in plain view on the lounge table. "She was only three when they were killed, for God's sake. Yet when I asked her if she remembered them, she went on and on like she was the *Encyclopaedia Britannica*. Some of the stories she got from movies. And I'm not just talking about obscure ones that maybe someone wouldn't recognize. She actually said that her parents used to take her to a place in another country called Casablanca, and her father would toast her mother by saying, 'Here's looking at you, kid.' "

"Is that from a movie?" Terry asked innocently.

Tru pointed and gave a fake laugh. "He's cute, Rick. He's got that deadpan sarcasm thing happening."

"That's why I keep him around." I gazed at Terry with all the warmth I could muster. "Anyway, what else did she say?"

"Some of it wasn't from movies, but it was just as pathetic. Like she went on about how her mother and she would go out to the beach at Pelham Bay, and how when her father found out they were having fun without him, he'd play hooky from work by telling his boss . . . Look, what difference does it make anymore? The point was that a *three*-year-old simply would never remember these things. And she was that way all the time. Never seeming to know the difference between what she made up, and what really happened."

"But you loved her?"

"She used me, I used her," Tru answered flatly. "We each got exactly what we wanted. We were together—what—four years? If you want to call it love, be my guest."

"You know, Tru, I never heard *why* you and Tara broke up."

I could tell it was still a sore spot, from the way he folded his arms and avoided eye contact. "It wasn't my attraction for men, if that's what you're thinking. Tara dug it when I brought home guys. She liked to watch."

I couldn't resist looking at Terry, who listened respectfully, as if he heard this kind of talk all the time.

"At first she did it in secret," Tru continued, "but after awhile she was right there in the room—sometimes even in bed with us. She especially got off on ordering us around. The dominatrix who commands one man to do stuff to the other man's body. She loved it when I could seduce a straight man—or supposedly straight, anyway. She'd even help me out. You know, pretend to come on to the guy herself, and then have me kind of hanging around, and little by little I'd make my move. One time we did it with the husband of one of the models in her agency. The girl really fell apart, but Tara just shrugged it off and said that if the girl couldn't take the heat she should stay out of the kitchen. And in a way Tara was right. The modeling world ain't the normal world, honey, and you better get used to it.

"No, we broke up because Tara had gone as far as she could with me. She was *the* supermodel, and she wanted to break into movies. And not just as a guest-star bimbo. She wanted to be taken seriously. She'd say how someday she'd win an Oscar. I was 'just' a fashion photographer, so what good was I? For the first and only time in my life, I begged. I actually got on my knees and pleaded for her not to go. I never got over how it felt when she walked away. She said, 'Truman, I really do know what's best for both of us.' Twenty years old at tops, and she *knows* this? I mean, where does she get off trying to tell *me* about *my* life?"

He rammed his fist into the palm of his other hand, the anger still fresh after twenty years. The dance music from the other side of the wall grew louder, and I could hear people stomping and shouting to the beat.

"She wasn't my one great love. I don't believe there is such a beast. But she was my one great something-or-another. Because I determined that night that I would be so successful in the movie business that Tara would be heartbroken over having left me. I'd saved a few bucks, so I checked around. I invested in a low-budget flick that I could tell would be a big hit. *Frat House Kegger.*"

"Say, you produced that movie?" Terry's face lit up. "I've always wondered how they did they that scene where the baby pig is swimming in the keg, and then the bad guy dean with food poisoning—"

"So, Tru—it's been one success after the next for you." I smiled extra-toothy at Terry.

"And in a way, I owe it all to Tara. I've been too pissed off to be anything but a big success. Now that she's gone . . . well, I guess I'll have to find someone new to hate."

My mind boggled at the number of people who would've assumed that such was already the case between Tru and themselves. But, then, he never was cognizant of the shoddy ways he treated people. Besides, he probably thought he had license to do whatever he wanted to anybody, since one person had the audacity to hurt his feelings twenty years ago.

"Well, Tru, I'm sure you didn't ask me over just to reminisce."

"You're right, Rick. I'm normally not so sentimental. I live in the now." He reached inside his robe to scratch his balls. "I need a good testicle massage."

Terry snorted. "I can relate to that."

"What Tru *means*," I rushed in pleasantly, "is a form of ancient—what? Chinese? Hindu?—stimulation of the groin as a spiritual cleansing."

"It's *not* a sex thing," assured Tru. "In fact, if it gives you an orgasm it's a sign of spiritual impurity."

"Huh?"

"I'll explain it later, Terry." Though in all honesty he pretty much took the words right out of my mouth.

"If you take up body massage, you might want to consider including testicle work in your repertoire," Tru offered helpfully. "Your top-paying male clients would pretty much expect it. I can't even *think* about a single film idea without it."

"Look, Mr. Shea, thanks and all, But I—"

"Call my secretary, Terry. He'll put you in touch with a good practitioner. It shouldn't cost too much. Maybe two hundred an hour. And it'll pay off in spades."

"I'm sure Terry appreciates that you've taken valuable time to be helpful to him. I think you were about to tell us something about Tara."

"Oh, right." He took a few deep breaths, and began flexing his body in a kind of harried executive's bastardized version of yoga. "You might hear a rumor about some recent dealings between Tara and myself. And you need to know that that's really all they are. Rumors." He bent his torso down to his knees, then raised his legs. His body was indeed remarkably limber.

"It's true, the last time I saw Tara we weren't all that chummy. I might've even said something in the heat of the moment. 'I'll kill you,' or what have you. But you know how it goes. We all say things like that all the time."

"What were you so mad about?" I asked. "The lawsuit?" I made it sound like it was common knowledge that Tara threatened to sue him. Whether it was over *Don't Leave Me This Way* or *Do That To Me One More Time*—or both—I could only now hope to find out. Tru grimaced as he held his legs in midair. "Lawsuits! They roll off your back. They're like parking tickets."

"Then what made you so angry?" I inquired.

"Blackmail, of course. And after all we'd been through together. After I *discovered* her."

"Blackmail?" I asked, trying to sound incredulous. "What could there be to blackmail *you* over?"

"She threatened to do damage to the reputation of a star I have under contract. That's all I'm going to say about it, Rick. The point is, I hope you can see why I would've been upset."

"Sure, Tru. I can see that."

"I'll tell you one good thing to come out of all this. At least she's not breathing down my neck anymore." He stretched and yawned, apparently finished with his exercises. "But I didn't kill her, of course."

"Of course," Terry and I agreed.

"The star in trouble was Bob Raflowitz, wasn't it?" I inquired, of course remembering what Terry said about Bob having filed a police report.

Tru stood up, shaking. "Damn you, Rick. If you say one word to anyone—"

"Easy, Tru. I'm just doing my job. Plus trying to keep myself from death row. It's *business*, that's all."

"I would've thought that after all these years, I was your *friend* Rick."

"Oh, you are, you are," I assured him. "But think about it, Tru. Could you honestly say you wouldn't have gone digging around in my predicament?"

Through trial and error, I'd learned that appealing to Tru's sense of fair play was often effective when he required the kid-glove treatment.

"You're right, Rick. But imagine when you have this actor under contract who's like this role model for Mr. Nice Guy, and you're even going to star him as a priest in *Joy to the World*, and this frigid-ass actress tells you that she knows about the porn movie."

Terry and I kept our cool.

"That must've been a shock," I commiserated. Then, going out on a limb: "I guess Bob was pretty hungry way back when to go the X-rated route."

Tru shook his head sadly. "So it would seem. Personally, I see nothing wrong with it. I *adore* porn. And lots of straight guys indulge in a little GFP when they're first starting out. I've always found it a real turn-on."

"GFP?" Terry pondered.

I nudged him in a "silly rabbit" sort of way. "Oh, Terry, you're always teasing. 'Gay for pay,' of course."

"Jesus," Terry muttered, "isn't anyone in this town—"

"What did Bob say about all this?"

"He denied being in the movie. He says he's antiporn." Tru reached for a remote, aiming it at the wall. From seemingly out of nowhere, a wardrobe of clothes opened before us. He padded over to hangers and drawers, and began getting dressed—sort of.

"I always figured it was just wishful thinking," he shared, slipping on a black leather harness and matching jockstrap. "To see that incredible bod putting out to another man. Talk about *hot*. But rumor or not, I can't sell him to the public as a kindly priest if everyone thinks he starred in something called *Beat Me, Daddy, Eight to the Balls*."

"Have you ever seen the movie, Tru?"

He laced up one of his tall black Harley boots. "Nope. Lord knows I've tried to find a copy. Maybe it doesn't even exist." He looked at me with threat in his eyes. "Have *you* ever seen it, Rick?"

"Can't say that I have." As casually as possible, I added: "Were you backstage much during the Oscars?"

"Numerous times, as a matter of fact." He laced up the other boot. "*Butterfly Kisses* won a lot of categories. I like to personally shake hands with winners from my pictures."

"And you wouldn't by chance know anything about a missing Oscar?" I figured it was worth a try.

"That was in the papers," Tru replied impatiently, sticking a cat-o'-nine-tails in his jockstrap. "Tara's Oscar is missing. Surely you already knew that."

Tru inspected his image in the full-length mirror. "Well, gentlemen. I trust that all that we've shared will be treated with the utmost discretion. I would hate to—well, you know."

"We know," I quickly responded. "You don't have to worry, Tru. It's a *given* that you're innocent. And thanks for donating so generously to the Save Rick Domino Foundation."

Tru laughed. 'Say, how'd you guys like a little peak into the party? *You* can't go in for obvious reasons, Rick. Although if Terry gets off-duty soon, perhaps he'd enjoy it? Bear types are very 'in,' you know."

"Let's just take a quick look," I suggested.

I wasn't just being polite. I wanted to see if Cinda or Jeep was there.

"Good!" Tru enthused. "I'll point out to you my newest girlfriend and boyfriend. I am *so* in love with them both, I can scarcely think of anything else. I feel like I don't even want to *look* at another man or woman ever again, that's how fulfilled I am."

Terry followed uncertainly behind as Tru pressed another button on the remote, and a wall panel began to slowly, almost imperceptibly slide open.

"Terry, get over here!" Tru scolded. "Don't be shy, I want you to see."

Through a crack of maybe three inches, we looked down into a veritable snake pit of omnisexual pleasure.

Oversized vases and pretentious wall frescoes did little to detract from the orgiastic scene before us in what can only be described as a ballroom. There were girls with girls, boys with boys, and boys and girls together. "Look," Tru pointed, "There they are. My new loves. Over in the Jacuzzi." And indeed, we saw an unclothed male and female enjoying more than mere jet sprays of water. "I love to watch them together, and then have them do me," Tru confided.

"Guess they're the bread, and you're the bacon, lettuce, and tomato."

Tru was too swept up watching to pay attention to what I said, though Terry gave a nervous chuckle.

Off in one corner, wearing his business shoes and socks and extra-large white cotton briefs, was my old pal Chauncey Riggs. He reached into one of his socks and presented a wad of cash to a young man who obviously wasn't but who probably tried to pass himself off as Freddie Prinze, Jr.

There were naked people and near-naked people in leather and latex. People chained to the wall, led on dog collars, handcuffed, tickled, Saran-wrapped, whipped, and practically everything but fricasséed. Pills were popped, powders snorted, liquids imbibed and injected. Buxom youths of five or six different sexes writhed from high cages, doing all kinds of swell tricks with rubber fire hydrants and real boa constrictors. A banquet table of food provided more bacchanalian fun and games as cream pastries were smeared on bodies to be licked off.

As my eyes grew accustomed to the wonders before them, I began to discern order in the anarchy. It was as if, like kids figuring out where to sit in the school cafeteria, certain activities were always held in certain areas of the massive room. I looked at what I came to think of as Bootlick Boulevard, and then glanced my eyes over to Rimming Road, and then a quick stop at Fellatio Falls.

In fact, I felt like I saw just about everything possible there was to see—except Cinda Sharpe and Jeep Andrews.

Terry nudged me. "Look over there." He pointed toward a far corner.

In a cage, dancing by himself, naked but for his military boots and a veritable rainbow of sex-code bandanas decorating each forearm, was none other than our own Brother Dennis. (Or at least I assumed it was Brother Dennis, and not the actual Shane.)

"Shane—I didn't expect him," commented Tru. "What a delightful surprise."

"How about that," I noted.

Even people in showbiz who knew Shane was gay didn't necessarily know anything about my relationship with him. It was but one of many things that made me so utterly joyful when I thought about all we meant to each other.

"Obviously he's not all that broken up over losing Tara," Tru noted sardonically. "Talk about a joke. But you know—maybe it's just my imagination, but his body isn't quite so buff anymore. Not a *bad* hunk of meat, but he looks like he might be going to seed." Tru opened the sliding wall wide enough to step out into the ballroom. "I'll have to lecture him about too much high living. He needs to do better than that if he wants to work for me."

Terry and I discretely lunged out of view as Tru entered the room, stepping down into the music and wild sex. As the door slid closed, we saw him walking over to Brother Dennis.

20

"Trust me, you wouldn't have liked the rest of the house, anyway."

I was walking along the nighttime Malibu shore with Terry. After we left Tru's, Terry said he needed a few minutes to think, and I figured I'd give it to him. I could see how he would've been bent out of shape by some of the more unfamiliar aspects of the visit. And while I didn't exactly have time on my hands, I needed Terry to be as functional as possible over the next couple of days. If he needed a moment to regroup, so be it.

It was peaceful surf, and Terry seemed to find it therapeutic. He was sadder and more thoughtful than I'd seen him before. The cold water ebbed and flowed around our ankles as we walked along the soft, wet sands. Terry's mighty ankles and feet were as hairy as the rest of his body presumably was. In a way, he reminded me of a fuzzy hobbit—only bigger, of course.

"Really, Terry. It's the truth. Tru's home is just room after room of nasty-looking kitsch. It's like a bordello version of a Fingerhut catalog."

He smiled, pausing to study a dead starfish on the sand. He

turned it over with his foot. "I don't know what you mean, Rick. But I appreciate that you're trying to cheer me up."

"It must've been hard for you to see all of that. Or *not* hard, if you know what I mean." I nudged him or so. "So—any thoughts about the porn movie? Personally, I doubt that Bob would've ever done something like that. Still, someone was blackmailing him about something."

When Terry didn't respond, I asked, "Was it seeing Brother Dennis that way?"

"Nothing necessarily happened," Terry answered. "All we saw was Truman Shea walking toward him."

"You're right," I agreed. "Maybe Tru is showing him how to do sit-ups."

Terry squatted down, absently toying with the starfish. "Darla Sue isn't coming back in three weeks." He looked at me with wounded eyes. "She left me."

"Terry, I had no idea. When did this happen?"

"Monday night, when I got off duty. I've been lying to myself. Pretending that it didn't happen. But it did. See, that's one of the reasons why I got involved in all this in the first place. I needed something different. To keep from going crazy."

"You must miss her a lot."

He stood up and looked out at the moon on the sea. "Not really."

"Look, I know you're a big tough guy and all, but it's okay to be unhappy once in awhile. You don't always have to be so macho."

He turned to me and smiled. "You mean like you, Rick? You act big and tough, too. Like nothing can ever hurt you."

"I know. But sometimes even I let it all hang out. Witness my bedside histrionics. And you, Terry, were right there for me."

"Thanks. I appreciate what you're trying to do. But you really don't understand. Darla Sue and I have never had much of a marriage. We got hitched because she was pregnant. We were never really in love. The baby might've brought us together, but she lost it. We've been sort of a bad habit posing as a marriage. I bring home the bacon. She keeps an all right house. We *do* make each other laugh. She can be a lot fun, after a lousy day on the beat. You'd *like* her, Rick. But it was never love. We never even told ourselves it was.

"I'm not sad the marriage ended—in a way, it never began. It's more that everything safe and familiar's ended. That I just spent twelve years dreading that I'd realize one day my life wasn't about very much, and now that's exactly what I am facing."

For a moment, we listened to the crashing waves.

"Gee, Terry, maybe you and Darla Sue can, you know, kind of patch things up or something. See a marriage counselor."

"She left me for another man, Rick." He started walking again. "You're the first person I've told this to. Actually, that's not right—she left because another man finally came along who can give her all the passion and romance she deserves. Darla Sue wants to be a country-and-western singer. And this guy, Bobby Earl Sykes, believes in her. He wants to be her manager, her husband—the whole enchilada. They've started driving around in his car, trying to get gigs along the coast. Sort of like—what'shername—Loretta Lynn and the guy who was in *The Fugitive*."

"Tommy Lee Jones."

"Yeah, whatever. Anyway, it wasn't that I was all that freaked out by Truman Shea's party. Some of it kind of looked like fun."

"Oh really?" I teased. "What is it about you straight men and lesbianism? What's the big turn on?"

"Never mind." Even in the moonlight I could tell he was blushing. "Seriously, though. What bugged me I guess was the way that Truman just seems to . . . I don't know. It's like he has no idea about all the loneliness there is in the world. I was thinking how everyone at that orgy thing couldn't possibly be very happy—not happy in a real way—but then I started thinking, well, who the fuck *is* happy? And I thought about how I could never be relaxed about sex the way these people were, but how I'd never *want* to be that relaxed about it. I'd never want to get to where sex has nothing to do with how I feel, but how I *hated* the way it made me feel . . . I don't know. I'm not making any sense."

I spotted an interesting shell. "Actually, I think I understand. I still get confused sometimes about what I want from sex and intimacy and all that nonsense. I thought I loved Shane, but now I'm doubting that I ever did. Not just that I don't love him anymore. It's this 'What was I thinking?' kind of feeling." The shell was chipped, so I tossed it aside. "So I've been wasting a lot of time myself."

Terry sat on a driftwood log. "Do you have family, Rick?"

I was taken aback by the question. No one I knew ever talked about anything so irrelevant as family. In TV interviews, sure. But not in private. Family was something you left behind someplace long ago, like your real name or birth nose.

"Gee, I *guess* I do. They're back in Iowa."

"Was it a large family?"

"My mom and dad. Two brothers. I was the oldest." I thought about sitting down next to him, but decided not to.

"What do your brothers do?"

"I dunno. Stuff. They're in *Iowa*." He just wasn't getting the point.

"I would've given anything to have brothers. I was an only child."

"You're welcome to mine." I kicked some sand around.

"Did they give you a bad time about being gay?"

"Let's not go there, okay? It's old. It's boring. I've made my peace with them. Big fucking deal."

"You don't sound too peaceful about it."

"As much as I'm likely to be." I accidentally kicked some sand in his face.

"Hey, *watch* it."

"Sorry."

He brushed the sand from his shoulders. "What about your parents?"

"What about them? They're alive. They sit around. They're *parents*."

Terry stood up and laughed. "I wish I could be more like you. I always take everything so seriously. My dad died when I was twelve, and I had to look after my mom. She hated that I became a cop, but it was something I just had to do. She and Darla Sue are like oil and water. Not a kind word to say about each other in twelve years."

"Doesn't sound like too much fun."

Terry picked up a stone and threw it out to sea. "You learn to live with it."

He touched my shoulder. "Thanks, Rick."

A honking sound was coming from behind. Before I could respond to Terry, we both turned to look.

A white Explorer pulled up, its brakes screeching as it came to dead halt. I recognized the sandy, windblown hair of Cinda Sharpe.

"I never do this. It's *so* illegal. But I needed to find you, Rick."

"Why, Cinda?" I tried to sound surprised that such would be the case.

"Because everyone is full of shit is why. *Get in.*"

21

$\mathcal{I}$n press interviews, Cinda Sharpe came across as warm and direct, but in real life she was doggedly enigmatic. Despite her alleged urgent need to talk to me, she revealed begging little as she sped across the beach to the coast highway.

"Who've you been talking to?" she asked challengingly, as though daring me to give an acceptable answer.

"Francine, Tru, Bob. Cleo, just a little." I made a point of not mentioning Zeke, or anything about Shane/Brother Dennis.

"Well, that figures. The only one of them who's worth listening to is Bob. And Cleo, if you can get past all of her love-peace-flowers BS."

From the determined way she shifted gears, her cowgirl-booted foot flooring the gas, I wondered if she wasn't going to drive us off a cliff or something.

"I think you should slow down," Terry offered, trying not to sound too much like a cop.

"And I think you should shut up. Who is this guy, anyway, Rick?" She crossed the double-yellow line to cut in front of a truck whose driver had the audacity to only be going about 70 MPH.

"My bodyguard, Terry Zane."

She turned to give him the "gimme five" with her hand. "Cinda," she cordially offered, giving no indication of having insulted him a second earlier.

Her right hand, I noticed, had a Band-Aid across the palm. "Stunt work," Cinda explained, when I asked her about it. "I do my own whenever possible."

"Do you jump out of windows and things?" Terry eagerly asked.

Cinda laughed. "Not *so* far. My movies are a little too 'human interest' for all that." She grabbed the stick shift; when it stuck in gear for a second, she swore under her breath. "If you're Rick's bodyguard, I assume you're cool."

"As an Eskimo Pie," I assured her.

"You guys diddlin' around?" She looked perturbedly out her rearview mirror, like she thought she might be followed.

"Hardly. Terry plays for that other team you might have heard about. Apparently, it has to do with a man inserting something into a woman, though I can't imagine what it would be."

I wondered if this would get Terry's goat, but he laughed good-naturedly.

"Cool," she affirmed, giving Terry her crinkle-eyed, engaging smile. Cinda got along famously with straight guys, the more conventionally masculine the better. (By contrast, she seemed to regard gay men as things to be eaten off the end of a toothpick.)

"Been doing security gigs a long time?"

"Pretty long," Terry obfuscated. "It pays the bills."

"Rick, I need you to tell me everything that Francine and Truman said to you." She rounded a hairpin turn in third gear.

"It's a deal, if you promise not to kill us."

She honked at a minivan driver who gave her the finger. "Relax, guys. I'm a great driver. If I weren't an actor, I'd race professionally."

"Then save your stunts for the racetrack," Terry admonished.

But at that moment, we abruptly pulled into a driveway, and stopped.

"I'm sorry, Terry, for changing the subject before. That was rude."

Cinda's digs were a little farther south toward Santa Monica. She lived year-round in what had once been a lighthouse, and which offered a luxuriant view of the ocean from its circular deck. That a lesbian lived in so phallic a home made for a few bad-taste jokes about penis envy that Cinda was a good sport about. "How can lesbianism be caused by penis envy?" she'd mock-rhetorically pose. "I *have* a penis, and it's a hundred feet long."

But such musings about lesbianism were limited to private discussions.

Not that there weren't rumors galore about her sexuality. There were women who all but creamed in their pants over the impish Cinda. On screen, she came across as girl-next-door wholesome— i.e., not very sexy to men, and historically such actresses have often been fodder for underground rumors as to their propensity for all things Gertrude. But Cinda came of age when the underground was not quite so under-, and the supermarket tabloids regularly sullied her well-scrubbed image with baseless and not-so-baseless rumors of her close encounters with la femme.

Thus, admired as she was for the forthright women she played, she'd also suffered her share of flack from the gay world. Euphemisms about her "independent spirit" wore thin, as did her tenacious refusal to answer questions about her personal life, as though it were a matter of principle. ("My only responsibility to the public is as an actor," etc.) Despite her supposed dedication to parts that "tell the truth first, and make money only as an afterthought," Cinda scrupulously avoided playing lesbians.

But the gay media was running out of patience fast. As I gleefully reported on TV with deadpan face, Cinda recently suffered negative publicity when gay activists protested her being honored for her AIDS work. The picket signs said things like: "Stick that prize in your closet, bitch!" and "Cinda Sharpe, Chickenshit of the Year."

Of course, the problem wasn't just that her on-screen image wasn't very sexy (for nonlesbians, anyway), and thus caused gossip, but that it translated into a decided lack of box-office clout. Cinda's camera karma was sadly mixed—the lens only kinda sorta liked her. Quite striking in person, ash blonde with vivid complexion and rich hazel eyes, on screen she looked merely so-so. Even after she won a much-deserved Oscar for playing a courageous Vietnam Army nurse in *Ruby Tuesday*, she failed to crack the box-office Top 25.

The upshot was that Cinda got big-budget work only if there were other stars to guarantee profit, and in a sour-grapes way she claimed to prefer indies with so-called important messages. (Though no doubt it was becoming increasingly difficult to find an indie script without any lesbian scenes.) She also was wont to decree that she enjoyed not having to worry about getting mobbed by fans when seen in public. "I would *hate* to be Tara Perez," she waxed philosophically to more than one reporter. "I wouldn't want to be inside her shoes for a minute." Though presumably Cinda could have withstood being inside something else of Tara's—and for considerably longer duration than a minute.

What made her Goody Two-shoes image all the more dubious was the not-so-secret fact that Cinda's sexual appetite ran toward exotic cuisine. I genuinely was surprised not to find her at Tru's orgy—if not leading it from a bell tower, amidst vampire bats and lightning bolts. When she wasn't linking arms at singalong rallies protesting lab animals or nuclear holocaust or whatever, Cinda was known to be one spunky little Kitten with a Whip. Leather was so much a part of her, claimed an underground joke, that she'd been declared a sacred cow in India.

Supposedly, Cinda remained single by choice. True, she certainly thought nothing of stringing along three or four women at a time—and not just figuratively speaking.

But many insiders assumed she was too busy pining away for Tara to ever commit to another woman.

In the meantime, Cinda drowned her sorrows in her shrewd investments. She made more money trading online between takes than she did acting before the camera. Her Wall Street savvy didn't jive with her ultraliberal image as Little Miss Save-the-Whales, but like most successful people, she didn't let her contradictions stop her. Her famous lighthouse was done up in a manner that reflected her mix-and-match approach to life: Tiffany glass beside worthless wood carvings from feminist music festivals. Featured on one wall was a paper pop-out from a children's book depicting a circus—alongside a signed Chagall lithograph. In a casual, whimsical touch, her dining table had mismatched chairs—but the value of each antique chair could've fed a family of six for a lifetime. Her rationale for installing a not-so-energy-efficient elevator into the tower was that it made it wheelchair accessible.

Still, since I never claimed to be Mr. Politically Correct, I had to say I didn't mind taking the elevator to the lighthouse deck. The only stairs I like come with a speed meter and an endorsement from Suzanne Sommers. And say what you wanted about Cinda, she had cushy outdoor furniture for us to sink into, with a tall pitcher of freshly made gin-and-tonics, festive with slices of those newfangled things that are half-lemon, half-lime. The potion, like the panoramic ocean view, was stupendous. Moreover, Cinda, whose moods disconcertingly fluctuated between self-righteous anger and palsy-walsy giggles, got all chummy as she served the lemonade, and told me how she just *knew* things were going to go well for me. Her fuzzy blue sweater made little gossamer flickers in the wind.

If I wasn't on trial for murder, I would've enjoyed myself.

But I was getting a little tired of everyone offering their fake showbiz sympathy, especially when the person cheering me up was so blatantly hiding something. That was Hollywood in a nutshell: a town where people *sort of* helped you while *sort of* tripping you up, smiling and blowing kisses all the way.

"Here's to friendship." She jovially offered, leaning against the railing, facing us, as she held up her tall glass.

"Hey, all right," Terry agreed. I got the impression that His Heteroness was predictably enough enjoying the company of a lesbian. Seldom had Terry seemed so relaxed as when he stretched out with his hands behind his head on the comfy outdoor lounge and looked out at the cinematic night sky and sea. I figured that's what straight guys liked so much about lesbians: for once they didn't have to prove what "men" they were, and could just relax.

"I know how important Rick's friends are to him," Terry couldn't resist adding. I could tell he was being a smartass, which wasn't like him at all.

"So what did Francine have to say?" Cinda interrogated, suddenly all business.

I thought about it. "Stuff," I finally answered.

"I can just imagine," she replied, as though we were on the same wavelength and I hadn't just tried to be defiantly sarcastic. "The poor old thing hasn't been able to walk in a straight line for decades. Believe me, I worked with her in *Papa Don't Preach*. It was before her quasi-comeback, so granted, her part stank to high heaven—she was this the-doctor-will-see-you-now receptionist—but would you believe it took something like eighty-seven million takes for her to get it right? She kept saying she was seeing things, like she had her decrepit little poodle in her lap when the fucking creature was at home sipping vodka. The old biddy hasn't a clue. She says anything that her bottle tells her to say."

"So then Zeke isn't going away to some fancy eastern prep school?" Terry shrewdly asked.

"Prep school?"

"That's what Miss Quick told us," Terry related. "She said he'd gotten some teenaged girl pregnant, so Bob and Cleo were sending him back east to get away from it all."

"Well, then, she got her facts only slightly garbled for once. The *girl* isn't pregnant, Lord help us all. She's—well, out of the picture for good. Connee Kellog, bless her soul-less soul. Bob nearly had a fit when he found out about her. I tell you, it was a blessing for all concerned when she kicked the bucket. Starting with poor Connee herself. The school for Zeke's on the west coast. But that's the general idea."

"No doubt," I agreed.

"And if by chance you talk to Zeke, ignore anything he says. The kid has a wild imagination, to say the least."

"Thanks, Cinda. I'll remember that."

"Hey, no sweat, Rick. We all have to help each other to survive, right?"

"Just out of curiosity," I began, "what's it all to you?"

"Bob's my friend. He's a great guy who doesn't fight dirty, so I'm willing to fight dirty for him. He and Cleo have enough to worry about." She broke into a sob; tears were welling in her eyes. "And then of course Tara. If Francine spread *any* poison about her, I'll crush that bitch's skull with *one hand.*" Good actress that she was, Cinda did a breathtakingly credible pantomime of said action. You could all but visualize Francine's brain matter oozing between Cinda's fingers.

"You make a helluva good drink," Terry commented, helping himself to the pitcher. He saluted her with his glass.

"Thanks." Cinda smiled. "I tended bar for years when I was a starving artiste in New York." She took a swallow of gin-and-tonic as if taking a vow. "And as for that pig of pigs, Truman Shea—he better just shut up if he knows what's good for him. He has no right to even say Tara's name after what he did."

"Actually, Tru had surprisingly little to say to us about Tara," I conveyed. "Her name barely came up."

"Mr. Shea talked business," Terry confirmed. "He wanted to feel out buying the rights to Rick's life story—is it okay that I said that, Rick?"

Cinda stared ruefully at her glass. "Figures. Mr. Moneybags. Mr. Step-on-Everyone-and-Everything-to-Make-a-Buck. You know, Tara never got over what he did to her. People said she was the ruthless, ambitious one, which was so unfair. She was a baby when they got together, and she thought he was her Prince Charming. It wasn't that he turned out to be gay or bi or whatever the fuck he turned out to be. But he'd shove it in her face. I mean literally. He'd force her to watch while he'd be going down on some man or woman or whatever. Especially given the terrible time she had as a child—can you imagine how that just make might someone a little more hard on the outside, a little less willing to trust?"

It looked like Cinda was starting to cry hard, but then I realized she was laughing.

"Tara was so much fun," she shared. "We knew each other *forever.* From the time she first came to Hollywood. We had the same acting coach, Billy What'shisname. The rest of us kept saying how we wanted to achieve truth about human nature and blahbidy-blah-blah-blah. Not Tara. She'd say, 'I'm here to win an Oscar, baby.'

It got to be a big joke. She'd do a scene and Billy would say, 'The envelope, please,' when Tara was good. And damn, even back then, she could be so very, very good. I liked that about her, though. Nothing about Tara was false."

"It must have been quite a moment for her," I commented. "To win after all those years."

"You're fucking right it was. It drove me nuts when I saw Tara huddled up in a corner backstage, more upset than I'd ever seen her. It should've been the happiest night of her life. Shane was trying to comfort her—not that he could do much good. I was trying to get her to tell me what was wrong, but next thing I knew, I had to present Best Actor. When I came back, Tara was . . . gone. And, in his way, so was Shane." She studied me intently. "By the way, how *are* things with Shane? Have you been seeing him since all this started?"

I couldn't change the subject fast enough. "Did you see Tara talking with Connee Kellogg backstage? Or with Bob?"

"Bob told me that Tara talked with some blonde he didn't know. Why *should* he have known Connee Kellogg? She was lucky to have someone like Bob even breathe the same air."

"What about Bob—did he tell you that he said anything to Tara?"

"He said *nothing* to her," Cinda replied evenly. "Nothing besides congratulations."

"That's weird about the missing Oscar, isn't it," Terry commented. "What do you suppose happened to it?"

"Truman Shea is probably sitting on it as we speak."

"Rumor has it that a leading actor once made a gay porn movie," I offered.

Cinda was unimpressed. "The really interesting rumor would be that there was a leading actor *who hadn't* done gay porn. Serious actors—the ones who make it—don't want something like that to come back and bite them on the ass. I'd be very surprised if this rumor were true."

"What if it was about Bob?"

She tossed down her drink like medicine. "Then I'd say it was an even bigger crock of shit than I already thought it was."

I decided to go for broke: "I don't pretend to understand your unwavering loyalty to Bob. But I do know you were in love with Tara. You'd say anything to protect her."

"Tara and I were friends, dammit. Men turn everything into porn. But women can just hang out together, without it meaning anything. We don't have that male competition thing happening. Us women *like* each other. Now, I can't say I'd have kicked Tara out of bed for eating crackers. But it would've needed to be *consensual*. I would never for a moment even consider forcing myself—"

Someone was ringing the front door.

"Shit," Cinda commented, running inside to see who was there. "Just when I was getting to the good part."

Terry laughed. "She's got a good sense of humor."

"At times," I agreed.

Jeep Andrews stepped out of the elevator. His face was flustered as he angrily shook his fist at Cinda—who slapped him across the face in response.

Through the thick glass, we couldn't hear what they were saying to each other. But I felt confident in assuming it wasn't a difference of opinion concerning a recipe for guacamole.

I'll say this: they both made histrionics enough for a whole row of Oscars. Jeep pounded his fist on a table, and with mad eyes ran his fingers through his hair. Cinda winced and covered her ears, refusing to listen; then she pointed toward the elevator for him to leave.

"Sorry, fellas." Cinda distractedly slid the glass door shut, and made a face. "Someone is on the rag." She sighed, sipping her fresh drink to calm herself.

"Tara came over here almost every night leading up to the Oscars," she stated firmly. "And *no*, nothing happened. For someone who supposedly was always putting out, I must say it's funny that Tara spent most nights alone in her Bullwinkle bedroom slippers with a good book. But you see, I knew the *real* Tara. Rumor had it she was finally going to win Best Actress, and she just about drove me nuts with all her insecurities. We'd come out here to relax, stretched out just like you guys, and Tara would say, 'I know I'm not going to win, anyway, so why should I bother going?' Then the next minute she'd say, 'What if I wear the wrong dress?' Then she'd get angry that she didn't win the last time she was nominated. 'I deserved to win for *Kiss from a Rose*,' she'd tell me. 'Even if I win now, it's going to feel like a consolation prize.'

"So here you have that big, manipulative, oh-so-sure-of-herself total bitch that some people claim to have known so much about. Tara was *bewildered* by her good fortune. She took things as they came to her. Any story about her trying to steal a part or fuck for a part or fuck someone else out of a part if a total bunch of shit. I frankly don't even know that she *had* many sex partners. After Tru broke her heart, she lived for nothing but her career."

"So you admit that Saint Tara was just a teensy bit ambitious?" I queried.

"No one ever complains when a man wants a career," she lectured. "I can't believe it—the same old story after all these years. A woman wants more out of life than loading up the dishwasher, and everyone makes her out to be such despicable scum that she deserves to get brutally murdered. Sure, Tara made no apologies about wanting to be somebody. But that doesn't mean she still wasn't the sweetest, the dearest, the most fragile and delicate—"

Cinda stopped herself. "Let me show you guys something." Instructing us not to get out of our lounge chairs, she wheeled us around to face the glass doors. Then she stepped inside and opened a cabinet, revealing a wide-screen digital TV. She inserted a DVD. She scurried back out over to us, leaving the glass doors open.

"This used to be our favorite way of watching TV together," she explained.

"Meaning you and Tara?" I asked.

Cinda's cheeks flustered. "Yes, of course." She hit a button on the remote. A nondescript title announced: "*With or Without You.* Bedroom Remorse Scene."

"Our unfinished movie together," Cinda explained, with a mixture of pride and sorrow. "There's talk of recasting someone else in the other female lead. I'd rather see the project shut down. The role is just so much Tara's, no one else could play it."

A chalked slate gave way to what was obviously meant to be the bedroom of a rich, pampered girl. A voice yelled, "Action," and Cinda, lying on her stomach fully clothed atop a flowered bedspread, burst into tears. Her hair was in a bouncy flip, and she wore a simple good-girl type of dress with a Peter Pan collar. Tara entered, wearing glasses and a nurse's uniform, her hair in a tight bun. She looked appropriately concerned over Cinda's well-being.

The more predictable casting would've been for Cinda to play the good nurse, and for Tara to play the spoiled, troubled heroine on the brink of sexual discovery. But supposedly both actresses resented the typecasting, and actually made a screen test on their own time to prove to Truman Shea that they should switch parts. Maybe it really happened that way; maybe it was just a publicity stunt. But I also found it telling that the nurse was supposed to be a bit AC/DC. It certainly was an astonishing coincidence that Cinda did not want to play such a part.

Tara tentatively sat on the edge of Cinda's bed. She started to stroke her back, then thought the better of it.

"I'm not going to do it this time," pronounced Nurse Tara. "You act like Alice in Wonderland. A dreamy-eyed little girl, sleepwalking through a world where nothing makes sense—nothing but you and your greed. It's no wonder no one can trust anything you say. There's always some hidden meaning, some special little secret that the rest of us just aren't special enough to hear. Well, I have news for you, Missy. You're just a user. You're like a junkie, shooting up on people. You think that Brad is the bad guy—that he used you and lied to you. Well okay, he did. But Clarissa—you did the same thing, don't you see? You've got claws like the rest of us. You're just not honest enough to admit it."

Cinda/Clarissa turned to face Nurse Tara, her face one big red fire engine of tears. "Y-you think you u-understand me, but you d-don't." Her chin quavered. "All I've ever w-wanted was to be l-l-loved."

Nurse Tara wanted no part of this Pity Party. She grabbed the spoiled brat by the shoulders and shook her. As Tara did so, her tight bun began to unravel, and a delicious wisp of hair fell to her shoulder. "You think you're the only one in this world with a broken heart?" Tara posed rhetorically, yet with a smoldering undercurrent.

"Don't you know how I feel? Day and night, watching as you dust your golden skin with expensive French powder. The clean line of your back when you're bathing, soaping up your firm breasts, the water dripping down your nipples like Venus on the half-shell." Tara took off her glasses and became utterly gorgeous. "Clarissa, awaken to love."

Clarissa decided she'd pass, thanks all the same. She hissed through clenched teeth: "Get out!" Then, like a total schizo, she put her hands to her mouth in horror. "Oh *nurse*," she whimpered softly. "I am so sorry. I do love you, only not that way."

Nurse Tara held the fickle slut to her breast. "There, there," she softly murmured, her hair burying part of her face. "I love you in that other way, too."

Terry crossed his legs. I suspected this sojourn to Lesbo Heaven was making him hard.

Suddenly Tara burst out laughing. Cinda looked hurt and puzzled, but then she laughed, too.

"How was that?" Tara called out to the unseen director. She crinkled her nose at Cinda and gave her a friendly little punch on the arm. Cinda gave her a friendly little punch back.

The lispy-voiced director answered back, "You don't seem surprised enough, Cinda. Remember, you love *Brad*. Brad is this thing called a *man*. *I* should be playing your part."

Both women laughed, clapping their hands together in delight. Cinda quipped, "Maybe if there was a man on the set, it would inspire me."

The director indignantly cried, "You bitch!" Tara slumped over on the bed, exhausted with laughter.

A title flashed: "End of Scene."

Cinda hit the backwards button, freezing a frame of Tara and herself clowning around. "You see? Here you have the real Tara."

I felt like I wasn't getting anywhere. I decided to try a different approach.

"I almost hate to bring it up, Cinda," I began carefully. "But I've heard some rumors. That Tara tried to cajole you into a three-way with Tru to get the lead in *Don't Leave Me This Way*. That she said that if you really loved her, you'd back off from the part. Then she gave you a letter at the Oscars, telling you to bug off. Perhaps because you weren't cooperating. But maybe because she was just plain sick of you."

Cinda stared at me like a preying mantis. "Tara and I had an understanding. You saw for yourself, she was completely relaxed about lesbianism."

"Yes or no: Did she give you that letter?"

She smiled ruefully. "No."

I decided not to argue with her. "So, Cinda. Any future career plans?"

She laughed. "Still on the job, I see. If you must know, Rick, I've signed to play the lead in *Don't Leave Me This Way*. Tru wanted me for the part in the first place, but the pressure was on for him to consider Tara, since she was—well, you know—considered sexier. It was pure vindictiveness on Tru's part to say she was too old for the lead. Tara was the same age as me, and if anything looked younger. She was absolutely justified in taking legal action against Tru. But, anyway, now the part is mine for certain."

"That's certainly convenient."

"Rick, that was exceptionally low. I expect better from you. By the way, what did you guys think of the movie?"

"Interesting," I tactfully replied.

"I loved it," Terry announced. "It was so . . . so real."

She stood on tiptoe to kiss his cheek. "You're a sweetie." His face flustered, and he smiled like he just swallowed a six-pack.

As for me, I'd have to make do with a handshake. "Good luck, Rick. I have no idea who did it, but I know it wasn't you." She said this with all the conviction of a defendant in court stating that she had the utmost respect for the person she purposefully ran over with her car.

"Just out of curiosity—would *you* ever play a lesbian, Cinda?"

"If the right script came along, without question." Seeing the look on my face, she added, "I know you must think it's terrible of me not to come out to the world. But you know how this town works. Once people knew about me, I'd only get offered lesbian parts. And I want to portray the full range of women's experiences."

The ride back to my Cherokee was anticlimactic, to say the least. Cinda had hard-rock music blaring full blast, and she bopped along to the metallic beat, tapping her fingers on the steering wheel. I don't think any of us said anything.

Once or twice, I thought I saw a car following us from a discreet distance. The driver seemed to be playing "Follow the Leader" with Cinda, and would swerve and cross as she did.

I was not all that surprised when, just as Cinda drove off, Jeep Andrews pulled up beside a windswept Monterey cypress.

On screen, Jeep was a hunk and a half, but he looked at least as good in person. He was so handsome a vision he almost seemed unreal, like some comic book hero come to life. With his khaki shirt and pants setting off his blond hair, perfect tan, perfect teeth, and blue-green eyes, he could've just come back from a top secret military mission, or dangerous safari.

There was nothing effeminate about Jeep. Yet I couldn't help thinking that Terry must've been disconcerted when the first thing this walking and breathing action figure did was kiss me lightly on the lips and proclaim, in his husky bass-baritone, "Rick, *darling.*"

Terry, I figured, had to be dying a thousand deaths. But he put on a brave face and offered his hand—probably to insure that Jeep did not get too democratic with his kisses.

"Terry Zane. Rick's bodyguard."

"Don't get any ideas, Jeep," I merrily joked. "He's straight."

"Oh, one of those." Jeep rolled his eyes debonairly. "Only fooling. Hi, call me Jeep."

Despite the reality of who Jeep was, Terry still seemed honored to meet his fantasy macho hero. "I've really enjoyed your movies, Jeep. It is truly an honor to meet you."

Terry was so sincere, I almost felt sorry for him.

"Oh c'mon," Jeep answered. "You're embarrassing me."

"That'll be the day," I observed.

"Very cute, Rick. Now, how'd you guys like to follow me to my beach house for a night cap? I have a strange story to share, unlike any other you've heard. It's called The Truth."

22

"Never believe anything Cinda says," Jeep advised, sitting in an overstuffed tan leather chair in his beachfront living room, nursing a double shot of Jack Daniels. Jeep was one of those gay men who always sat in a single chair at parties, or slept in the one single bed on weekend ski trips. You always wondered if he did this intentionally or if it was an unconscious reflex.

Otherwise, Jeep's home was a welcoming place. The rugged leather furniture featured thickly padded armrests and hassocks. Prominently mounted on the log cabin walls were the numerous large sea bass he'd caught. But there were no mammal heads; Jeep fished but didn't hunt. The fireplace was made from no-frills rocks, such as you would find lying on the ground. On the mantle were pictures of himself shaking hands with the last few U.S. presidents. The coffee table was a sanded piece of slate mounted on unfinished boulders. Authentic Native American blankets were hung on the walls as art. His ocean-view deck was under tarps, as Jeep was building a new grill brick by brick.

The closest thing to fey in the room was his famous collection of antique pocket watches, the glass case that protected them taking up a corner wall. Also featured under glass was a large fossil of a delicately detailed prehistoric fern. He did not own any paintings or sculpture.

Terry and I sat on the matching sofa opposite Jeep. I was being semicareful by sticking to gin-and-tonic, while Terry, ever mindful of his role as designated driver, was making do with a Coke. The cocktail glasses were thick, rectangular cut glass.

"It's not just that Cinda doesn't want to be a dyke," Jeep elaborated. "It's that she doesn't want to have been in love with Tara—or should I say still be in love with her? And when someone is that out of touch with something so basic to who they are, you can't trust anything they say. She likes to act like she shoots straight from the hip. But her hip is crooked, if you follow me. Everything she says is stilted."

It was interesting to hear Jeep go on about Cinda's unrequited passion for Tara, since Jeep was whispered to harbor those exact same feelings toward Bob.

"You know she comes from old-biddy Eastern money," Jeep continued.

"What's wrong with that?" I wanted to know.

Jeep's two Great Danes—coyly named Skeet and Pete, the characters played by Jeep and Bob, respectively, in the *Detonation* series—were temporarily confined to the downstairs guest quarters, over which fate they barked their protest. Jeep thumped the knotty wood floor with his Doc Martens boot to quiet them.

"Not a damn thing's wrong with old money. Unless you try to deny it, and act like you're some no-frills, no-shit everywoman. You can tell she's a totally snooty bitch, though. Every now and then, when Cinda's feeling testy—if you'll pardon the expression—she emphasizes certain words. 'If a *man* happened to live in a lighthouse, I'm sure you'd never be making these *adolescent* remarks.' Like she's telling the maid to *please* hurry up and *vacuum*."

For a leading man who never got a crack at accents or character parts, Jeep did a commendable job capturing Cinda's manner of speech. And there was nothing campy about it—the performance was matter-of-fact, beyond the labels of gender and sexuality.

"Say, that *does* sound like her," Terry remarked. "I'm impressed."

In fairness to Cinda, Jeep had a much easier time of it, gaywise. There wasn't any pressure for him to come out, because other than some to-be-expected rumors, it wasn't "obvious" that he was gay. He even did a "special guest appearance" turn as a gay character in a suburban comedy called *Party Lights*. Jeep was this ultra-butch cop who busts up a teenaged beer bash (hence the title), whereby it was a ha-ha, what's-this-crazy-world-coming-to gimmick that this hyper-macho cop could be *gay*. A pleasantly competent star said to always "play himself," Jeep got characteristically pleasant reviews. The critics used phrases like "amiably low key" and "good sport" to describe how America's most likable action hero handled a gay role.

Jeep had the decency to not pretend to date women, unlike the ultraparanoid Shane Kirks of this world. But then again, since he was a guy, Jeep—unlike Cinda—could get away with being labeled a "private" person who either shunned premieres or attended them solo. It was all part of his brooding testosterone. The loner Marlboro Man. The Man with a Secret Past. The way Jeep carried it off, the absence of a woman on his arm made him seem all the more intensely hetero.

If there were one antigay person left on the planet, Shane Kirk still would've been afraid to come out. By contrast, Jeep talked in terms of one day meeting his Great Love, at which time—or so he claimed—he would come out proud as a peacock. "I've made more money than I know what to do with," he'd philosophize, "so sure, when I've met that one special guy, I'll let my rainbow colors fly."

Even when discussing outing himself, Jeep somehow made it sound like he was this brave but modest cowboy or air force pilot preparing for his most important mission.

Maybe it was all a bunch of you-know-what, but it still put Jeep ahead of the pack. Many gay celebs didn't even pay lip service to the idea of coming out, and instead kept trying to rationalize why it showed more integrity to stay in the closet. Cinda was a case in point—but then again, Jeep didn't know what it was like to have the tabloids telling millions he was not only gay but a glorified coward.

Since he was rich, handsome, and a nice guy, Jeep might've seemed the biggest catch since Willy the Whale. But Jeep was one of those cursed souls—be they gay or straight—who made a great friend but were utterly hapless at handling relationships. Tens of thousands of dollars spent on head-shrinking had done little to alter the clingy, whiny dope he became when dating.

When it came to falling in love, Jeep had more neuroses than all the characters in Woody Allen's movies put together. Glenn Close in *Fatal Attraction* was Miss Manners by comparison. He literally broke up with guys for calling at ten-fifteen when they said they'd call at ten, because they really didn't care if they couldn't keep a simple commitment, and so on. Fun stuff like that.

Of course, Jeep's chances of finding true love were further limited by being what you might call a One-Note Johnny in the boudoir. He was the proverbial old dog who could not be taught any new tricks, as it were. There were underground jokes aplenty about Jeep's doorbell buzzer playing *You're the Top*, and in truth he was a confirmed, fanatical, relentless bottom. Any variations to this scenario meant that you didn't love him—indeed, that the two of you hadn't even had "sex." In his movies, Jeep often made shaming, inspirational speech to the men under his command, rallying them to climb that muddy hill in the torrential rains after not eating or sleeping for days so that they could kill a few slimeballs for Uncle Sam. You couldn't help conjuring a similar mental image of Jeep waving his fist and yelling at the men leaving his bedside: "Quitters! Every last one of you."

But romancewise, the final nail in Jeep's coffin was his tortured love for Bob Raflowitz. No other man could ever truly be his. It's all fine and well to be Joan Fontaine in *Rebecca*, gothically jealous of the phantom presence of the other Mrs. DeWinter, but to play a similar role in real life would leave something to be desired.

"So what did Cinda say?" Jeep asked rhetorically. "That after finding a cure for cancer and healing invalid children with her touch, Tara would drop over for Bible study?"

"That was pretty much the gist of it," I admitted. "But in all honesty, she talked the same way about Bob."

I waited to see Jeep's reaction.

"I'm sure there was a difference," Jeep insisted. "Bob's the greatest guy in the *world*, but he'd be the first to admit he's human."

Actually, my impression of Bob suggested otherwise, but I didn't want to go there.

"Jeep, I have to ask you. Who do you think killed Tara?"

"Cinda," he replied without hesitation.

When neither Terry nor myself said anything, Jeep elaborated: "Well, Rick, for one million dollars: Who else would've been pissed off enough to kill Tara?"

"It's my general impression that the correct answer would be: the entire white-page listings in greater Los Angeles."

"Okay, so everyone hated her guts. But we're talking *murder*. And I know what I saw. I went backstage a little while before presenting Best Picture. You know, to kind of savor the moment. I've never been nominated—have never *deserved* to be, let's face it—so when they let me present a major category, I think of it as my honorary Oscar. That all the billions I make for those fuckface bastards counts for something. Anyway, it would've been just a few minutes before Tara got shot." He looked at Terry and then at me. "If the news reports were correct, that is."

"Yes, of course," I agreed. (It hadn't yet been announced to the public that it was the Oscar that killed Tara.)

"Shane was trying to calm Tara down—I'm not sure over what. I heard him tell her, plain as day, 'I want to marry you, dammit.' Those were his exact words. That engagement ring was for Tara, all right. I saw him give it to her."

Jeep tactfully paused. He knew something about my relationship with Shane.

"Of course," Jeep continued, "Shane being Shane, he had the ring in a paper bag, like he just bought it at the 7-Eleven. But I presume the stone was real."

"Yes, I've heard that Chauncey found the ring with the receipt backstage." I did my best to sound neutral about the whole thing. "But I thought that Tara was planning on running off with Zeke Raflowitz."

"Please, Rick. Tara must choose between an eighteen-year-old mental case and the hottest young actor in town—gee, who do you think she's going to pick?"

"But supposedly she made this speech to Bob, all about how she wanted to make Zeke happy."

"Are you trying to convince me or yourself?"

"That's not the point," I insisted.

"Rick, remember where we are? This is the planet Earth, and we're talking about *Tara*. She fucked people's minds even more than any other part of the human anatomy. And in her case, that's saying something."

He smiled at me with sad understanding. "When Cinda saw Shane giving Tara the engagement ring, she went ballistic. It came out in that sick, smarmy way she has of making it seem like she couldn't care less about herself, it's all about wanting to help *you*. She was all 'Oh Tara, are you sure this is what you want right now?' Or, 'Shane, are you sure you can make Tara happy?' But you could just *tell* that she was going totally berserk. Her fist was clenched so tight that you could see little drops of blood dripping down from her palm. It's like she was digging into her own flesh and not even noticing."

Terry and I quickly made eye contact. Cinda, after all, claimed she hurt her hand doing stunt work.

"Tara said, 'Cinda, don't you get it? Please, just leave me alone.' She handed her an envelope. I don't think it was for Best Actor. Well, Cinda reads this thing and burst into tears. Alas, a stage technician wanted to go over something in the green room—they were jerking around the Best Picture graphics at the last minute—so I missed what happened next. But in a matter of minutes, Cinda was out there presenting Best Actor—to *Shane*, of all people—only Shane and Tara were nowhere to be found. You do the math."

"Am I safe in assuming that this is what you and Cinda were fighting about just now?"

"Actually, Rick, there's more to it than that." Jeep stretched, cracking his knuckles. "I reported her to the police."

Terry and I damn near did one of those Danny Thomas spit scenes with our respective drinks.

"Say *what?*"

"I went to the police. I told them everything: Cinda was in love with Tara, Shane proposed to Tara, Cinda's bleeding fist, the letter. The whole ball of wax. Except that Shane was gay." He took a sip of Jack Daniels and mockingly added, "Oops. How forgetful of me."

"What did the police say?" Terry asked.

"They were kind of ho-hum about it. Like they already had

their prime suspect, and weren't going to go out of their way to complicate matters. They did want to know if I was going public with this information. I said I'd have to think about it. You know—talk to my lawyer and all that crapola. Mostly they wanted my autograph."

"And Cinda found out?"

"From what I gathered, the cops went through the motions, and questioned her for like five minutes. They were satisfied she was clean. We'll see about *that*. But she wasn't the world's happiest camper. She called me to say that some fuckbrain told the cops she killed Tara, and what nerve, and I said, 'Well, Cinda, *I'm* the fuckbrain who told the cops you killed Tara, because I *know* you killed Tara.' There was like this long pause on the other end. Then she hung up. Then the fucking lunatic left these crazed messages on my answering machine."

Without getting up from his chair, Jeep was able to hit a button on a remote and play back Cinda's voice:

Jeep, you fucking asshole. How could you do this to me? Are you that jealous that I'm Bob's friend, too? Has your psychosis reached such pathetic heights? Are you on drugs? Have you not gotten your daily ass fuck? Did you have a burning desire to out me in the most degrading way possible? Have you—

A beep brought the message to an abrupt end.

"Wait, there's more," Jeep promised.

Jeep, this is Cinda again. You really need to set your machine to leave longer messages. I am so fucking mad at you I can't even see. I am so fucking pissed off. What if the press gets hold of this? What if the cocksucking press finds out what you said? Consider your ass sued to Kingdom Come. Or make that Kingdom No-Cum. I'm going to mow you down the next time I see you prancing down the street. I'm going eat your fucking balls for lunch. I'm going to—

Jeep was unmistakably amused.

"Needless to say, I couldn't just sit back and let her think she could get away with this type of horse shit. So I went to her place to tell her to fuck off."

"And when you stormed into her house, you weren't worried that Cinda would kill *you*?" Terry asked.

Jeep considered. "Now that you put it that way—no. I hadn't

even thought of that. I was so pissed at her that it never occurred to me to be scared."

"But you said she just got angry enough to kill someone else."

Jeep smiled charmingly. "Rick, who is this guy? A bodyguard, or a detective?"

"Last time I checked, it wasn't illegal for a bodyguard to have a brain."

"Touché, Terry." Jeep poured himself a small refill. "God, did I really just say, 'touché'? Anyway, to answer your question—Cinda is not dumb. She wouldn't bump me off five seconds after I told the cops she's a homicidal maniac. For me, it was the principle of the thing. Maybe she and certain other people can withhold evidence, but I just can't. I've played too many cops to not feel something for what they go through trying to solve crimes."

"That's a good attitude," Terry decreed. "Still, what if you're wrong about Cinda? To accuse someone of murder—that's awfully serious."

Jeep shrugged. "She'll get over it."

"You seem to be *enjoying* all this," Terry remarked.

"Personally, it's hard to mourn for Tara. You've probably heard of the shit fit she caused about not getting enough close-ups in some stupid chick flick we made. I *hated* working with her. She gave new meaning to the word 'difficult.' She gave new meaning to the word 'fucking cunt bitch.' Every goddamn time I'd try to get out of work-ing with her, she'd threaten to out me. With this sick-O lilt in her voice, she'd tell me, 'I know something about Jeepie-kins.' She even fucked up a relationship I was having, just to amuse herself. We were on the set together and I made the fatal error of saying I thought some technician was cute, and the next thing you know she's blab-bing to my boyfriend that I have the hots for this other guy."

He savored a slow sip of Jack Daniels, rolling it over his tongue. "Still, murder's always wrong. The killer has to pay."

First one dog, then the other, started barking. Jeep stomped both feet. "Shut the fuck up!" He looked at us. "Not you, the dogs."

"We knew that," I assured him. "When you say 'certain people' are withholding evidence, who do you mean?"

Jeep yawned. "Bob of course. And Cleo."

"What do you mean?" asked Terry.

"He's being a real mother hen toward his son, Zeke. The poor kid was in some kind of stink with Tara. Tara tried to use Bob sexually, and when that didn't work I guess she figured Zeke was better than nothing. Bob talked to a bunch of us after the Oscars and said he needed to protect his son. He liked you, he knew you were innocent, and he'd try to help, but he wanted all of us to promise that whatever we told the cops we'd keep his son out of it."

"And you promised?"

"Sure. Why not? Other than having had the bad luck to have known Tara 'personally,' as they say, the kid *did* have nothing to do with it."

Terry polished off the dregs of his Coke. "Zeke could've freaked out if he heard that Tara was going to marry Shane. What makes you so certain that Zeke didn't kill her?"

"Because that poor kid couldn't have *held* a gun, let alone fire one. I don't mean this in a gay way—he's straight, God bless his unfortunate soul—but the kid really is a *wimp*. I mean, you've met him, right?"

"I have, but not Terry."

"Then I'm sure you'll agree: He might've pulled a scene with Tara. He might've threatened to OD on happy pills unless she sucked his dick. But that boy is no killer. Not in a million years."

"So all told, who did you see backstage?" Terry inquired.

"Bob. Zeke. Francine and her flask, feeling no pain. And of course Tara, Cinda, and Shane. And about a million prop and lighting people."

"Did you see Connee Kellogg?" I asked.

"Briefly, now that you mention it. She was in a big hurry. She was trying to look elegant, the poor dear. Basic black was a little *too* basic, the way she wore it. And at the risk of sounding foo-foo, it wasn't the year of basic black, anyway. Connee was always behind the times. She was funny, though. She had a sense of humor about her tacky little career. Used to love to shake her stuff at gay bars. And she could really *shake*. Drag queens worshiped her."

"Do you believe she OD'd?" Terry inquired.

"There he goes again, Rick, with the probing questions." Jeep shook his head and smiled. "Terry, if you fancy yourself to be some sort of detective, listen carefully. Connee died of an overdose. She almost did the same thing a million different times. I was trying to get her a small part in my next movie, but Tru said no one would insure her anymore. I didn't have the heart to tell her. I was going to put up the insurance money myself."

I helped myself to another gin-and-tonic. "Tell me, Jeep—did you *really* cry at Tara's memorial?"

Jeep smiled. "What can I say? I'm a bit of a drama queen at times. It was an emotional moment. Who knows what's real?"

"What was it that you wanted to tell to Tara after she won the Oscar?"

He rubbed his eyes; I was getting the impression he'd had a fair amount to drink. "I'm not sure what you mean, Rick."

"At the memorial, when you were making your speech, and then the mike went dead."

Jeep laughed. "Oh, right! And everyone and their brother came on stage to comfort me. It's funny, that seems like such a long time ago. To be honest, Rick, it wasn't anything much. Just that I wanted to congratulate her—you know, showbiz talk. It's always a pleasure, though, to cop a feel from Bob." He paused to study our reactions. "Bob's a dreamboat. He's *stunning*. I make no apologies about finding him attractive. We joke about it all the time.

"Cinda, I suspect, cut the mike. She was afraid I'd start getting into who said what to whom that night. Which might've included the way Cinda yelled at Tara. Which might've brought up who killed Tara."

"She *yelled* at her? You didn't mention that before." Terry leaned forward on the coach.

"That's kind of a given, isn't it? I mean, before you shoot somebody in a jealous rage, you just might yell at them, wouldn't you?"

"Actually, not," Terry informed us. "According to several studies, jealous rage murders usually involve—" he stopped himself.

"Bodyguards get trained in all kinds of studies about the psychological state of killers. But I guess it gets a little technical."

Jeep yawned. "With all due respect, I don't trust studies. Real life gives me all the facts I need. But yeah, I heard her yelling on my way to the green room. Something like, 'Why can't you love me when no one could ever love you more?' Nothing too surprising. Just . . . *loud*."

"Speaking of Bob, did you ever hear anything about him making a porn movie?"

Jeep's face lit up. "You can't possibly mean *Beat Me, Daddy, Eight to the Balls?*"

"Well, actually . . . yeah."

He roared with laughter. "When they aren't saying Bob's in it, they're saying I'm in it. Neither of us ever did anything like that. Not in a million years."

"Do you have a copy of it?"

"Gimme a break. I have good taste in porn."

My cell phone rang.

Upon answering it, I could feel myself turning pale.

"What is it?" Terry asked, when I got off the phone.

"It was a computer."

Jeep grinned mischievously. "Rick, you *are* getting desperate, aren't you?"

"A computer was just programmed to tell me that . . ."

"That what?" Terry asked.

"Jeep, I'm sorry, but I need to talk to Terry alone for a moment."

"I'll check on the pups." He kissed my cheek on his way out, and gave Terry a friendly pat on the back.

"The Oscar. Someone has it. They want to give it to me. Right now."

23

I feel like I'm in *The Maltese Falcon*," I shared with Terry, seated next to me in the Cherokee along a glitzy, mean side street off of Sunset.

"Huh?"

"Never mind." I long ago resigned myself to the sad little fact that unless it was one of the ten shittiest movies of all time, Terry never had heard of it.

But in actuality, here I was in the dead of night, awaiting a mysterious statuette. Countless particulars differed from *The Maltese Falcon*, but I look for my classic movie parallels where I can. It helps the day go by, especially when everything isn't exactly coming up roses.

"Here it comes," I noted. "Number Four."

A cross-dressing prostitute knocked on the rolled-up window. Terry and I shook our heads negatively. It was the fourth time in the half-hour we'd been waiting that we'd been propositioned thusly.

"First drag queen, though," Terry pointed out.

"Maybe we should keep two separate lists. It could make the time go faster."

"You're *sure* they said—that the computer said, 'Be there by one-thirty.'"

"No, Terry, I'm not. I could barely even pay attention to so trivial a phone call."

"Sorry. Jeez, no need to get all bent out of shape."

On the radio came the two A.M. news report. There was a new crisis in the Middle East, and stocks were down. Then this: *Oscar-*

*winning actor Shane Kirk announced this evening his plans to launch
the Tara Perez Memorial Fund, a nonprofit charity for terminally ill
children. Mr. Kirk was quoted as saying: "Tara was the light of my life.
Now I want to share that light with the masses." Earlier this week, Ms.
Perez was murdered—*

I turned off the radio. "What a fucking lunatic."

Terry turned the radio back on. "We should keep listening."

"You're right."

"But of course."

It was such a dumb joke that I laughed. As the newscaster
droned on, I studied Terry. "You don't believe Jeep, did you?"

Terry considered. "We'll have to see."

"Is it that hard to conceive that your beloved Cinda could be
guilty?"

"Very funny. I don't have a thing for her, okay? Or for lesbians."

I gave him a little shove. "Coulda fooled me, big guy."

I didn't know if it was residual longing for Darla Sue, or that it
was possibly the first time I—the gay one—initiated some form of
physical contact, or what. But Terry just about snapped my head off.
"Look, you don't know what you're talking about," he barked. "Give
it a rest."

"Okay, okay." Whatever it was all about, I'd leave it alone. "The
thing is, Jeep's story makes sense. She lied about the bandaged hand.
She has some sort of creepy denial thing happening about Tara's
having been something other than virginal. And the letter—Jeep
and Zeke talked about it. Besides, it's—"

"Someone else to pin it on? Rick, I want you to beat this thing
as much as anybody. But we can't afford to go jumping to conclusions. First, let's get our paws on the Oscar. Tomorrow we can do
some digging on Cinda. Firearms purchases, unusual bank transac-
tions—the whole song and dance."

"Well, *maybe*," I allowed. "But I still say Jeep might be on to
something."

The radio newscaster stated: "On Monday, the trial of gossip
kingpin Rick Domino is expected to begin at the Superior Courthouse in—"

"Holy fuck," I proclaimed. "It's Brother Dennis."

The newscaster blathered away about my wondrous trial as we watched Brother Dennis gad about in the classic gay male hustler ensemble: black leather jacket, tight white T-shirt, faded 501s, and butch hiking boots. He walked up to a couple of street-punk whores standing under a fizzling neon sign for something called the Hospitality Inn—though the "s," "p," and "i" were not lit. (I assumed there were lame jokes about "Ho'tality Inn.") Brother Dennis showed the punks a photo; we assumed he was telling them he was looking for Shane. A red Porsche pulled up. The two boys walked over to it, and after a moment of discussion with the driver began to climb in. Brother Dennis ran over to the car, shouting, "I'm Shane Kirk!"

The car drove off. Brother Dennis collapsed into a heap of tears.

"I better go help him." I reached for the door handle.

There was a tap at Terry's window.

Someone wearing a ski mask, with medium-stature body swaddled in clothes—so you couldn't even be sure of the sex of the person—breathed onto the window. With gloved hand, the person painstakingly spelled onto the glass: O-S-C-A-R. Then the person wiped the window, and pulled on the door handle, indicating we should let him or her in.

"We both better stick around," Terry decided, reaching for the door handle. "They'll be suspicious if you're not here. And you could use protection." He quietly pulled out his gun, setting it between us, with a dark sweater thrown over it.

I looked regretfully at poor Brother Dennis. "You're right."

The phantom androgen entered the car.

Climbing into the backseat, the person pulled out a gun of his or her own. With a garbled, heavily disguised voice, he/she began barking directions. But that was all the mysterious stranger would say. And when a gun is pointed at your head, this weird thing happens where you don't feel much like generating idle chitchat.

I don't know if it was fear, or the incredible labyrinth of turns we were directed to make, but though I've lived in L.A. for years I couldn't tell you where exactly we ended up.

We were at a T. There were no street signs, though one signpost had been sawed in half, and the other bent over to the ground. The night sky gave the omnipresent broken glass an iridescence, though in daylight it must've looked ugly. Getting out of the Cherokee, we had to step over a sleeping street person who, I couldn't help noticing, was lying in vomit. At the cross of the T was nothing but a ruddy field, as if maybe twenty years ago something was going to be built there but then the contractor ran out of money. On the right-hand side was a boarded-up little clapboard house, the roof half-naked with tar paper. On the other side of the street was a barbed wire fence, with some long-abandoned factory on the other side of it. The safety-glass windows were smashed, and the crumbling brick exterior had been heavily graffiti'd.

The masked person silently led us across the street to the boarded-up house.

At the rickety front steps, he/she held up an index finger, indicating we should stay put.

It felt like we waited outside for an eternity, though when I checked my watch, it was only about ten minutes later when the person emerged from the door.

From the steps, the masked individual tossed down a package wrapped in brown paper.

I caught it—and nearly fell over. It was heavier than I thought it would be.

I undid the string, understanding for the first time why Maria von Trapp would list this among her Favorite Things. I opened the gift box inside.

Amidst balled-up newspaper for padding, there it was—an Academy Award, glistening in all its gold-plated splendor. Catching the light of a cracked streetlamp, it gleamed all the more brilliantly, like captured rays of sun.

The phantom personage turned back around on the steps.

"Wait!" I called out. "Who are you? How'd you get this? Why are you giving it me?"

The mysterious figured slammed the door upon re-entering the house.

For about a minute, we just stood there, waiting for I don't know what. The sound of gunshots? The house exploding into flames?

"Let's just get out of here and quit while we're ahead," Terry reasoned.

"Not a bad idea," I agreed. That a large rat was scurrying not ten feet away from me did little to encourage me to linger.

As we climbed into the Cherokee, Terry fastened his seat belt and said, "Now all we have to do is figure out how to get the hell out of here."

I was careful not to touch the Oscar, but kept staring at it. Would it exonerate me or damn me? I had to take the risk. There was no point in concealing evidence—that could only make matters worse.

Terry's cell phone rang. As he listened, he looked puzzled and pleased at the same time, as if being given an all-expense-paid vacation to a place he'd never thought about going to.

"Well, I guess that's that." He put away his cell phone.

"What do you mean, 'that's that'? That's *what?*"

Terry revved up the engine. "Zeke Raflowitz." He pulled out, thought for an instant, and decided to turn left at the T. "He's confessed to murdering Tara Perez."

24

*T*erry drove us straight to the police station, and turned in the Oscar as evidence while I waited in the car. I didn't even ask what outlandish story he came up with to explain how it came into his possession. My mind was reeling for all that was happening.

Would the state buy the confession of a mixed-up teenager, with his highly respected father no doubt making extremely serious threats of legal action against the state? I kept fighting the urge to call Benji. I'd be seeing him in a few hours, anyway, when the poor guy got out of the hospital. So it was best to wait until I knew what was up with Zeke.

Terry came back out to the car. "Good news," he decreed,

expertly pulling out of the parking place. "I saw a few flecks of blood on the Oscar thingamajig when I brought it into the bright light."

I was too much on edge to be cheered up. "Tara's blood. So what?"

"Well, maybe someone else's blood, too, if there was a struggle. That's what's so what."

"Oh." I hated it when Terry made me sound foolish.

"You have to tell me how to get to the Raflowitz place. He made a big to-do and said the whole thing's a joke—you know, a teenager pulling a telephone prank—and he'd have it all straightened out in a jiffy. So in some special-treatment, PR move, they said they'd keep a plainclothes cop car outside the house tonight, and he didn't have to bring the kid in till morning. We can't let Bob pull off a cover-up. According to my sources, the kid sounded pretty believable when he phoned."

"Believable? How do you mean?"

"Well, for starters, he said he clubbed Tara to death with her Oscar." He honked angrily at an overly aggressive driver.

"Jeepers."

Terry laughed. " 'Jeepers?' Is that the best you can do?"

"Sorry. I'll make up for it next time."

"Anyway, Bob threatened massive lawsuits if anyone blabs to the press in the meanwhile, so mum's the official word."

"I won't tell a soul," I promised. "Now all we have to do is figure out how to get past the guards into the house."

"Shouldn't be too difficult, seeing as how I volunteered to relieve the schlep on duty."

It was Saturday dawn as we pulled up at the Raflowitz–Simone compound. A red scar of cloud rose above the sagebrush. Under normal circumstances, it probably was mighty pleasant to wake up here, but I doubted that Bob, Cleo, and their children were feeling particularly invigorated. I ducked out of sight in the front seat while Terry chatted cavalierly with the cop on duty, who soon sped off.

"Kinda nice up this way, huh?" Terry rhapsodized. "Wow, look at that—a hawk. No, two hawks."

Sure enough, two mighty yet graceful birds swooped and glided about the conflagration of mountains and valleys. They'd fly off separately, cross each other, and then come back again.

Despite all that was happening, we took a few seconds to watch them dip and turn.

"You know, I think I can guard better from the inside," Terry mock-decided. "Let's go."

We knocked on the door, we rang the buzzer, but we got no answer.

"I could break down the door," Terry offered, "and drum up some excuse for it later."

"I have a better idea."

I led us over to the huge glass tent where Cleo conducted her classes. Sure enough, Cleo was in full lotus at the center of the dome, as if in some egomaniacal way she was worshipping herself. In her purple leotard, she rested on a mass of pillows as she merged with the sunrise.

She heard us enter, yet she kept her eyes closed.

"Good morning, kind souls!" she cheerily called out.

"Good morning, Cleo. It's Rick. And my bodyguard."

I waited for all hell to break loose.

"Rick! How wonderful that you've dropped by. And a bodyguard. That's every bit as wonderful. We need to guard our bodies, whether it be on the physical, astral, or ethereal level."

She still did not open her eyes, or move from her meditative position.

"Cleo, we need to talk to Bob. And to Zeke. I'm sure you know what it's about. Please, this is very important."

"Oh, I know," agreed the blissed-out meditator. "But they aren't here."

"Not here?" Terry puzzled. "There was supposed to be a police guard—"

Cleo laughed. "There was, there was. But we can make ourselves invisible, you know. It is a matter of harnessing *all* of your energy on *all* levels of existence. Think to yourself, 'I am shadow. I am a child of the Moon Goddess. I am of the unseen.' Lo and behold, you are . . . gone."

She opened her eyes, smiling warmly. "Cleo Simone," She offered her hand to Terry, then ended up giving him a hug. I, too, was embraced, but in a longer, more contemplative way. Every gesture, every breath she took, seemed focused on reinforcing the notion that Today would be a Good Day. Terry and I were but the first of Many Treasures that awaited her.

Standing upright, she did a few yoga movements with her legs. "They've gone to Tru's place. In town. I should expect you'd find quite a party there."

There was an undercurrent of irony to her last statement—I wondered if there hadn't been a disagreement with Bob over going to Tru's, or having certain people there—but I could always find that out later. Besides, who could really say what went through Cleo's mind—especially at so understandably stressed-out a time as this? I could only hope that she wasn't just hallucinating that everyone went over to Tru's.

We made as hasty a retreat as we could—Cleo insisted on several more hugs from us both—and hot-footed it over to Tru's Beverly Hills mansion.

"Turn yourself invisible, my ass," Terry complained the whole way over. "That officer either fell asleep on the job, got loaded, or took a payoff. Totally unacceptable."

"Small potatoes," I tried to assure him.

"It's the *principle* of the thing," Terry insisted.

At one point I managed to ask Terry what he thought of Cleo.

"I dunno," he decided. "Rich, a little dinghy."

"Too dinghy to know what really happened?"

"Nope. If anything, too rich to know—or at least to admit to knowing. She's not about to get her fingernails dirty. But she's not totally out of touch."

Just as Jupiter is larger than all the other planets put together, so could all of the impressive residences I'd inhabited over the lest few days—including my own—have fit snugly into but a corner of Tru's Beverly Hills mansion. Like his beach house, it was imposing and surreal, only more so. It had been built for a highly eccentric European silent-movie goddess, but she was said to have sold it for almost nothing once it was finished because she found it "depressing." It wasn't hard to see why.

You all but expected moats and drawbridges as you drove up the steep, private hill past the gargoyle lions and *then* the gargoyle angels to the gray, gnarly looking, four-storied eyesore. From a distance, the exterior gave the impression of having been inspired by fingers badly disfigured by arthritis, with ivy climbing up the sides like twists of thorns. But up close, you saw that the exterior was a chaos of human faces and figures, all chalky, frozen-looking, and snakily interwoven—yet somehow too realistic, as if real people had been buried alive under plaster, or hexed by an evil spell.

You stepped inside relieved that you didn't have to look at those trapped, gaping people anymore—and you found out you were wrong. In the corners of the walls and ceilings, in a kind of art nouveau gingerbread effect, were *more* faces and figures, all done in dark gray marble, all seeming to stare with their blank eyes. No amount of furnishings—and Tru overdecorated every room with love seats and window seats and divans and bric-a-brac enough to make a Victorian home seem sparse—could diminish the overpowering effect of these monstrosities.

I wasn't the only one who hated the house. Quite a few guests had freaked out on drugs over the years—as in, needing to be hospitalized after screaming that some omnipresent marble personage was trying to kill them or read their minds. One time Tru himself reportedly freaked out, saying these were all the people he'd screwed over come back to get him. (About once every five years, something happened to shake up Tru enough to give him a conscience for about a day and a half.) I didn't think the house was haunted, or anything like that. It was just so damned ugly.

One of Tru's more endearing traits was his inability to admit to a mistake. In fact, he'd go out of his way to keep committing the offensive deed (sabotage, extortion, whatever) to show how unwrong he was. The same held true for his home. He filled it with even *more* sculpted renderings of the human form. Given his bisexuality, both sexes were amply represented. Of course, no one ever came right out and said the place was creepy, just like no one was ever dumb enough to outright accuse him of ripping them off. But in his slick, showbiz way Tru could tell what was on people's minds—when he felt like paying attention, that is.

So in the average room of the house, there was maybe a couple of dozen marble people, big and small, staring at you from every which way.

"Not my kind of place," Terry whispered to me, as the butler directed us to a drawing room. From each corner of the room there emerged, like freakish stalactites, a gray marble female body intended to depict one of the four seasons. Spring wore a nightmarish garland of wildflowers, Summer played creepily with a stalled butterfly, Autumn had leaves falling in her hair like leeches, and Winter wore an ominous shroud that partially covered her nude form. Along the mantle and various tabletops were a plethora of additional figurines and busts.

The slate gray walls and listless, gray-to-black furniture added little reflected light to the room. Though it was morning, an overbearing crystal chandelier needed to be turned on. It was encircled by a crown of tiny marble people, whose shadows loomed large on the high ceiling.

His drug freakouts notwithstanding, Tru seemed to love the home. Spying him in the room, sipping cognac as he looked about with dreamy, squinting eyes, he seemed highly impressed with himself. I wondered if Tru would be annoyed—or worse—to see me, but he acted, anyway, like he couldn't have been more pleased.

"Rick! What a delightful surprise." He was wearing what used to be called a smoking jacket, plum-colored silk with black silk pajamas. I got the impression that he hadn't slept all night. "And your friend is . . . ?"

"You remember Terry," I encouraged. "My bodyguard?"

"Oh, right. The one who does the massages. I should give you a call sometime." He extended his hand, and Terry gamely shook it.

"Thanks, Mr. Shea."

As I stepped further into the room, I peered beyond an imposing iron sculpture of a Hindu elephant-god, its trunk triumphantly curled out, to see several personages tucked away on a sofa. In the center was Zeke Raflowitz, who was crying too hard to make cognizance of Terry and myself. To one side of him was his father, Bob, who gently smiled at me as he held his son's hand. As he stroked his son's hair and rubbed his back, I realized how many light-years away from Bob's consciousness was the notion that I might have to suffer for a crime I didn't commit. I could tell Bob had been crying, too. It could've been an act, but I didn't think so. In spite of my anger, I found myself feeling a little sorry for him.

On the other side of Zeke sat Cinda Sharpe, who held Zeke's other hand with tightly clenched jaw, and refused to acknowledge me—though I caught her grinning at Terry. I guessed that she found me to be a nuisance, a nosy reporter messing up this marvelous Kodak moment. But Terry was one of the Working People, so it wasn't his fault he was there.

A silver tray was piled high with used coffee cups and an empty espresso maker.

"We've been doing some very intense hypnotherapy," Tru chipperly conveyed, as if reporting encouraging X-rays concerning a broken leg. "We're almost *there*, I think. Almost back at what really happened. Zeke's just a little scared, that's all."

I had no idea if hypnosis was for real or not. But I obviously needed to take it most seriously. That is, assuming that everyone else was taking it seriously, that Bob in particular believed this was a way to get at the truth, and he therefore would be beholden to whatever that truth revealed. But maybe it was all just for show. Maybe they expected me, and once the supposed hypnosis revealed that Zeke didn't do it, that would be that.

Still, if Zeke was truly facing something fearful, I couldn't think of a worse environment to be doing it in.

Tru—who had a way of knowing what you were thinking—stated, "Zeke *asked* to come here. He said he's always felt safe in my house. It was quite a production, sneaking him out."

I turned quizzically to Terry, who gave me a "let's see what happens" look in response.

"Good idea," I declared. "Anything to get at the truth."

"Have a seat, Rick," Bob offered quietly. "And your friend, too." As if we were all on the same side.

Terry briefly introduced himself to Bob, and then joined me on a divan in the corner.

"Did I miss anything?" The jovial voice of Jeep Andrews filled the room. He did a mock double-take at the sight of Terry and me. "Hey, guys. Long time no see." He genially held out his hand to Terry and gave me a quick kiss.

I couldn't help noticing that this time Terry seemed unfazed by the sight of two men kissing. (Unless he, too, was putting on an act.)

"I thought *he* was leaving," Cinda complained to Bob.

"No, way, babe," Jeep cheerfully answered. "Our love is here to stay."

Bob frowned like a scolding parent. "Now, you both promised me you'd bury the hatchet for the time being. I need you right now. I need you all." He turned to me. "Even you, Rick, now that you're here. You are ingenious, my friend. We were—well, *half*-expecting you, I guess you could say."

Jeep was holding a tall glass of (spiked?) juice. He sipped it through a bright red straw. "I have no hatchet to bury, Bob." He became self-conscious of everyone watching him drink. "Just pineapple juice, folks," he assured us. "If there was rum in it I'd need one of those little umbrellas. As I think of it, I've plumb run out of them at home. Maybe I can drive up to Cinda's to borrow some. I'll bet she keeps plenty around for those festive occasions."

"There—you see how he is?"

"Now, now." Bob patted Cinda's arm. "Jeep's just having his fun."

"Fun!? Accusing me of—"

Bob put his hand over her mouth. "Not now, remember? That's why we're here. For the *truth.*"

Jeep sat down in a broad-backed, spindly looking chair opposite Terry and myself, and toyed with his straw. "How's the boy?" he asked.

"He's . . . he's getting there," Bob answered.

"He's very brave." Cinda kissed Zeke's forehead. "Isn't he, *Bob?*" She shifted her back slightly to avoid suggesting cordiality toward Jeep.

"I'm sorry," Zeke managed to sputter between sobs. "Oh, Daddy, I'm so sorry I was born. I've made so much trouble."

"Shh." Bob patted his son's hand and smiled. "Silly talk."

"By the way, I assume one of you is the hypnotist?"

"Not quite, Rick," Tru answered cheerfully. "But you're warm."

Into the room wobbled Francine Quick, looking rather worse for the wear. Her mascara was streaking down her face à la Tammy Faye. There was a sponged-up stain of some kind on the front of her pale blue dress, which looked like something that Queen Elizabeth II would've rejected for being too matronly. It wasn't Francine's usual style, but then her mission at hand was hardly her usual one, either—though doubtless she was drunk just the same.

"Presenting Madame Francine!" Tru proclaimed.

Jeep raised his glass to Francine in a gesture both good-natured and sarcastic, while Cinda flashed her all-women-like-each-other smile. Bob gallantly kissed Francine's hand and murmured, "Thank you." She took a smaller, spindly chair and pulled it up in front of Zeke—though not before shooting Jeep the evil eye for not helping her into it.

"Seriously, Rick—Francine is a *brilliant* hypnotist," Tru assured me. "She's been doing this for *years*."

At her most likable when she let her Brooklynese all hang out, Francine was excruciating when she feigned sophistication or intellect, as she now did. "I learned the technique on a location shoot in India back in the early—I mean, late 1950s. Rick, it *totally changed my life*."

"I'm impressed," I replied.

Francine made a little kiss with her lips. "How's my favorite bodyguard tonight?"

Actually, it was morning, of course, but you couldn't blame her for being confused. The room was dark, and she'd clearly been up all night.

Terry kind of half stood up. "Fine, Francine. How nice of you to remember me."

She made a pathetic effort to smile sexily. "Honey, the main thing is, do you remember ol' Francine?"

Terry blushed, which made Francine laugh. "Rick, don't let this one get away."

"Oh, I won't," I answered, rolling my eyes at the curious Jeep to signify this was just Francine getting it all botched up.

"Are we ready?" Cinda asked quietly.

"We sure are, toots." Francine took a swallow from her drink. "I still can't believe this new Hollywood etiquette. Imagine not being able to smoke indoors. It's worse than . . . barbaric." The corners of her mouth turned downward with centuries of bitterness. "But let's give it a whirl."

Tru rushed over to a camcorder in the corner of the room, and switched it on.

"Before we begin," Bob interjected, "I just want to say thanks again to everyone. Cleo needs to be with the kids, of course, but if she were here, I know she'd be . . . well, you know."

"We know." Cinda reached across Zeke to put her hand to Bob's cheek.

"And thanks to Rick, too," Bob continued. "And Terry, his bodyguard."

"Thanks, Bob." I couldn't decide if he was pissing me off or making me feel better.

"Here, here." Francine agreed. "Now, Zack—I mean, Zeke. We need you to be *quiet* again. Can you do that? All that screaming and shaking like the last few times simply won't do if we're to continue. Perhaps we should try something else." She passed her hand a few times over his face; his sobbing stopped completely, like it never even happened. He looked blank, but not zonked out—simply rested and at peace. "We'll go back to your very first fear," Francine continued. "What is your oldest bad memory?"

Zeke began to breathe hard; his eyes grew wide.

"Not *that*," Bob grimaced. "Zeke, if you're thinking what I—"

Francine frowned at him. "I keep *telling* you, dodo-brain—let me do the talking."

"Sorry," Bob murmured. But he nervously fidgeted with his free hand.

Zeke started to whimper. "Mommy," he murmured. "Mommy's

in a box. Mommy has no colors. Mommy is crazy. They're taking Mommy away. Everything is . . . it's . . ."

Bob stood up from the sofa, and turned away with his hands in his pockets. "I can't go through all this again. I can't do it."

Francine looked up at Bob, then back at Zeke. "Keep going, Zeke. You're doing fine."

"Mommy," he repeated. "I can't touch Mommy. Mommy is cold and hard. It *hurts*. Blood . . . I make blood . . ." He started crying— not just hard, but like a toddler.

"Fine." Francine held Zeke's hand with all her strength. "Now you walk right through that, whatever it is you are walking past it. *I am here with you,* and you are walking through it."

Zeke kept wailing like a four-alarm fire engine. It was one of those instances that made me glad I never had kids.

"I am here with you," Francine repeated. "You are not alone. We are walking together through the hurt and the pain and the fear."

"Jesus!" Bob cried. "That's enough, dammit."

Francine stared right back at him. He was King of New Hollywood while she but a battered serf from Old Hollywood, yet there was no doubt who was the regal one. She held up her liver-spotted index finger, its false nail generously painted deepest red, as she mouthed the word *Wait* with such authority that Bob backed down.

"*Together,*" Francine told Zeke, squeezing his hand. "We are walking together."

Cinda gripped Zeke's other hand more tightly.

"Together," he whispered, barely audibly.

"Yes, yes, together."

"Together," he repeated, laughing a little this time.

"Yes, yes, we're walking through it all."

"We're walking through it."

"Wave good-bye. 'Good-bye, fear!'"

"Good-bye fear!" Zeke repeated back.

"We're thumbing our noses at the fear. We're mooning at it with our bare behinds."

"Yeah, we sure are." Zeke was laughing. "We're like . . . on a sailboat. It's all sparkly."

"Yes, yes, and now we're pulling into port. What's this? Why, it's Monday night, and we're backstage at the Oscars—just where we left off before. Now you're sorry, aren't you?, that you didn't tell that nice Mr. Domino all that you saw, isn't that right? And he's right here, and he's *very* nice, and knows how sorry you are and he forgives you." She looked over at me meaningfully; Francine had, after all, earlier told me she believed Zeke killed Tara. "Now, you saw your father kiss Tara and it hurt your feelings and so you ran off. Tara comforted you, but then Shane talked to her, and you saw him give Tara a ring"—Francine had to grip Zeke's hand extra-tight—"and you ran off to cry, and then you thought you saw Connee. You thought you saw her slip out back so you peeped through the door and . . . ?"

Zeke became very still. Then he screamed.

"Walk through it," Francine told him. "I'm here, remember? We just got off our beautiful, beautiful sailboat and we're walking together through the fear. What do we see?"

"Tara . . . hitting Tara . . . with the funny little man . . ."

"The Oscar," Francine encouraged..

"The Oscar hitting Tara. On her head. On her *throat*." Zeke grabbed his own throat, as if choking for the memory. It comes down and down on her . . . Cracking sounds . . . Cracking sounds . . . Blood . . . it hurts." Zeke clutched his head in pain. "Then the gun . . . So much blood."

He started crying hard, only more like a young adult this time.

Cinda, I noticed, was crying hard, too. Jeep looked respectful but indifferent, as if attending a function of a political party he didn't belong to, while Tru stared with his usual self-absorbed fascination: Was there a movie script in this?

"Zeke, who is killing Tara?"

"Mommy is in the box. Mommy has no colors."

"Yes, yes, Mommy is in the box. Who is killing Tara?"

"It's the same, but it's different. It's a different person."

"You're right, it isn't Mommy. Who is it?"

"No colors. Dark. I can't see."

"Maybe he only saw their shadows," Tru offered.

"Are they shadows? Zeke? Do you only see their shadows?"

"I'm scared. I want to go look but I'm scared."

"So you *did* just see their shadows? Can you remember anything about the other person?"

"It's always my fault. Everything. 'It's your fault I never loved you.' Mommy screaming at me. 'It's all your fault.' I should've helped Tara. Tara's dead. Connee's dead. She wanted to me to come over, and I didn't. I should've helped. I was afraid. Everyone dies."

"Zeke, *who was the other person in the alley?*"

"No colors. Like Mommy. A different person. Tara. Funny little Oscar man. The gun."

"C'mon, Zeke. You can do it."

"C'mon, Zeke," I urged.

"No colors. I can't see. No colors." He whimpered like a child. "I can't see," he repeated. "I didn't go see."

Francine sighed. "I'm afraid that's it." She looked up at me with a sad kindness. "I'm so sorry, Rick."

Bob patted my shoulder. I was too drained to know what to think or feel.

She waved her hand over Zeke's face. He drank in a deep, calming breath.

"What just happened?"

Bob gave his son a big hug. "You're clean, kid. You didn't do it. You just get your jollies by blaming yourself for everything. You see, you have this tendency to—"

"Dad, I'm *so* tired. Can I just lie down for awhile?"

"Of course, son."

"We'll get your bed ready," Tru offered, meaning one of the servants would.

On his way out of the room, Zeke turned to me and smiled. "Hi, Mr. Domino."

I gamely waved in reply.

Did Zeke really see what he claimed to see, not see what he claimed not to see? Was he really not guilty after all? I didn't know what to believe for certain, but I had to admit I found it all pretty convincing.

Though of course it made for even more questions.

"Boys act tough," Francine philosophized, returning to her drink. "Men do, too, which is why they're still boys. But *no one* enjoys watching someone die. Years ago, I visited the troops in Korea—as a juvenile performer, you understand—and I saw first-hand how traumatized those brave soldiers were by slaughter happening all around them. Dying is lousy enough, but killing . . ." Francine shuddered, steadying her nerves with a refill of gin.

"I'm . . . leaving," Bob announced, as though making a momentous decision. "I need to talk to Cleo, and check on the kids." He reached for his hand-woven hooded jacket. Tired and frustrated as I was, I couldn't help noticing how elegantly the folds of the material clung and then slipped around his tight T-shirt. "I also need to talk to the police department, and put this to rest once and for all." He held out his hand to me. "I'm sorry, Rick, that we couldn't have been more help. But you know I'm pulling for you." I shook his hand; he clasped my hand with his other hand to emphasize his good will.

"Wait a sec, Bob," Tru called. "What was the bit about 'Mommy in the box with no colors'?" He asked this as if he were idly curious, in a kids-say-the-darnedest-things kind of way.

"He was watching Cleo on TV, of course," I heard myself say. Everyone looked at me like I was incredibly psychic or something, but I thought it was pretty obvious. "And as I think of it, she was in this black-and-white experimental movie years ago called *Psychotic Reaction*—"

"Rick, *please*," Bob beseeched me. "We can talk later, I promise."

"She was in a movie where she played a mother who goes crazy and tells her son everything's his fault and she doesn't love him, and then he grows up to be . . ."

"A killer?" asked Terry.

"No, actually he grows up to be this boring psychiatrist who dedicates his life to helping others. But Cleo's big scene—she had like ten minutes of screen time, so she had to make them count—was looking right into the camera and screaming all this 'You did it' type of stuff."

Jeep loudly slurped the dregs of his pineapple juice. "God, poor kid. He must've seen the movie on TV in his playpen or something, and thought it was real. Bob, I had no idea."

Bob walked to the center of the room. "Nobody knew. Not even our closest friends. We were afraid that if people knew too much about Zeke in advance, they'd prejudge him." He sat back down on the sofa. "But there's a little more to it. I don't blame you, Rick, for forgetting some of that awful movie. The mother incested the son. There were scary close-ups of Cleo saying things like 'Isn't that Momma's good boy?' But the worst part was . . ." Bob wiped a tear from his face. "Tara."

It took him a moment to compose himself. Cinda started to say something about poor Tara always finding herself in messes, but Jeep hushed her to be quiet, and let Bob speak.

"I know those were different times, and she must've tried in a million different ways to say she was sorry. We were having a party—an afternoon thing—and Cleo had her hands full. Besides Zeke, Naomi-Flower was in diapers and Cleo was pregnant again. Tara offered to mind Zeke for a few minutes while Cleo changed the baby. I was . . . oh, probably wheeling and dealing with Tru or some other hotshot producer out back. I can't really blame Tara, it was our fault for trusting her for even five minutes. She took Zeke by the hand and plunked him down in front of the TV, and reached for any old video, the first one she found—which turned out to be *Psychotic Reaction*. See, there was some big shot at the party she wanted to win over."

"Unfortunately, the TV room was where we were putting all the coats and things. Zeke was only five, after all. He snooped around the pockets of the coats, and found what looked like a bunch of candy."

"Oh, my word." Francine shivered. "How strong was the stuff?"

"He swallowed the equivalent of ten acid trips, or so the doctors guessed. They pumped his little stomach. They gave him sedatives. They had to give him twenty stitches for his hands. He put them through the TV set, and cut his veins but good. If you can imagine a three-year-old nearly bleeding to death on ten hits of acid . . ."

"Oh, Bob," Cinda whimpered, kissing his cheek.

"Zeke screamed for days on end," Bob continued. "He kept saying how Mommy was doing this or that. We figured out it was the movie. The doctors couldn't promise anything. They said that if there was a propensity for mental illness within Zeke, this experience might set it off. They said he was like a time bomb. The teen years would be especially tricky."

"So then Cleo didn't . . . ?"

Bob gently smiled. "Did Zeke tell you she molested him, Rick? That she was crazy? That was the movie talking. The movie and the drugs. *Any* drug—even cough medicine—can set him off into that crazy world. Even his fancy medication is touch-and-go. We've been to four different doctors, and they all agree he's starting to show symptoms of paranoid schizophrenia. It may have happened anyway, but we'll never know, will we?"

"Poor Tara," Cinda pondered. "She must've felt so awful."

"Oh please." Jeep rolled his eyes.

"I believe she did feel awful," Bob stated. "She gave all kinds of money to children's causes. She insisted in setting up a college fund for Zeke. But sometimes Tara had inappropriate ways of showing that she cared."

"Boy, I'll say," Jeep agreed.

Cinda frowned. "What do you mean, Bob?"

"He means *sex*, you dummy," Jeep explained.

Bob rubbed Cinda's arm. "Jeep's a bit indelicate, but he's right. I don't even begin to know what the truth was about Tara's past. She changed the story around so many times over the years. But I guess *something* happened to her at some point, and well, when she felt very guilty about something, she wasn't beyond using her body to make it better."

Jeep grinned meanly. "With a *man*, that is."

Cinda shot back at him, "That must've made *you* very happy."

I walked around the room in thought. "So in other words, Bob, that's why Tara wanted to get up close and personal with Zeke?"

"And even me, sometimes." Bob sadly nodded his head. "When Zeke became a young man and felt attracted to Tara, she thought it was her big chance to help him heal. Or so I figured out at the Oscars. The other day, I didn't quite tell you everything, Rick—I wasn't ready to. But Tara and I had quite a row backstage."

"I know that, Bob," I replied quietly.

"Tara kept saying this was her chance to make it all better, and I told her it was much more complicated than that, and that she knew better, and to get a grip. It got ugly and emotional, but at one point, we actually kissed. Naturally, Zeke had to see it. It wasn't that type of kiss, not really, but still—you can imagine.

"But I guess I'd sort of forgiven Tara. When you work with someone, you form an artistic bond, and that changes things. Cleo had a much harder time. That was one of the reasons she welcomed Tara as a student—to learn true forgiveness. But in her heart she never succeeded. That's the *real* reason, though, why Cleo never pursued her career all that much. After the incident with the acid, she really began to question the effects movies have on people. I did, too, but . . . I can't help it, I just have to act."

"Does Zeke know Tara did all this?"

"As of the other day. We told him in the presence of his psychiatrist, and just sort of kept our fingers crossed. We all thought that maybe if he knew the whole story, it'd help him to understand better. Our timing couldn't have been worse. About an hour later, it was announced that Connee Kellogg had died. Zeke started blaming himself for not being there for Connee. Then he started saying he killed Tara.

"I hated having to cover things up, Rick. If you ever become a father yourself, you'll understand. On Oscar night, Zeke talked in his sleep about that funny little Oscar man and all the blood. I figured out what he meant—that he saw Tara getting killed. That was why I made the statement about how 'if her Oscar could talk.' I knew you'd be putting it all together, and I wanted to give you *something* to go on. Until hopefully I could find out what really happened."

"My poor Bobby." Cinda gave him a long hug.

"How touching," Jeep remarked. "She could become a new doll— excuse me, action figure—for the kiddies. Cinda, The Hug-a-Killer."

"I'm not even going to dignify that with a comment," Cinda replied.

"I do need to go," Bob reiterated.

"Later, Bob." Jeep stared straight ahead with his empty glass.

"A pleasure as always, Bob." Tru stepped forward to give Bob one of his famous weak, awkward embraces—"like being enveloped in mediocrity," commented a hotshot writer from New York. "We'll just let Zeke rest for now."

Francine did a full diva as she remained seated with her arms extended, palms down. Bob dutifully kissed her hands, deciding that silence was the most eloquent farewell of all.

"Wait."

I must've said it pretty forcefully because Bob stopped dead in his tracks.

"I know this has all been very meaningful, and Bob, I appreciate your sorrow, but in case you all haven't forgotten, I have a murder trial starting in . . ." I looked down at my watch. "About forty-six hours. Now, everyone keeps saying and saying they know I didn't do it. Well, who the fuck did? Sure, I hated Tara's guts. So did all of you. But I had *less* reason to hate her. Okay, so she was the cover date for my boyfriend. But he was a total shit, anyway. And if it's true the engagement ring was for Tara, I didn't know about it.

"But the rest of you? Blackmail, broken hearts, broken careers, more blackmail. Fucking up your child, in Bob's case. Now *that's* the stuff that makes for murder. There's about a hundred loose ends, and we're going to start putting them together now. I don't care how tired everyone is. I'm tired, too. Tired in ways you'll never know."

I was waiting for someone to protest or make an excuse, but nobody said anything, Nobody even moved.

"I have questions, and Terry, my bodyguard, might have a few, too. He's pretty good at this stuff himself." I smiled at him, and felt reassured when he smiled back. "Now then—"

"Rick, I couldn't be angrier."

Benji Malone came stomping into the room, all business. "Does a little something called 'breakfast with your attorney' ring a dim bell?"

"Benji, I'm sorry, but so much has happened—"

"Yeah, yeah, yeah. Cleo told me you were here." He looked about the room like a Marine Corps drill sergeant inspecting an especially pathetic group of new recruits. "Howdy, y'all."

"Hi Benji," the roomful chorused—a bit a lamely, like children ashamed of themselves. He really knew how to protect his client of the moment. It was as if he dared anyone in the room to even sneeze at me.

"Don't feel bad, Rick. Actually, you've saved me a great deal of time." He shoved aside the coffee tray, and clicked open his briefcase. "One for you, one for you . . ." He walked about the room handing Francine, Cinda, Bob, Tru, and Jeep manila envelopes.

"A subpoena," Francine declared, her face turning white as she opened her envelope. "Christ, I need a smoke."

"Yes, that's right," Benji declared with relish. "You are all star defense witnesses. I *know* how eager you'll be to help my client."

"Fuck," Cinda reflected, upon seeing hers. "This is all I need." She looked at me and quickly added, "Not that I don't want to *help*, Rick."

"Why Benji, you shouldn't have," Jeep demurred.

"Malone, if you think you can fuck with me," Tru warned, "you better think again."

Benji didn't bother looking up at Tru as he clicked his briefcase shut. "And if you think you can commit perjury under oath, think again."

"I have nothing more to hide," Bob reflected. "Might as well get it over with. I suppose you have one to deliver to my wife?"

"And to your son, I'm afraid."

Bob put his hands to his face, then slid them together at his chin. "I understand."

"I appreciate that, Bob. But even if you didn't, I leave no stone unturned for a client."

"Benji, you don't understand. I was just about to—"

"Rick—I know what you were about to do. I remember you telling me that back in high school you wanted to be an actor. I can see why you never made it. Your timing stinks."

Before I could speak, Benji continued: "I've been digging around, too. We need to compare notes if we're going to get these jokers to come clean. And in a court of law, where there can be no monkey business."

"Plus that way the lawyer gets all the credit," Jeep wryly noted.

Benji ignored him. "C'mon, Rick. We have work to do."

25

*B*enji insisted that he and I have breakfast alone—as in, without Terry. I pulled Benji aside to say that Terry had been a major help, and that even though he was a cop, he was totally cool. Benji replied that it didn't matter if Terry was a goddamned cucumber, as a *cop* he couldn't be present during our private consultations and I had to stop being such a ninny.

On that charming note, I sent Terry off on his merry way—no doubt to a hearty truck driver's breakfast trough someplace—while Benji and I partook of a rarified repast at my poolside patio. As the careful, Zenlike geometry of the waters spilled down into the smaller, bluer pool below, we sat in the mild morning sunlight at my table of hand-painted tiles from Lisbon, fueling up on state-of-the-art takeout: egg-white-only Eggs Benedict on a millet muffin with fresh starfruit-ugli juice and raspberry-almond espresso, half-decaf.

Whether it was exhaustion, the fact that the food really wasn't good, or just some unconscious urge to prepare myself for prison cuisine, I oddly found myself envying Terry. I pictured him with his friendly elbows on the table as he indulged in, say, a big stack of hotcakes dripping with syrup with a side of hash, and cup after cup of Maxwell House. He sure had been a pal over these—what? Glorified two days, not counting the time I'd been sick? Cliché though it was, it seemed so much longer than that.

But it was good to see Benji, too, and as always I was fascinated to watch how his mind worked. It seemed he'd done what he could to dig up some dirt himself, given the constraints of his recent injuries—which he claimed to be completely untroubled by, though I caught him wincing and clutching his ribs more than once. If I had any fears that he'd scold me for sticking my nose where it didn't belong, I needn't have worried. I felt like a kid who broke a window with a baseball, but because he brings Dad his breakfast in bed, he doesn't get in trouble. Benji could hardly wait to dig into it all.

He'd been duly informed of the retrieved Oscar, and was awaiting word on blood and fingerprint tests. He more or less repeated what Terry said: that blood or a fingerprint from a third party essentially handed us the case on a silver platter. In the meantime, he hired a private dick to sniff around the Connee Kellogg caper. He told me it was a long shot, anyway, so not to waste time on it, seeing as how a "pro" was working on it. ("No offense, Rick.")

Benji had not known the Zeke Raflowitz story, but expressed interest in it only to the extent that it helped the case. When I reflected for a moment on how sad a tale it was, he scolded me to get to the point, dammit. He said he'd heard a rumor about Bob having done a porn movie, though not that Tara might've blackmailed him over it, and he doubted the movie ever existed. But he allowed that it never hurt to poke around. In any event, Bob, Cleo, and Zeke sure had enough reasons already for wanting Tara dead. Thinking out loud, Benji said he'd probably not mention the porn movie when Bob took the stand unless we had something really specific by then. Otherwise, it could turn jury sympathy against us.

He'd long known about Francine's chopped-up part in *That Girl—The Movie*. It was common knowledge about town, though of course Francine and Tara both always denied it when interviewed. Benji said that Francine was unlikely to have wanted to spoil her night of a special Oscar by offing someone. When I suggested that her little moment as Queen Bee might've been exactly what did push her over the edge if Tara said something exceptionally bitchy, the best Benji could muster up was a shrug and a "Maybe."

As for all the garbage between Tara and Tru, Benji couldn't have cared less. "If Truman Shea's going to kill someone," Benji elaborated, "it's not going to be over some penny ante crap." When I suggested that when it came to Tara, nothing was penny ante crap for Tru, Benji accused me of being a "sentimentalist," which, coming from Benji, was a supreme insult. He did, however, say that he'd heard something about some exceptionally questionable business deals on Tru's part around the financing of *On the Road Again.* Benji said that if Tara had gotten wind of said dealings, this—and none of the things I'd mentioned—might well have made for an exceptionally unpleasant encounter between herself and Mr. Shea.

Jeep's issues with Tara—the outing blackmail, the botched relationship, the movie close-ups—weren't of much interest to Benji, either. ("Rick, don't tell me about every little time you find a dime on the sidewalk," was how he put it.) But then there was the matter of Jeep's pinning it all on Cinda, which he seemed to regard more like finding a hundred-dollar bill. He said it was the best news he heard all day—it implicated both Cinda and Jeep, and so deflected the guilt away from me that much more. Cinda's possibilities as the killer intrigued him, and he lit up when I told him about the way she made her own hand bleed from her anger. (He also, I thought, got a wee bit turned on at the thought of Cinda and Tara having a three-way with Tru, or just a two-way with each other.)

"Wait a sec, Benji. I thought you were convinced the murderer was Shane."

"I still *am,* pretty much. But, hey—reasonable doubt is reasonable doubt."

"You'll hear no complaining out of me," I admitted. "But I still need to get to the bottom of things. Until it's known for certain who did it, people will think I did. And, anyway, it's—it's just *right* that a murder get solved."

"God, Rick, don't tell me you've become one of *them.*" He poured a container of half-and-half into his espresso, and stirred the spirals of brown and white.

"One of what?"

He took a loud sip. "One of those people with a conscience. You've been hanging around that dopey cop too long."

"Terry's not a dope. He's got good instincts—better, I think, than he realizes. And he's a kind, decent, hard-working guy."

"Well, when all this is over, maybe the two of you can take a luxury cruise."

"Obviously, he's not my type of person," I admitted, setting aside my flavorless eggs. "But I have to say we work together well."

Benji sighed with mild exasperation. "I suppose it's understandable. I'm no shrink, but a cop probably represents stability at this time and blah-blah-blah. Sort of like when people find God when their careers go down the toilet. I'm sure you'll come to your senses once you're acquitted. Which, I might point out, will not exactly cramp your style any in cracking the case. You might find it hard to do much sleuthing around from Death Row."

I had to admit he had a point.

"Of course, there's also Brother Dennis." I took a deep breath. "I don't know if you've been paying attention to the news. That press conference Shane gave?—it was really Brother Dennis. I let him talk me into it. I know it was wrong, but he said it was just for that one time. Except now he's kind of gone crazy. And Shane's still nowhere to be found."

Benji smiled devilishly. "Brother *who?* Oh, you mean Shane Kirk. After all, the man *says* he's Shane Kirk, and he certainly *looks* like Shane Kirk. Who am I to disbelieve?"

I laughed in spite of myself. "Benji, you're a genius."

" 'Tis true," he concurred. "Of course, Shane's reputation will be but mincemeat by the time I'm finished. Brother Dennis shouldn't be a very tough nut to crack."

I laughed again. "Tell me something, Benji. If your mother were on her deathbed but was the sole witness to a jaywalking incident that your client was being accused of, would you force your mother into court, or have your client pay the fifty-dollar fine?"

He ignored my superfluous question. "Keep on digging around, Rick," he encouraged, finishing his coffee. "Do it with that Terry joker, if it makes you feel better. Lord only knows what his game is. But the more 'I don't knows' and contradictions and pleading of the fifths we can get out of all those witnesses, the more your acquittal's in the bag." He reached across the table and patted my hand, an unusually kind gesture for him. "My friend, I think you need to realize that the case will not be solved by Monday morning. I'm not going to tell you to stop trying, because I know it wouldn't do any good. But do me a favor, and don't have a nervous breakdown in"— he glanced at his watch—"forty-four hours. Deal?"

We shook hands. "Deal."

But if anything, I was all the more determined to find the killer before Monday.

Benji stood up. "I know the way out."

"Benji, wait."

He sighed with impatience; once Benji was ready to *go*, you didn't stop him.

"Go easy on the Raflowitz kid, okay? He's been through a lot."

"Rick, I'm your *attorney*. You have to *trust* me."

"I know, I know. Forget I even said it."

But though I was fairly sure I could trust Benji, I wasn't at all sure that Zeke could.

26

*O*nce Benji drove off, I retreated to my study. I saw Terry, his arms folded across his belly, sleeping soundly in a chair beside the laptop. I quietly shut down the computer. After thinking about it, I resisted the urge to lead him over to the sofa, unlace his boots, and bring him a blanket and pillow. It was hard to predict these sorts of boundaries with a straight guy.

Telling myself that I'd only close my eyes for five, ten, maybe fifteen minutes, I took Terry's blissful-looking nap as an omen that I needed a little shut-eye myself. After all, I did have to sleep at some point.

Terry woke me by lightly touching my shoulder with one finger—which is the one way of waking me that just about gives me a heart attack. Once my shriek was no longer reverberating, and the bed no longer shaking for the height of my jump, I looked at the clock.

"Two in the afternoon. Fuck."

"And a good afternoon to you, too." He handed me a cup of coffee. "You're welcome."

"Oh, right—thanks." I blew on the coffee and tasted it. "You make a good cup of coffee." I was tempted to add a dumb little joke about what great secretary he'd make, but he never responded when I crossed gender boundaries with him, so I didn't bother. It probably wouldn't have been very funny, anyway.

"Everyone says that. Anyway, I only just got up myself, so don't go biting my head off." He sat up at the nightstand with his own coffee, and a bag of donuts. "Want one?" He held up the bright paper bag.

I sat up in bed. "This bedroom looks like a fucking Tide commercial." I squinted for all the blinding white.

"I think it's nice. Simple. I like that." Terry broke his buttermilk donut in half, dipped a piece in his coffee, and ate it with pleasure. "Sure you don't want one?"

"What are you, some sort of Donut Diety who conjures up cream-filled extravaganzas?"

Terry laughed. "I picked them up when I had breakfast."

"Fine, I'll take one." I reached for the bag and took a French cruller. If I *have to* have a donut, I always have a French cruller. I feel it shows "good taste."

"I made this thing," Terry explained, booting up the laptop. "It's kind of a Sim City of the goings-on backstage."

"Looks more like a game of Ms. Pacman," I teased. Actually, they were more like Lego figures, crudely geometric and seeming to be all shoulders. Utilizing some sort of bizarre clip art, Terry depicted the key players in the manner of one with an adolescent sense of melodrama. Bob was a generic male with a thin moustache, while Jeep had puffy blond hair reminiscent of "Crackle" in the old Rice Crispies ads. Tru was depicted as a Tyrannosaurus rex. Shane wore bathing trunks and a life preserver labeled "Life Guard"—I guess to indicate he was a "hunk." Francine was rounder than she was in real life as a way of making her seem "older." Cinda looked like a Wonder Woman-ish superhero. Connee had huge white hair, and Cleo was a sunflower. Zeke was depicted as a little bouncing peg.

Tara was a silhouette with a question mark on it.

"Now, when you put everyone's story together," Terry explained, "here's what you have. Bob presents the Best Actress award. He goes off into the green room; Tara meets the press. Then Bob sees Tara and Connee have it out—he said didn't know who Connee was at the time, but other people like Francine, Zeke, and Jeep did."

I watched the screen as Terry's crude figures hobbled about.

"Connee leaves in a huff. Bob yells at Tara. Bob kisses Tara. Zeke appears. Tara goes after Zeke. Francine is off behind the curtain, getting potted. Shane comes backstage after presenting Best Song. He gives Tara the engagement ring"—a sparkly gem probably lifted from a role-play game appeared with musical fanfare—"which Zeke sees, and which freaks him out. Then Cinda enters the scene, getting ready to present Best Actor. Now *Cinda* flips out—or at least according to Jeep, who's also hanging around by this time, getting ready to do Best Picture.

"Now, here's where we kind of have to improvise: Tara and Shane go outside, for some reason without the ring. And *maybe* with some other person"—Terry clicked on a storm cloud with a lightning bolt across it—"who kills Tara. Unless Shane does. Zeke thinks he sees Connee, but ends up looking outside, going bonkers. He runs off. Cinda goes to the stage to present Best Actor. *You* go outside, Rick"—I was depicted as a chess knight—"and this other person takes a shot at you. Shane appears, and then disappears. While all the time Tru is lurking about everywhere."

"Great. So what does all this mean?"

"It means," Terry stated, "that unless I've missed something, *anyone* really and truly could've done it. Because anyone could've had the time it took to kill Tara during the commercial break before Best Actor."

A ridiculous and terrible thought entered into my head: If it weren't for those interminably long commercial breaks between Oscar categories, Tara would still be alive.

Terry flicked on the TV. The DVD I'd made of the Oscars flickered into view. We watched all the audience shots during the major categories frame by frame. At commercial breaks, it was hard to see beyond all the superimposed graphics, but we did our best. Just as I recalled, Cleo Simone remained glued to her seat. Truman Shea got up and returned to his seat a half-dozen times before he claimed Best Picture.

Of course, we could not see what happened during the commercials themselves.

From the corner of the frame, I spied a diehard blonde in a black dress. Just before Best Actress, she walked toward the seats; then she had a change of heart, and walked backstage.

"Connee Kellogg," Terry noted.

It was the last time the blonde in question appeared on the recording.

"I get this terrible sinking feeling sometimes," I shared. "What if Connee did it? Only since she's dead, there's no way of really pinning it on her."

"She could've OD'd out of guilt—or maybe fear," Terry concurred.

"Thanks for the vote of confidence."

"You know I didn't mean it like that. Look, let's just get to work, okay?"

And so we did.

We went over Terry's little simulation about a million times, seeing if there was any sort of glaring inconstancy we were missing. When that proved fruitless, we went back over the recording of the Oscars—to similar frustration.

Next, we checked out every Web site we could find that had anything to do with the key players. Remembering Benji's lead, I found several Web pages about Tru's corrupt business dealings in his quest to take over the world, but none seemed worth taking seriously. They were all a bit too *Pinky and the Brain*. We did find two Web sites dedicated to the alleged dirty movie, *Beat Me, Daddy, Eight to the Balls*. One of them claimed that it starred a different pair of actors, while the other site strove to "set the record straight" by claiming that it was a family picture starring Flipper, the dolphin. Otherwise, there was nothing new to add to Tru's list of motives.

I'd never paid very close attention to the career of Francine Quick—why should I have?—but I discovered that she'd been arrested back in the early 1960s for impersonating a hypnotist at a "B" list party. The charges were dropped almost immediately—it was all a "big misunderstanding" and part of a "practical joke"—but it did cast doubt as to the authenticity of Dr. Quick's highly dramatic journey into the psyche of Zeke Raflowitz. In which case who could say if Zeke didn't do it after all? And of course if Francine lied about her powers of hypnosis, who knew what else she'd lied about?

Hacking into police records, Terry made an interesting discovery. Cinda Sharpe had been arrested the day before the Oscars for disturbing the peace—and at the residence of none other than her closest chum, Tara Perez. It seemed the enthusiastic Cinda was screaming at the top of her lungs that Tara had better get outside and "talk" to her. Truly, the human thirst for lively conversation knows no bounds. In any event, the charges were immediately dropped by the fair-minded Ms. Perez—who, one might hazard a guess, did not want the police sniffing around to much into her general direction. This did not bode well for poor Cinda, but, then again, it wasn't the same thing as irrefutable evidence against her.

As for the cursed Raflowitz–Simone dynasty, there was even more to add to the already foul-tasting mix: Hacking into bank records, we discovered that Bob made a cash withdrawal of fifty Gs on the day of the Oscars.

As for Jeep, there was nothing more that we could find, other than the relatively mild threats and squabbles with Tara that he'd had to contend with. Even the porn movie, if for real, would not have concerned him the way it would've concerned Bob.

But in a way, that almost made us more suspicious of Jeep.

What it all boiled down to was even more reasons why all of these people could've done it. But there was nothing that told us that one of them *had to* have been the murderer.

While I couldn't say I was having fun—time was running out

before Monday morning, and I was starting to feel the pinch—the time flew by nonetheless.

"Jesus, it's eleven." I took off my glasses and rubbed my eyes. "Officer Zane, what say we go to a gay bar."

Terry was tired, too, and he got a little snippy.

"Rick, I thought we were way past all that teasing crap."

"I'm serious. Shane is still the key. Unless he's taken Dennis's place among the Jesuits in Ohio—which ain't too likely—he's out there someplace, biding his time. And someplace just might be a gay bar—preferably of the twink, call-boyish variety. I think I know the place. Shane talked about it awhile back." I quickly added, " 'Twink' means a young guy."

"I *know* what it means," Terry replied, deeply offended. "I'm a cop. I'm not naïve."

"Sorry," I answered back. "Forgive me if my manners are slipping when I've got about five minutes left to live. But Shane's still got that sugar daddy mentality. If he's depending on the kindness of strangers, that's the kind of place we'll find him."

"But what about that man in the white car that Brother Dennis talked about?"

"What about him? Terry, I'm not in a position to take anything Brother Dennis said too seriously. It was just a story that some street kid told him, anyway. Maybe I won't find Shane, but I have to try."

Terry thought about it. "We might at least stumble across Dennis."

"Whom we better not let out of our sight for any number of reasons."

"You're right." Terry stood up and stretched. "So let's go."

"Is it going to be weird for you, being in a gay bar?"

Terry reached for his construction boots. "I've been to gay bars before, Rick. Once on duty I had to check something out. And Darla Sue, when her sister and husband were visiting, took us all to a drag show."

"Well, you look okay," I commented. And he did. T-shirt, jeans, construction boots, buzz cut—you can't go wrong with that.

"Okay for what?" Terry looked a bit concerned.

"To fit in. You know—to not look like a cop or anything."

I didn't feel like being recognized, either, so I put on a broad-brimmed baseball cap to shadow my face, or hopefully shade it enough.

Once in the Cherokee, it annoyingly took a little extra time for Terry to ditch all the reporters, but at last he managed to do so. It was nearly one A.M. by the time we pulled up at a trashy-chic sawdust bar called Dawson's, off Wilshire in West Hollywood. It was *the* hot pickup bar for old men with money to burn on young guys with expensive tastes.

The bar was an old furniture warehouse that had been converted into a multistoried affair, with two dance floors: disco pop on the second floor, country-and-western on the third. On the main floor were the pool tables and hardcore drunks. It was Saturday night at its peak, and it took several minutes to push our way through the crowds and noise.

In obvious and not-so-obvious locales throughout the bar, young men stood watchfully about. Some opted for the wholesome look, like they just stepped out of a Tommy Hilfiger ad, while others were into the Calvin Klein bad boy thing. Barely legal or able to pass for such, they no doubt called themselves models and told themselves that their porn shoots and "escort" gigs were but stepping-stones for better times to come. Still, they were social classes above the underage unfortunates walking the streets.

At the second floor, an extremely inebriated fellow with eyes so bloodshot they could've been used in a transfusion leaned his killer whiskey breath in close to Terry and uttered, "Hey there, big guy. What are you, a cop?" He touched Terry's chest in wonder.

Terry was a good sport. "Sure," he smiled, removing the guy's hand. "I'm a cop."

"God, what a killer smile," the drunk noted. "What a real hunk of *man.*"

Terry took a sip of his ginger ale. "Thank you."

"Dance with me, big guy. Whadya say?"

A go-go boy climbed up onto the bar, and began gyrating down the length of it.

"Say, look at that." Terry pointed helpfully at the dancer.

"Been there, done that." The drunk dismissed the dancer with his hand. "C'mon."

Terry tried to ease the man's grip off his arm, but the drunk took it as a sign of encouragement, and attempted to lace his fingers with Terry's.

"He's with me," I shouted above the noise. "Scram."

"Uh, that's right," Terry agreed. "C'mon, let's go."

To make it look good, I kind of grabbed Terry's arm.

"Well, you certainly are the belle of the ball," I noted, as we climbed up to the third story.

"Very funny."

The predominant music changed from Madonna to George Straight as we entered into the pseudo-country setting. Various male couples in cowboy drag were line-dancing across the floor with a Rockette-like precision.

"I imagine you're quite the whiz at all this western two-stepping."

"Actually, I don't know the first thing about it. It looks like they're having fun, though."

We looked around for a minute or two.

"Say, they're pretty good dancers," Terry commented, noting a showy couple doing all sorts of twirls and things.

"Let's go," I decided. "This was a waste of time."

Terry nudged my shoulder. "I'm sorry, Rick. We can try driving around."

We shuffled through the crowds back down to the second floor, and were turning to go to the first floor when I thought I saw a ghost.

I tapped Terry on the back and pointed to the far end of the dance floor.

"Shane?" he asked me.

"I *think* so. Unless it's Dennis?"

With a bad-dream frustration, we inched our way through the crowd. Shane/Dennis bobbed out of sight. By the time we reached the opposite side of the dance floor, he was nowhere to be seen.

Someone tapped Terry's shoulder. "Dance with me," ordered the voice, like a cop might tell you to drop your weapon.

It was Truman Shea. "Rick, I'm borrowing your bodyguard," he informed me, in a manner that indicated I had no choice. He wore a black leather vest over his bare chest.

From behind Tru there emerged none other than Dennis—unless it was Shane? He wore a white shirt that dazzled in the dance floor light. He seemed in a state of ecstasy as he mouthed along to the lyrics of the oldie that was playing: "Only In My Dreams" by Debbie Gibson.

Terry looked at me searchingly, but I could only subtly shrug in return. I honestly could not tell if it was Shane or Dennis.

"Uh, sure, Mr. Shea," Terry decided. "I'll dance with you." He gamely let Tru link arms with him as he led him over but a few inches of crowded dance floor. I was amused to see Terry being so very much an Officer in the Line of Duty that he would force himself to dance with a man. Ironically, I had to say that Terry was the much better dancer. Like a lot of big guys, he was surprisingly light on his feet. Tru, by contrast, did his usual stiff, odd dance that gave no indication of responding to the rhythm of the music. Tru gazed at him with a quirked eyebrow and asked, "Do you swing both ways, or are you only into guys?" Terry replied with a friendly but non-committal smile.

I turned my attention to the man in the white shirt.

"So, Shane—where have you been staying?" I tried to sound casual.

"Back at my place." There was scorn in how he said it, like it was too obvious that that was where he'd be staying.

"Do you still want the mirror?" I asked, hoping to determine from his answer if he really was Shane.

"Of course," he answered obtusely. "I love mirrors."

"Where's your twin brother these days?"

He grinned determinedly. "I don't know."

"Dance with me, Shane." I stared at him unblinkingly.

He stared right back. "Sure, Rick."

Whoever this really was, he *danced* like Shane—slow and sexy, with a rugged intensity in his hips.

"I got a subpoena," he shouted above the music. He smiled

brightly, as though conveying a cheery bit of casual news. "I hope you're not *too* mad at me, Rick." He turned, dancing with his back-side to me. Then he spun back around to face me. "Don't worry, I'll set the record straight." He reached over to tweak my nose.

Normally, these little flourishes would've aroused me, but Shane's charms—or at least Dennis's charms—were not working their intended spell.

"Shane, what *is* the record? What happened in the parking lot?"

Of course, I didn't know for certain if this *was* Shane, but I needed to take the chance.

He leaned over to whisper in my ear: *"I want to surprise you."*

I stared at him in disbelief.

"Trust me, Rick."

"Shane, what the hell happened? *Who murdered Tara?*"

He laughed. "You've always worried too much."

It was all I could do not to grab him by the neck and shake him—or even worse. But some voice of reason told me that the last thing I needed was to be spotted acting violently toward Shane Kirk.

I could see that Terry, though, was watching me with some concern. Tru danced up close to him, and Terry politely moved a bit away, as if he did so for being swept up by the music.

A tap to my shoulder made me all but jump through the roof.

"Rick, I can barely see you under that cap. Is this your new look?"

It was Chauncey Riggs, sweating as usual in an unsuccessful attempt to look festive in a Hawaiian shirt. He bobbed his head slightly to the beat.

"Are you ready, Shane?" He made a point of staring at me as he asked the question.

"Sure, Chauncey." Shane leaned over to me. "I have an interview, Rick. Sorry."

"Shane, you can't just—"

But the two began to walk away.

"I'll be right back, Rick," Shane promised.

I glanced over at Tru, who seemed oblivious to my plight. He was trying to score with Terry, so nothing else in the universe mattered. That I knew his quest to be utterly futile added to my frustration toward him.

I decided to follow behind Chauncey and Shane, but in the crowd I couldn't find them. By the time I got back over to the dance floor, Terry and Tru had stopped dancing, and were talking. I saw Chauncey nearby nursing a beer.

"Where's Shane?" I asked him.

"I have no idea, Rick." He took a big swallow of beer.

"What do you mean?"

"I turned my back for one second, and he was gone." He indicated to the bartender that he wanted a refill. "I guess he saw some hot number." Chauncey looked at me to study my response. "Why, Rick? Are you concerned about the trial, or is it something else?"

"Fuck you, Chauncey." I picked up his beer and poured it over his head.

I'd always wanted to do that to somebody.

"C'mon, Terry. Let's go."

27

*B*ack at my house I got righteously drunk.

I don't remember too much of what happened. There was a whole lot of cursing and swearing—much of which was directed at Shane—and then, as if part of a logical progression of ideas, I performed for Terry one of my old high school football fight songs. Way back when, I never even went to any of the football games, but the song lingered in some back alley of memory, I suppose out of some long-suppressed desire to have been a cheerleader. There I was, singing away, replete with gestures, about how the Perkins, Iowa, Minks—yes, our mascot was the mink—were bound for V-I-C-T-O-R-Y. Terry kept working away on the laptop throughout, periodically giving me a patient smile or "uh-huh."

At some point I passed out on the sofa. Terry threw a blanket over me.

Sunday I felt like hell, but we drove over to Shane's place—no one was there—and then we drove around to whatever gay haunts were open. We scanned the prostitute-riddled sidewalks. We then drove back to Shane's. But there was no sign of Shane/Dennis anywhere.

I napped to take the edge off my hangover.

We did some more Web surfing, to no particular avail.

I cried for about two hours. Terry patted my back.

Suddenly, there it was: Monday morning.

As I put on my dark blue suit for the courthouse, Terry advised, "Try not to be so afraid it destroys you."

"Thanks, Officer." I appreciated that he was not so blasé as to suggest I be fearless.

"I'll keep at it."

"I know." After an awkward moment, we awkwardly kind of hugged.

Benji wore a dark blue suit, too, as he drove up to take me to court. In between whistling along to the adult contemporary songs on the radio, he talked a mile a minute about all the witnesses he was calling, how weak the prosecution's argument was, and how he wouldn't be at all surprised if the judge dismissed the charges for the state's failure to establish its case.

None of it really made me feel any better.

Throughout the previous week, I clung to the hope that it would never have to come to this. My hope was what kept me sane. Now that I was actually going on trial for murder—on live TV, no less—I felt numb. It was all beyond my comprehension.

It seemed impossible that it had only been a week since I last saw Judge Ruetha Hopkins, not to mention prosecutors extraordinaire Carolyn Caruthers and Marion Goober. They both were wearing blue suits, as well. Benji exchanged words with Ms. Caruthers. Then he sat down next to me, got a folder from his briefcase, and whispered, "You have to look *calm,* Rick. Like you have nothing to hide." He put a restraining hand to my jittering leg.

The jury selection took two days. The major obstacle was finding people who seemed even remotely believable when they said that they didn't know *anything* about the trial. They just hadn't paid *any* attention to everything blared over the TV, radio, and print media nonstop for the past week. Of course, you could then make the argument that anyone that ignorant wasn't bright enough to sit on a jury. But what did I know? I was only the defendant.

On Wednesday, the welfare crackheads who comprised the jury were seated to hear the opening statements. According to sweet Carolyn, the State would prove beyond a shadow of a doubt that I was this "openly homosexual" beast of a reporter who was not content to ruin people through malicious words, but who also determined that Tara would have to literally pay with her life for having won the love of Shane. My obsessive love for Shane drove me over the edge like a herd of lemmings at the Grand Canyon. While I thought I was so clever and privileged I could get away with anything, the jury had this neat-O opportunity to send a different message to me and all the other murderous scumbags out there who had to always get our own way.

It was difficult to listen to this garbage. Leaning back in my chair with uppity defiance, I felt like Jessica Lange in *Frances.* I could only hope that a kinder fate awaited me.

Benji—normally in such a rush—dramatically took his time once he performed in a courtroom. He stood up slowly, then briefly contemplated while chewing one end of his reading glasses, before finally walking over to the jury. "Someone murdered Tara Perez," he began, "but it wasn't Rick Domino. The flimsy case against him is built on purely circumstantial evidence. He was not jealous of Ms. Perez, and he is not a vindictive individual. There *are* vindictive people in this town"—he looked down and away from the jury, as if deep in thought—"and one of them did kill Tara Perez. You'll want to send a message loud and clear to the State: Find the real killer, and stop wasting taxpayer's time and money with the first convenient scapegoat."

When asked if the State was ready to call its first witness, Carolyn replied, "Yes, Your Honor. The State calls Police Officer Terry Zane."

Terry never discussed this with me, I guessed because it was a mighty ticklish issue, but I realized that of course he'd have to take the stand as the arresting officer.

He made a point of never looking at me as he got sworn in.

The State's interrogation of him was short but thorough: Tara was in fact found lying dead, and I was indeed seen holding the smoking gun.

On cross-examination, Benji asked Terry, "Did you see Mr. Domino fire the gun?"

"No, sir, I did not."

"And as a police officer, what was your professional opinion—your gut instinct, if you will—as to Mr. Domino's guilt or innocence?"

An outraged Carolyn interrupted. "Objection, Your Honor. The witness's 'gut instinct' is not relevant." She looked truly perplexed; why would the defense ask this of the arresting officer? What sort of underhanded scheme was Benji trying to pull?

"I can see how this would fall within the purview of professional experience," stated the judge. "But I hardly feel it could be in your client's best interests to pursue this line of questioning, Mr. Malone."

"We're willing to take that chance, Your Honor."

"Very well." She sighed. "Objection overruled. The witness will answer."

"In my professional opinion, sir, Mr. Domino displayed none of the traits associated with a murderer."

"Please explain."

"Quite often a murderer acts more upset than he really is—fake tears, fake outrage. Mr. Domino was . . . well, just himself. Upset that he'd been arrested, to be sure, but very matter-of-fact. He looked right at you when he spoke. No mind games or manipulation. He had no telltale nervous tics about him, either, which someone who just committed murder often has. He wasn't shaking, shifty-eyed, or perspiring profusely. He was neither too hot nor too cold."

On redirect, Marion Goober asked, "Still, Officer Zane, it is *pos-*

sible for someone to commit murder without perspiring afterwards—or any of these other relatively minor behavioral patterns you are describing?"

"Yes, it is," Terry began, "but—"

"Thank you, Officer Zane."

My instincts told me that the State won the battle but lost the war, so to speak, by cutting Terry off. Technically, they got the answer they wanted, but the jury must've seen that it was a manipulative tactic, as if the State had something to hide.

The next witness was a police detective who testified that the gun fired on Tara was the exact same one that I was holding at the crime scene, and that residue on my hands determined that I'd fired the gun. Benji asked him if the only reason someone would fire a gun was to commit cold-blooded murder. After Carolyn's objection was overruled, the detective replied that of course it was not. Benji's sarcastic "thank you" drew titters from the audience.

Next was a different detective who examined the crime scene, and who asserted that there was no evidence of a third party involved in a struggle. No shell casings from a different gun were found. This last bit of info distressed me no end, but I felt a little better when, on cross, Benji asked him if the Oscar won by Ms. Perez was found anywhere at the scene. The detective answered that it had not been.

Then a doctor from the coroner's office testified that Tara actually died from getting clobbered with a blunt object, and that traces of her blood were found on the Oscar she'd won. Benji had no questions for him. Then another detective stated that only two sets of fingerprints on the statuette could be identified: Tara's and mine. Benji asked the detective if he didn't think it odd that no one else's fingerprints—such as those belonging to Bob Raflowitz, or the startlets who helped hand out the awards—were found on the Oscar. The detective made a major blooper in replying that fingerprints easily got smeared.

The police shrink who'd interviewed me testified that I was about as Looney Toons as they came, and definitely capable of offing Tara. My little joke about masturbation and anger management became grounds for him to determine that I confused sexual fantasy with violent impulses. When Benji questioned him, though, it was learned that this shrink was rabidly homophobic, active in the Christian Right, and therefore unlikely to be an objective judge of an openly gay man's character.

The next witness was none other than Chauncey Riggs, looking relatively dapper in a navy pinstriped suit. He melodramatically conveyed how he found the engagement ring and sales receipt in a paper bag backstage, and turned said paraphernalia over to the police. In stating this, he made more faces than Sally Field as *Sybil*. Benji asked Chauncey if he had offered to post bail on my behalf. Chauncey mopped his forehead with his Italian hankie to reply that he had. Benji then asked him if he was in the habit of posting bail for people he believed to be murderers. Carolyn objected; the objection was sustained. Chauncey looked utterly heartbroken when Benji stated he had no more questions for him.

Finally, they showed a brief film clip of me interviewing Tara and Shane at the pre-Oscar show. They repeated for the jury the little bit when I said that Tara could play a Sumo wrestler and whatnot to show what a mean-spirited little shit I was.

And that took one full day—some actual advancement of the case amidst a million objections and sidebars. Yet I was reluctantly granting myself permission to feel elated. The State really didn't have a case, and surely even the ninnies on the jury could see that this was so. I took a luxuriously long bubble bath that evening, and got a much-needed long night's sleep.

First thing Thursday morning, the State was to call its next witness: Shane Kirk.

But saving someone's life is much more important than accepting a prize."

"What about Ms. Perez?"

"She was helping, too. She set down her Oscar, and was saying soothing words. 'We love you, Rick, we want you to live.' That type of thing."

"And what did Mr. Domino do?"

"He looked at her Oscar and said, 'I've always wanted just to hold one.' Then he reached down for it. For a second, I thought he was coming to his senses. But in one swift motion he picked up the Oscar, and hit Tara over the head with it. She instantly fell to the ground. I said, 'Rick, oh my God, what are you doing?' He hit her again and again. Then he took the gun and shot her. He shot her and shot her and shot her."

Shane wept hard—or at least pretended to—with his face to the railing.

After letting him cry for a minute or so, Carolyn asked, "And then what happened?"

Shane lifted his head, and rubbed his face with both hands. "Rick—Mr. Domino—said that he planned to kill Tara all along. That he faked wanting to kill himself to trick us, and kill her with the Oscar instead. He said it was poetic justice to kill Tara with the very prize she'd fought all her life to win. He took the ring off her finger. He said it was *his* ring, not Tara's. But I suppose now he ran back inside to put it on the chair, to make it look like—like I don't know what. Maybe to make it seem like *I* did it. As if Tara had turned me down. I think I did leave the bag inside—you know, being happy about getting engaged and all, I guess I got a bit absentminded."

"What did you do then?"

Shane lowered his head in remorse. "I am very ashamed to say that I went into shock. Maybe if it had been someone else, anyone but *Tara* . . . well, my doctor keeps telling me not to blame myself, that it was a physiological reaction over which I had no control. But I ran. Like a coward, I ran. I got a hotel room under a different name. I lay with the blankets over my head, too paralyzed with shock and depression to move. It took about a day to find the strength to reappear—and with the help of so many close friends, I found the courage to face up to it all."

"And you are certain that this is what happened—that what you have told us was not distorted by any sort of shock or trauma?"

"Absolutely, Ms. Caruthers. I have told you *exactly* what happened."

"Your witness."

Benji took his characteristic time walking over to Shane. I sensed that Benji was going to have to walk a mighty thin line in his cross-examination. He couldn't openly accuse him of being Brother Dennis, because it opened all sorts of stinky cans of worms that would make me look bad. And he also couldn't casually accuse Shane of being gay or having slept with me, because he was likely to lose the sympathy of the jury—not to mention all of America.

"So, Mr. Kirk," Benji finally began, all smiling and friendly. "You're an actor. I'm trying to remember—what was the first movie you appeared in?"

Marion rose to object, disputing the relevance of such a line of questioning. Benji countered that he needed to establish the credibility of a witness who so recently suffered such traumatic "shock." The judge allowed the question.

Shane's hand shook slightly as he held it to his chin in thought. "I'm terribly, sorry, Mr. Malone. Could you please repeat the question?"

"Certainly. Your first film role. What was it?"

"I . . . I'm sorry, but with all that's happened, I'm afraid I can't think of what it was. *Gypsies, Tramps, and Thieves?*"

"Actually, it was *Every Breath You Take.*"

"Of course," Shane replied. "*Every Breath You Take.* I . . . all this is just too much. My career just seems so unimportant right now."

"And you next movie?"

"I . . ."

"It was *Everyday People.*

"Right, *Everyday People.*

"Actually, it wasn't. I just remembered. It was *Boogie-Woogie Bugle Boy*."

"Oh, right. *Boogie-Woogie Bugle Boy*. That one was fun."

"No, wait—I'm sorry. I was right before. It was *Everyday People*." Shane got red in the face. "Look, I told you, I'm upset."

"Upset enough to not remember what happened when Tara got murdered?"

"Objection," chimed Marion and Carolyn.

"Overruled."

"Mr. Malone, I can assure you that I remember something that important."

"Did you or did you not just state that you went into shock Monday night, such overwhelming shock that you could not move out of bed?"

"Yes, but as I explained, I'm better now."

"Are you on medication?"

"*No.*"

"So let me get this straight. One week ago, the love of your life is brutally murdered before your very eyes. You are so traumatized that you disappear. But, as if by magic, you're all better now. Is that correct?"

"You're twisting it all around. You're making it sound like . . ."

"Like what, Mr. Kirk? That you're lying?"

Shane sat there with his mouth open, utterly dumbfounded.

"Never mind. Let us move on. You stated that you got an engagement ring for Ms. Perez, correct?"

"Yes, that is correct," Shane answered with defiance.

"It must have been a lovely ring. A large diamond, I imagine?"

"Yes. The biggest, brightest one I could find."

Benji walked over to his briefcase. "Mr. Kirk, would you be so kind as to read aloud this document?" He handed him a sheet of paper. "The highlighted sections only, please."

Shane cleared his throat. If he was the real Shane, he'd probably stumble over any big words there might be.

But the message was straightforward enough.

In a memo from Truman Shea to the costume designer of *On*

The Road Again, it was noted that Tara had it expressly written into her contract that she would never wear diamonds or faux diamonds on screen, just as she never wore them in real life: "Ms. Perez is unyieldingly firm in her belief that diamonds do not become her," Shane read aloud. "She furthermore associates them with an unspecified traumatic incident from her past and considers them bad luck. Hence, her insistence on wearing sapphires, emeralds, and rubies only, which preference, Ms. Perez strongly believes, has become one of her most recognizable trademarks."

Shane was quiet for a moment. "What can I say?" he finally answered. "I'm a guy. I don't notice these things."

"Apparently not," Benji agreed. "No more questions—for now."

Marion rose to briefly get Shane to reiterate that he'd told the truth, regardless of the tactics Benji had just used on him.

For my part, I was reasonably convinced that Shane was really Dennis, but not absolutely so—the real Shane might have been just as big a dodo about remembering his movies and whatnot. In any event, whichever one it was, it certainly looked good for me that Shane would be perceived as such a ditz. A crazed ditz if he were Dennis, and a nasty, scheming one if he were Shane, but a ditz in either case.

Having provided an alibi, hard if somewhat circumstantial evidence, and an eyewitness adored by the public, the State rested its case.

I managed to get to sleep that night after drinking a whole bunch of gin. Both Benji and Terry called to comfort me, but I couldn't even bring myself to pick up the phone to speak to either one.

The next day, Friday, a group of unhappy faces—namely, Bob, Cleo, Zeke, Francine, Cinda, Tru, and Jeep—were seated in the courtroom, as if awaiting execution by guillotine. Benji, they feared, would grill them mercilessly to get at the truth. All sorts of skeletons were about to come marching out of any number of closets.

Benji called Bob as his first witness. Carolyn rose to object. The upshot was a meeting in the judge's chambers with Her Honor, Carolyn, Marion, and Benji. From what I could piece together after-wards, the State argued that none of these witnesses were relevant to the case unless they could cast reasonable doubt on Shane Kirk's testimony. Since Benji could not guarantee that any of these wit-nesses would in fact swear under oath that they saw Tara's murder, the judge ruled that there was no reason for them to testify. Merely blowing smoke, she told Benji, by pointing out that other people had issues with Tara, was not an appropriate line of defense. Even Jeep's having told the police Cinda did it was deemed irrelevant—unless Jeep could state that he had conclusive evidence to offer, which—to the judge's mind—he could not do.

To say that Bob and the other looked relieved when they were told they were excused from testifying would be like saying that movies had once or twice found it profitable to include scenes of sex and violence. Bob did have the decency to kind of tighten his lips together in sympathy for my plight on his way out, and Jeep winked at me.

I tried to be fair: In their position, what would I have done—if, after all, I really didn't know who killed Tara? Still, they were all cowards, as far as I was concerned. And how did I know that none of them knew who killed Tara—let alone was the killer?

So there in one fell swoop went over half of our case.

Benji called a couple of experts to the stand. First was my shrink, who testified that I didn't have a murderous neurosis in my psyche. Next he called a former D.A. now working as a private con-sultant, who stated that given my height, the blow to Tara's head should have been at a different angle.

Then came the moment I dreaded most of all.

Originally, Benji wasn't planning on calling me to testify, but now he had no choice.

I stated exactly what happened—how I crept outside and stum-bled across the body, how someone shot at me so I picked up the gun and fired, how Shane appeared then ran off, how I stumbled upon the Oscar in Shane's closet and that that was why my finger-prints were on it.

Beyond that, I never lied, but was necessarily selective with the truth. I never mentioned Terry or Brother Dennis, though I stated I left Shane's house shortly after I thought I "heard something"—which was technically true. When Benji asked what Tara's Oscar was doing in Shane's domicile, I replied that I didn't know. We avoided mention of how Benji got injured, and the Oscar stolen from his car. Benji said it would sound "fishy and paranoid" to the jury, and to keep it simple. The Oscar was brought into police custody, period, and we left it at that.

Benji treaded carefully over my personal life. He asked me if I had any sort of personal vendetta against Tara Perez, and I replied that I did not. When he asked me about the pre-Oscar show clip, I answered that it was common for gossip columnists to get cagey with the stars. He asked me if Shane Kirk ever lived in my house, and I replied that he had done so on and off for several years. Again, Benji was careful to not make it seem like we were "accusing" Shane of being gay; we'd say just enough of the facts, and let the jury add two and two for themselves.

If I achieved no other victory, from now on at least some people would wonder why Shane Kirk was living with an openly gay man. My only regret was that Shane/Dennis was not in court. I couldn't watch him squirm—or better yet, make a scene as he tried to deny it all.

I felt a sharp jab of pain in my stomach as Carolyn stood up to cross-examine me.

"So, Mr. Domino," she began, "you cannot tell us what actually happened. If your testimony is to be believed, you conveniently enough were out of view from the TV cameras as you sneaked outside and got there just a moment too late to have seen it all. Is that correct?"

"Yes," I answered, thinking to myself: *Don't say a single extra word.*

"You stated that Mr. Kirk lived in your home. Were you in love with him?"

"Yes."

"And did you believe that Mr. Kirk in love with you in return?"

"Sometimes I tried to think he was. But I suppose he wasn't."

Carolyn walked leisurely about the courtroom, confident of her victory. "Whatever made you think he might've been?" she asked condescendingly.

"We were lovers," I replied boldly.

"Order in the court," insisted the judge, when the room erupted in a stir of voices.

Carolyn had committed the classic error of asking a witness a question she didn't know the answer to.

"You and Shane Kirk were lovers," she repeated back, as if unable to fully comprehend the words. Marion stood up for his utter incredulity, nodding at me in exasperation: to what depths of sleaziness would I not stoop to get myself acquitted?

"Yes, that's right. To the best of my knowledge, Shane was never sexual with Tara or any other woman. He's a highly closeted gay man. That was one of the problems in our relationship. He was always so afraid of being outed."

"Why should anyone believe you?"

"Would you like me to describe his body in the minutest detail?"

Carolyn was flustered and desperate as she turned to face me. "Well, if what you say is true, you *really* would have been upset, then, if Shane proposed marriage to Tara. To have believed he had these feelings for you . . . ?"

"I might well have been upset," I answered evenly, "but I didn't kill Tara. And why should anyone believe Shane? He's lied his entire career about who he is."

"That's up to the jury to decide."

I shrugged. "You'll get no argument out of me."

There were giggles in the courtroom.

Carolyn pronounced, in a most sarcastic and rueful tone of voice, "No more questions." She said this in a way that suggested I was such a waste of time to question when I was so obviously guilty, she was done with me.

On redirect, Benji asked me more about my relationship with Shane. Since the State opened the door, Benji didn't have any qualms about assassinating his character.

"Shane was a prostitute when I met him," I conveyed. "He slept with male producers to get parts. I can document this. He was, in my experience, an extremely dishonest person who used people to get ahead. Tara was just a cover, so no one would know he was gay."

Carolyn fiercely objected. "Your Honor, Mr. Kirk's sexual life history is not what's on trial here."

Benji looked at her triumphantly. "Would you like us to recall him to the stand, so that he could swear under oath that none of this is true? Would you like us to ask him about an arrest for solicitation back in—"

"Objection withdrawn," Carolyn decided, waving her hands in frustration. Marion had his hands over his face, presumably in a similar state of mind.

Benji then showed the same pre-Oscar show clip, only he asked the jury to note how Shane Kirk was subtly handing me something. Benji asked me what this was; I replied that it was a note to meet him in the men's room, where Shane and I passionately kissed.

The shock of having just heard scandal permeated the courtroom. Imagine two men kissing in a *public* men's room.

"Do you still love Mr. Kirk?" Benji inquired.

"No. I don't know who really murdered Tara, but after Mr. Kirk has lied about what really happened that night, after he disappeared when he could've helped me . . . I'm sorry, Mr. Malone. But my opinion of Mr. Kirk and anything he might have to say could not be lower."

Carolyn declined the opportunity to ask me any more questions.

"Defense rests."

And that was Friday.

At Benji's instance, I spent the weekend at a Palm Springs health spa, his treat. I was forced to relax—at least somewhat—whether I liked it or not. Benji said we were in great shape. That we had reasonable doubt up the wazoo. I firmly agreed with him, but I couldn't resist bringing along my laptop anyway, and putting in a few calls to Terry—who, though he kept on trying to come up with some new piece of evidence, arrived at nothing but dead ends, just like me. Oh well, at least I'd get acquitted, and could keep working on the case.

If nothing else, I'd hurt Shane's career. Not only would people, at very least, question his sexuality from hereon out, but the you-know-what had hit the fan in a most ignoble way. Over the course of the weekend, the best he could muster was a lame "no comment" to the press. And of course if Shane was really Dennis, I showed that I wasn't about to just sit back and let him lie me into the death chamber. Even if I were found guilty—unlikely a possibility though it was—I'd walk to my death tasting sweet revenge, in a twisted, Bette Davis sort of way.

29

On Monday morning, the jury heard the closing arguments.

Carolyn essentially reprised what she'd been saying all along: fingerprints on Oscar, smoking gun, motive, ring, eyewitness. She added that whatever jurors might want to speculate about Shane Kirk's personal life, it did not detract from the integrity of his testimony—that he saw what he saw. She concluded by reminding them what a beloved star Tara was, how she'd brought joy to millions and all but walked on water during her all-to-brief stay on earth.

Benji, I thought, made mincemeat out of her arguments.

He reminded the jury of the circumstantial nature of the evidence, and the expert witnesses who cast doubts upon it, as well as my own testimony as to what happened. He discussed the stupid Christian Right shrink versus the normal shrink that said I was not capable of murder—as had Officer Terry Zane. Most of all, Benji emphasized that Shane Kirk's testimony was obviously not to be trusted. "Reasonable doubt," he emphasized time and again.

And so the jury adjourned to deliberate.

One hour and twenty minutes later, they came back with a verdict.

"Great sign," Benji stated, give me a friendly jab in the ribs. "It was a no-brainer."

With virtually the entire world watching, Judge Hopkins instructed me to rise and face the jury. Benji of course rose with me, looking cavalier. He was as close as he got to non-homely when he just won a case, and I could see him getting ready to savor victory as if salivating before a T-bone steak.

From the corner of my eye, I spotted Terry seated in the back of the courtroom, encouraging me with his eyes.

The clerk read the verdict: *In the case of Richard Domino vs. the People of the State of California, we the People find the defendant guilty of murdering Tara Perez, a human being, in the first degree.*

Benji lost his balance, like he was going to faint. Oddly enough, my very first thought was to hold him steady.

When your body is severely injured you go into a state of shock, and even if you've just lost an arm you might walk around as though nothing is wrong. In a way, that was me at that moment. A strength I never knew I had welled inside, a liquid-like sensation that warmed me all over. I was shattered, destroyed, my life was ruined, and yet I never had more fight in me.

As if understanding, Terry clasped his hands together and did a sort of champ gesture. I could sense his strength and caring.

"Rick," Benji whispered. "I just can't . . ."

"I know," I whispered back.

The victory had little visible effect on Carolyn, who modestly shuffled through papers, but Marion Goober wore a most obnoxious smirk.

The judge silenced the courtroom with her gavel. "Thank you, members of the jury. Having been found guilty of murder in the first degree, the defendant is remanded into custody. Sentencing will begin tomorrow."

"There's gotta be something we missed."

Terry was in uniform as he paced the concrete floor of my prison cell that afternoon while Benji was off hunting for character witnesses on my behalf. I told Benji not to bother flying in members of my family, so it was up to the charitable instincts of the showbiz community to convince the court that just convicted me what a swell guy I was.

Terry was firm that we not give up. "Let's go over it all again, Rick. If Shane really is Shane, he probably did it, right? But if he's Dennis—"

"Then Dennis is either nuts and having fun, or else nuts and covering for Shane. But since there *is* no Shane if he's Dennis—" I stopped myself, falling in a heap onto the rickety, lumpy bed in exhaustion. "It's hopeless, Terry. Everyone in this town is so full of shit, there's no getting through. Whoever really did it probably *forgot* by now. It was too many drinks ago. Too many lies ago."

"Let's talk about Bob again," Terry insisted. "There's lots of evidence against Bob. Maybe there's something we missed." He clicked on the laptop. "I've been doing *hundreds* of Web searches."

"I know. And it all just proves I'm right. You haven't come up with anything—not really." I sat up in bed. "Maybe Benji can get the verdict overturned on appeal. Some sort of technicality. People will still think I did it, but I could go low profile. Write a book and buy a little house in the country someplace. At least I wouldn't be in prison."

"Bob made four movies with Tara," Terry stated, ignoring all I'd said.

"And I'll bet you never saw any of them." I laughed in spite of myself.

"C'mon, Rick. Stay with me here. Bob and Tara. Lots of bad blood."

There was a polite knock against the bars of my cell.

"Hi, Mr. Domino."

It was Calvin, whom I'd met the night of my arrest—the guy who did not try to poison a kindergarten class. He was accompanied by a guard.

"Hello, Calvin." I stood up to shake hands with him.

"Tough break for you," he commented.

I shrugged. "Win some, lose some."

Calvin laughed. "I have to get a move on. A meeting with my lawyer."

"Good luck."

"Thanks. And please thank Mr. Malone, too. For being such a help to us both." When I registered puzzlement, he added: "You know, me and Ed."

"Oh, right, Ed. As in, grandmother and hammer. I'll be sure to give Benji your message." I couldn't decide whether to be impressed that Benji was so surprisingly generous as to give his time to Calvin and Ed, or to be angry that he took time away from defending me.

Calvin reached into the front of his uniform, and pulled out a rubbery pale blond wig. "We put on quite a show last night." He started laughing as the guard grabbed the silly wig from him, admonishing Calvin that he wasn't supposed to have had it in his possession.

"Guess it takes all kinds," Terry politely noted, as Calvin was led away.

"Sure does," I agreed. I found myself deep in thought, suddenly excited about solving the case like I'd never been.

"Now, where were we? Bob and Tara—"

"And what Bob said to me," I thought out loud. "What he said in the first place."

Terry looked up from the screen. "What do you mean?"

"Did you bring the DVD of the Oscars?"

"Sure, I have it right here."

"Then what are you waiting for? Let's watch it and find the killer."

30

*B*enji had rounded up what you might call the usual suspects to speak on my behalf. Francine, Cinda, Bob, Jeep, and Tru might not have relished testifying that I didn't kill Tara, but in a pang of something approaching conscience, they were willing to tell the court I shouldn't be given the death penalty for it.

Terry was not in court that morning—yet. I hoped he'd arrive in time with what we needed.

Bob was the first one called to the stand. He said I was a "warm and charming man," and that I could still "make a meaningful contribution to society."

"That's all," Benji declared. "Thank you, Mr. Raflowitz."

Carolyn was ready to do business. I could just imagine the sympathetic comments she'd force Bob to make about Tara.

"Excuse me, Your Honor." I stood up. "Before the State questions the witness, could I ask him a question myself?"

Benji put a restraining hand on my arm. "Your Honor, my client is understandably upset. I apologize for this unexpected display."

I removed Benji's hand. "Please, your honor. My life is on the line. Could I have just one minute?" I looked at her with all the earnestness and integrity I could muster.

There was a flicker of a smile in her eyes for me. "Very well, Mr. Domino. You understand your attorney has advised you against speaking at this time?"

"Yes, I do."

"And you still would like to address the witness?"

"Yes, Your Honor. Very much so."

Bob made a point of remaining very calm on the witness stand, like he was this Zen sort of guy who would go with the flow either way.

"Mr. Raflowitz," I stated, "you and I discussed this case over the past couple of weeks, have we not?"

"Yes, Rick." Bob smiled at me.

"And you remember telling me that Tara was arguing backstage with a woman you thought looked slightly familiar, but couldn't quite place?"

"Yes, that is correct."

"Was *this* the woman?" I handed Bob a somewhat blurred close-up of a woman from the crowds at the Oscars.

"Yes," Bob decided at once. "Yes, it was."

Terry entered the courtroom. He nodded affirmatively.

"Your honor," complained Carolyn, "I would like to remind the defendant that the jury has already reached its verdict. This picture, whatever it is, is not evidence, it isn't anything. The trial is over."

"*I only asked him,*" I replied to Carolyn, "if this was who he saw arguing with Tara."

"If you have a point to make, Mr. Domino, do get on with it," admonished the judge.

"Very well. Thank you, Mr. Raflowitz." I looked up again at Judge Hopkins. "Your Honor, may I now please make a brief statement?"

"Your *Honor*," Marion complained. "This is turning into a circus."

Judge Hopkins banged her gavel. "Mr. Goober, are you suggesting that I run my courtroom like a circus?"

"Uh . . . no, Your Honor." He sat back down.

"Make it fast, Mr. Domino."

The cinematic dimensions of the moment were not lost on me. One of my movie star fantasies was to play a hotshot lawyer, and have the judge tell me to make it fast, that I was on a short leash, or whatnot. Here was my big chance—and on live TV at that.

"Thank you, Judge. I know the jury had a job to do, and did it to the best of their ability. I don't blame them, I really don't. Because up until yesterday"—I looked over at Terry—"Or in a way, until just now, I was stumped myself. But I can tell you now what happened on Oscar night." I walked over to where Francine, Cinda, Jeep, and Tru were seated. "All these leading citizens of our fine community, willing to testify on my behalf. You, too, Bob. But I don't need you anymore."

I handed the image of the woman's face to the judge. "Your Honor, this is the person who murdered Tara Perez." I turned to face the courtroom. "My attorney, Benji Malone."

The judge banged on her gavel to silence the court as Benji stood up. "Your Honor, my client is clearly traumatized. Please do not permit this irrational outburst—"

"Your Honor," Marion interrupted, "this must not continue." Carolyn put a restraining hand on his arm. I heard her mutter: "*Let him dig his own grave.*"

"Excuse, me, Judge," Terry spoke up. "Officer Terry Zane, wit-

ness for the State. May I approach? I have information that I promise is vital to the matter at hand."

The judge looked at Carolyn. "Do you want to say anything?"

"Fine," she smiled politely. "Let Officer Zane approach." After
all, she couldn't very well censor a police officer in front of millions
of people.

The judge scowled as she put on her glasses to study the document.

"I have been presented with a registration," she announced,
"for the gun that shot Tara Perez. It is made out to Benji Malone."
She took off her glasses and rubbed her eyes. "Ms. Caruthers,
would you care to explain why you never checked to see who
owned the gun?"

Carolyn glared at Marion. He stood up reluctantly, looking
away from the judge. "I couldn't find it, Your Honor."

"Or you didn't want to?"

"Your Honor, we *knew* the defend*ant* fired the gun. How
important was it whether he owned it or not?"

"I'm not sure I like what I'm hearing, Mr. Goober. When this is
all over, I'll want to meet with you in my chambers."

He lowered his head. "Yes, Your Honor."

"Now then, Mr. Malone. Would you care to explain?"

"Surely you can understand, Your Honor," Benji began. "I
didn't want to implicate my client by making it known that I knew
he stole my gun. I realize it was wrong. That as an officer of the
court I was obligated—"

"Shut up, Benji."

"Mr. Domino, may I remind you are not the one who deter-
mines who speaks when in this courtroom?"

"I'm sorry, Your Honor. But please, may I address Mr. Malone?"

"Very well." She looked down at me sternly, but with a glint of
kindness.

I turned to face Benji. "I should be forced to resign from the gay
community," I began. "Imagine not spotting a drag queen when I
saw one. But you're good, Benji. The best I've ever seen. You really
pass for a woman. A washed-up, over-the-hill woman, but a

woman. Though unlike any other cross-dresser I've known, I'd say you've got some pretty serious problems."

I pulled out the blond wig from my inside suit pocket.

"We got this from a guard last night. It's the same wig in the photo. *He* got it from an inmate, Calvin Dickerson, who's willing to testify you gave it to him, Benji, for a prison drag show. You almost had it licked, didn't you?, but you couldn't resist that last little festive touch. All along you've been trying to throw me off track. So eager to pin it all on Shane. Even this joke of a trial—moving up the start date so that I wouldn't have time to crack the case. And then encouraging me to interview all these witnesses, knowing they had nothing to do with it. Stopping me when I had them all in one room for questioning. Making up false leads. You probably even knew we had a bogus defense lined up. Yet so much *nicer* to me than normal. Was it your guilty conscience?

"You planted the Oscar at Shane's, didn't you? To throw me off the trail, and maybe get my fingerprints on the murder weapon in the bargain. And then you staged the car accident, the one where you supposedly lost the Oscar. Good Lord, you were willing to *injure* yourself. Was it you under the ski mask who brought it back just to make it look good? After all, you were discharged from the hospital by then—though I guess I wasn't supposed to know that.

"But it was you all along. The bald, 'funny little Oscar man' that Zeke Raflowitz said he saw. 'The same only different,' he said —you, only as a woman. And then Bob saying he didn't know who the blonde was in the green room, while other people said it *was* Connee. They were all telling the truth. It was *you* backstage, before Connee ever got there. Though maybe you disposed of Connee afterwards, so that I'd never get a chance to talk to her, and could keep confusing her with you." I looked at him unflinchingly. "What about Shane? Or should I say Brother Dennis? Who is he, really? And how did you get to him? Did you pay him off? Threaten him? Dope him up?"

Carolyn and Marion were frantically writing things down; they didn't understand half of what I was talking about.

Benji calmly looked away from me, and closed his briefcase. A prison guard stood nearby.

He swung his briefcase at the guard, knocking him in the head. As the guard lost his balance, Benji grabbed the man's gun from its holster.

Terry drew his gun on Benji. "Easy now," Terry tried to soothe.

"I love you, Rick," Benji murmured, obliviously waving the gun. "I couldn't help it. I never had these types of feelings for a man before. Sure, I liked to dress as a woman. It *relaxed* me. Even if it cost me five wives out of five. But what I felt for you, Rick—it was something different. First I started thinking of you when I was a woman. But then, it was even when I was dressed as a man. I couldn't believe that I might've been . . . you know, *gay*. Or least gay with you. Dealing with clients was one thing. But to be that way myself. A fruit. A fag . . ."

Benji let out a self-pitying sob, as though the only thing that mattered out of all this was that he not have to suffer for his sexual identity.

"I wanted Shane out of the way. I wanted to comfort you in your grief and then have you to myself. Shane's ring was for *you*, Rick. He told me so in the hallway just as the Oscars were starting. But I convinced him that would never do. That he should propose to Tara if he proposed to anyone. Otherwise, his career would be ruined. Then I told him . . . things about you, Rick, that weren't true. How you could never be a reliable partner, how you'd break his heart once the thrill of the chase was over. Shane was dumb. He was easy to manipulate."

"Shit," I could not help reflecting. Then I quickly added, "Sorry, Your Honor."

"Do be careful, Mr. Domino," admonished the judge.

"I felt this urge to change into a woman," Benji continued, gesturing absently with the gun in his hand. "It was stronger than it ever was before. I was *very* excited, Rick. So very turned-on by the thought of being with you in that special way. So I became Wendy. That's what I call myself, Wendy. I think she's quite pretty. It hurts my feeling so much when you call her all washed up. Wendy, to me, is . . . just so wonderful. I decided I'd come on to you as Wendy. That *that* was how I could be with you.

"Tara and I had a few words in the green room. I passed for the real thing with other people, but not Tara. She instantly knew who I was. At first, she was just delighted to see me as a woman. She told me she especially liked my long black velvet gloves, and how they matched my gown. I can't tell you how many shops Wendy and I had to go to find the exact right pair.

"But then things got dicey. I told Tara that she needed to marry Shane. She said it was dishonest. That there was so much dishonesty in her life she couldn't take anymore. But I kept harping on it. At one point, I grabbed her Oscar away from her. I asked her how she felt without it. And before she could speak, I told her, 'If you don't play ball, in a few years it will be as if this never even happened.' She told me to go away and mind my own business. She said that she'd done enough crappy things for one lifetime. That she was tired of having to threaten and cheat to get people to like her. Now that she'd won the Oscar, things would be different. She didn't need to prove herself anymore. She wanted a life of integrity and all that bullshit. 'From now on,' she said, 'I'm going to be a good person.' I laughed in her face. She slapped me and started to cry. She told me to go away.

"I *did* go away. I needed to think. But then I came back. I saw Tara with Shane, just after he proposed. Cinda was all bent out of shape—she didn't get that Tara had turned him down, and there was no time to explain. She had to get ready to do Best Actor. But all that was just a mixup, like any of the rest of it. Who was black-mailing whom, this one in love with that one—it didn't mean *anything*, really. Just Hollywood business as usual. I hadn't given up, though. I wanted to change Tara's mind. Shane didn't recognize me, but when I told him who I was, he laughed. I think it made him feel better—you know, that other people lived with secrets, too. I proposed we all go outside for a quick line of coke before Best Actor.

"From the moment he tooted up, Shane became *so* tiresome. He was saying how Tara was right, maybe it was time to start being honest. *Honest!*—I couldn't believe it. Tara agreed. She said that she didn't need a cover marriage to convince the public of her appeal, and that neither did Shane. I got so *mad*, I can't explain it. I picked up Tara's Oscar. I wanted to slam it into Shane's head. But Tara, damn her soul to hell, got in the way. On purpose."

Benji started to cry. "She jumped in front of Shane to shield him. To save his life."

He composed himself, and continued. "I didn't mean to hit her so hard. But her head started bleeding. It was awful. I was so scared. I didn't know what to do. So I hit her again. And again. And then I shot her."

For a few seconds, everyone was quiet. I could hear Cinda Sharpe softly weeping.

"Bumping into you backstage like that broke my heart—I wanted you to love me, and instead I had to run because Tara was dead. But *then* I realized I had go back outside. Stir things up. Find Shane and . . . and scare him or kill him or make sure it looked like he did it. But then it all began to unravel. I couldn't find him. And *you* were there, instead. I purposefully aimed away from you, Rick. I had to scare you off for your own good. So that you wouldn't be involved. But then I picked up the shell—I *had* to. I mean, what do you do when you *love* someone, but you don't want to go to jail for murder? I'm sorry I had to make it harder for you. Like the engagement ring—Shane left it on the chair by accident, and when you started asking questions about it, I had to work like hell to blow smoke. To make it seem like it was part of Shane's plan. But I tried to help you, too. I *did* try to get you off. Sometimes. I just . . . well, it's hard to know what to do when you're two different people."

"Why did you have the gun?" Terry asked.

"Because my last wife threatened to kill me," Benji replied. "She made fun of me as Wendy, so I got a little rough with her. I started carrying it with me all the time." He choked back a flood of tears. "It fit into my p-purse."

It was a pathetic admission, but some of the people in court started laughing.

Benji looked slowly around the room, pale and bug-eyed.

"I didn't kill Connee. The fucking bitch OD'd fair and square." He aimed the gun at me. "I'm so sorry, Rick."

"Easy, Benji," called Terry, gently walking toward him. "Let's talk about it, okay?" In one graceful dive, Terry tackled Benji, landing flat on top of him, and knocked the gun from his hand.

"Fuck you," Benji hissed.

31

 &ℱ;rom all of us here at Hollywood Network," enthused Mitzi McGuire, her eyes but mere slits for the glee she feigned, "I can only say, 'Welcome back, Rick Domino.'"

"Thank you, Mitzi," I replied, seated beside her at my evening broadcast desk. "And thank you as well for doing such a great job filling in for me these past couple of weeks."

"Oh, I could never take *your* place, Rick." She two-facedly leaned over to kiss my cheek; like the bitch was really glad to see me back. I felt the strange sensation of collagen against my skin. "What a hero you've turned out to be. They'll never say anything against us gossip columnists again."

"Maybe you're right," I replied thoughtfully, wondering if that would be a good thing.

"So tell us, Rick. Is a book in the works?"

"Maybe," I demurred.

"Will it have the inside scoop on any big-name stars?"

"I'll have to see," I replied.

"It is all just *too* dramatic," Mitzi gushed. "What with Shane Kirk fleeing the Oscars in fear for his life, and Benji catching him. And then the police finding Shane tied, gagged, and starved but gallantly fighting for life in Benji's closet, behind all those sad little off-the-rack gowns. And Shane's twin brother, the Jesuit Brother Dennis, mentally ill for *years*, and then getting a call from Shane that scares him into coming to L.A. A call that Benji, of course, forced Shane to make, as part of his scheme to confuse you. None of us even knew Shane *had* a Brother Dennis—except Benji, it would seem, as Shane's attorney. I think we're all still a little confused, Rick. Was it that Benji told Brother Dennis exactly what to say and do if he wanted to see Shane alive again? Or did Brother Dennis really believe he *was* Shane?"

I cleared my throat. "I believe it was a little of both, Mitzi. Most everything was orchestrated by Benji. He had Dennis meet with me to win my trust. So that when Dennis offered to pose as Shane for one press conference, I'd go along with it. And I'd be kept on a wild goose chase looking for the *real* Shane, with those made-up stories about someone seeing Shane in a white car. When Dennis betrayed me, I'd be doubly thrown off track—baffled that he'd do this to me, plus wondering if maybe he really was Shane. And of course Benji could look like the hero, gallantly trying to save my neck in the face of this crazed liar. Dennis got cold feet from time to time—he didn't think it was right to keep lying like that. Having to memorize all that false testimony especially got to him, from what I understand—knowing he'd have to lie after swearing on the Bible. But Benji would remind him that if he didn't play ball with him, Shane would be dead.

"But apparently Dennis also got confused—has often gotten confused—about thinking he *was* Shane. And Benji knew this about him from talking to Shane. So when all else failed, he could also psych Dennis into believing he was Shane for a few more hours here and there. Now and then Dennis got a bit carried away with impersonating his brother, and really did attempt to enact certain—shall we say?—fantasies."

I didn't go into any of the specifics here. Though Brother Dennis was supposed to be scouring the streets looking for Shane—preferably with me watching—he was not supposed to be getting himself arrested for solicitation. But Benji unwittingly created something of a Frankenstein monster, who alternated between thinking he was Shane the rich movie star and Shane the street hustler. Still, Dennis apparently had his lucid moments. He really did figure out on his own about Terry's involvement in the case, for example. And as far as I knew, he never did say anything about it to Benji.

"Did he ever succeed in enacting any of those fantasies?" Mitzi couldn't wait to know.

"I really have no idea."

Mitzi shook her head sadly. "Unbelievable, isn't it?"

"It is quite a tale," I admitted. "But he's back with the Jesuits now. I bear him no malice."

"And Officer Terry Zane helped you through all this, am I right?"

"He sure did, Mitzi." I gave the thumbs-up. "He's a credit to the LAPD."

She patted my hand to fake an interest in my well-being. "Tell us, Rick. What about Shane? Have you been to see him at the hospital?"

"Not yet."

"Do you think that the two of you might . . . ?"

"I don't think so, Mitzi."

"Why, Rick. You're blushing."

"So I am, Mitzi. So I am."

"Tell us, Rick"—Mitzi frowned slightly for a moment's lag in the teleprompter—"Do you have any new insights to give us?"

I was tempted to mention that no sooner had I gotten home from the courthouse than did a package arrive anonymously at my front door. It was a video of *Beat Me, Daddy, Eight to the Balls*. The blurry, low budget, pre-condom production did in fact feature a scene with two models who somewhat resembled Bob Raflowitz and Jeep Andrews. Tacky as it sounds, I noted that circumcision-wise—among other things—the models matched up well to Bob and Jeep. But otherwise, I honestly didn't believe it was them. The resemblances were not all that convincing. As far as I could see, the matter was closed. Bob made that huge withdrawal from his savings at the same time he reported being blackmailed, but I could only guess if it was over the porn movie, or over something else that being a movie star had brought into his life. (I also got a voice-mail from Bob telling me that Zeke was doing much better, and that they'd be sending him to a progressive school Zeke himself selected in Vancouver, B.C.)

Like Tara's letter to Cinda and so many other things, I might never know the whole story. After ten years of covering the Hollywood scene, it occurred to me that for all the dozens of people whose job it was to dig up dirt on the stars, most things about them remained a mystery. Actors took their work home with them. Just as they could convince you on-screen that they were starving across a desert or falling in love or robbing a bank, they could conjure up their own reality off-screen. After awhile, it was impossible to know what really happened.

"I just have one thing to say," I improvised. "That the real hero out of all this is Tara Perez. Like all of us, she was not perfect, but like very few of us, she redeemed herself in the ultimate sacrifice you can make in this world. She literally lost her life to save someone else's."

I signaled to the off-camera technician. "Please roll the tape."

And there was Tara, telling Chauncey Riggs: *"You might think I'm crazy, but in all honesty my life hasn't gone the way I planned. I've always wanted to find something very simple, and very honest and sincere. And no matter what sort of adventures I've had in this world, I've never found what I've been looking for."*

"Tara Perez wanted to win an Oscar," I told the TV audience. "And in the end, her Oscar killed her. But most of all, she wanted a life of integrity. However tragic her death, I know she found what she was seeking." I swallowed hard. "Wherever she may be."

I never thought I'd hear myself say such things about Tara, but it was all true.

"That was just so beautiful, Rick." Mitzi wiped away an imaginary tear.

"Thank you, Mitzi."

"Next, we have an exclusive interview with Cinda Sharpe and Jeep Andrews on the set of their hot new romantic comedy *Afternoon Delight*. The big question is: Will the fireworks on-screen ignite these two sexy stars off-screen, or will they simply remain the best of friends?"

Later, after the show—after Mitzi coolly told me to go to hell once we were off the air—I made my way to Shane's hospital room at Cedars-Sinai.

His voice was hoarse and weak, it took obvious effort for him to even turn his head, and he was hooked up to an IV. But he was expected to make a full recovery.

"I heard you outed me, Rick." He smiled wanly. "Now what am I going to do?"

"In a way, I want to say I'm sorry, Shane. But in a different way, I'm not sorry at all."

"I'm not *mad*." He coughed, the pain of so doing apparent from the grimace on his face. "When you almost die, it puts things in perspective."

"I know what you mean."

He groaned as he attempted in vain to sit up on his elbows. "Rick, maybe it's not too late. Maybe we can still make a go of it. I *was* going to ask you to marry me, you know."

"I realize that. But you didn't." I helped him ease back into his original position. "You strung me along. Then you believed Benji. You proposed to Tara, instead. And then you ran off in fear, rather than trust me—or try to help me. You're not a bad man, Shane. And I'm sorry for your ordeal. But you're self-protective in a way that causes harm to others. Even when you don't mean to be. I know you're still young—you'll probably change over time. But I can never feel the same about you. Maybe what I felt was never even what I thought it was."

Shane looked at me with an honesty that was new to his face. "I'm sorry, Rick."

"I know. I'm sorry, too." I reached down to kiss his forehead.

He extended his hand. "Friends?"

"You know it."

He kissed my hand and squeezed it. "Just out of curiosity: Did my brother tell you a story about my being molested and then killing the man?"

I nodded affirmatively.

"I figured. It happened the other way around. That creepy guy in the ski masked looked us both over, and *I* was the one he let go free. Dennis was the one who got raped. And who killed the guy. There was even a hearing about it. As a juvenile, Dennis's name was kept out of the papers. His record was permanently sealed. But the judge could see he was losing it, and sent him to a mental hospital. Dennis said he found God while he was there, and started hanging out with the Jesuits. They've been very kind to him over the years." He coughed, then struggled to stop. "Dennis means well, but he gets mixed up. I imagine he's gay—or would be, if he wasn't celibate. Or whatever."

Shane reached for a glass of water. I handed it to him. "It's strange, isn't it, Shane? What we sometimes think people are, and who they turn out to be. All this dirt on Tara, and the people she sullied herself with. Blackmail, run-ins with police, mental illness, drugs, obsessive love, kinky sex, backstabbing to get this or that part, rumors of X-rated movies. And it all came to nothing. Like Benji said, just another day in Hollywood."

"*What* people, Rick?"

"Oh, don't worry about it just now. You can read about it soon enough."

"You know, one of my nurses is pretty hot. Maybe we'll fall madly in love, and I'll become an advocate for crime victims and buy an asparagus farm with him in Fresno."

I laughed. "By all means help people, Shane. And please do fall madly in love. It would work wonders in your life. But I'm sure you still have a career. You may be surprised."

I pulled up in my driveway to see Terry Zane waiting outside my door. He was in his standard civvies: T-shirt, 501s, and the jacket with all the pockets.

"You could've let yourself in," I chided.

"The case is over. I thought that would be rude."

It felt really good to see him.

"Terry, I haven't even really had a chance to thank you. The other day, there was such insanity in court, and since then everything's gotten ever nuttier."

Our handshake gave way to an embrace. He kind of patted my back or so.

"You're looking at Terry Zane, Junior Detective," he announced. "Or at least I hope so. They're letting me take the qualifying exam next time it comes up."

"That's great." I turned the key to the front door. "You got what you wanted."

Dasher saw us and hissed, jumping across the room out of sight.

"It feels great to be home," I noted. "And I couldn't have done it without you."

"Same here."

"Tell you what, Terry." I slipped off my suit jacket and loosened my tie. "Let me buy you dinner. Someplace fancy. Or better yet, someplace you'd enjoy."

"Fancy sounds fine." He stooped down to get the cat's attention. "I have to confess your tastes have been rubbing off on me a little." Dasher condescendingly permitted Terry to pet him once or twice.

"You'll need to change your clothes. As usual."

Terry laughed. "I have a dinner jacket in my car."

"So, what else are you going to do?" I sorted through a stack of junk mail.

"How do you mean?"

"You know—a new lady friend to drown your sorrows over Darla Sue."

Terry sighed, and looked down at the floor. "I don't think so, Rick."

"Why not? You can't keep moping over your losses forever. Are there any nice single girls on the police force?" I frowned, taking out my palm pal to key in things I'd need to do the next day.

"I'm sure there are."

"Well, then. That's a start, isn't it? Ask one of them out."

Terry took my arm. "Rick, before we go out, I need to tell you something."

"What—you got someone pregnant? You have the clap?"

Terry sat on the white muslin window seat and ran his fingers through his virtually nonexistent hair. "Rick, when I told you about Darla Sue, how I didn't have a very fulfilling married life with her—"

"But you got her pregnant, so you married her."

"No, I said she *got* pregnant, and I married her. But someone else got her pregnant. He was my best friend, Andy. Only he died. Killed in a motorcycle accident."

"Well then, that really was nice of you, Terry. You do seem to be an exceptionally nice guy." I smiled at him and returned to my palm pal, which was beeping for a decision about my interview schedule.

He knitted his thick eyebrows with earnestness. "What I mean is, I never much . . . you know, had sex with Darla Sue. I've always liked her a lot, but she's never turned me on."

"Well then, I guess it wasn't much of a basis for a marriage. Most problems begin in the bedroom, you know. Just recently, I read this article about—"

"Rick, damnit. Don't you get it? I loved Andy. I married Darla Sue out of my love for him. He never let me have him that way, though he used to tease and torment me when he got drunk. When he died, it broke my heart, but I thought if I became father to his child . . . only she lost the baby."

I set down the keypad. "Terry, do you mean to tell me . . . ?"

"I've always known it. I've been fighting it all my life. It's never worked with a woman."

"What about . . . uh, guys?" I was having trouble believing what I just heard.

He shyly played with his boot lace. "I've never really made love, Rick. Not ever in my life. I've fooled around for five minutes here and ten minutes there. But love, real love, lying close all night with someone that I care about . . . That's never happened to me."

"Terry, how sad." I walked over to him and patted his shoulder.

"I almost told you so many times before. I was bursting at the seams when we walked on the beach. The timing was never right. All that murder stuff kept getting in the way. But I wanted to tell you that being around you has made me feel . . . okay about myself. That being gay is part of who I am. And I'm ready now to face it."

"That's great, Terry," And I supposed it was, though the news was still such a surprise it was barely sinking in. "I'm sure there are gay cop clubs and bowling leagues and whatnot. I can introduce you to a nice guy myself, if I ever meet one."

He blushed to bright crimson. "Thanks, Rick." He smiled in an inner-directed way, like he was feeling lightheaded.

I offered him my hand and smiled. "Welcome to the club, bro.' "

But I *still* couldn't believe it.

"Thanks." He shook my hand, then placed his other hand on top of mine. Then he clasped my chin between his fingers, and lightly kissed my lips.

I had to admit that it felt a little nice, considering that Terry was not at all my type.

"Um, I hope that was okay."

I thought about it. "Sure, why not? I kiss my friends all the time. This *is* Hollywood, after all."

I felt self-conscious as I returned to sorting the mail. "I promise to be the worst possible influence. In fact, I think I'll call Truman Shea right now and tell him you're moonlighting as a paid escort."

"Very funny."

I lost track of what I was doing. "I thought so."

"Well, then, I think it only fair that I return the favor. Maybe Marion Goober is gay. I'll bet he's just your type."

"That was pretty good. You're improving."

Terry awkwardly shifted about. "I guess we should get ready."

"You're right. We should." For some reason, I was feeling kind of spacey.

I turned to go to my bedroom to shower and change.

"Rick?"

I stopped, and faced him. "Yes, Terry?"

"Never mind. Let's just have a good time tonight, okay?"